DISCLAIMER

Fictional Work

The characters and events portrayed in this book are fictitious. Any similarity to real persons, living or dead, is coincidental and not intended by the author.

COPYRIGHT © 2023 BY ZARAH DETAND

All rights reserved.

No part of this book may be reproduced, or stored in a retrieval system, or transmitted in any form or by any means, electronic, mechanical, photocopying, recording, or otherwise, without express written permission of the publisher.

Cover design ©Zarah Detand

CHANGE MY TICKET

ZARAH DETAND

1

Skeletons. Bloody *skeletons*.

This is what Ray gets for having blatantly devious friends who are willing to exploit his inability to walk away from a dare—any dare, ever. On the bright side, the university building won't be busy today. The seminar rooms on the upper floors are empty on Sundays, and the research lab is nominally closed, even though stragglers are common because, well, *scientists*.

He hitches his backpack higher up on his shoulder, peers left and right, then swipes his badge. The door buzzes open.

All right, no time like the present. Also, if this stunt torpedoes his job, he'll make Patrick and Andrew feed him until he finds a new gig—contrary to popular opinion, twenty-something med school dropouts don't thrive on coffee, booze, and quiet shame alone. On a related note, the claim that you can survive on just beer is patently untrue, as Ray had to explain to Patrick just last night, when his friend staggered into their shared flat at one in the morning, three sheets to the wind. Yes, beer contains some minerals, but with very little protein and no vitamin C, you'd be dead in six months.

Incidentally, that's the discussion that took them straight to the topic of skeletons, which in turn led Ray here. Somehow, arguing with Patrick never turns out well.

Instead of following his usual path to the lab, Ray checks the hallway to his left, confirms that it lies abandoned, and pads along, sticking close to the wall, sneakers silent on the linoleum floor. The historical anatomy collection hides behind the fourth door on the right—two floors and several interconnected rooms that house shelves lined with odd specimens in glass jars, an entire row of skulls, pelvic bones in all shapes and sizes, mummified limbs, and hundred-plus-year-old skeletons. Ray isn't supposed to know the door code, but his lab supervisor organises occasional anatomy tours for students and interested members of the public, and once in a blue moon, Ray manages to pay attention when it counts.

He enters the code and holds his breath for the second it takes until the status light switches to green and the door snicks open. So far, so good. With another deep breath, he slips into the adjacent corridor.

The smell is instantly noticeable: dried chalk and dust, mixed with something sweetly cloying and the stench of alcohol. He lets the door fall shut behind him and takes a moment to get his bearings. Faint daylight slants through a window at the far end of the corridor.

Is that...voices?

His heart jumps into his throat, and he stands still like a rabbit caught in the headlights. Voices, yes.

Fuck.

They're off to his left, at least three people. Not drawing closer, though.

The smart thing, the *right* thing, would be to back the hell away, tuck tail, and run. Except Patrick would tease Ray mercilessly for not even trying, at least after resurfacing from what's bound to be a sizable hangover, and Andrew might slip a crack about testicular fortitude into his next opinion piece for the *Evening Standard*.

It's not that Ray's got anything to prove, but... But. He lets go of the door and takes one step to the right, towards the room with the child-sized skeletons that date back to the sixteenth century. This is very, very stupid. But also, it's a dare, and what is Ray supposed to do other than follow through?

Tea time, man! Make it proper romantic, will ya? Give us doilies, cute little cups, the works. Oh, and just so we're clear: the romantic couple is two skeletons, and there better be pictures.

Kudos to Patrick and Andrew for, one, creative slyness under the influence, and two, being terrible influences on Ray. If this blows up in his face, they are *so* buying all the groceries and covering his share of the rent until he finds some other form of steady employment.

Well then. A dare is a dare, and Ray didn't bring a backpack of supplies for nothing.

∼

IT FEELS LIKE A COSTUME.

Which it is, of course—a white lab coat topped off with make-up is not Gabe's everyday attire. But ideally, he'd already sense a spark of magic, the one that lets him know it's just a matter of time before it clicks and he becomes someone else, temporarily steps out of his own skin and into that of his character.

James Watson: young and brash counterpart to Francis Crick's brilliant magpie mind, both of them obsessed with beating their US competition to the finishing line, first to decode the DNA structure. Like mountaineers racing to the peak, come hell or high water.

Instead, he's still just Gabe Duke in a lab coat.

Good thing they're only doing production stills today—according to some critics, 'shut up and look pretty' is Gabe's true calling. And he's not alone in having a bad day either: Gordon, the seasoned character actor cast as Francis Crick, is still recovering from a nasty flu and visibly sweating under the lights. The guy has been nothing but gracious to Gabe—to a much younger actor whose primary credentials are looking good in spandex—so there is no joy in seeing him struggle, but the breaks? The breaks Gabe will take.

"Everyone!" The photographer has the dramatic air of someone creating ART in big neon letters, never mind that his *sujet du jour* are variations of Gordon and Gabe in serious conversation against a backdrop of apothecary jars filled with wet specimens that creep Gabe out just a little. "Fifteen minute break. *You!*" Directed at a make-up artist ready to spring into action. "Fix this!"

'This' being, miraculously, not Gabe, but Gordon's wilting appearance.

"I'm just—" Gabe takes a step back, points a thumb over his shoulder at the door. "Loo."

Since no one is paying attention to him, he nods once for emphasis, then slips out into the corridor. His breathing eases the moment he leaves the bustle of activity behind.

They picked him for a reason. Yes, his acting experience is limited to school plays and being part of a superhero franchise that received a far better audience than critics response. Still, they saw something in him that went beyond the ability to bring in a teenage crowd.

All right, deep breaths. He's fine; this is fine. He just needs a minute, is all. Being surrounded by skulls and bones is not helping, but he's fine.

A mummified hand reaches for him with fingers curled like claws.

Fine. Splash a bit of water on his face, don't ruin the make-up, and he'll be good to go. Did anyone mention where the toilets are?

He tries the closest door and finds another room with wet specimens that he doesn't want to examine too closely—are those *testicles*? —and moves on to the next one. There's a weird sort of resistance when he presses down on the door handle, not quite like it's locked, more like it's somehow jammed. He puts a bit more effort into it, and the door gives quite suddenly.

He stumbles forward and hears a pained grunt. What the...? Oh.

Dark eyes blink at him from a face with the kind of bone structure that could move Michelangelo to tears: cheekbones to cut glass, straight eyebrows, light-brown skin and a full mouth, coupled with a sophisticated five o'clock shadow that would make Gabe look like a little boy playing at being an adult.

"Um," Gabe says, quite eloquently. Thousands of miles away, all the way across the Atlantic, his media coach just woke up in a cold sweat.

"*Ouch,*" says the boy. Man? He doesn't look much older than Gabe, who feels like a boy about seventy per cent of the time, and like an old man for most of the rest.

"Hi." Gabe flashes his eyebrows, smiles, and tilts his head just like media training taught him. *See? Not a total waste of your time.* "I'm sorry if I hit you. The door seemed stuck, and I didn't see you there."

"Well, obviously," the guy mumbles, but the severe lines of his frown fade a little. The usual spark of recognition is absent as he gives Gabe a once-over that could mean anything and likely means nothing.

"Didn't think there'd be any people around," Gabe says because clearly it's on him to keep the conversation going.

"Ah, yeah." The frown is back. "Just checking on a thing. Was about to leave, actually."

Gabe nods like he understands when really, he has no clue what 'thing' this guy could possibly be checking on a Sunday morning in an anatomy collection. Might be why Gabe is only pretending to be a scientist—although honestly, this guy looks a little young to be a fully certified researcher. PhD student, maybe?

Also, the silence is threatening to turn awkward. When in doubt, use an empathetic statement. "So you're about to leave?"

"Yeah, just, y'know." The guy flutters one hand in a gesture that could mean anything. "Finishing up."

"Finishing up?"

"Yeah, just need to put a few things away, and then I'll be on my way. I'll be just a couple of minutes, yeah?"

Now that Gabe deviates attention away from his own personal crisis and to his surroundings, he can tell that there is something decidedly fishy about the guy's behaviour. It's in the way he won't quite meet Gabe's eyes and keeps glancing over his shoulder, in how he's still blocking part of the doorway with his body. He's also not dressed like a lab rat: battered sneakers, low-slung jeans, and a loose T-shirt that might look baggy on someone just a little less beautiful.

Gabe has seen enough beautiful faces that he's developed a moderate case of immunity, and if this guy is here to rob the collection—seriously, though, what does a jar of bollocks fetch on the black market?

No matter. The point is, if the guy is here to rob the collection, Gabe isn't afraid to ... call for help. Because that's just how much of a badass he is.

"I was wondering if you could point me towards the loo?" As he asks the question, he takes a step to the side that lets him peer around the guy and into the room, and while the guy shifts to mimic him, he's too late.

A pause.

"Um," the guy says, in a throwback to how this conversation started. "Loo is" —he raises a hand and points down the corridor, back to where Gabe came— "that way."

Another pause.

"Did you know," Gabe begins, "that there are two baby skeletons having a picnic on that table over there?"

"They must have been more, like, five-year-olds or so," the guy protests, before he falls silent and looks pained, his eyebrows drawing together, near-black eyes narrowing. "And, uh. Yeah, I'm aware."

"You're aware," Gabe repeats slowly. He leans further around the guy and studies the scene: a bath towel that serves as the picnic blanket, one of the skeletons reclining against some box, the other sitting with one leg folded over the other, glasses and plates between them that are at odds with their size. Also... "Surely they're too young to be having wine?"

Silence reigns for a few seconds, then the guy cracks his first smile. It turns him from beautiful into devastating. "Well, see, they're from the sixteenth century. Back then, wine was probably safer than water, so..."

"The unfortunate historical reality of drinking from the sewers?"

"'Don't defecate where you drink' didn't gain traction until some two-hundred years later, yeah."

Gabe nods sagely. "So by drinking wine, these two are safe from, like, bacteria, even if they might die of alcohol poisoning?"

"Pretty much, yeah."

"Except for how they're already dead."

"Well, yes." The guy's smile persists longer this time. "Except for that."

As far as conversations go, this one ranks fairly high on the weirdness scale. Gabe loves every second of it. "So, okay. I can't help but ask. Did you wake up this morning and just randomly decide that this was the day to scratch a premature Halloween itch?"

"Uh. So, funny story." The guy tugs at a sole stud earring. Usually, Gabe's not into that, but this guy makes it look like a gentle act of rebellion. In a classy way. Also, Gabe should probably get the guy's name, but then again, what's the point?

"Funny story?" Gabe echoes.

"I've got these friends. Who are a bit crazy, I guess."

Friends? Yeah, Gabe used to have that. He's down to one now, partially through fault of his own. Rather than share that sorry fact about his life and have this guy possibly sell it to the papers, Gabe makes a sympathetic sound and waits for more.

"And a dare is a dare, right?" At this, the guy widens his eyes, as though he's asking for Gabe's agreement.

"Right," Gabe says slowly. "So, just to confirm, you're here because your friends dared you to do ... this." He indicates the skeleton arrangement. "Not because you're robbing the collection."

"Robbing the collection?" The guy's surprise sounds genuine. "Who'd even buy any of this shit?" He hesitates. "No offence intended, if you're somehow affiliated with this stuff."

Good to know that the lab coat makes Gabe look like he could belong. Theoretically. "I'm not. But I thought you were?"

"Uh, yeah. Kind of." The guy crosses his arms and shifts his weight from one leg to the other, gaze skittering away like a cockroach fleeing the light. Right—robber or not, he's clearly breaking some kind of ethical protocol by playing around with human antiques.

"You work here?" Gabe guesses.

"Not ... exactly." The guy rubs a hand over his head, dark hair cropped short at the sides and longer at the top.

"Not exactly?"

The sheer amount of discomfort in the guy's posture makes Gabe experience a second-hand sense of unease, much like when the camera in a shitty reality TV show starts shaking to the steps of an overweight contestant. "I just ... work around here."

"Like, in this building?"

Gabe can pinpoint the exact moment the guy decides that resistance is futile. "In the research lab, yeah. Just ... maybe we can forget this happened?"

"And by 'we,' you mean 'me'?" Gabe asks, genuinely curious.

"Please?" The guy has the puppy dog eyes down pat, and honestly, it's not like Gabe is about to report him. Who'd he even tell, for Christ's sake? He's just an actor in a lab coat, not a real researcher.

Which—huh. Now *there's* an idea. Instead of waiting around for that magical spark to ignite, maybe he could help things along by talking to someone who actually lives what Gabe aims to emulate.

He flashes the guy his best grin, dimples and all. "How about a deal? I keep my mouth shut and, in return, you tell me all about working in a lab. Like, all the mundane little things, like staying late to catch the growth cycle of some tribe of bacteria—or species. I guess it's species of bacteria?"

When the guy merely blinks at him, Gabe reviews his words, and oh, shit. Yeah, he can just see the headline: *'Shock: Gabe Duke's Indecent Proposal'*.

"Wait, that sounded bad, didn't it?" He softens his grin and drops his arms. "I didn't mean to make it seem like..."

"Blackmail?" the guy suggests, and for the first time, he looks almost cheerful.

"Yeah, that." Gabe lets one corner of his mouth tug up further. "I'll keep my mouth shut either way. But I would also *really* appreciate it if you could spare an hour or two and tell me how things work in a lab."

The guy juts his chin at Gabe's attire. "I thought you were a researcher yourself?"

"Not quite, just ... trying it on for size, you know? The idea of being one, not the lab coat." It's not a lie, strictly speaking. It's also not the truth, the whole truth, and nothing but the truth—but there's something awfully refreshing about talking to a beautiful stranger who has no preconceived notion of what Gabe is and isn't like.

It's not a random notion, either—Gabe has seen the media briefing his agent put together, inviting the press to describe Gabe as British, sweet, and in possession of boyish charm and killer abs. Nowhere does it mention bouts of insecurity and loneliness.

"Oh, okay." The guy nods like that makes sense. "Sure, man. Thanks for not ratting me out, and happy to tell you more about life in the lab. From one potential future colleague to another, right?"

"Right," Gabe says vaguely.

"So, what do you want to know?"

How does it feel to be obsessed with finding an answer to the secret of life? What does a lab sound like first thing in the morning and when you leave at night? Do people compete and look over their shoulders, or do you collaborate and ask for help?

"A lot." After a glance down the corridor, Gabe hesitates. "I should probably make my way back, but, uh, are you possibly free this afternoon?"

Something passes behind the guy's eyes. Intrigue, possibly even a hint of flirtation? "I should be, yeah. Do you want to meet up somewhere?"

'Somewhere' is uncomfortably close to 'somewhere public.' Briefly, Gabe considers his hotel suite, but there might be fans hanging around, and river view notwithstanding, this guy doesn't look like he'd be at home in a nineteenth century throwback setting.

"Sounds good, yeah. I'm part of a group here, though, so I can't quite predict how much longer I'll be. I could just come over to your place when things wrap up, in a couple of hours or so?" He follows it up with his most guileless smile. "Also, by the way, I'm Gabriel."

"Ray," the guy says, and unless he's the kind of actor who could give Gabe a run for his money, there's still no recognition.

"Nice to meet you, Ray." Gabe widens his smile. "Odd, but nice."

"Same, I guess." Ray's chuckle is low and a little raspy, just like his voice. He sounds like someone who isn't used to people paying attention when he speaks, and while that's none of Gabe's business, it makes him a little sad all the same.

For a second, they're both quiet, just watching each other. Then Ray tugs a phone out of his jeans that just barely passes for a smartphone, like he either can't afford better, or he doesn't give a damn about carrying a pocket computer around at all times. Gabe suspects it's a mix of both.

"Why don't you" —Ray offers the phone to Gabe, already opened to a new contact page— "give me your number, and I'll text you my address? I don't have plans this afternoon, so anytime is fine."

"Sounds great." Gabe decidedly doesn't notice the way their fingers brush as he accepts the phone and saves his number under 'Gabriel Jacob.' His full first and middle name is as close to the truth as he's willing to skirt. "I'll bring coffee." Wait, this is London, not Los Angeles. "Or tea, if you prefer?"

"Coffee's good," Ray tells him. "Just black, please. There's a place just around the corner from where I live that's more than half-decent."

A coffee date with an actual researcher who also happens to be bloody *fit*—Gabe's feeling pretty good about how he spent this allotted break, which is almost certainly drawing to a close. Since he doesn't want to be the wanker who makes everyone else wait, he casts one last look at the honestly quite hilarious skeleton picnic before he takes a reluctant step back into the corridor.

"Text me the address," he says, by way of taking his leave.

"Will do." Ray's smile is bright against the honeyed tone of his skin. "Thanks for being cool, mate."

On his best days, Gabe and 'cool' are passing acquaintances. He sees no need to volunteer as much, not if there's a chance to maintain the illusion until he and Ray part ways later today. That way, if Ray goes to the press once he realises who Gabe is, he might paint the kind of picture that will make Gabe's agent happy.

"See you later," Gabe says, cool.

He's back in position, warm under the spotlights, before he realises that the restless itch of energy from before has faded to almost nothing.

2

Ray is about sixty per cent sure that it's not a date. Gabriel is bringing coffee, yes, and he suggested they meet in private—as in, conveniently close to Ray's bed. On the other hand, he wasn't openly flirty, and for all that he seemed to enjoy their conversation, he didn't propose to extend it until Ray mentioned that he works in the lab.

Most likely, then, he's a potential colleague. Honestly, it would be nice to work with at least one person who could maybe, eventually, turn into a friend. That's not too much to ask for, is it?

Granted, Gabriel looked young for a PhD student, but he might be one of those superbrains who complete their A-levels at age sixteen and then set out to be brilliant and capable because the world is their oyster. If Ray hadn't been quite so distracted by a dimpled smile and potentially losing his job, he could have bloody *asked*.

But, alas.

Even though Ray expects it, he startles at the sound of the doorbell. It's right around the time Gabriel said it would be—which is good, because Patrick won't be back for a while yet, so Ray has a chance to make a decent second impression before his flatmate barges in and inevitably becomes the loudest voice in the room.

Maybe a date.

"Fifth floor," Ray tells the intercom. "If the door doesn't open when I buzz you in, try harder."

"Brute force," crackles the response. "Got it."

"And only take the elevator if you're okay with getting stuck."

"Cheers. Think I'll stick with the stairs."

"Where's your sense of adventure, mate?"

"Took it to the dry cleaners for a thorough scrub."

Ray is smiling when he presses the button for the door.

A couple of minutes later, Gabriel takes the last flight of stairs. He doesn't seem out of breath, which confirms Ray's suspicion that he was hiding a rather fit body under that lab coat earlier. Not that Ray still needs to rely on his imagination: Gabriel has ditched the lab coat to expose tailored jeans and a simple yet equally well-fitting white T-shirt with a pair of sunglasses dangling from the front. He looks ... expensive, for lack of a better word—as though he should be sitting on a piazza in Rome, sipping espresso while debating the merits of buying another Jaguar to match his belt.

That's until Ray's gaze drops from the two cups Gabe carries in one hand, and he spies the baseball cap tucked into the waistband of Gabriel's jeans.

"Manchester United? *Really*?" Ray doesn't bother moderating the disdain in his voice.

"Why, you an Arsenal fan?" With a grin, Gabriel offers Ray one of the two coffees—seems like he sprung for reusable cups that have flowers and leaves printed over some bamboo type of material. His green eyes are bright, his dark curls sticking up in odd little tufts. "Because if so, mate, we flattened you in that last match."

"3:1 hardly qualifies as flattening," Ray protests even as he accepts the coffee and waves Gabriel into the flat.

"*Flattened*," Gabriel repeats, with an inappropriate measure of boyish glee.

"We had way more possession than you."

"And yet our shots were on target."

"At least" —Ray sighs and takes a sip of his coffee— "you actually know something about the game. Nothing worse than a supposed fan who can't name a single player and only shows up for the Champions League final."

"I catch a match whenever I can." Gabriel toes off his shoes, exposing a pair of bright green socks, before he follows Ray towards the kitchen. His voice carries a smile. "Had a soft spot for them ever since Jake Quinn and then Ben Jimmer joined the squad."

Huh. Ray makes it a point not to react. "So you were in favour when Jimmer took over as coach?"

"Eh, I was on the fence for a bit there. A great player doesn't always make for a great coach, you know?"

"Fair point," Ray says, and it is. However, it might be a mere excuse to justify criticism.

When Jimmer was initially announced, it caused a media wave that washed up all sorts of old stories about that time he lost his temper on the field, about that time he sassed reporters, and, most notably, about that time he came out as the first gay player in the Premier League. Did he have the right level of maturity to coach a team like Manchester United? Only *The Daily Mail* was blunt enough to outright ask whether a bunch of millionaire star players would take orders from a gay coach.

Five matches and four wins later, the talk mostly died down—it must have helped, too, that Jimmer has been married to the same guy for about a century. There's something to be said for being the right kind of gay.

"I've come around, though," Gabriel says, tone light. "He seems to have a good head for strategy, and like I said, I've always had a soft spot for him."

So that's a hint, maybe. At the very least, Gabriel isn't wildly homophobic.

"He's okay," Ray allows. "For, you know, a person affiliated with Manchester United."

"Careful there. Next thing you know, you'll wake up with a red devil tattoo on your forehead." Gabriel's grin is the brightest thing around—which isn't saying much given the scarcity of natural daylight in the kitchen. It might have helped if the sole window next to the table had seen a cleaning rag at any point in the last five years. Since all it would improve is an abysmal view of the ageing office building across the road, Ray's motivation is lacking, and he doesn't think Patrick even knows what to do with a rag. As for Andrew, well, he probably considers the layers of dirt some kind of experiment that he blogs about in secret.

"If you're only here to mock my team affiliation..." Ray plops into a chair and gestures for Gabriel to do the same.

"I did also bring you coffee," Gabriel tells him, and there is that.

"There is that." Ray lets his own grin show. "Honestly, it's kind of nice to talk footie. I live with a physical therapist who claims that playing football sets you on a statistical fast track to getting injured, and a political scientist who calls it a weapon of mass appeasement."

Gabriel's laugh could melt glaciers, and if Ray was the type to believe in love, he'd be halfway there. Fortunately, he's been weaned off his illusions. "Those the same friends," Gabriel asks, "who sent you on a Halloween mission?"

"The very same."

"They sound like fun." There's a wistful quality to Gabriel's smile, but before Ray can ask, Gabriel continues. "So you've got a background in ... medicine? Biology?"

This is the moment for Ray to clarify that he's a uni dropout—that, as a guy without a PhD under his belt, he's not exactly doing research that will change the course of the world as we know it, that mostly he just does as the real scientists tell him, and takes care of the dishes. Hardly the kind of thing that justifies Gabriel buying him coffee in return for his limited insights.

It's nice, though. To have someone looking at him like he didn't blithely bin his scholarship along with his future. Like his opinion *matters*.

"Medicine," is what he says. It's not a lie, after all. "What about you?"

"Oh." A sheepish look passes over Gabriel's face as he takes a sip of coffee. "Actually, I'm kind of trying to get into a character's head.

Hence the lab coat. And the whole" —he gestures at Ray and the room at large— "barging in on you."

Okay, so it really isn't a date, then. Which is *good*, because Ray doesn't do dates; he does mutually beneficial one-night stands that leave no one disappointed or emotionally compromised, and he likes it that way.

Also, *hence*. He raises a brow. "Writer?"

"Actor."

Given Gabriel's apparent affluence, Ray wouldn't have pegged him for a job that is usually pursued as a teenage hobby and dropped once paying bills becomes a thing. "Film or stage? Anything I might have seen?"

"Ah." Gabriel lifts one shoulder and glances away, down at his hands. "Probably not."

He seems almost embarrassed, so Ray considers a crack about how it's not porn, is it? Except if it was, that would dial the awkwardness level up to eleven. It almost certainly isn't because what porn actor would be … uh, *performing* in a lab coat and care about getting into the right headspace—and ha, headspace, now that's another pun right there.

Ray clears his throat. "Yeah, I guess I'd remember. But it pays the bills?"

"I do all right," Gabriel says with this little shrug that suggests he does more than that. Good for him.

"Brilliant." Ray raises his cup in a mock toast. "Means I won't have to feel bad about bumming this coffee off a starving artist."

"Well. It does set me back by about a month's salary, but…" Gabriel follows it up with what Ray is pretty sure is supposed to be a wink but is really more Gabriel squinting in an asymmetrical way.

"Mate." Ray sinks a world of meaning into the word. "Who taught you how to wink, and can you fire them?"

For a beat, Gabriel fixes him with a steady gaze. It lasts just long enough that Ray thinks he went too far, got comfortable too fast—not usually among his social failings, but meeting over skeletons might have short-circuited any concern about embarrassing himself in front of Gabriel because been there, done that.

Then Gabriel gives another laugh that's softer this time, almost shy. It's only when his shoulders relax that Ray realises they weren't before. "Afraid that firing my sister is out of the question."

"I see how that could pose a challenge."

"I don't think you truly do. Not until you've met her."

"As someone who has three of them, I doubt my imagination is that far off."

"Three?" Gabriel purses his lips, eyes sparkling like he's a fucking Disney prince or something. "You are a stronger man than I am."

"You rise to the occasion."

"No, what you do is fall to your lowest level of preparation."

"That's a rather sobering outlook on life."

"Life is not a Christmas wish list, mate. Also, I like to think of it as motivating." Gabriel's lips curve around the rim of his cup. "Take this, for example. I wouldn't be here if I wasn't trying to prepare for my role."

"So you'd have missed out on me insulting your winking skills," Ray says dryly. "Tragic."

"Hey, I could use more people like that." Gabriel's easy tone is at odds with the way the corners of his mouth pull down, just briefly, before he catches himself. For an actor, his poker face is aggressively average.

Ray chuckles to gloss over the awkward moment. "You mean people who insult you?"

"I mean people who are honest."

And isn't that just dandy given Gabriel is here on the incorrect assumption that Ray is a legit researcher with valuable insights to offer? Ray washes the bitter taste in his mouth down with some coffee.

Okay, all better now. "And on the topic of being prepared, how can I help? What do you want to know?"

"Well." Gabriel leans forward, elbows on the table and fingers wrapped around his cup. He's got nice hands that would look good wrapped around—*hold it right there*. "How much time do you have?"

I've got all night.

"As much time as you need," Ray says instead, and he's rewarded with another one of those smiles that brighten up the entire room.

～

THE DOOR BANGS open halfway through Ray's explanation about cell replication cycles and the way they dictate whether you have to work late. "I'm home, motherfuckers!" Patrick calls out. "And you better not be having sex on the sofa!"

They did indeed move to the sofa some ten minutes ago, but there is no sex involved. It's just been ... comfortable, in spite of the lumpy state of this particular piece of furniture that Andrew found at a yard sale approximately five-hundred years ago. He refuses to part with it because he objects to 'consumption on steroids that treats consumers like a small detour on the way to the rubbish heap.'

Sadly, Gabriel's sense of ease seems to have evaporated: he's gone rigid at Patrick unmistakably announcing his presence. Is it the implication of gay sex? Ray shoots Gabriel a probing glance, but keeps his tone flat. "I'm very sorry about Patrick. I wish I could say this is unusual, but unfortunately, it's the everyday cross I have to bear."

"I can hear you muttering about me." Patrick's statement is underlined by the twin thuds of him kicking off his running shoes.

"Just apologising for your general existence," Ray volleys back. "While trying to assure Gabriel that you are mostly harmless."

"Don't even *think* about constructing an intergalactic bypass anywhere near or through my person!"

The corners of Gabriel's mouth twitch a second before Ray himself catches the *Hitchhiker's Guide to the Galaxy* reference. Gabriel seems to relax by a fraction, but he's still sitting with his back unnaturally straight when he was slouching just moments ago.

"I'm not a Vogon." Ray directs it at the doorway, where Patrick is due to appear any moment.

"And yet you do rather resemble a slug first thing in the morning," Patrick calls back. "In addition to authoring terrible poetry."

While Ray may have written an angst-filled verse or two in Sixth Form, he had the good sense to keep it hidden. He is about to accuse Patrick of blatant slander when his flatmate strolls into the room, shirt sticky with sweat to prove that he works for his body—unlike Ray, who nowadays gets by on good genes and semi-watching what he eats.

Angling himself towards Gabriel, Ray heaves the sigh of the world-weary. "This is Patrick. I'm really very sorry about him."

Gabriel nods, clearly uneasy. It's a little strange; while Ray understands that Patrick can be a lot, most people find him entertaining rather than unsettling.

Frowning, Ray turns his attention to Patrick. "So, Patrick, this is Gabriel—"

"Whoa," Patrick interrupts, wild-eyed. "*Gabe Duke?*"

"No, that's not..." Ray trails off, suddenly unsure. Gabe Duke? It's not what Gabriel entered into Ray's contacts, and yet ... it sounds familiar?

"Yeah, um." Gabriel's smile looks strained. "Just Gabe is fine, really."

Gabe? Gabe Duke?

While Ray's brain knots itself into decorative shape, Patrick stands squinting at Gabriel, at *Gabe*, for a heavy second before he transfers his attention to Ray. "Mate. *Ray.* Why is there a movie star in our kitchen?"

"A..." Ray inhales through his teeth as it finally clicks. *Gabe Duke.* Breakout sensation from the latest instalment of some superhero franchise that Ray knows only because Patrick and Andrew watch it ironically—or so they claim. "The Green ... something?"

"Hunter." Gabriel—*Gabe* accomplishes the feat of looking gracefully sheepish. Maybe that's something they teach at acting school. "The Green Hunter."

"So when you said you were doing all right..."

"I am." An affable shrug. "For, you know. Someone with just two movies under his belt, and the third one still in post-production."

"Is it true you auditioned on a dare?" Patrick breaks in. "Always thought it was a pile of bollocks."

"Nah, that part's true."

"Oh?" Patrick's sharp blue eyes narrow in on Gabe. "So which part isn't?"

Gabe seems to weigh his response for a long beat, his silence turned more pronounced by the flush of a toilet from a neighbouring flat. Then he grins. "I don't have a rose tattooed on my arse."

Patrick mirrors Gabe's grin, and it's a real one, crinkling the corners of his eyes. "I'll alert *The Sun*."

"Might also want to let them know I'm not allergic to peanuts," Gabe says.

"Allergic to peanuts?" Ray finally rejoins the conversation. He tucks one foot underneath his body as he shifts to face Gabe. *Gabe Duke, movie star.* On Andrew's old sofa. Holy shit. "Who even comes up with stuff like that?"

"According to my mate Charlie?" Warmth touches Gabe's eyes, just at the mention of the name. "Whoever's drunkest at the morning editorial meeting."

"Does it bother you?" Ray didn't mean to sound quite so serious, but he gets his answer in the form of Gabe's gaze shuffling away like a sideways-walking crab fleeing the light. Gabe's shoulders pull back even though his tone is deliberately light.

"I'm not complaining."

"Why the hell not?" Patrick breaks in. "If people made it their business whether I splurge on scented three-ply toilet paper or enjoy an extra dash of soy milk in my tea, I'd sure feel like telling them where to stick it."

"I could do that," Gabe says evenly. "If, you know, I want to make an enemy of the press, which would then have no qualms about painting me in the worst possible light."

"Sounds like blackmail."

"It just is what it is." Gabe's careless shrug is almost believable.

"I'm new in town. I need to earn my keep before I get to complain about the rules of the game."

That sounds mildly depressing. But then, Gabe could walk away if he so chose.

Ray pokes him with a socked foot. "Pretty sure your metaphors are all over the place, mate."

"Pretty sure you're no English teacher, mate," Gabe returns, but he's smiling a little as he pushes up from the sofa and pauses to stretch. "Anyway, I should get going."

"Peanuts to eat, tattoos to choose?" Patrick puts in.

Gabe nods sagely. "I was thinking 'snake coming out of the eye of a skull'."

"Classy." Ray gets up too, unsure for a moment. He should walk Gabe to the door, shouldn't he? It's what you do with a one-afternoon friend who's not a date. Right? Right. "I'll walk you to the door."

"Thanks," Gabe says, and fuck, he's pretty when he smiles at Ray like that, all dimples and white teeth. "And thank you, too, for the tutoring session."

"Anytime," Ray tells him. It comes out a tad too grave for the occasion, and he makes it a point to avoid Patrick's eyes as he scrambles off the couch. For a moment, it brings him way too close to Gabe, close enough to spot tiny flecks of gold in the bright green of Gabe's irises.

Patrick coughs, and Ray takes a step to the side, towards the door.

"Thanks," Gabe repeats quietly, and when Ray glances at him, his smile has turned distant and a little sad. He directs a "Nice to meet you" at Patrick before he follows Ray and stops to put his shoes on in a hallway that's so tiny Ray has to lean back against the wall so Gabe has space to kneel.

Inappropriately, Ray's mind flashes back to a quip about acting in porn. He exhales and looks away. "So, uh. See you around, I guess?"

He won't. Of course he won't.

And that's okay. If circumstances were different, maybe they could be friends—but circumstances aren't different. On the bright side, it doesn't matter that Ray bent the truth just a bit.

"Yeah." Gabe straightens and brushes some dust off the knees of his jeans. "Can I... If I have more questions, is it okay if I give you a call?"

Yeah, Ray's not exactly holding his breath waiting for that to happen. It's nice of Gabe to pretend this isn't goodbye, though.

"Sure," Ray tells him, sending a smile after it. "Like I said, anytime."

An answering smile coupled with an awkward moment of stillness. Ray wonders whether he should shake Gabe's hand, or if that would make him look like a proper wanker. He's saved from his indecision when Gabe reaches out for a one-armed hug, complete with a manly pat on the back. Okay, this is fine. Ray can roll with this.

Gabe smells like expensive cologne, all warm and spicy. Which alerts Ray to the fact that he himself probably smells like eau de own-brand shower gel mixed with coffee breath.

It's fine, though. Not a date, after all.

And since it is fine, and since it isn't a date, Ray doesn't linger by the door after Gabe's walked out of the flat and his life. While it's rare that in between his bouts of awkwardness and introvert tendencies, he clicks with someone quite this quickly... Well, he wouldn't be surprised if Gabe had lessons in how to connect with people, in making them feel like they're the only person in the room. All part of the job, right?

Yeah.

Ray shuts the door.

To exactly no one's surprise, Patrick pounces at the sound, appearing in the hallway as though he was hiding just around the corner, eavesdropping. He probably was. "So," he says loudly.

Fortunately, Ray speaks fluent Patrick. "Nothing happened. He wanted some advice for a role, is all."

"You two seemed awfully chummy when I walked in."

The way Ray remembers it, Gabe turned into a statue the moment Patrick made his presence known. "We were just sitting on the sofa. It's what you and I do most nights, and I have yet to hear you refer to *us* as chummy."

Patrick tilts his head, assessing Ray with the clear look of someone who knows him far too well—knows about every stupid, sorry time Ray had his heart crushed just a little because he actually believed people who claimed that they saw more than just his pretty face.

"I've known you since we were both in diapers," is all Patrick says, after a beat too long. "We're the chummiest, and no random superhero actor can take that away from us."

It's an easy out that Patrick doesn't grant often, and Ray is grateful. "Not a chance," he agrees. "Although it might help if you took a shower."

"Please. You love the smell of my musky maleness."

"Did you dip into the waiting room's stash of *OK! Magazine* again?"

"Kate" —Patrick strikes a dramatic pose— "is rumoured to find William's personal hygiene lacking."

"I find *your* personal hygiene lacking," Ray grumbles.

"Is that your best shot?" Patrick sounds like a disappointed father.

"I'm saving all my gems for a special occasion."

"Like what?"

"Like my speech at your wedding."

It serves its intended purpose, that is: it shuts Patrick right up, save for some half-arsed mumblings about how it's all still new with Lauren and that Ray is really not funny. Underneath, Patrick looks pleased, though—pleased and uncharacteristically sheepish, just like when he first told Ray that he maybe might have met someone, but he doesn't want to risk exposing her to Ray's face just yet or she'll realise she could do so much better.

Ray's happy for him. Really, he is.

And if there's a moment of envy, just the tiniest spark of it as he puts away the reusable cups Gabe brought—well. Ray's human, and he still wants certain things even though he should know by now that they're not for him.

He'll learn eventually.

3

'When Watson and Crick proposed their model of the DNA, did they do it by cheating Rosalind Franklin out of her research? Discuss.'

Gabe rereads his draft message: casual tone, no glaring typos that would make him look like an idiot if Ray decided to sell him out. After a brief bout of hesitation, Gabe sends it.

It's been three days since they first met, and while this is the latest of five messages he's written, it's the first that he allows himself to send.

Gabe has always been quick to latch onto people. There was Charlie on the first day of school; there was the preacher's son who hosted the after-church Bible study course; there was Gabe's first girlfriend that he tried so hard to fall in love with; there was the captain of his swim team, and his first Hollywood friend, and the American singer Gabe publicly dated for about five seconds. Out of them all, the only one who remains is Charlie.

The point is, Gabe is susceptible to the new-and-shiny disease, and Ray is both. He's also model gorgeous, which doesn't exactly dampen Gabe's enthusiasm. Not that Gabe would be stupid enough to try anything with someone outside the business, but ... he's got eyes.

Gabe tucks his phone away as Gordon wanders past with one of those mayonnaise-loaded salmon sandwiches that make Gabe feel as though he's gained weight just by being in the same room. He's glad that his nutritionist-approved special catering will save him from having to double his gym time tonight, even if it makes him look like a spoiled brat.

He rises when he's called to the make-up chair and ignores the buzz of his phone in favour of chatting with Kelsey, the make-up artist who reminds him of his sister. God, he misses Deborah. But at least they talk, if only on the phone, and while it's been a few months since he managed to see her, that's because she's studying in France for the year rather than because he betrayed Jesus by erring down the wrong end of the Kinsey scale.

"Pretty as a picture," Kelsey tells him once she's done, and he smacks a kiss to her cheek.

"Just your magic, love."

"Don't 'love' me, love," she says, but she's smiling.

He checks his phone on the way to the set. Three messages from Charlie that detail everything that's wrong with paprika crisps, and one from Ray.

'Ooooooh, one of science's favourite controversies! If you ask me, it's like a Facebook status: complicated.'

Gabe blames growing up in a conservative family for how much he loves a grammatically correct message. *'Please elaborate?'*

'Might be easier on the phone?'

'How about in person?'

Ray has yet to reply when Gabe has to leave his phone behind for a scene with Gordon and the guy who plays shy Maurice Wilkins. Prior to filming, Gabe takes a moment to examine the replica of the infamous Photo 51—an X-ray of DNA diffraction patterns taken by a student under the supervision of Rosalind Franklin, crucial in shaping a better idea of the structure of DNA. Out of the corner of his eye, Gabe catches a crew member wearing a shirt with the same photo printed on the chest. Got to love a geek.

By the time they're done with the scene—Wilkins presenting them with the forbidden fruit of someone else's research, and Watson and Crick jumping on the clue like a cat that spotted a mouse—it's late in the afternoon and the director calls it a day.

Costume ditched and make-up removed, Gabe steps out into another unseasonably warm October day. After the windowless studio, his eyes need a moment to adjust. Sunlight paints the nearby river a muddy green.

"Exciting plans for tonight?" Gordon asks as they wait for a car to take them back to the hotel. It's not the first time he's inquired, like he expects Gabe to have a string of willing sex partners lined up outside the door to his hotel room—there's no malice in Gordon's tone, though, just plain curiosity about the supposed perks of being a teenage heartthrob. He never quite seems to believe it when Gabe shrugs and cites a hot date with a book, and fair enough: if Gabe were just a little less gay and a little more extroverted, he could find a different girl at a different party every night.

Too bad for him.

"Meeting a friend later," Gabe says. It feels like a lie even though it's not—Ray is a friend, if a new one, and he agreed to meet Gabe with a *'Your place or mine?'* followed by a wink.

He sent a second message almost right after: 'Just kidding! I didn't mean to imply anything.'

And then: 'Except I totally, totally do!!'

Another few seconds later: 'SORRY! That was Patrick. Please ignore anything that originates with him, always.'

Half an hour later: *'Gabe?'*

Gabe really should have responded the moment he got his hands on his phone again, put Ray's mind at ease. Privacy is at a premium on a busy movie set, though, and just when Gabe finally found a quiet corner to wait for his turn in the make-up chair, Karine wanted to discuss an aspect of his take on Watson. Days ago, it would have sent Gabe tumbling down a rabbit hole of insecurities, but he feels more at ease now in Watson's skin than he did before. *Thanks, Ray.*

"A friend?" Gordon sounds distracted, frowning at something on his phone. "That's nice."

"You?" Gabe asks.

"Oh, just—" Gordon glances up. "Liverpool match and an early night, I think. Still not over that bloody flu."

"The hotel serves chicken broth," Gabe suggests.

"Got it coming out of my ears, at this point." Tucking his phone away, Gordon turns his full attention to Gabe, weighing him for a moment. "How you doing, lad? I know this is a tad lower on explosions than what you're used to."

Gabe's first instinct is to lift his chin and cross his arms, but he stops himself. There is no judgement in Gordon's eyes, only curiosity and a touch of warmth.

Gabe exhales. "I'm doing all right, I think. Thank you for asking. Better now I've had a chance to … really dig into the role, learn more about life in a lab and all that." He hesitates, then squares his shoulders. "Any advice?"

"You're doing fine. Relax a little and try to enjoy the ride, and you'll do even better." Crow's feet bloom around Gordon's eyes. He isn't classically handsome, but he's got a face for the stage: strong, expressive lines and pale skin that contrasts with his dark hair. "I'll be the first to admit I held out some reservations when I saw they cast you, but you're good. Guess that bow and arrow didn't show off your full range."

"Guess not. Running around in front of a green screen can be fun too, though—don't think I want to do only serious roles from now on." Gabe sends Gordon a smile, then realises he might have just insulted him. "Not that there's anything wrong with that! I just, you know. I like both. Like, I'm probably still a bit young to know what I really want to do with the rest of my career—if I get to have a proper career, you know. So…"

He trails off, uncertain, as Gordon arches one eloquent brow. "Are you calling me old?"

"No!" Gabe raises both hands. He thinks Gordon is kidding, but what if he's not? "You're only, what, ten years older than me? Twelve?" It's thirteen, but who's counting. "It's just, you know, you've just got all this experience that I don't have. Years and years of it, and also stage acting, which I've never really done. And you've been nominated for an Oscar, and you won a BAFTA Award, and—"

Mercifully, Gordon stops him with a laugh. "Breathe, Gabe. I'm not actually bothered. Hitting thirty was rough for a second there, yeah, but that's because everyone around me started having kids. Meanwhile, I was still on stage every night, coming home well past midnight to an empty flat."

Given he regales everyone who'll listen with tales of his pregnant fiancée, those days are behind him.

"And soon, you'll be a daddy," Gabe tells him with a grin. "Life's funny that way, isn't it?"

"You're too young to spout fortune cookie wisdom about how life goes."

"I'm twenty-one!"

"My point precisely."

The car's arrival interrupts their playful argument that Gabe is bound to lose based on lack of seniority, pun intended. He lets Gordon take the passenger seat and clambers into the back, folding his long legs into the narrow space behind the driver. It's the same guy who picked them up this morning, and while Gordon launches into a conversation about the state of the weather and the world, Gabe finally has a chance to turn to his phone.

'My place?' he suggests. 'No wining and dining, I'm afraid, but the hotel has room service. My treat.'

It's suitably light in tone, he hopes—he can't risk flirting with someone outside the industry, no matter how hot that person may be, but he can respond with a touch of humour.

Ray answers within seconds, as though he's been waiting. *'Room service? Is that the stuff I've seen in movies?'*

'It's fish and chips or tomato soup cooked by someone else. What's not to like?'

It's also lobster, oysters, and truffle tortelloni, but Gabe suspects Ray would be disconcerted rather than impressed. While Gabe never made it to uni and therefore missed out on the starving student experience, he was raised on sourdough bread and cereal. So ... he gets it.

'Tell me where and when,' Ray replies.

Gabe is smiling when he types his response.

∽

ENTERING the Savoy feels like stepping onto the set of an old movie. From the bellboy at the entrance to the wooden revolving doors with their domed roofs to the chessboard floor—all of it combines to inform Ray that he does not belong. As a partial second-generation Moroccan immigrant, Ray is a pro at not belonging.

Treat it like a dare.

He raises his head, squares his shoulders, and strolls forward in his scuffed-up sneakers and secondhand sweater that he bought off eBay. No one stops him.

He shares the elevator with a pair of suits who don't spare him more than a brief glance, then exits on what he assumes is the correct floor. *Just come on up and knock on the door* has a slightly different feel when it's cream walls, plush carpets, and gold-framed paintings rather than some standard hallway in some standard building on some standard street.

This is fine.

Ray knocks once, decisively, then shoves his hands into his pockets as he takes a step back. Ten seconds, fifteen—he knows because he counts them in his head.

No Gabe.

Should Ray knock again? He doesn't want to look desperate, but he also doesn't want hotel security descending upon him because he's loitering outside *the* Gabe Duke's room. He's about to pull his phone out when Gabe finally opens the door, a sheepish smile lighting his eyes to a translucent shade of green, signalling for Ray to stay quiet even as he waves him into a room cast in golden hues by the early evening sun.

"Sorry," Gabe mouths, then appears to listen to something, his gaze sliding past Ray. "Not at the moment, no. I'm travelling too much, you see? There is simply not much space for romance when I'm gone for weeks at a time."

His voice is smoother, more confident than Ray remembers, and Ray is confused for a second before he realises that Gabe's got headphones in. Okay then. Just another thing Ray can roll with.

While Gabe keeps talking about things he looks for in a girl—at least that's what Ray gets from Gabe's side of the conversation—Ray takes off his shoes to inspect the suite. Big windows, river view, decorative fireplace facing the sofa, and a half-open door leading to a separate bedroom. Art books are stacked up on an antique side table, and a faint scent of pine needles hangs in the air.

It's very, very nice, albeit in a retro, heavy-drapes-layered-over-curtains kind of way. There's a difference between drapes and curtains, right? Like ... fabric weight, possibly? And will Ray have to hand in his gay card if he doesn't have a proper answer?

Talk about internalised stereotyping.

He steps up to the window to enjoy what is a rather spectacular panorama of the Thames. Clearly, there are perks to having your own line of merchandise.

"Sorry," Gabe says as soon as he's said his goodbyes. "Thought I'd be done with the interview by now, but I had the time wrong."

"No problem." Ray turns around, hands still in his pockets, and shoots him a grin. "Did you know there's a Green Hunter action figure that makes you look like the Hulk?"

Gabe assesses him with a sharp look before he relaxes. "Just wait for the next batch. For the third movie, they make it look like I doubled my body weight, and it's all muscle."

As far as Ray is concerned, Gabe's body is perfectly proportioned just as it is—no need for dramatic enhancement. Which just goes to show that Ray is not the intended audience for cheap plastic figures made in China, hopefully while respecting human rights. Since Ray is not Patrick, he knows when to hold his tongue along with his aesthetic opinions, though.

"Your parents must be so proud," he says instead, letting the corners of his mouth tug up into a deliberately cheesy smile.

Something twitches around Gabe's eyes, too fast to catch. "Not really."

Found mouth, put foot in it. Bloody awesome.

Before Ray can correct course, Gabe pastes on a smile that doesn't quite reach his eyes. "What about your parents, though? Doesn't get much better than a future doctor for a son, does it?"

Right, about that.

Ray rolls his upper lip over his teeth and rocks back on his heels, sounding out the words in his head. "It's ... more complicated than that, actually. You see, my dad died a couple of years back."

"I am so sorry." Gabe reaches out as if to touch Ray's shoulder, then seems to reconsider and drops his hand. "That must have been difficult. Was it ... unexpected?"

"Cardiac arrest. Came out of nowhere." The words taste like ash on Ray's tongue, even now. He can't quite meet Gabe's eyes, so he turns to face the spectacular view without seeing much of anything. "After that..." *I lost the plot and my scholarship.* "It was... I needed a break from uni, you know? Wanted to be with my mum and sisters."

Gabe steps up beside him, quiet for a moment, a warm presence. "Sounds like your family is close."

"Yeah." Ray swallows around a wistful smile. "My dad was the best. Just ... everything you could possibly want in a dad? He was all that, and more. Like..." He hesitates, just for a beat, the silent hotel room expanding around him—spreading out further and further, much like the ever-growing universe, the sofa shrinking away, the armchair retreating.

Stop. Breathe.

Ray breathes. Glances at Gabe, just long enough to find Gabe's attention anchored to him, calmly waiting, giving Ray all the time he needs.

"Like," Ray begins again, and this won't be a surprise to Gabe, surely. "How many Muslim fathers would be one-hundred per cent cool with a gay son, right? Mine was. Never even batted an eye."

Gabe does. His gaze grows distant, slipping past Ray to settle on a passing tourist boat, brows pulling together. *Well, fuck.*

Ray takes a step back, the icy touch of spider legs skittering down his spine. "Sorry. I'll go."

"What?" Gabe's eyes clear as his focus snaps back to Ray. "No, *I'm* sorry. Just blanked out there for a minute, nothing to do with you." His lips curve up. "Patrick isn't subtle, so it's not like I didn't know."

"Oh. Yeah." Ray nods, face too warm all of a sudden. "Patrick is what happens when you cross a sledgehammer with a particularly talkative poodle: tiny, adorable, but packs a punch and has no filter."

Gabe smiles, and it's like flicking on a light. "That's the kind of friend you want in your corner." Then his expression softens, his voice dipping low. "I really am sorry about your dad, Ray. He sounds like a great man."

"He was." Ray allows it to linger between them for a few breaths before he lets it go. "Anyway, so. The Franklin controversy?"

"The Franklin controversy," Gabe repeats slowly, as though he just about forgot why Ray is here.

"You wanted my opinion?"

"Right, yeah." Gabe nods quickly. "So, my current project. Cinema logic means we're playing it up for drama, of course, but it's about Watson and Crick, and today, we filmed the scene when Wilkins shows them that image taken by Franklin's student. The director wants me to turn up the controversial side of my character—James Watson—and I can do that, but... I'm just curious about how you see the whole thing."

That's a lot of words for a guy Ray would not describe as verbose. It's as though Gabe's nervous, except there's no particular reason why he would be. Ray dismisses the thought. "You mean: did they steal Franklin's research?" he clarifies.

Gabe nods. "Exactly. What do you think?"

"I think" —Ray grins— "that people love a good story."

"As in chemtrails? Flat earth?"

"I was thinking more like true crime, that type of thing. Good and evil, lies and betrayal and intrigue, white knights and villains and ugly henchmen."

"Superheroes in green spandex." Gabe is grinning back now, dimples pressing twin shadows into his cheeks. The fading daylight mutes the vibrance of his eyes.

"Superheroes in green spandex," Ray agrees. "All the good things."

Gabe ponders this for a moment, then seems to realise they're both just standing around when they could be getting comfortable. He waves Ray over to the mustard-coloured sofa, and since Ray's been mostly on his feet since eight in the morning, he accepts the invitation gladly. It doesn't escape his notice that Gabe chooses to share the sofa, tucking his feet under his body, when he could have escaped to the armchair. No need for a bro-type safety distance, it seems, and that's enough to loosen the band around Ray's chest.

"So," Gabe says. "Just a good story, then?"

"Mostly. Scientists love to gossip as much as anyone else, and don't believe anyone who tells you differently." Ray sinks further into the cushions, shifting sideways so he's facing Gabe. "I think there are scattered bits of truth, though."

"Which are?"

"They definitely were ... questionable in how they got their hands on some of her research. Not just the photo, but also some numbers, measurements she did." Ray pauses, briefly trapped in the spotlight of Gabe's attention on him—as though right here, right now, there is nothing that could be more interesting than whatever Ray plans to say next. "They didn't have permission to interpret her data, and best guess? She never even knew how much it helped them."

Gabe tilts his head. "So far, I'm not on Team Crick and Watson."

"Fair enough. But when their model was ready, they did actually invite both Franklin and Wilkins, and they all agreed that Watson and Crick should publish the model, and the other two would provide some supporting data separately."

"Because she didn't *know* they'd looked at her data," Gabe argues.

"They didn't exactly have to steal it, though—she apparently shared most of it herself in a lecture, a few months before Watson and Crick saw her report."

"So?" The stubborn tilt to Gabe's mouth remains. "Bet you that if she was a man, they would have treated her with more respect."

Ray snorts. "It was the fifties. Of *course* they'd have treated her with more respect if she was a man. That said, I think they wanted to win the DNA decoding race badly enough to bulldozer right over anyone who stood in their way, male or female."

"Fair." With a lopsided smile, Gabe switches on the lamp next to the sofa. It casts a gentle glow that doesn't reach far past them, and there's something intimate about sharing a sofa like this, their little island of light with the sky darkening outside.

Just this morning, Ray was convinced he'd never see Gabe again. He'd been fine with it.

"Like I said..." Ray draws a breath and locks that thought away for another day—Patrick keeps telling him to live more in the moment, and if there's one thing Ray enjoys, it's being allowed to geek out in peace. Patrick and Andrew usually stop him two minutes in. "There is *some* truth to the myth that they weren't the most ethical of guys. But also, her research kind of belonged to the institute, so there's an argument there as well."

"So it's just like you said: complicated."

"Pretty much." Ray flutters a hand in a so-so gesture. "Also, keep in mind that Franklin made for a perfect martyr when she died, and then the others all got the Nobel prize without her. *Also*, Watson was an easy target, what with those comments about how white people are smarter, and insulting everyone left and right in his biography."

"Well, I don't know." Gabe attempts another one of his awkward winks. "If I ever write my biography, *Avoid Boring People* will definitely be in the running for the title."

Ray shouldn't be surprised that Gabe bothered to read Watson's memoir—after all, Ray is here because Gabe takes his character research seriously. It might be Gabe's way of combating anxiety; if so, Ray isn't judging.

"Is that my cue to leave?" he asks, mostly joking.

"You're not boring," Gabe tells him with another flash of dimples.

"My ex would beg to differ."

"Your ex sounds like a dickhead. No offence."

"None taken—he kind of was."

Gabe purses his mouth, studying Ray with a thoughtful weight to his gaze that makes Ray feel a little warm, a little nervous. In the end, though, all Gabe says is, "Well, I'm sorry you had to put up with that. Now, I believe I promised you food?"

It's a change of topic if Ray ever saw one, but a lot of straight guys are much more comfortable with the theory of hanging out with a rainbow acquaintance than they are with the reality of discussing gay relationships. Disappointing? Sure. Unusual? Not so much. Not if Sixth Form was any indication—or some of Ray's current colleagues, for that matter.

There's no way to win that battle other than to give it time, Ray has learned. So he shifts marginally further away on the sofa and tucks his knees up against his chest, smiling at Gabe across the divide. "Yeah, you did. In fact, I believe you promised me fish and chips."

Maybe Gabe hears something in his tone because for a second, he frowns. Then his forehead smoothes over. "Fish and chips it is," he says lightly. "Want some ice cream to wash it down? Or the Savoy's take on a Black Forest cake?"

When Ray smiles, he's surprised to find that it's genuine, his disappointment melting away already. And really, why hold on to it? It is free food, after all, and an attractive view to boot. After this, he's about as likely to see Gabe again as his mum is to win The Great British Bake Off, meaning borderline impossible, won't happen, keep on dreaming—so he might as well enjoy the ride.

"Only if you plan on wheeling me out of here later," he tells Gabe.

Gabe's grin is all mischief, eyes sparkling like they're in some stupid movie or something. "That's what butler service is for."

Butler service. Of course.

"Not that this is news, but ... you and I live in *very* different worlds."

One corner of Gabe's mouth pulls down. "I don't really live here, you know? Just turn off the stage lights, wash off the make-up, and there's nothing all that special about me."

Strangely, it sounds like he believes his own bullshit. Since there is no way Ray can argue the point without sounding like a drivelling fan boy, all he does is shake his head. "Either you're a fantastic liar, or you don't see yourself very clearly."

Brief silence precedes Gabe's answer. "Well, I *am* an actor," he says then, his tone bright as he mimes flicking back his hair in a diva toss.

Somehow, Ray is not convinced.

"That you are," he agrees gently, and whatever Gabe hears in his voice causes him to stare at Ray for a beat too long, both of them tucked into their respective corner of the sofa. Then Gabe blinks, smiles, and looks away, picks up the menu.

Ray feels oddly cold without the weight of Gabe's attention on him.

∾

"Are you okay?" Gabe sounds more amused than worried, and Ray raises a hand to shush him.

"Not a *word*. I'm having an out-of-body experience, and if the price is that I'll be leaving here ten pounds heavier, I want to enjoy every bloody *second* of it." He's briefly worried whether that was too familiar, as though he and Gabe are actual friends when Ray's just the guy who offers some insight into lab life. When he glances up from his magical Savoy Black Forest dessert, though, he finds Gabe smirking at him.

"D'you need the room? I can give you some privacy."

"'M all right." With a happy sigh, Ray lets the spoon slip from his mouth. Gabe's gaze seems to flicker for an instant, but it might be just a trick of the light—or lack thereof, rather, the room bathed in shadows that are softened here and there by golden pools of lamp light.

Brief silence spools out between them as Ray sections off another spoonful. This time, though, he pauses before taking another bite. "Okay, question for you: how do you reconcile constant access to food like this with looking the way you do?"

Too flirty?

Before Ray can tie himself into a decorative mental knot, Gabe's huffed laugh dispels any tension. "Iron-clad discipline at breakfast and lunch, and a penchant for overcorrecting any nutrition missteps in the gym."

It's said lightly, but doesn't feel like a joke. Ray weighs his options before he goes with, "I don't know about you, but this?" He nods at his plate. "This is a spiritual experience, not a misstep."

The corners of Gabe's mouth tug up. "I can see that."

"You should *taste* that." Ray sends Gabe's sensible sorbet a dismissive look before he offers his Black Forest to Gabe. "C'mon. You know you want to."

"If you're applying for the 'devil on my shoulder' spot, I'm afraid that's already taken by my friend Charlie."

Ray waves the plate under Gabe's nose, smiling his toothiest smile. "He and I can take turns."

Gabe glances from Ray's eyes down at the plate, then back up again, and pulls his bottom lip between his teeth. "This is cruel and unusual."

"You only live once, mate."

Gabe inhales deeply, glancing back down at the plate. When he picks up his spoon and scoops up a delicate bite, Ray mimes a stadium cheer.

"Human after all!"

The look Gabe sends him is equal parts shrewd and wistful. "Expect a strongly worded message if it turns out my Green Hunter costume won't fit me anymore."

"It's one little bite, Gabe."

"Two," Gabe says, and scoops up some more. Ray lets him. While he grew up with three sisters and Patrick to train him in being protective of what's his, he figures Gabe doesn't indulge very often.

They share the rest of Ray's dessert without much commentary, other than occasional declarations of love for the kitchen genius who whipped this up. Once they're done, Gabe's sorbet a forgotten, melted puddle, Ray sags back into the cushions with a satisfied sigh and tips his head to the side.

"Hey, can I ask a personal question?"

"Sure." Gabe mimics Ray's pose, hands loosely curled on his thighs. Not for the first time, Ray notes that he's got nice hands—long and slender, healthy-looking nails, and maybe that's part of the job description for an actor who made his debut shooting poisoned arrows with the accuracy and speed of a sniper. "I reserve the right not to answer, though."

"Ah, so your sense of adventure is still with the dry cleaners?" Ray asks lightly.

"Lost the collection slip," Gabe returns in precisely the same tone.

"Rest in peace, I guess." Ray tucks one foot under his thigh as he carefully chooses his words. "So, I'm just ... wondering. I mean, someone like you, right? You've got it all: money, fame, looks—you name it. So, you've got every reason to be conceited, but you're just ... not."

"Thanks, I think?" Gabe makes it sound like a question, but continues before Ray gets a chance to react. "I guess it's like... My sister's got this theory, right, how fame doesn't make you a different person. It just elevates who you were before."

"Meaning if you're an arsehole, you stay an arsehole, but you can get away with it even more?"

Gabe frowns. "Something like that, yeah. And if you're essentially a nice person, you stay like that, but maybe you get a few more opportunities to help others out."

"Okay, fine. I get that. But." Ray waves a hand at nothing in particular. "You have people chanting your name, singing your praises, throwing themselves at you. Easy to grow your ego to the size of an average cruise ship—like one of those that pulls into a town like

Venice and it's twice the height of the tallest building there? I mean, I haven't been, right, but I've seen the pictures."

What is Ray's mouth doing? He's pretty sure he didn't grant it permission to say all this.

Gabe doesn't seem to mind, if the amused glint in his eyes is any indication. "There are moments when I feel on top of the world, yeah. Like walking down a red carpet with people cheering, and everyone's just happy to be there? That can be addictive, not gonna lie." His voice tilts down. "But then, just give me thirty seconds, and I can easily find you ten Tik Tok rants about how much I suck."

"Trolls will be trolls?" Ray offers. "I bet anyone even halfway famous has legions of haters trailing behind them, just because they've got nothing better to do than to spew poison on the internet." He pauses, then admits, "I'd hate that, though, if I were you."

Ray would hate it. He'd deliberately seek it out because that's just how his brain works, and then he'd obsess over whether they're right about, like, his teeth not being one-hundred per cent white and straight—incidentally, neither is Ray—or his smile making him look like a smug prick, or how he's a generally talentless sack of wasted space who should just do everyone a favour and crawl back into whatever dark corner he came from.

Gabe must have seen all of that and worse. A gentle swell of secondhand sadness leaves a bitter film on Ray's tongue.

"I do hate it." Gabe averts his gaze to his hands. "Some people are really good at shrugging it off, and I know that's what I should do, too. It's just... I was kind of raised to believe that I'm just, like, failing all the time. That I'm never quite enough. So."

The words hang between them for a few seconds while Ray fishes around for something useful to say. He draws a blank and ends up settling on, "I'm really sorry. That must be tough. The way I see it, parents should prop their kids up, not tear them down."

"Yeah, mine didn't get the memo." Gabe's tone is bleak, his eyes distant.

"I'm really sorry," Ray repeats. It's perfectly inadequate, but he can't quite fathom what it's like to grow up with parents like that.

While his family might not be perfect—his mum and dad had their ups and downs, and Ray was an angsty teenager, and there are no angels to be found among his sisters—he knows deep in his bones that if he needs them, they'll be on the next train. It's part of why losing his dad punched him straight in the teeth.

"Thanks." Gabe draws a deep breath and smiles. "At least my sister's in my corner, you know?"

"She sounds great."

"She's the bane of my existence," Gabe corrects, in the tone of voice people reserve for those they love deeply. It resonates somewhere in Ray's chest, sparking a warm glow.

"And yet..." He extends a leg to poke Gabe with his foot, then wonders if the gesture was too familiar. No way to take it back. "And yet, admit it: you wouldn't change a thing about her."

"Not a thing." Gabe's smile settles in the corners of his eyes. "Sound familiar?"

"Very." Ray retreats back into his corner, studying Gabe's face for what might be a beat too long. In the golden lamp light, he looks like something out of a movie. "Can I ask another personal question?"

"Only if I get one, too."

"Uh, sure?" Ray can't fathom what Gabe could possibly want to know about him—hopefully nothing to do with when he's planning to return to med school because... Yeah, well. 'Never' just doesn't have a sexy ring to it, now does it?

"Go ahead, then," Gabe tells him.

"No disclaimer this time?"

Grinning, Gabe tips his head back against the sofa, exposing the column of his throat. Christ, it's like he *wants* Ray to look. "Terms and conditions apply."

"Terms and conditions," Ray echoes vaguely, before he pulls his attention away. "Right. The way you're talking about what you do—guess it's got me wondering whether you actually enjoy it."

Gabe's response comes with a delay. "You know, no one's ever asked me that. Most people just tend to assume."

"You don't have to answer. Obviously." Ray lifts one shoulder and grins. "In fact, this is your room, so you can kick me out anytime you want."

"Why would I do that?" Gabe sounds genuinely baffled.

Ray raises a hand to tick off his fingers. "Eating your food, taking up your valuable time, asking intrusive questions. I can go on?"

"You're not a bother." Annoyance steals its way across Gabe's face, but it doesn't seem directed at Ray. "Anyway, as for whether I enjoy acting? I do, yeah. I love slipping into someone else's skin—like, not in a creepy way, but immersing myself into a character, trying to see the world through their eyes. And the money doesn't hurt, either. I mean, show me the twenty-something guy who wouldn't love owning a house and a Porsche."

Ray wiggles his fingers. "You're talking to someone who never got around to getting his driver's licence. Although I would enjoy *selling* the Porsche."

"No driver's licence?" Said in the same tone of voice one would reserve for things like 'you fell into a crevice and *survived*?' or 'a bear attack?' It makes Ray laugh.

"Contrary to popular belief, driving is not an essential skill. At least I've survived this far."

"Okay." Gabe shakes his head. "But *why*?"

Ray shrugs. "Cost of driving lessons, lack of interest, lack of likelihood I'll be owning a car anytime soon,..."

"You grew up in the city, didn't you?"

"Not exactly. Small town east of Leeds, some fifteen thousand inhabitants. You wouldn't have heard of it."

"Train connections to Leeds?"

"Every twenty minutes."

"How long does it take?"

"Ten minutes."

"And this, right there?" Gabe nods, seemingly satisfied. "Is why you can be forgiven for your mistaken belief that life without a car is worth living: you haven't grown up in a village where it takes forty minutes to the nearest movie theatre, and if you miss the train, the next one won't be for another hour. Where daily church service is the only entertainment within walking distance."

Ah, yeah. Ray can see how that would impact a teenager. "Speaking from experience, I take it?"

"Speaking from trauma, more like." Gabe sounds like he's joking, but there's a hint of truth in the tilt of his mouth.

Ray might be paying too much attention.

"Anyway," Gabe continues. "Moving on from all the reasons I should be in therapy—here's my personal question: why Arsenal?"

"Is that" —Ray squints at him— "an insult?"

"Most definitely." Gabe sends him a sunny smile. "But I'm also genuinely curious. I mean, we just established you're not even from around here. Leeds United would have been the natural choice."

"Yeah, but it's actually nice to win sometimes. Also..." Ray lets his gaze wander away from Gabe, to the pearly lights of traffic on Westminster Bridge and the brightly lit windows of Canary Wharf that rise against the dark sky. "My last couple years in school weren't awesome. I don't regret coming out, but not everyone was a fan—including the guy I was kind of dating at the time. At least until he ended up on Team Mock the Gay Brown Kid."

"Ouch." Gabe sounds genuinely sorry, and when Ray chances a glance at him, he looks it, too. "Is it just me, or do you have a track record of dating dickheads?"

"Not just you." Ray huffs out a breath. "You and Patrick should have a chat sometime."

Gabe's grin teases Ray with a hint of dimples. "That should be interesting."

"Interesting sounds about right." Ray shifts and grins back. "So, yeah. Unlike Jennifer Grey in *Dirty Dancing*, I did not have the time of my life those last couple of years. Arriving in London felt like I could breathe for the first time, and somehow, I liked Arsenal better than Chelsea."

Gabe opens his mouth as if to say something, then appears to think better of it.

"What?" Ray asks.

"Just..." Gabe's dimples stage a barnstorming return. "Comparing yourself to Jennifer Grey? That might be the gayest thing you've said so far."

"*Dirty Dancing* is a classic." Ray leans forward, and he's possibly proving Gabe's point by waving his hands around, but this bears emphasis. "Just think—show me the Hollywood boss who would nowadays approve a movie where a Jewish teenager hooks up with a working-class Catholic boy, and the middle-class parents approve, and there's possible statutory rape, and a botched abortion with Baby's dad to the rescue, and Johnny is sexually harassed by hotel guests and wrongly accused of being a thief because, you know, prejudice."

Gabe digests this, head tilted as he studies Ray. "Wow, you're good. Almost makes me want to watch it."

"You haven't seen it?"

"I have not."

Without a word, Ray gets up.

"Are you walking out on me?" Laughter warms Gabe's voice.

"No, although maybe I should." Ray collects the remote from the mantelpiece of the fake fireplace and clicks on the TV. "They must have pay-per-view here, right?"

"You want me to watch *Dirty Dancing*?" The warmth in Gabe's voice persists, so Ray feels on solid ground when he throws a narrow look over his shoulder.

"Yes. You will watch it, and you will enjoy it."

Gabe purses his mouth, but his eyes are dancing. "Fine. Guess I should order us a couple of beers, then."

"Guess you should," Ray agrees.

Another laugh as Gabe scrambles off the couch to pick up the phone. It's when Ray browses the selection of movies that it occurs to him that he basically invited himself for a movie night when Gabe might have had different plans.

"Hey," he says as soon as Gabe's done placing the order. "You know you don't have to, right? I mean, I really do think you should watch it sometime, but it doesn't have to be tonight."

"I know it doesn't have to be tonight." Gabe falls back onto the couch and smiles up at Ray. "It sounds like fun, though."

Slowly, Ray returns to his side of the sofa. "If you're sure?"

"I am." Gabe's smile softens, but doesn't fade entirely. "Now, come on. Let's get this party started."

After watching Gabe for what might be just a beat too long, Ray turns to face the TV and hits play.

∼

It's past ten when Ray leaves the hotel, exiting into a night that carries the first bite of winter. In just his sweater, he's severely underdressed—the temperature must have dropped by several degrees since he arrived earlier this evening.

He didn't count on staying this long. He certainly didn't count on Gabe letting him hang around for several hours, well past the agreed purpose of food and discussing the Franklin controversy.

Wrapping his arms around himself, Ray turns to follow the riverwalk. At this hour, there's a magical feel to it, the path lit by a string of Victorian lamps, the London Eye glimmering in the distance, and very few people still out. He pauses to gaze out at the dark waters of the Thames, bright boats dotting it here and there.

This, here, is the London he first fell in love with: historical parks and side streets off the beaten tourist path, far removed from the bustle of Leicester Square and Chinatown. He wonders if Gabe ever got a chance to enjoy this, or whether he was catapulted from his village straight into the kind of fame that likely won't allow for casual city strolls. Ray wouldn't want to trade places.

With the river to his left and a tall row of trees to his right, separating him from traffic, he inhales on a deep, slow breath. Releases it after a beat, along with the memory of Gabe's rumbled laugh, of his elegant hands and the way he pays attention.

Starts walking again, ready to make his way home—back to reality.

4

Patrick leans in, close enough for Ray to smell his coffee breath. "I dare you."

Ray counters with a bored look. "Wait your turn."

"I'm taking my turn preemptively. Like shorting stocks."

"You," Andrew contributes from where he's assessing their supply of tea bags, "don't know the first thing about shorting stocks."

"I've seen the movie." Patrick barrels on before anyone gets a word in. "My point is: seriously, just fucking text him. You've been checking your phone every six seconds, and honestly, mate, that's just sad. You're not the heroine in some bloody story waiting for her prince to come calling."

"One, I'm pretty sure that's vaguely sexist as well as vaguely homophobic." Ray parks his bum on their kitchen table. "Two, I don't want to bother him."

Patrick throws up his hands with what might be a mumbled insult to Ray's lineage. He turns sharply, pointing at Andrew.

"*You*. Back me up here."

Andrew takes his sweet time inspecting a bag of ginger tea. Only once he's satisfied does he glance over, his eyes as grey as the morning sky. "Yeah, all right. I'm with Patrick on this one, Ray. You claim that all you want to be is friends? Then call him."

Clearly, two out of three people in this kitchen have gone mad. Ray crosses his arms and raises his chin in a stubborn tilt. "I can't just call him."

"My *God*," Andrew says. "You are such a millennial."

"So are you," Ray tells him.

"I was born in the eighties. It's totally different."

"Because you're old?" Ray suggests blithely.

Andrew adjusts his glasses, his tone dignified. "Because I remember a time when you called someone's house, not their mobile."

It's Patrick who accepts the silver-platter offer. "Because you're old."

While Andrew grumbles, Ray grins at Patrick, Patrick grins back, and in that instant, their little squabble is all but forgotten. Unfortunately, Patrick isn't easily deterred—he hones in on Ray as soon as the first flash of amusement fades. "You heard Andrew: he's with me."

"I fail to see how your opinions matter." Ray raises a haughty brow. "You just want me to befriend him so you get free tickets to the premiere of his next film."

"The thought never crossed my mind." Patrick looks momentarily shifty, then recovers. "No, here's the point: if I catch you staring out the window with a wistful sigh just one more time—"

"I don't do that," Ray cuts in.

True to form, Patrick ignores him. "—I will personally call the shelter and tell them there's a lost puppy in my flat."

In the background, Andrew laughs quietly. *Bastard*. Ray's attempt at a glare falls flat because Patrick leans right back in his face, close enough that Ray goes cross-eyed.

"Tell me, Ray..." Patrick has perfected the art of the ominous pause. "What've you got to lose?"

"He could think I'm a desperate loser who's trying to hit on him?" Ray means for it to come out like a joke, he really does, but his voice twists halfway through and gives him away.

"Oh, Ray." Patrick's tone is equal parts exasperated and affectionate. "And what's the evidence to suggest he'd think that?"

"Well." Absently, Ray runs his finger over a nick in the table wood, back and forth.

There's how Gabe was yawning when they said goodbye on Wednesday—but Gabe mentioned that he's an early bird trapped in a night owl job, at least when his promo obligations force him to attend premieres for an upcoming film, a different city every night. There's how both times they met, Gabe led with questions related to his current role—but their conversations went well beyond that, and Ray suspects Gabe shared more than just public knowledge about himself. There's how Gabe hasn't reached out since—but he must be busy, and he also doesn't seem the type to spend every waking minute glued to his phone; as far as Ray remembers, Gabe barely touched it the last time they met.

"The evidence is circumstantial," Ray decides because it sounds better than admitting his fears are grounded in nothing.

"Which is a fancy way to say there's none." Patrick knows him too well.

"It's more of a feeling I have."

Patrick looks entirely unimpressed. "All right, mate—a feeling. Colour me convinced."

Sometimes, the best defence is to go on the offence, so Ray pushes away from the table and straightens his back. "What's your stake in this, anyway?"

Whenever Patrick is deliberating a lie, he pushes his tongue against the back of his teeth. It's a tell that Ray has come to recognise over the years, and Patrick is doing it now.

"I'll know when you're lying," Ray reminds him.

Patrick scrunches up his face. "Fine. I just think—you know how I've got this sixth sense for when people are interested in you?"

It's a bit of a joke between them: Patrick likes to pretend that over the years, he's developed a Raydar that allows him to suss out whether he's wasting his time on someone who's mostly interested in getting Ray alone. Self-defence is what Patrick calls it, and whenever

Ray maintains that it's a ridiculous notion, Patrick counters that Ray's face is what's ridiculous.

"Or so you claim," Ray says slowly. It takes no genius to see where Patrick is leading and, lost scholarship notwithstanding, Ray isn't stupid.

"Oh ye of little faith." Patrick sighs. "My point is that I know when someone is into you. And Gabe? He's into you."

Yep, he went there. Ray shakes his head and tries not to even entertain the idea that Patrick could be right—there's no way. "One, you saw us for all of five seconds. Two, I understand that you are in the honeymoon stage of a new relationship, but that doesn't mean you need to set me up with someone."

"One, five seconds was enough. And two" —Patrick's smile is distinctly shark-like— "who said anything about relationships? I'm just trying to get you laid."

"With Gabe Duke." Ray says it slowly, in the vain hope that it will make Patrick realise just how unlikely that sounds.

Patrick pumps his fist. "Exactly!"

All right, no intelligent life on that side of the kitchen. Ray turns imploring eyes to Andrew. "Help me out here, mate."

"Yeah, I don't know." Andrew sways his head. "Isn't he dating that model? You know, the one with the body and the eyebrows?"

Patrick snorts. "Be less specific, I dare you."

"I'm just saying—if Duke is used to dating female models, I'm not sure Ray here will be his type. No offence, mate."

"None taken," Ray tells him, quite honestly, and nods at Patrick. "See?"

"No offence, mate" —Patrick waves his hand at Andrew— "but you don't know shite. If your argument is that no one in Hollywood could be bisexual or closeted, boy, do I have news for you. And if your argument is that Ray is no match for some random model, well, you weren't around when he grew from a teenage geek into a hot med school student who worked out six times a week and turned heads wherever he went."

"And then I reverted into a lab geek," Ray says. "It's like I have a case of the midnight pumpkin."

"Untrue," Patrick says. "You're still hot. You just don't act like it anymore."

Ray widens his eyes. "Excuse me, have you seen my six-pack lately? Because I sure haven't."

"Fine, maybe you dialled it down to a notch. Took your eleven down to a nine-point-five or so."

"You know, Patrick," Andrew puts in. "If I didn't know better, I'd think you're half in love with him."

A few years ago, for about five minutes, Ray would have welcomed that idea because Patrick was *safe*. Then Ray realised that dating him would, at some point down the line, imply sex, and while he's seen Patrick starkers more times than he cares to remember, he just couldn't fathom touching Patrick with the intent of getting his rocks off.

"I," Patrick states with an air of grandeur, "am very secure in my sexuality. I can admit when another guy is fit without worrying whether it'll turn me gay."

"Good for you." Ray applauds, and it's only a little mocking.

Patrick takes a bow. "Thank you, thank you. Knickers to the left, bras to the right, please."

"Sorry, mate." Andrew's drawl is unparalleled. "My bra's in the wash, and I'm down to my last-chance undies. They are pink lace, though."

"Excuse me while I go scrub my brain with bleach," Patrick tells him, but a second later, he's laughing, eyes reduced to happy half-moon slits. Ray lets himself be swept up in Patrick's mirth, and it isn't until he's getting ready for a shortened Saturday shift at the lab that he picks up his phone and stops, staring at his silent screen as he examines the idea of texting Gabe from multiple angles.

What've you got to lose?

'Hi. I'll be at the lab for a couple of hours if you want to join me for some hands-on experience?'

He rereads it once, then forces himself to send it off without another review. If Gabe is busy... Hey, then at least Ray can say he tried.

∽

"Trypsi...what?" Clad in a hoodie and loose jeans, a knit beanie covering his curls, Gabe bears little resemblance to his superhero alter ego—which is part of the idea, of course. Behind the horn-rimmed glasses, Ray barely recognised him from afar, and neither of the two PhD students hanging around the lab today gave Gabe so much as a second glance.

Which, incidentally, is much like how they tend to treat Ray, too.

"Trypsinisation," Ray repeats. "From trypsin. It's an enzyme that breaks down protein."

"Okay..." The way Gabe scrunches up his face makes him look ten years younger. Ray chuckles.

"Okay, see, what we try to do here is grow more of these cells." He points at the plastic flasks that contain the cell cultures. "In order to do that, we feed them the good stuff so that they grow into nice, healthy, happily proliferating cells. With me so far?"

"So far, so good." Gabe's knee bumps Ray's when he wheels his chair a little closer. He peers at the flasks as though they hold the secrets of the universe. "I thought labs used these round Petri dish thingies?"

"We use those as well, yeah." Ray nods at an unopened box on a shelf. "Plates are cheaper, and they're better for some tasks, like when you want to harvest small amounts of cells. Flasks are easier to handle and better when you want to grow a bigger amount of cells."

"Makes sense." Gabe is close enough that each time Ray inhales, he catches a shadow of Gabe's aftershave. "So, you feed stuff to the cells to make them proliferate."

"Exactly. Thing is, once we've got a certain amount, we want to split them up into two flasks. They're clingy bastards, though, so we need something that'll make them let go of their container and each other."

"Tryptin," Gabe supplies.

"Trypsin, yeah."

"Trypsin." Gabe leans in until his nose almost touches the flask in Ray's hand. "How long does it take for a cell culture to grow enough?"

"Depends on the cells. Some need a couple of hours to double the population, for others, it's three days."

One corner of Gabe's mouth lifts, eyes glinting behind the glasses. "Bunnies versus pandas?"

"Thanks, mate. My perception of yeast cells has been permanently altered."

"You're welcome."

As Ray prepares the biosafety cabinet, Gabe watches with rapt attention. He doesn't ask any questions, just soaks it all up as though he's trying to imprint it in his mind—the snap of Ray's gloves when he puts them on, the alcoholic stench of the disinfectant, the bright pink of the medium.

"It's like a dance," Gabe says when Ray switches one pipette out for the next. "Like you've done this a million times."

"Not quite, but it is a fairly standard procedure." Ray sends him a smile before he focuses back on the task at hand, namely rocking the flask back and forth before it goes into the incubator.

"There's this almost dreamlike precision in how you move around this stuff," Gabe observes. "It's pretty cool to see. I know it's just a temporary thing, but you seem to like it here, right?"

Ray chooses not to correct Gabe's assumption that this is a temporary gig—there's no shame in working as a lab assistant, none at all; the shame is in admitting that Ray gave his original plans a mighty shove out the window and never even bothered to check how they landed.

"I like it here, yeah," he says instead. "At least when it's quiet like today, less so when it's busy on a normal workday. Not great with people, me." He's not sure why he added that last part—maybe offering a slice of truth in the face of omitting another.

"Oh, I don't know about that." Gabe leans his hip against a workbench, hoodie pulling tight across his chest. "You seem to be doing just fine with me."

"That's because we immediately skipped to the part where I embarrass myself, so I didn't have to worry about it anymore." Ray shoots Gabe a quick grin to show he's kidding. Mostly. "Also, you're just a person. I mean, you're a great person! But there's just one of you—"

"Are you calling me a unique and special snowflake?" Quiet laughter is tucked into the corners of Gabe's eyes.

"Stop making fun of me," Ray demands, even though he can't help but smile. "No, what I mean is that I struggle with groups. There's much more to take in, and the mood swings more quickly, and somehow I always end up just listening to everyone else shout over each other while I try to find something clever to say and draw a blank."

"The beauty of being an introvert?" Gabe suggests, and he sounds like he understands.

"I guess so, yeah." Ray busies himself with sorting the common solutions on one side of the workbench by alphabet, close to Gabe yet granting an excuse not to look at him. "But, you know, maybe it's also easy to talk to you because this is an impossible friendship?"

Gabe is silent for a beat. "An impossible friendship?"

"Well, you're you." Ray glances over and away again. "And I'm me. It's like… Like talking to a stranger on the train, and you can be brutally honest because you know that at the end of the journey, they'll go their way and you'll go yours."

In the pause that follows Ray's words, he grows uncomfortably aware of how he's curled in on himself, back hunched, when his mum always taught him to stand up straight and project confidence. He doesn't dare glance at Gabe again.

"So," Gabe says eventually, after what might have been a minute of silence. "Funny story. You know how Arsenal is playing West Ham later today? My agent fixed me up with a couple of free tickets. I thought you might want to join me?"

Fuck, that's not fair. That's just really, really, *really* not fair. Because there's no way Ray can possibly accept that.

Can he?

"You're not doing this to prove something, are you?" He turns to properly face Gabe, mirroring Gabe's lean against the workbench and crossing his legs at the ankle. "I mean, it's okay if you only hang around for some advice."

Gabe quirks a brow at him. "Mate, just... I don't get it. How can you look like this" —he indicates Ray's general person— "and yet your self-esteem is crap?"

"*Hey.*" Ray remembers to straighten his shoulders, and that was a compliment wrapped in an insult, wasn't it? Kind of. He purses his lips. "Pot, meet kettle?"

Gabe's shrug is off-handed. "Yeah, but enough about me—let's talk about you."

Briefly, Ray entertains the notion of laughing it off. Gabe's eyes are sharp, though, gaze intently focused on Ray, and anyway, strangers on the train, right? Ray checks to find the two PhD students in different aisles, safely out of earshot, then turns back to Gabe.

"Maybe I've learned that my face can only fool people for so long."

Gabe looks like Ray personally offended him. "And what the hell is that supposed to mean?"

"Just that most people don't hang around for long. They like me well enough at first sight, but less so once they realise I'd rather be home with a book than boozing it up at some shitty party at some shitty club."

"People?" Gabe asks evenly. "Or guys?"

"Guys, I guess." Ray tries for a smile. "Much as I tried to get rid of Patrick and Andrew, they're remarkably persistent."

"Or maybe you just have better taste in friends than guys."

"Maybe," Ray admits because truth is, he did tend to date guys who come on strong enough to bowl him over, who compete with Patrick for the spotlight—guys who know how to dial the charm up to thirteen until they lose interest. "Honestly, there's a reason I've sworn off dating."

Gabe narrows his eyes, expression pinched as he studies Ray. The stark overhead light intensifies the green of his irises, brings out flecks of brown and gold, and Ray shouldn't notice any of this because that way lies madness.

"So." He clears his throat and glances at the clock: almost time to take the flask back out of the incubator. "About the match. Thought you were a ManU man?"

"Yeah, but I'll take what I can get these days." Gabe affects a dramatic shudder. "Tried to get my fix at a Major League Soccer match—L.A. versus Austin, supposedly the top dogs of the western conference. Let's just say that Leeds United could have beat them two-nil, and with one of the goalie's hands tied behind his back."

"That bad, huh?" Ray exhales a short laugh. "You realise that Manchester is only, like, a three-hour train ride away, right?"

"You realise that I can't exactly hop on a train and pray that no one will see through my disguise, right?" Gabe's voice is as dry as chalk.

Ray nudges him. "Oh, please. Live a little."

"Only if I want my agent to kill me later."

"You could rent a car."

"I just might." Gabe says it like he's rising to a dare.

"See that you do." Ray holds Gabe's gaze and lets his grin fade. "So, about the Arsenal match. You really got those tickets for free?"

"Yeah, really." Gabe dips his head. "I mean, so to speak. I'm obliged to show my face at some point, present the cameras with my best side."

"Fame is a gift that keeps on giving, isn't it?" Ray asks lightly, rather than point out just how far removed Gabe's life is from most people's day-to-day—somehow, Gabe doesn't seem to appreciate those reminders.

"Guess so," Gabe says. "But I'm offering to share, so ... please? I'll have more fun with you there, plus you actually *like* the club."

It's hard to believe that Gabe couldn't find someone else who'd jump at the chance to pick up the extra ticket. He's asking Ray, though, and while Greek mythology suggests that it's an excellent idea to look a gift horse in the mouth... Fuck, but it's been *two years* since Ray last went to see a match.

"If you're sure?" He can't help the way his voice tilts up at the end, a blend of hopeful and uncertain because Gabe is still Gabe Duke, and Ray is just Ray.

"Absolutely." Gabe's smile is brilliant. "Pick you up at half six?"

"Thought the match starts at a quarter to eight?" Again with the upwards tilt. "We can meet at the stadium if it's easier."

"Pick you up at half six," Gabe confirms his own proposal. Ray could put up a fight, just for the hell of it, but now that he's wheeled this particular gift horse all the way into his city, he might as well enjoy the view and pretend it can last.

Six thirty it is.

5

Ray looks...

Yeah.

It's not like Gabe didn't notice that Ray's a good-looking chap—he's got *eyes*—but the first time they met, Gabe was too distracted by picnicking skeletons and his own personal confidence crisis. The second time, Ray came straight from work, and the third time, earlier today, they actually met at the lab. So, Gabe is only now confronted with the sight of Ray putting effort into his appearance.

And what a sight it is.

In Gabe's view, black leather jackets should be used sparingly because most people don't pull them off nearly as well as they think they do. Gabe, for one, tends to look like he's trying too hard. Ray, on the other hand? Christ, he makes it work. Coupled with his dark eyes and jet-black hair that he styled into a quiff, and offset by the silver glint of his stud earring, he could have walked straight out of a wet dream.

Ray is almost at the car by the time Gabe remembers to lean across the backseat and push the door open for him.

"A chauffeur?" Ray asks as he ducks inside. "Way to make me feel like the protagonist of some American prom movie." Catching the eye of the driver, Ray adds, "No offence, mate."

The rearview mirror shows the driver's professional smile. "That's quite all right."

"Sorry," Gabe says. "Should've warned you, I guess: my agent instructed me to arrive in style."

"Your agent." In the shadows of the car, Ray's eyes appear nearly black. He leans back into the seat when they pull away from the kerb, Arsenal team colours peeking out from underneath his leather jacket.

"Agent, yeah. As in, the guy who gets me roles? And, in this case, tickets to a Premier League match?" On short notice, too, given that Gabe asked Walter to find a way just this morning, as soon as he saw Ray's text about meeting at the lab. He had the tickets an hour later, confirming Gabe's suspicion that Walter is either magic or a prominent underworld figure. Gabe shoots Ray a lopsided grin. "Not to be confused with my PA, of course, who makes sure I know where to be when, and how to dress so I don't embarrass myself."

"Your agent and your PA. Sure." Ray nods. "Because that's a normal thing for any self-respecting twenty-one-year-old."

This is the kind of discussion that will take them straight back to Ray's belief that they can't be friends. With Gabe's time in London drawing to a close, he'd rather not head down that particular road, so he steers them onto a different path by circling back to their earlier conversation about lab cleaning protocols.

Ray is still detailing the intricacies of efficient organisation by the time they arrive at the stadium. He falls silent once he notices it's a side entrance, shooting Gabe a sidelong glance as they are ushered inside and along a corridor plastered with Herbert Chapman trivia. Gabe doesn't scoff at all the Arsenal wank, but it's a close thing.

A lady in red welcomes them to the top-tier members-only restaurant and guides them to an equally red leather booth, leaving them to get settled after promising that their welcome cocktails will be just a minute.

"*Gabe*," Ray hisses the moment she's gone.

"Yes, Ray?" With a beatific smile, Gabe leans back and laces his hands on the table. On the edge of his vision, he catches the telltale shift of people's heads turning towards him, but he pointedly keeps his attention on Ray.

"This is…" Apparently, Ray doesn't know how to finish that sentence and instead jerks his chin at their general surroundings. "You should have warned me! I'm *underdressed*!"

"Eh." Gabe gives him a once-over that errs on the side of platonic. "The leather is stylish, the team colours you're wearing underneath are encouraged, and as far as I could tell, your jeans fit and are in one piece." There: casual. Not like Gabe has been checking Ray out or anything, nuh-uh.

Ray appears to need several deep breaths before his shoulders come down by a margin. "Okay. Sure, this is fine. You just invited me to, like, a thousand-quid kind of experience, but it's fine. Like, look, here's your personal screen, just in case you don't feel like getting up from the table because the food's too good. You want the best seats in the stadium? But of course, sir, please just walk right through that door."

Gabe stifles a laugh. "Hey, I meant it: I'd rather not be here all by myself, so you're really doing me a favour."

"A favour. Sure." Ray's gaze skitters over the room and the neighbouring tables that pretend not to pay them any mind—the nice thing about the truly wealthy is that they would never gawk at someone as plebeian as Gabe.

When their champagne arrives, Ray throws his back with the air of someone taking a leap into the unknown.

"Can I ask you something?" Gabe waits for Ray's cautious nod before he continues. "And please tell me if this is somehow insensitive or whatever, but you said your dad was Muslim, right? Does that mean no alcohol when you grew up?"

A shadow of sadness passes over Ray's face. "Nah. My mum is vaguely Catholic, and my dad was… I think my grandparents were quite strict with him and his brother, and at some point, he rebelled and veered the other way—always said that conversations between

Allah and him are private, and the same was true for any conversation his children chose to have with Him. Or not."

Gabe is glad that at least one of them enjoyed that kind of upbringing. "He really does sound great."

"He was," Ray says simply. He's quiet for a beat before he adds, "So, in response to your question: he'd drink on special occasions, but not, like, regularly."

"Is that common in the Muslim community?"

"More common than you'd think." Ray runs a finger along the rim of his glass, smiling a little and seeming more at ease by the second. "Okay, now, explain me a thing."

Gabe is more than happy to comply. "Bananas are radioactive because of potassium. But it's so low that you'd have to eat, like, fifty million for a lethal dose."

"Funny," Ray says flatly, but the smile stays in his eyes. "No, but really, explain this to me: you're not some random Hollywood actor who's in London for a couple of days and thinks that chips are crisps."

"Or mistakenly believes it's vulgar to ask where the toilets are," Gabe contributes.

"Exactly." Ray points at him. "Which is to say that you're actually *from* here, so you must know people. Are you seriously telling me that no one wanted to come? You don't even have to be an Arsenal fan to enjoy this!"

"It's..." Grounds for depression? Gabe hesitates. "Complicated."

"Complicated." Ray's voice is devoid of judgement. He sounds like he *cares*, and Gabe has never told anyone this story because he didn't need to, because he chose to keep his sister in the dark while Charlie was there for every minute of it, and they're all Gabe's got left.

He could tell his story, just this once.

Not all of it, mind—he's not that brave, nor is he that stupid. But ... some. A half-truth, if you will, which is more than he's shared with anyone since he hopped on a bus to follow Charlie to Manchester and never looked back.

After a quick glance at their surroundings, Gabe leans in, voice low. "I mentioned that things with my parents are difficult, right?"

Ray's dark brows pinch together. "Yeah."

Gabe waits while their appetisers are served along with some water and a menu of their food choices, thanking the waitress with a smile. Once she's gone, he leans back in. "So, what that really means is that they're deeply, *deeply* religious, and my life is incompatible with their expectations for me."

"*Gabriel Jacob.*" Ray sounds like he just had a revelation.

"Yeah. One an archangel and one a sinner who's seen the light of God." Gabe feels his mouth twist into a bitter smile. "Bet you they pray there's an omen somewhere in there."

Ray sets his water glass down with a clank. He's mindful to keep his voice down, though. "But it's not like you're snorting coke and fucking hookers left and right!"

This is where things could swerve into dangerous territory. Gabe spears a bite of delicately steamed scallop as he chooses his words with great care. "True. But, see, they'd already picked out a propaedeutic course for me, and instead, I run off to don skin-tight pants and a bow and arrow."

"Priesthood?" Ray asks, as though the mere thought is absurd. "I mean, don't take this the wrong way, but I don't really picture you as a man of the faith."

"You should have seen me at sixteen." It's not a lie—Gabe came close, *so* close: trying his damned hardest to please his parents, to stifle that contrarian little voice at the back of his mind. In the end, all it took was an evening with Charlie, sharing a pizza on a bench outside the church, greasy fingers and the smell of cheese, Charlie's murmured question whether Gabe really was prepared to spend the rest of his life miserable.

"I'll take your word for it." Ray's eyes are thoughtful, maybe even sad. "So you don't talk to them at all?"

"They call me once a year, shortly before Christmas, to see whether I've changed my errant ways. Last year, it was a two-minute conversation." Even now, Gabe feels chilled at the memory of his father's cool tone as he inquired whether Gabe still insisted on choosing homosexuality over his family. Somehow, 'it's not a choice; it's who I am' didn't land too well.

"Wow." It's barely more than an exhalation. "That's... I don't even know what that is."

"Suboptimal parenting?" Gabe suggests.

"To say the least."

"Yeah." Gabe places his fork on the table and leans back, crossing his legs at the ankle. A glance at the screen reveals the first players warming up on the pitch. "Well, all this is to explain why I couldn't wait to get the hell out of there. Followed Charlie to uni and slept on his floor with no plan for my future, until Charlie dared me to audition for the Green Hunter role. Think he just wanted me to get showered and shaved, for a change—probably used some psychology mind trick from his intro course on me. But ... here I am."

"Here you are," Ray echoes softly, and for just a moment, the warmth in his eyes makes something tighten around Gabe's chest.

He breathes through it. Smiles back and ignores the fact that he's leaving tomorrow.

~

THE COLD EVENING air packs a punch when they take their seats in time for the match. Gabe wraps the Burberry scarf more tightly around his neck and buttons up the wool coat, also Burberry, that his assistant had dropped off at the hotel earlier today—promotional agreements don't honour themselves.

Next to Gabe, Ray has his hands tucked into his leather jacket. He's beaming at the panoramic view of the pitch, practically buzzing with excitement as he takes it all in. Once the match starts, he's quivering with each failed pass, halfway out of his seat at the slightest hint of a chance for Arsenal, fully immersed in the game.

Gabe, on the other hand, divides his attention between Ray and the pitch. The past three years have honed his spider-sense for when there's a camera on him, and he can feel the telltale weight of glass eyes at various moments throughout the first half. When they return inside during halftime, Gabe is stopped for several pictures while Ray waits patiently outside the frame, expression hard to read. Probably polishing his strangers-on-a-train concept.

"Sorry about that," Gabe says once they're back at their appointed table.

"No worries. Part of the job, isn't it?" The corners of Ray's mouth lift in a genuine smile. "Can't complain when you're essentially paying for both of us being here with your body."

"Way to make me sound like a gentleman of the night."

Ray smirks. "Mario Magdalene?"

"Incidentally, Mary Magdalene is the name of my sister," Gabe says, straight-faced, and Ray's smirk drops.

"Tell me you're joking."

Gabe holds on to his grave expression for another second before he laughs. "No, I'm joking. It's Deborah."

Ray's reply gets cut off by the buzz of Gabe's phone.

"I should take this," Gabe tells Ray, after a glance at the screen. "It's Charlie. Experience says that if I ignore him, he'll just keep calling every two minutes until I pick up."

"By all means, don't make him wait." Ray's mouth quirks. "He and Patrick should get together sometime, though."

"It might be the end of the world as we know it," Gabe shoots back before he picks up with a "Magic Carpet Cleaners—how may we serve you today?"

"Who's your date?" Charlie asks.

Gabe's gaze skitters to Ray and away. How did Charlie...? Ah. "Since when do you watch Arsenal matches?"

"You wouldn't believe how motivating it is when a football crowd cheers you on as you're writing a paper. Not that you'd know, right, what with how you never got around to getting a proper education." Laughter rings bright in Charlie's voice. "Also, a little birdie told me you were going to be there."

Gabe never should have introduced Charlie to his personal assistant Jade; they hit it off like a pair of firecrackers and enjoy teasing Gabe way too much. "The little birdie needs to watch its beak."

"We mock because we care."

"You mock because you dare."

"Same difference." It's easy to picture Charlie's dismissive head jerk. "Now, who's your date?"

There's no point in evading the answer. Once he's honed in on a topic, Charlie is like one of the Green Hunter's arrows: he always finds his target.

"I think you mean my friend Ray." Gabe places subtle emphasis on 'friend' that will escape most, yet Charlie is bound to understand due to years of living in each other's pockets. "Black leather jacket, black hair, dark eyes?"

"Sounds about right."

From across the table, Ray raises a quizzical brow. "Dark eyes?"

Hey, if the opportunity is offered on a silver platter... Gabe leans forward to peer closely at Ray's face, taking in the straight nose and full mouth, the amused gleam in his eyes. "Almond," Gabe decides.

"Almond what?" Charlie asks.

"Eyes." For Ray's sake, Gabe adds, "Charlie saw us on the telly."

"On the telly? Like, both of us?" Ray startles as a snack is placed in front of him, glancing up at the waitress with a mumbled thanks.

Gabe utters his own thanks coupled with a brief smile before he focuses back on Ray. "Uh, yeah. Sorry? It's the price of standing next to me in a public setting, I'm afraid."

"I expect a full report," Charlie interjects. "Just so we're clear, yeah? As soon as he's gone, I want *all* the details."

"Sure, whatever," Gabe tells Charlie absently, most of his focus on how Ray's features have tightened, discomfort plain to read. After disconnecting the call, Gabe slides the phone back into his pocket and tilts a smile at Ray. "Hey, you okay?"

"Yeah, I'm fine," Ray says, too quickly.

Gabe spears a bite of chicken satay and chews thoughtfully. "You sure? Because you don't seem okay."

"I'm just..." Ray exhales in a rush, setting his fork aside to drum his fingers on the table. He's got a tiny tattoo of a crescent moon on the side of his thumb that makes Gabe want to ask him all sorts of questions. "I'm just not all that comfortable with being in the spotlight."

Gabe sets his fork down too. "You know what's interesting?"

"Me?" Ray twists his voice to show he's kidding, and Gabe slides him a smile.

"Actually, yeah. I find it interesting how, on the one hand, you're up for sneaking into places you shouldn't be just because your friends dared you. But on the other hand, you have no interest in being the centre of attention."

"It's different. Like, I don't carry out a dare for attention, you know? It's just this thing that Patrick, Andrew, and I started doing for fun, and it forces me a little outside of my comfort zone sometimes, yeah, but they would never ask me to do something embarrassing and public like stand on a street corner and hand out free hugs."

"I'm sure there'd be takers."

"Honestly, hugging a bunch of strangers sounds like a scene straight out of a nightmare to me." Ray scrunches up his nose. It's a boyish gesture at odds with the delicate scruff he's rocking, and Christ, Gabe wants to kiss him. *Breathe through it.*

"Welcome to my world: hugging strangers comes with the territory." Gabe finishes his last bite of chicken and sets the fork aside. "Also, you seemed okay with giving *me* a hug the first day we met."

Maybe he's said too much. It was just a brief contact—one arm, pat on the back, deliberately casual and over before it really started. But for that short moment, Gabe got a glimpse of what it would be like to feel Ray against him.

"You're not a stranger," Ray says.

"Ha!" Gabe exclaims. "My point exactly, thanks for the validation, case closed."

"Do your fans know you're a bit of a moron?" At odds with the words, Ray's tone is coloured by a note of affection. It's why Gabe gives him his best smile, the one that makes his dimples pop.

"My fans think I'm gorgeous and lovable, thank you very much."

"They must be mad and misled," Ray tells him, but the warmth in his voice persists.

"Darling, you say the sweetest things."

Too much, Gabe thinks, a beat too late. *Too much, too flirty.* Until he's ready for the fallout, anyone outside the industry is a risk he cannot take—and he isn't ready, not yet, maybe not for a long time. It's just that Ray makes it easy to forget that there's a world out there, and it isn't kind.

Ray hasn't responded yet, is staring at Gabe from across the table, dark eyes unreadable. He knows. He *knows*.

"Anyway," Gabe begins with no clear idea how to continue that sentence, what topic to pivot to. 'Boy, it sure got cold, didn't it?' 'How 'bout them Red Devils, huh?' "Second half is about to start, isn't it?"

"Think we got another couple of minutes." Ray is still studying Gabe with slightly too much focus, and Gabe shifts, picks up his napkin, and takes great care folding it on the table.

Fortunately, the waitress appears to read it as a cue to manifest next to Gabe and refill first his glass with champagne, then Ray's. Gabe engages her in a conversation about how she feels the game is going, and by the time she moves on to another table, the match is about to resume, and the moment has passed.

Saved by the bell.

∽

ARSENAL WON. And Ray had one of the best seats in the stadium to see it.

In the car, on the way back, he can't stop grinning. He's riding a comfortable buzz, and even as he and Gabe are debating potential ideas for dares Ray could push on Patrick or Andrew, half of Ray's mind is stuck on the way Gabe's voice curled around the word 'darling'.

"You said his relationship is quite new, right?" Gabe chews on his bottom lip, grin just waiting to break through. "Have him call his parents and say he got engaged."

Since Patrick's parents are hippie types who are repulsed by the institution of marriage, that could actually be hilarious. Ray looks away from Gabe's mouth. "I like the way your brain works."

He's hit with the full force of Gabe's smile. "It's a weird and haunted place, granted, but people know me there."

What would Gabe do? If Ray kissed him—just unbuckled his seatbelt and slid across to take Gabe's face in his hands, breathe him in for a second, give Gabe a chance to retreat. If Gabe stayed still, waiting, and Ray leaned in to kiss him... Would Gabe turn his head away? Or would he open for Ray, maybe even push in closer?

Ray inhales, champagne courage swirling in his blood. What would Gabe *do*?

It takes a small cough from the driver for Ray to realise that the car has pulled to a halt. A glance out the window reveals Ray's building, and right: back to the real world, where the lift isn't working and Andrew's blue cheese is stinking up the fridge.

Ray lets his gaze rest on Gabe's face and doesn't move. "Thank you for this, Gabe. It's been an amazing treat."

"You're really very welcome." The shadows inside the car seem to colour Gabe's voice, making him seem both nearer and further away. "I'm glad you came."

Ray still doesn't move. Now that reality has crept back in, he knows that there's nothing he can do, not really, not while the driver is right there. Even if the guy signed some kind of contract—he probably did, because that's how the rich and famous do things, isn't it? But even so, this is not the time, not the place.

"So." Ray hesitates. "You want to hang out, like, next week?"

"I'd love to." Gabe glances away, his voice dropping. "But I'm actually leaving tomorrow. Location shooting first, then we move to another studio."

Oh.

Okay, then.

So that's ... it. That's it.

Gabe is leaving—of course he is. He was always going to leave because that's what people like him *do*. They're not looking for a home; they're looking for the next flight out.

There's a shard of glass stuck in Ray's throat. He swallows around it and fights to locate a smile, his voice, *something*. "I ... guess we should say goodbye, then."

"I'll be back in December," Gabe offers. "Close to Christmas, for the premiere of the third movie. If you want to meet up?"

That's six weeks away, or seven. By then, Gabe will have forgotten all about that guy he hung out with for a bit there, back in London. Ray was foolish to ever think otherwise.

He grapples for a smile that sits wrong on his face. "Sure, that'd be nice."

"Yeah." Gabe releases the word on a long exhale, nodding as if to himself. Then he's the one who unbuckles his seatbelt and slides across—but only to pull Ray into a hug that's made a little awkward by the lack of space and Ray's seatbelt digging into the side of his neck. He still curls into Gabe, allows himself one moment of breathing him in, of closing his eyes so he can commit it all to memory: Gabe's warm weight and the spiciness of his aftershave, the whisper of a sigh against Ray's cheek.

Ray pulls back first because he knows that there's no use in holding on.

Gabe's arm tightens around Ray's middle for another breath before he lets Ray go. "So, I'll see you soon."

No, he won't.

Pain radiates from behind Ray's ribcage, but he knows it's only temporary. He'll get over it. It's not like he's in love with Gabe or anything ridiculous like that because, really, who falls in love in a week? And sure, it felt longer than that, bigger and brighter, but it's over now.

It's over.

Ray blinks a couple of times and drags another smile up from where it sits by the soles of his feet. "See you soon, yeah. Good luck with the rest of filming."

"Thanks. But if you think I'm done peppering you with questions, think again." Gabe's answering smile gleams like fool's gold. "Got to keep my personal consultant busy, right?"

"Anytime," Ray says, and it comes out too quiet, too honest. He ducks his head to unbuckle his seatbelt, shoves the car door open, and scrambles out into the cold night before he chances a look back at Gabe—Gabe, who isn't smiling anymore. Maybe he caught on to the unwarranted sweep of emotion in Ray's voice—is, right now, pondering how to let Ray down gently because Gabe isn't the type to be cruel about it.

"Thanks again," Ray rushes out. "It's been really cool to see the match like that, so thank you. Have a good night, yeah?"

"Ray," Gabe begins, and Ray pauses with his hand on the outside of the door, ready to nudge it shut. He waits for a second, and another. When Gabe still doesn't continue, Ray inhales deeply and lets the cold November air soothe the burn in his chest.

"See you, Gabe," he manages.

This time, he doesn't wait for a response. Just closes the car door and turns away, starts walking towards his building. Three steps. Four. Behind him, the car hums to life.

Ray doesn't watch it drive away.

6

Ray spends his Sunday on the sofa, emulating a bag of potatoes. He must look truly pitiful because Andrew brings him tea without being asked, and Patrick sits with him for a while, uncharacteristically quiet even when a commercial break shows the trailer for Gabe's third movie. Ray stares straight ahead and holds his breath until it's over.

He's fine, though.

He's still fine when he rolls out of bed on Monday and drags himself to the bathroom, avoiding his own eyes in the mirror. Even though he's getting on the Tube half an hour later than usual, it's packed. He has to squeeze in next to a teenage girl who's bopping along to music from her oversized headphones and a middle-aged guy with a huge backpack who must have skipped a shower this morning.

Two stops into the ride, Ray grows aware of a businesswoman staring at him from the other side of the carriage. As soon as he meets her eyes, she looks away, back down at today's copy of *City A.M.* that's open in her lap. It happens again with a much younger woman who gets on one stop later, and then a pimply-faced teenage boy who flushes as soon as he notices Ray looking back.

Odd.

While Ray is no stranger to catching glances, his hair needs a wash, and he woke up at four a.m. and didn't fall back asleep until minutes before his alarm went off—meaning he's not looking his best today, and also, there was nothing coy about either the businesswoman or the teenage boy. Ray uses the screen of his phone to make sure there's nothing weird on his face, then spends the rest of the ride with his head down, careful to evade further attention.

It works. Right up until he arrives at work and is cornered by one of the PhD students who was there last Saturday, too.

"Tell me it wasn't him," she says, by way of a greeting.

A tinge of unease winds itself around Ray. "Who's 'him'?" he asks, afraid that he already knows the answer because there's another copy of *City A.M.* on her desk, and Gabe is the kind of person who makes headlines.

"Gabe Duke." She tosses her head. "Tell me you didn't bring him in on Saturday, and I totally missed it."

"Um." Embarrassingly, Ray realises he doesn't remember her name. "Listen, I'd appreciate it if, you know, it wasn't made into a big deal. He just had some questions for a role he's playing, that's all. I don't even know him that well."

It feels like a lie, because it is. Ray may not have known Gabe for long, but he can tell when Gabe's smile is fake, has seen his curious mind and quirky sense of humour.

"But you know him well enough to go to a game together," she says, and he can't quite tell if her tone is envious or admiring.

"We met just a week ago," Ray tells her because that, at least, is true. "He had a free ticket and no friends in town. It's really no big deal."

"It's Gabe Duke," she says. "Of *course* it's a big deal. I mean, you're gay, right? So I'm sure you can understand my point of view."

Fuck, he needs to nip this in the bud. He may never talk to Gabe again, but he doesn't want to be the reason for rumours, no matter how unlikely they are to get back to Gabe.

"I mean, yeah. Objectively? Sure." Ray hopes his shrug looks suitably unaffected. "Shame I've got the wrong equipment."

She squints at him for a second before a sunny smile takes over her face. "You know what? You're not too bad. Ray, is it?"

"Yeah. And you're..." Katie? Kelly? "Cassie?"

"Carrie," she corrects, seeming unbothered by his mistake.

"Carrie, right." Ray sends her a tentative smile and decides she's not too bad either. Even if the only reason she's speaking to him is his newfound secondhand fame.

⁓

BY THE END of the day, Ray is tired, cranky, and embarrassed—tired because that's how he started and it didn't improve; cranky because he'll scream if he has one more bloody person come up to him with an innocuous question when they really just want the scoop; and embarrassed because out of all the photos they could have chosen of him and Gabe at the match, they chose one in which Gabe is laughing, bundled up in his expensive scarf and coat, and Ray is looking at him like he hung the stars.

Fuck his life.

When he finally makes it home, after a day that lasted two weeks, Patrick takes one look at him and abandons his dinner preparations. "That bad?"

"Wine?" Andrew offers from where he's seated at the table, laptop open in front of him, likely working on some piece for his blog or the *Evening Standard*. Fuck, and now there's a thought.

"You're not writing about me, are you?" Ray realises he sounds like an arsehole the second it's out, but by then, the damage is done.

Andrew closes his laptop with deliberate slowness. "I," he says, carefully enunciating, "am your *friend*, Ray. And because I'm your friend, and because your heart's a bit broken and you had a rough day on top, I will let this slide."

My heart's not broken.

Ray swallows the words back down and ducks his head, exhaling in a rush. "I'm sorry. I'm just ... paranoid today. People have been staring at me all day, and everyone wanted to talk to me at the lab when they normally can't be bothered, and I'm just..."

"Having a Grumpy Cat day?" Patrick suggests.

Ray ducks his head further, nodding with his chin against his chest. "Yeah."

"Apology accepted," Andrew tells him. "Now: wine?"

Alcohol is part of what got Ray into this mess in the first place. If he hadn't been buzzed on champagne and an Arsenal win that he got to experience live, he never would have fooled himself into believing that he and Gabe could be more than passing ships in the night.

"Hot chocolate?" he asks, and fuck, he's tired. So, so tired.

Out of the corner of his eye, he catches Patrick's smile. "Like your mum does it, yeah?"

"Please," Ray says, and of course Patrick would get it. Ray's mum has never been great with emotional conversations—that was his dad—but she showed her love in other ways: help him carve the scariest Halloween pumpkin for a school competition, humour his long-gone obsession with Spider-Man with themed bed sheets and red-and-blue socks, and sit him and Patrick down for a hot chocolate whenever they'd had a rough day.

Maybe he should go home for a weekend.

Ten minutes later, he's sitting next to Andrew at the kitchen table, both hands wrapped around his cup of hot chocolate, the tension of the day ebbing away in increments. Lids drifting shut, he inhales the nutty vanilla scent that takes him right back to his mum's kitchen. "You know," he mumbles, "I'm not sure how Gabe does it. Like, how does he not resent all those people who only want a piece of him because he's Gabe Duke? I had just the barest hint of it today, and it *sucks*."

"Maybe," Patrick suggests, voice dry, "that's why he was happy to be Gabriel for a little while."

"Yeah, well." Ray raises the mug to his mouth. The first sip tastes like home, like there's nothing that can't be fixed with a hug and a sugar-infused beverage. "Didn't last long, now did it?"

"But the point is that you met Gabriel before you met Gabe Duke."

"I don't know what that means."

"It means you weren't too impressed with him because when you met, he was just a normal guy."

Ray takes another sip that lingers sweetly. "But I *was* impressed."

"With Gabe, or with Gabe Duke?" Andrew this time, and Ray throws him a glance from underneath his lashes before focusing back on the mug in his hands.

"Does it matter?"

"Of course it does," Patrick says. "And I bet it mattered to him."

"Not enough to stay." Even as he says it, Ray knows how silly it sounds. They were starting to become friends, maybe, but you don't throw your entire life overboard just to spend a little more time with someone you met a week ago. Gabe's life follows a plan, and Ray has no right to resent him for that. He has no right to be disappointed.

And yet he is.

He huffs out a breath. "I'm being ridiculous, right?"

"No, not ridiculous. Just..." Patrick stops to adjust his own mug so that its handle sits parallel to the edge of the table. "You haven't let yourself fall for anyone since Xander."

Wow, okay. Bring it on—it's not like Ray's day could get much worse.

"Xander is Fuckface, right?" Andrew puts in before Ray locates a suitable response. "The guy you were in love with in school, who turned out to be an utter twat?"

"First off" —Ray inhales harshly— "I'm not in love with Gabe. Secondly, I was *definitely* never in love with Xander. I was just ... young, and it's not like I was overwhelmed by choices."

"You were a little bit in love with Xander." Patrick's eyes are sad, and Ray looks away after a beat.

"If so, then it was only because I thought he was someone different."

"As in someone who wasn't a snivelling, two-faced dickhead?" Patrick asks.

"Sounds about right."

The stupid thing is that initially, when Xander dropped Ray like a hot potato, Ray defended him. Xander was scared; he just wasn't quite ready yet to come out, and it wasn't fair to blame him for that. His family situation was tough; he had a harder time in school than Ray and needed to hunker down.

Then Xander told everyone that the gawky gay kid had a pathetic little crush on him. When Ray tried to counter with the truth, everyone believed the best forward on the football team over Ray, the lanky defender who had yet to grow into his new height. He left the team a week later and threw himself into his schoolwork instead, which earned him the kind of grades he needed for med school—shame he couldn't hold on to the scholarship.

The chocolate didn't taste this bitter a minute ago.

Ray takes another sip anyway, staring out of the dirty window that might start suing them for neglect sometime soon. He startles at the buzz of his phone and pulls it out before he can consciously tell himself it won't be a text from Gabe.

It isn't.

It's his youngest sister Allie, who sent an image along with a simple '*WHAT*'. Even before Ray opens the message, he knows what the picture will show, and really, he should have seen it coming because Allie and her friends just about live on the internet. It still hurts, though, when he's faced with another variation of himself with Gabe, both of them laughing this time, Ray with his arms up in a cheer, maybe right after Arsenal scored the first goal.

"Took her long enough," Patrick says when Ray shows him the message. "Tell her I said she's slipping."

"Stop flirting with my sister."

"I will do no such thing."

"I'll tell Lauren."

"You will do no such thing."

"Watch me."

"Fine." Patrick huffs like it's a big imposition. "You're no fun anymore."

It's said in jest. Rationally, Ray knows that, but it veers dangerously close to how his last boyfriend justified their breakup, so it echoes in that quiet, melancholic space in his head that's reserved for cataloguing all the way he fails.

"Hey." Patrick must have noticed Ray's sudden stillness because he taps their feet together. "I'm kidding, mate. You know I am."

Ray releases a long breath and nods. "I know, yeah."

"Good. Now go on, don't make Allie wait, or she'll explode."

Since Allie has no patience at the best of times, Patrick may be on to something. After another sip of hot chocolate that warms him up from the inside, Ray stares at his phone for a full minute before he settles on a response.

'Down, girl. I met him by chance, helped him out a bit for a role that's got to do with working in a lab. He had a spare ticket for the match, so he took me as a thank you. Doubt I'll hear from him again.'

He sends it and lingers for another moment before he adds, in a second message: *'It's nothing.'*

It hurts because it's true.

∼

LOCATION SHOOTING IS BRUTAL.

Usually, Gabe enjoys trading the stuffy studio air in for something more natural—what can he say; he's a country boy at heart. But they catch a patch of rough weather, icy wind sweeping across peatland that's been chosen for cinematic appeal rather than historical accuracy, and it feels like he spends fifty per cent of his waking time trying to get his frozen fingers to move, and the other fifty per cent divided between taking long, hot showers, learning his lines, and checking his phone.

The pictures must have hit the press on Monday. By Wednesday morning, there's still no peep from Ray, nothing that suggests he's going to take this chance to sell Gabe out.

Gabe knew he wouldn't. Somehow, it still feels like a weight off his shoulders.

Wednesday is also when the weather turns, and in between filming, Gabe captures several amazing impressions of sweeping peatlands interspersed with bog pools, caught between golden sunlight and cloud-cast shade. He sends the second-best image to the woman who runs his social media accounts and asks her to include a note about the importance of peatlands in mitigating climate change.

The best image he claims for himself, editing it later that evening, stretched out on his stomach on the quilt-covered queen bed that dominates his quaint hotel room. A massive antique wardrobe takes up much of the remaining space, leaving just enough of a gap for the window that, during the day, offers a view of the rolling landscape.

Once Gabe is satisfied, he sends the image to Charlie because it's been too long since Charlie got a chance to rib Gabe about his pretentious photography aspirations. *'Scotland is cold this time of year,'* he adds in the caption.

Then he rolls onto his back and stares at the pastel green ceiling. Nothing stops him from sending the picture to Ray, too—except he misses Ray more than he should, and staying away is the safer choice. Also, it's not like Ray tried to reach out.

Gabe is saved from further rabbit-hole musings by the ringing of his phone. Since it's still in his hand, it makes him jolt.

Charlie.

Of course it's Charlie. And Gabe loves Charlie, he does—Charlie is his closest friend, his only close friend, as a matter of fact. So whatever traitorous corner of Gabe's heart was hoping for someone else? He blocks it off from the light.

"Gary's Ginormous Gardening..." Damn, he didn't think that through to the end.

"Gang?" Charlie suggests.

"Not bad." Gabe considers putting the call on speaker, but it's an old house, and the soundproofing of the walls can't be trusted. "How are you this fine evening?"

"About to shave my head, move to Tibet, and join a monastery." Since Charlie is in the middle of a Bachelor thesis about the impact of background music on buyer behaviour, this is within the range of expected answers.

"I'm not sure you should base your life choices on a Brad Pitt movie."

"He didn't shave his head, so it's not the same at all. Plus, you thought he was hot when we saw the film, don't lie."

"So." Gabe slips a grin into his tone. "What you're saying is that you want to be like a movie character that teenage me found hot. Is there something you're trying to tell me, mate?"

"Let me think." Charlie gives it two seconds. "Right, yeah! How's the lab geek that adult you finds hot?"

"Still hot, I assume."

A perfect world would let Gabe get away with that answer. Charlie, of course, doesn't. "Meaning you haven't spoken to him."

"I've been busy."

"You sent me a selection of your favourite pictures from the Comedy Wildlife Photography Awards yesterday, along with an article on ... sea cucumbers, I think?"

"Their impact on ocean health is vastly underrated!"

Charlie, predictably undeterred, starts making squawking chicken sounds.

"Very funny." Gabe rolls back onto his stomach and shoves a pillow under his chest. "And I'm not a coward. It's just... What's the point?"

"The point is that you like him."

"Doesn't matter." Gabe releases a sigh, then feels like a drama queen immediately after. "I mean, it matters, sure. But I can't start anything with him, and I thought I'd be good with being friends, but it's like... I don't know."

"Okay." Charlie uses the kind of tone one would choose for a particularly obtuse child. "Explain to me why you can't start anything with him?"

Gabe aims for exactly the same tone. "Because he could go to the press?"

"And would he?"

No. Ray wouldn't.

"He might," Gabe says anyway.

Charlie makes a dismissive sound. "You wanna know what I think?"

"Not really."

"Too bad." Charlie pauses long enough to make a point. "Here it is: he's not part of your plan, and you don't know what to make of that."

"My plan." Gabe means to sound unimpressed, but likely lands on constipated. The green pastel of the room makes him feel just a tiny bit ill.

"Yep, your plan. He's something you didn't expect, and it throws you for a loop."

"I'm not a control freak," Gabe protests.

"Um." Charlie fills the word with a world of meaning, most of it unflattering to Gabe and his ancestry.

"I just like it when things go my way."

"That's the literal definition of being a control freak."

"For a psychology student, that was a remarkably incompetent statement."

"Oh, fuck off." Charlie huffs, and for the first time, he sounds genuinely impatient. Since just about nothing can shake Charlie's chill, it makes Gabe sit up and drop all attempts at humour.

"Hey, man. Talk to me. What's really going on here?"

"Look, mate." Charlie's voice is low. "You like him. I mean, when's the last time you genuinely liked someone? And Timothée Chalamet in *Dune* doesn't count."

"How does that not count?" Gabe asks because it's better than his actual answer, which would bring them back to the preacher's son, and that was years ago.

"It just doesn't."

"My, aren't we fussy tonight?"

"Gabe." Something in Charlie's tone stops Gabe cold. "You *like* him. And you're about to just throw it away because... Why?"

It's just a case of the shiny new disease.

The token protest sparks and dies. While Gabe prefers his introspection in carefully controlled dribs and drabs, he knows that he misses Ray more than he can easily justify—and that's not even getting into the fact that Ray is the first outside person Gabe told about the fallout with his parents.

He must have been quiet for too long because Charlie exhales. "Look, can we switch to video?"

"Are you breaking up with me?" Gabe means it as a joke, but he knows it falls flat the second it's out. "Yeah, sure. Just let me get my headphones, all right?"

"'Course. Just dial me when you're ready."

Two minutes later, Gabe is sitting back against the headboard, his phone propped up against the pillow. When the call connects, the first thing he sees is a close-up of Charlie's nostrils, followed by a slow pan shot of Charlie's neck down to his naked belly.

"For God's sake, man!" Gabe covers his eyes. "Put some clothes on!"

"Got some pants on, don't I?" Charlie plops down on his sofa, in full view now, and he is indeed wearing a pair of tight boxers along with red socks. "Also," he adds, "don't lie: this is the most action you've seen in a while."

He's not wrong. That said, Gabe doesn't want Charlie anywhere close to any action he may or may not be getting.

"You don't know that," he says, with dignity.

"Oh, please. Like I haven't seen how much of a number your parents did on you." Charlie leans closer to the camera, squinting. "Hell, you still can't have casual sex without feeling guilty about it."

"I have casual sex!" Gabe protests. He does, too. It's rare, granted, but options are limited when you're trying to keep the media spotlight away from your closet.

"Yeah. And then you mope about it the next day."

This is not a conversation they've had before, and Gabe wonders how long Charlie's been bottling it up. "Okay, let's say you're ten per cent right. What's it to you?"

"I'm your *friend*." Charlie shoves a hand through his blond hair. "I care about these things. Like, honestly, when's the last time you felt truly good about yourself?"

The Arsenal match. Ray's shoulder pressed against Gabe's as they were sitting out in the stands, cold hands and cold noses, but Ray so warm and real next to him that, for a few moments here and there, Gabe could almost pretend that he might get to have this.

"Charlie..."

"Don't *Charlie* me." Charlie shuffles closer to the camera, peering at Gabe, blue eyes shadowed. "Mate, I love you. And you've got to talk to someone."

Gabe swallows. Media training taught him to face any difficult remark with a smile, but this is *Charlie*—the person who knows him at his best and worst, and everything in between.

"I'm talking to you," Gabe offers quietly.

"Well." Charlie's lips quirk into the tiniest of smiles. "I'm a therapist, true, but I'm not your therapist."

Gabe snorts. "You're not a therapist."

"I will be."

"Maybe one day, if you stop griping about your Bachelor thesis. Until then: not the same thing."

"Ha!" Charlie points finger guns at him. "You just made my point for me."

"Which is?"

"Bloody *talk* to someone."

Gabe can admit when he's been outmanoeuvred. Also, it's not like the concept of therapy never occurred to him—if your dad's parting words are that he'd rather you be dead than gay, it does make a boy wonder. He's even joked about it on occasion, mostly with Charlie and about all the money he'll save on therapists by sticking with the right kind of friend.

But.

He never got to the point where he actually saw himself walk into a stranger's office, sit down on a sofa, and share his sob story about how he wasn't hugged enough as a child. Surely he's in a pretty decent mental place, isn't he? He's successful; he keeps himself in shape; he doesn't drink or drug himself into oblivion.

When's the last time you felt truly good about yourself?

He brings the phone closer to his face and abruptly wishes Charlie were right there. Sure, Charlie snores and hogs the covers, and he always claims it's an accident when his cold feet press against Gabe's shins—but their late-night conversations are the closest Gabe has ever felt to another person. He *misses* his friend.

"How long have you been wanting to tell me that?" he asks quietly.

Charlie lifts a bony shoulder. "'Bout three years, give or take."

"Why now?"

"Because this is the first time I've seen you open up to someone other than me or Debbie." Charlie's voice is hushed, as though he's sharing a secret. "And you're about to give it up without even trying."

There is nothing Gabe can say in response because fuck, yeah, maybe Charlie's right.

They're both silent for a short while. It's the kind of silence that settles Gabe's thoughts, that lets him breathe for a minute or two while he sorts through the storm in his head.

"I can't just walk into some random therapist's waiting room," he says eventually, voice just as hushed as Charlie's was earlier.

Charlie flashes him his first genuine smile of the evening. "Because you'd be the first Hollywood A-lister ever to need therapy. Ask your agent, mate."

Right, Walter would know. In fact, Walter could probably set Gabe up with an appointment in two seconds flat.

"Fine." Gabe inhales. "On one condition."

"No, you can't have my firstborn."

"What?" Gabe asks.

"*What?*" Charlie asks.

"Sometimes, your brain is a scary place." But Gabe's grinning, chest a little wider than before, and maybe that was Charlie's intention. "No, here's my condition: I'm back in L.A. on the twenty-ninth. Visit me. You can work on your Bachelor thesis at my house—you might even make some progress that way instead of wanking off to porn five times a day."

"Fuck you very much," Charlie tells him cheerfully. "Also, I accept your terms."

Something akin to joy wiggles in Gabe's stomach. "So you'll come?"

"I'll come. If—"

"You already accepted!"

"—you not only set up a therapy appointment like you just promised, but also send a message to the lab geek."

One message. Gabe doesn't know why it feels like such a big deal when he really, truly meant it when he told Ray he'd see him in December.

"Gabe?"

Gabe startles. "His name's Ray," he tells Charlie, mostly to buy some time.

Charlie doesn't miss a beat. "Right, sure. You'll send a message to Ray, and we've got ourselves a deal."

For a moment, Gabe allows himself to remember almond eyes and honey skin, a brilliant smile and a slightly raspy voice that doesn't expect to be heard. Gabe's the one who left, and he'd be a fool to expect Ray to reach out first.

Maybe it's okay for Gabe to want this.

"I'll send him a message," he agrees. "But only one. And if I don't hear back, that's it, okay?"

"All right," Charlie agrees happily, as if the mere notion of Ray failing to reply is ridiculous. Well, Charlie didn't see the look on Ray's face when they said goodbye in the car—like that was it, like there was no way they could possibly meet again.

"All right," Gabe echoes, and when he smiles, it feels like the first time in days.

Later—once he and Charlie solidified the plan for Charlie's visit and hung up after their traditional round of creative insults—Gabe opens the thread of messages he exchanged with Ray. The last one, at the bottom, is just a simple *'See you there'*, sent by Ray last Saturday morning, before Gabe went to meet him at the lab.

Four days of nothing.

Gabe pulls up the picture he already sent to Charlie. He considers just copying his earlier caption, then decides that Ray is worth more effort.

'Traded London for the Flow Country and my suite at the Savoy for a room in a B&B that barely fits more than my bed. It's brilliant, now that the sun's come out. Hope the lab is treating you well and the cells do as they're told.'

Should he finish with an exclamation mark? He puts one in place of the full stop, rereads the message, and switches back to a full stop. Instead of rereading it a second time like he wants to, he takes a deep breath and holds it in his lungs for a second.

Then he hits send, shuts down his phone, and goes to brush his teeth.

∼

GABE WAKES up to the sun sending tentative rays past his curtains, a cat-related joke from Charlie, and two new messages from Ray.

Consciously dragging out the anticipation, Gabe first replies to Charlie—a picture of boiling water with the caption *'You will be mist.'* Only then does he open Ray's first message.

'Wow, I'm jealous! Looks like a great place to get lost in for a week or two. But how do you survive without Savoy dessert?!'

The second text is longer, sent a couple of minutes after the first. 'Thanks for checking - the cells are fine. Bonus: they don't care that I'm suddenly Mr Popular because apparently, being photographed next to you is like achieving knighthood. Not sure how you handle it on a daily basis, mate - you're a better man than me.'

Gabe sincerely doubts that. Or maybe that's his parents talking— not in the sense that he is or isn't better than Ray, but in the sense that he's been taught he could never possibly measure up. If 'love the sinner' was an actual Bible phrase, maybe he might have stood a chance.

'Is it the attention itself that bothers you?' Gabe replies. 'Or that it's fake? I've found I've become quite apt at telling real from false.' He hesitates, letting his gaze sweep over the miles and miles of open land outside the window. 'Although it was kind of nice how when we met, you thought I was just some weirdo in a lab coat.'

Pretty sure I was the weirdo,' Ray shoots back almost immediately.

Gabe chews on the inside of his cheek to stifle a grin. 'In your defence, it was a very inspired display of Halloween cheer.'

'Come on, be honest: you thought I was a nutter.'

I thought you were hot.

'Nah,' Gabe answers instead, because he does have a functioning brain-to-text filter. 'But I did wonder if you were trying to make off with a jar of bollocks.'

Ray doesn't respond, so Gabe assumes he arrived at work and put his phone away for now. Which is Gabe's cue to get his own day started—he isn't needed on set until eleven, so if he hurries, he can get in a one-hour run ahead of a rushed late breakfast.

Right. Up and at 'em.

7

'Hate to break it to you, mate: fruit does not count as dessert.'
    'Dessert is in the eye of the beholder.'
    'Is that what your nutritionist told you?'
'Don't knock it till you've tried it.'
'Fruit?'
'Healthy eating.'
'I'd rather go back to the gym.'
'Why don't you?'
'Rumour has it you get sweaty in there.'
'Who told you I skipped my shower today?! But seriously, I love hitting the gym. Makes me feel like I did something that's just for me, you know?'
'Uh. Your legion of fans would beg to differ. They would also like to thank you for your time and dedication.'

∼

"What do you think?"

"Hmm?" Ray drags his gaze away from Gabe's opinion about the general overuse of abbreviations in text messages—not a fan—and finds Patrick staring at him with an eloquently arched eyebrow.

"Gabe again?" Patrick asks.

Making a mental note to pepper his next message to Gabe with YOLOs, IDKs and TTYLs, Ray locks his phone and gives Patrick his full attention. "Sorry. You were saying?"

"*I*" —Patrick puts pointed emphasis on the word— "am trying to brainstorm what evil thing we can dare Andrew to do. *You*, on the other hand, are clearly more interested in projecting 'call me maybe' through the power of text."

"Thanks, man. I'm going to have that song stuck in my head for the next five days now."

"I live to cause havoc." Patrick tips his chair onto its hind legs, but his focus stays on Ray. "And I can't help but notice your evasive tactics."

While Patrick's tone is cheerful, there's an undercurrent of concern. Ray takes a slow sip of coffee from one of the bamboo cups that Gabe brought. "Okay, Pat. Spit it out."

Patrick's brow furrows. "You sure you want to hear this?"

"No. But I'm sure you want to tell me anyway, so..."

"Fair." Patrick sets his chair back down on all four legs. "Right, here we go. How long are we going to pretend that you don't want to have his babies?"

"Very funny." Ray drops his gaze to his hands. "I don't even know him that well."

"You've been texting multiple times a day for the past three weeks."

For once, Patrick is not exaggerating. After Gabe broke the initial silence following his departure from London, they fell into a rhythm that's come to frame Ray's days. Since Gabe is an early riser, Ray wakes up to a message from him most mornings, then they exchange one or two texts while Ray is on his way to work, and then some more in the evening, with Gabe usually off to bed first.

"Well, yeah." There's no use denying a fact, so Ray doesn't bother. "But it's all just in good fun. It's not like we're flirting or anything—we just happen to like some of the same things, is all."

"The same things?"

"Like..." Ray actually needs to consider his answer because their exchange has ranged from grammar jokes to that socially awkward moment when you're meant to remember someone's name but don't, from how Gabe's assistant secretly runs his life, to literature discussions because in spite of his profession, Gabe resembles Ray in that he'd rather spend his evening with a good book than in front of a screen.

Ray must have drifted for a second, staring into the murky depths of his coffee, because Patrick gives him a sock-muffled kick under the kitchen table. "Like?"

"Nothing important," Ray says. "Just random stuff, you know? Like books, or ribbing each other about football. Commiserating about our crazy friends."

"Okay, fine." Patrick's lips press together. "Just be careful, okay? That's all I'm asking."

The fact that Ray feels instantly defensive might be an indication of things he'd rather not examine too closely in the full light of day. "I thought you were Team Gabe."

"I was. I *am*." Patrick waves a hand to punctuate the statement. "It's just... When those pictures came out, the ones from the game—you hated the attention. It would be a thousand times worse if you were to date him."

Ray ignores the flutter of unease in his belly. "As far as I know, he's straight."

"Doubt it, mate. No straight guy would invest that much time into texting a queer friend he just met."

"You text me multiple times a day, and we live together."

"What part of 'he just met' wasn't clear?" Patrick leans forward, eyes sharp and serious. "I saw what happened the last time you dated someone stuck in a closet. I don't care for a repeat."

After a beat, Ray averts his gaze. "Point taken," he mutters, and while he knows that Patrick means well, it's ... fuck, Ray isn't stupid. He knows that Gabe is way out of his league—or rather, Gabe is in a different league altogether, say English Premier League versus American Major League Soccer, Hollywood star versus lab technician, a couple million dollars per movie versus thirty-three thousand a year.

It's not going to happen. Ray knows that; he's prepared for it.

But until Gabe decides there are more productive uses of his time than to argue with Ray about the predictability of *Gone Girl*, Ray is happy to pretend that he doesn't feel a quiver of warmth at each new message.

At least he is until he screws up.

Specifically, he takes a lunch break by himself in a corner of the lab and decides to spend some of it Googling Gabe. He thinks it'll be a laugh—maybe he can tease Gabe about a silly sweater he was wearing to some show, or about a bad haircut he sported a couple of years ago. In all honesty, it's more of a spontaneous impulse than a well-reflected plan.

The first picture that pops up shows Gabe on some millionaire's yacht: shirtless, muscular chest and clearly defined abs, smoothly tanned skin. He's gorgeous, and while Ray knew this already, there's something different about seeing Gabe on full display like this, offered up like a delicious taste of the proverbial forbidden fruit.

The second picture shows him happy and smiling, dimples out in full force, next to a stunning woman Ray vaguely recognises from flipping through *Metro*. While it's linked to some kind of breakup story, the point has been well and truly made.

Gabe isn't Ray's. He belongs to the world, belongs with beautiful women and rich men who own yachts and football clubs.

What can Ray offer him, other than some scientific tidbits and a daily supply of marginally witty exchanges via text message?

Nothing, that's what.

Absolutely nothing.

∼

"Stop ignoring me," Charlie says.

"I'm not." Gabe keeps his attention on his phone, absently scrolling through his emails. In London, it should be right around the time Ray leaves work, so Gabe expects a response to his last message any moment now. "I'm just choosing to direct my attention elsewhere, at least until you're done writing one full page."

"Friends enable their friends' procrastinating ways."

"Is that your professional psychological opinion? Oh, wait." Gabe pauses for effect, then slowly lifts his head to level Charlie with a hard stare. "You won't be a professional if you don't work on your bloody thesis."

Charlie flops back onto Gabe's living room carpet with a dramatic groan, laptop abandoned on the sofa table next to a small stack of books. "Who died and made you my mum?"

"Hey, just making sure my investment in our friendship will reap me future benefits in the form of free, qualified counselling."

"Right." Charlie tips his head to the side, staring up at Gabe, who's perched on an armchair. "And how's that going for you? The counselling."

"Well." Gabe drapes his legs over one side of the armchair and sends Charlie a crooked smile. "For one, it isn't free. So that's a downer."

"You can afford it," Charlie says, unmoved.

"Can't be too careful with your money. It's amazing, the proportion of professional NFL players that go bankrupt within, like, two years of retirement. Think it's about a third or so."

Frowning, Charlie sits up. "You are being deliberately evasive."

"It's going ... fine. I think." Gabe shifts his shoulders in a semi-shrug. "Don't have much experience, what with being a therapy virgin, but ... Walter handpicked her and swears she can be trusted, and I like that she's not just, 'Please lie down on a couch, close your eyes, and tell me all about your childhood while I take notes in silence.'"

There's no couch at all, in fact, just two people in their respective homes connected by the marvel of technology. At first, Gabe felt strange making himself the sole topic of conversation, tried to ask return questions and learn about her life, too. She let him get away with it for about five minutes before she leaned back, fixed him with a look, and told him that she was willing to answer any questions that would make him feel more at ease with her and the situation. But if his aim was to deflect attention from himself—that was not what they were there for.

"So it's been a good start?" Charlie sounds pleased.

"I think so." Gabe sneaks a covert glance at his phone—still nothing from Ray. Maybe he decided to work late today. "I mean, three sessions won't fix me—"

"Who said anything about fixing you?" Charlie interrupts.

Gabe raises his eyebrows. "Um. Pretty sure *you* did."

"I never said you needed fixing." Charlie sits up. "What you need is a nudge. Something to make you believe that your parents are the problem, not you."

"I know that."

"Sure you do. But do you *believe* it?"

Gabe wants to say yes. Instead, he exhales a long, harsh breath through his nose. "Fine, you made your point. Now go back to that thesis you were going to write."

"Why? So you can stare forlornly at your phone?"

"Don't you have an academic degree to complete?"

"For someone with your level of media training, you're really bad at subtle topic changes."

"Oh, piss off."

Charlie snorts. "I rest my case."

For a moment, they're both quiet. Then Gabe rolls off the armchair and onto the carpet, draping himself over Charlie in a half-hug. "Hey, I'm really glad you're here. Thank you for coming."

"'Course." Charlie's hand finds its way into Gabe's hair, fingers tugging on an errant curl. "Takes more than you moving to the US to get rid of me."

"Not trying to get rid of you, ever."

Charlie makes a sarcastic cooing noise, but his hand stays in Gabe's hair.

Another moment of silence, then Gabe cranes his neck so he can look at Charlie. "I'm thinking it could be nice to buy a place back in the UK. Like, maybe a flat in London. Two and a half hours by train from Manchester instead of an eleven-hour flight."

"London, huh?" A smile has crept into Charlie's voice. "Any particular reason for that choice?"

Since it's London, there are plenty of reasons Gabe could cite—it's the capital, the art and theatre scene is thriving, and it's got the best Indian food out of all the places where Gabe actually speaks the language. What he says instead is, "Nothing that wouldn't sound ridiculous."

"Newsflash: feelings aren't meant to be rational."

"I know. And it's not like I'm in love with him or anything, right? I don't know him *that* well." Gabe takes a second to sort through the words that tumble through his head. "It just feels like maybe, given time, I could. Fall in love with him, I mean."

Usually, this is when the little voice in his head, the one that always asks 'what if', would pipe up with all the reasons this is a bad idea. And maybe it is—Gabe hasn't exactly thought this all the way through, starting with the small matter of Gabe not being exactly out and proud, and ending with the question of whether Ray would even be interested. Gabe thinks yes because ... well. Mainly because of the look in Ray's eyes when Gabe said he was leaving, but also because it takes two to tango, and Ray is keeping their ongoing exchange of texts alive just as much as Gabe is.

With promo season right around the corner, Gabe will soon be swept up in a two-week tornado, too fucking busy to breathe, let alone sleep or think. After, though? The premiere in London is on the 21st of December, followed by a week of absolutely *nothing* before he plans to even consider his next project. Talk about a light at the end of the tunnel.

Also, Charlie is staring at him with a soppy smile.

"What?" Gabe asks.

"Nothing. Just..." Charlie pretends to wipe at his eyes. "My little boy, all grown up and ready to fall in love."

"You're not half as funny as you think you are."

"That's still pretty damn funny, so I'll take it."

With a sigh, Gabe relaxes further into the carpet. He spares an errant thought for what his fans would say if they could see him now—in ratty jeans and a hoodie that's a size too big, unshowered and sprawled on the ground like a teenager who objects to societal norms represented by seating furniture. Living the glamorous life of the rich and famous, he is.

He adjusts his position so his head is pillowed more comfortably on Charlie's stomach. "So you think this is a good thing, right?"

"Me being funny?" Charlie's stomach moves with the words, and Gabe considers protesting that Charlie isn't appropriately fulfilling his pillow duties, but decides he's got bigger fish to fry.

"Ray. Or, like, me taking a real interest in someone." Gabe draws a breath and blinks up at the huge ceiling fan that aspires to be an airplane propeller, installed by the previous owner of the house. "It's kind of complicated, isn't it, with me being, you know ... me."

"Can't really help being you, now can you?" Charlie's comforting drawl rumbles under Gabe's head.

"I guess not." Gabe considers it for a moment. "And it's not like I really want to. I mean, hey, nothing forces me to do another movie ever in my life, but I do enjoy it, you know? I get paid for doing something I love, and yeah, privacy is a bit of an issue sometimes, maybe I can't take a leisurely stroll down Fifth Avenue, but some people have real problems."

"Part of the package?" Charlie suggests.

"Privacy being an issue?"

"Being you and doing what you do. But also being part of your life." Charlie reaches down to tug on Gabe's ear. "Like, as your best mate, I have to be okay with having my picture taken sometimes when I'm with you, and people stopping you for selfies while I'm twiddling my thumbs. I've also had my fair share of strangers trying to use me to get to you."

Sickness flutters in Gabe's stomach. "You never told me that."

"No point, was there?" Charlie doesn't sound upset. "I've become good at screening, don't worry. The good ones in the pot, the bad ones in your crop."

It's on the tip of Gabe's tongue to ask why Charlie's telling him now, but really, he already knows. His fame is like a dusting of glitter that sticks to everything he touches, and while he might be worried about people stalking him for pictures or some former classmate he barely remembers selling stories about him, people like Charlie or his sister are affected in other ways.

If he ever chose to date someone normal, that person wouldn't escape untouched.

"Cat got your tongue?" Charlie asks, when Gabe has been quiet for a few moments.

"Nah." Gabe reaches for a conscious smile. He gets what Charlie is trying to tell him, he really does, but this conversation has taken a turn into the kind of serious territory Gabe isn't ready for yet. Another day, another time. "Just, I'm trying to shake the image of you kneeling in the soot in front of a firepit, humming to yourself as you sort through phone numbers you collected at a party."

"Well, I do have the blond hair and the blue eyes to pull it off."

"Missing the impossible hourglass figure, mate."

"You really know how to charm a boy."

Since Gabe is fresh out of a good response, he resorts to digging his fingers into Charlie's side, right below the ribs where Charlie is at his most ticklish. Charlie's shriek could cut glass. He retaliates by shoving his fingers into Gabe's hair, doing his best to turn Gabe's artfully tousled curls into a careless mess.

By the time they break apart, both grinning, any heaviness has dissipated.

∽

THREE HOURS LATER, Gabe still hasn't heard from Ray. It's getting close to bedtime in London, and Ray might be busy, maybe out with a friend, maybe out on a *date*.

Gabe should leave him be. It's not like they have an agreement that says Ray owes him a daily post-work message or anything.

In spite of his better judgement, Gabe pulls up their texts and types another one, right below his last comment about this creature called alot that seems to be running rampant online—look at all these people who care about alot more than they care about the space bar!

'Everything good back in London? Heard there might be snow in the coming days.'

After considering his draft, he deletes the second part—it's another two weeks before he'll return to the UK, so why would he care to check the weather report?

Should he delete the whole thing?

He counts to five and sends it.

It takes half an hour for Ray to reply, and when he does, it's short. 'Sorry, bit under the weather today. Nothing a good night's sleep can't fix.'

At this point, Gabe knows Ray's style well enough to sense the tiredness woven into the message. *'Need me to arrange for a soup delivery?'* he writes back.

He waits for a couple of minutes, but there's no response, so chances are Ray went to bed. Consciously dismissing the weird, twisty sense of unease in his gut, Gabe puts his phone aside and goes to challenge Charlie to a game of scrabble.

Living the Hollywood life, he is.

∽

Two weeks.

Five continents, twenty-seven cities.

Airplanes and limousines and taxis and one interview after the next. Smiling until his face hurts, words that blend together until they stop making sense, questions and answers and posing for cameras and never, ever enough sleep.

There are moments when Gabe wants to cry. Instead, he goes where he's pointed and stands where he's told and smiles, smiles, smiles.

Ray is pulling away.

It's nothing obvious, nothing Gabe can specifically point to. Ray doesn't suddenly ignore Gabe's messages or respond with one-liners, but there's a notable lag now, along with... It's not a lack of enthusiasm, not exactly. More like a sense of restraint that wasn't there before, as though Ray decided to put just a little more distance between them.

Or maybe Gabe is imagining it all. Given he's getting an average of three hours of sleep per night and running on enough caffeine to feel chronically jittery and start hearing colours, he might not be the best judge of reality at present.

'Back in the UK tomorrow,' he texts Ray in between an interview with a Spanish teen mag and an Italian radio show. Possibly the other way—it all starts blending together, after a while. *'Will be a crazy schedule until the premiere, but you could come? Or it would be nice to see you after. I may just need to sleep for about a century first.'*

Maybe it's too much.

Since the Italian radio host is entering the room with a beaming smile, Gabe sends the message without further edits and forces his facial muscles into something appropriately friendly.

Eye contact? Check.

Dimples? Check.

About to keel over from exhaustion? Not today.

He gets through the interview, and then two more, without saying anything horribly embarrassing. At least that's what he hopes; the last interview he remembers with any amount of clarity was for the final episode of *The Daily Show* with Trevor Noah, mostly because he read the guy's autobiography and is just a little in awe of him. After that, it all goes a bit soupy in Gabe's head: it's a string of similar questions that he answers with similar words, different places that he forgets the moment he leaves.

Ray replies at some point, but Gabe doesn't get a chance to read it until he's back in his hotel room, getting ready for bed so he can rise again, too soon, for a brutally early flight.

'Not sure I'll have time to watch the first two movies before the premiere of your third. Plus alot (see what I did there?) of people aren't quite my scene.' Ray added a smiley after the words, as though it's enough to soften the rejection. 'Off to see my family on the 23rd, but if you have time to hang out before, sure! Just let me know.'

It's a brush-off.

Isn't it?

Gabe's head is stuffed with wool. He leaves the phone on the bedside table, sluggish as he brushes his teeth, sluggish as he takes off his socks and then his jeans, sluggish when his phone rings and he picks it up without even checking because his vision is a little bit blurry and a little bit grey.

"Yeah?" he squeezes out, and if it's his assistant with any more instructions about where to be when, he'll either scream or cry. Maybe both.

"Son."

Gabe's stomach drops to his knees.

He sits down where he stands, right there on the floor of an objectively nice hotel room that looks just like the one from yesterday, and the day before. *Not tonight,* he thinks in a sad, stubborn kind of almost-prayer. *Please, not tonight.*

"Gabriel. Are you there?"

Tonight, then.

He locates his voice somewhere around the soles of his feet and drags it all the way back up to where it belongs. "Dad. I'm here, yeah."

Silence.

Gabe isn't the one who called, so he refuses to break first.

"Your sister is coming home for Christmas."

I know.

Gabe doesn't say it. Deborah has always been so much better at letting their parents believe whatever they needed to believe, be it the focus of her studies or her intact virginity. He isn't going to ruin that for her—not now, and not back when their parents kicked him out and he convinced her he left of his own volition and made her swear to avoid all discussions about it.

"That's nice," Gabe says vaguely.

"You know you would be equally welcome in our home. God loves a repentant sinner."

And there's the catch.

"I'm not repentant." Usually, Gabe would leave it at that—apologise, even, just to keep that door the slightest hint open. Tonight, though, he's tired. So, so tired, down to the very core of his bones. Too tired to cling onto the vain hope that maybe, one day, his parents won't need him to change who he is so they can love him again. "You can ask me tomorrow, and next month, and a year and five from now, and I'll still be me—and yes, that includes the simple truth that I am gay. You might as well stop waiting for that to change."

"I see." His dad sounds grim. "So you insist on your choice."

It's not a choice.

There's no point. There simply isn't, and last year, Gabe just about broke down when defeat sunk in. Now, he just feels numb. "Yeah. I guess I do insist on my choice."

"I see," his dad repeats even though no, he doesn't see at all.

Gabe stares at the lamp on the bedside table until his vision grows foggy. He stays silent.

"Is there truly nothing you have to say for yourself?"

"I don't think there's any point," he replies, toneless.

His dad has more to say after that, something about family and faith and duty, but Gabe's just ... done. It's all noise, syllables mashed together that don't add up to anything. He could hang up, he thinks, but the idea feels distant, like it occurred to someone else.

Eventually, all that's left is the dial tone.

He ends the call on his side and keeps his fingers wrapped around his phone, blinking a few times until the room shifts back into focus. He still feels dazed, like it was someone else who just had that conversation. Is this progress? Maybe he should ask his therapist.

Instead, he sends a quick text to Charlie, his fingers numb but somehow capable of finding the right spots. *Just had my traditional Christmas call with my dad.'*

For a second, he lets himself think about sending a similar message to Ray. Except Ray has been pulling away, doesn't want to hang out while Gabe is in London, and Gabe has been rejected enough for one night.

He's about to crawl into bed when his phone rings again. Charlie, this time, and Gabe should get some bloody sleep, but he picks up instead and lets Charlie ramble, the familiar cadence of his best friend's voice soothing him into a bone-deep state of exhaustion that eventually lets him slide into a dreamless sleep.

Still exhausted, he wakes up to his alarm far too early the next morning. Drags himself out of bed, out of his room, out of the hotel and into the car meant to take him to the airport. Spends the flight with his eyes closed and his headphones blocking out the world. There's a distant ache in his chest when he steps off the plane in Heathrow.

Two more days.

He throws a blanket over the dark corners of his mind and prepares to smile for the cameras.

8

It's the day after the premiere, and Gabe has yet to answer Ray's message. Good thing that Ray spent the last couple of weeks working on slowly, painstakingly, lowering his expectations. It didn't stop him from watching the first two movies Gabe did, of course—motivated by that tiny, treacherous part of his brain that was fully prepared to attend the premiere if Gabe doubled down on the invitation.

Not so.

But now Ray's mind is full of Gabe all over again, tangled up with images of Gabe in his Green Hunter role: the way real Gabe laughs, head thrown back and mirth crinkling the corners of his eyes, in contrast to the rare and fleeting smiles offered by the Green Hunter, who was kidnapped off the streets and subjected to some traumatising military enhancement procedure. How real Gabe listens with his whole body, compared to the faraway look in the Green Hunter's eyes as he gazes out over the ruins of his childhood village. Gabe sneaking a bite of dessert, grinning around the spoon, and the Green Hunter narrowing in on a target, tension in the generous curve of his mouth.

Rationally, Ray knows this is pathetic. Gabe was never more than a beautiful dream, and from the very beginning, Ray was prepared for the ending—strangers on a train, an impossible friendship. He knew it wouldn't last.

But now that it's over, it turns out he isn't ready at all.

With a hissed breath exhaled through his teeth, he sets about filling the kettle for a cup of tea. At two in the afternoon, it's pathetic that he's still bumming around in a pair of jogging bottoms and his sleep T-shirt, yeah, but that's okay because his clothes aren't the only thing that's pathetic—he's just matching what's inside to his outer appearance.

When the bell rings, he ignores it. Not his problem if the neighbour is never home to accept his packages; Ray has a day job too, and he schedules his deliveries accordingly, while next-door dick Richard habitually bets on Andrew accepting his frequent Amazon purchases. Andrew bears it with patience, but he's currently taking care of some last-minute Christmas shopping, and Ray is fresh out of neighbourly goodwill.

The bell falls silent. Thank you, postman, and a merry Christmas to you.

Then Ray's phone starts buzzing.

He considers ignoring that, too, but his oldest sister meant to call him about the Christmas menu, and Farah doesn't suffer being ignored.

It isn't Farah.

For a beat, Ray stares at the screen, his sense of balance knocked off-kilter. Weeks of text messages followed by three days of utter silence, and *now* Gabe's calling? Yeah, Ray gets that Gabe is busy—it's why he kept his invitation casual enough that Gabe would feel no obligation.

He's not sure when he decides to pick up, but he does so with a tentative, "Hi?"

"*Ray.*" Gabe's voice is croaky, as though he hasn't used it in a while. Too much drinking last night? "I'm—there's no one home. I know you don't want me here, but I didn't know where else... But there's no one home."

Ray speaks fluent babble, but this is beyond his level of certification. "Okay, slow down. What's going on?"

"There's no one home." A momentary pause and a sniffle. On pure instinct, Ray's gut twists before he even realises that Gabe might be ... *crying*? "Sorry. I shouldn't have come."

"Home meaning..." And then it finally clicks for Ray. "You're *here* here. You just rang the bell?"

"Yeah." More exhalation than a word.

"I thought you were the postman. I'll buzz you in right now, just give me a sec."

"Thank you." Again, it's barely audible.

What happened?

Later.

Ray presses the button for the door, and it's only when he hears Gabe's drudging steps travel up the stairs that it hits him: he's about to see Gabe again. He didn't think he would, and it's been six weeks, and he looks sloppy and unshaven, and this is the first impression he'll make after their time apart.

None of that matters once he catches sight of Gabe, though. Gabe looks... He's still *Gabe*, so 'awful' doesn't sit quite right—but he looks as though he hasn't slept in weeks. His eyes are red-rimmed, his hair flattened on one side and sticking up in odd tufts on the other, most likely a result of the wool hat he's clutching in one hand.

Whatever Ray meant to say dries up. Wordlessly, he holds open the door, catching a whiff of Gabe's aftershave as Gabe squeezes past him into the narrow entrance area. In the kitchen, the kettle starts whistling.

"Tea?" Ray asks in lieu of all the other questions that are tripping over each other in his mind.

"Please?" Gabe dips his head, eyes hidden as he kneels to take off his shoes. "I'm sorry to barge in on you like this."

I know you don't want me here.

That's what Gabe said, isn't it? He couldn't be more wrong, of course—Ray wants it too much, is the problem.

"You're welcome here, Gabe. You know that, right?"

"Yeah?" It's a quick, shy glance from underneath lowered lids, then Gabe ducks his head again.

"One hundred per cent," Ray says, with enough emphasis to hopefully get the point across. "Now, come on. Let's get a cup of tea into your hands, and then you can tell me what's wrong."

Gabe blinks, gaze sliding away, and nods.

He's silent when he trails Ray into the kitchen, silent when he leans against the counter, still silent even as he approves the bag of green tea that Ray holds up with the ghost of a smile, so fleeting it's barely there at all.

Ray pours water into the two bamboo cups Gabe brought the first time he was here, adds the tea bags, and hands one cup to Gabe.

"You kept them?" Gabe's voice sounds faded, like an old photograph bleached by the light.

"'Course I did." Ray leaves it at that. While he could make some excuse about how they're useful, nothing to do with the memory of Gabe right here in this flat, looking too good to be true because he was—well, it doesn't feel like the moment for excuses.

Gabe's only response is an upwards tug to one corner of his mouth, gone as quickly as it came. Bloody hell, he's starting to really worry Ray.

After a second's consideration, Ray jerks his chin towards his own bedroom instead of the sofa in the living room. "You look like you could use a break from ... everything, really. Andrew and Patrick will be back at some point, so let's go to my room, yeah?"

For the first time since he arrived, Gabe seems to relax, if only by a fraction. "Thank you."

"You're welcome." Ray sends a smile after the words, and while Gabe doesn't quite smile back, he seems to relax by another fraction. Again, he's silent when he trails Ray into the bedroom, his gaze briefly assessing the fairly functional, yet neatly kept space: a desk, a bookshelf, a wardrobe, a window that's slightly bigger and cleaner than the one in the kitchen, and the bed.

Only now does Ray realise his mistake: there's no neutral piece of furniture to sit on that's big enough for two people.

He plops down on the desk chair and waves Gabe towards the bed. "Come on, make yourself comfortable."

Gabe hesitates for the shortest of moments before he sags down onto the bed. He sits like that for an instant, head bent and eyes closed to inhale the scent of the tea, before he blinks back to alertness and shuffles further up the mattress. His thighs fall open as he leans against the headboard.

If the mood felt a little less heavy, Ray's brain would stutter-stop over the image.

As it is, he takes a sip of tea—still too weak, of course—and spins the desk chair to better face Gabe. "Okay, you're kind of scaring me here. What's going on?"

"I'm sorry." Pale-faced, eyes wide, Gabe looks younger than he is. "I shouldn't have shown up like this. I just... I didn't know where else to go, and you probably had a different idea for your day, so ... thank you for inviting me in anyway."

This must be the third time Gabe implied that Ray wouldn't want to see him.

"Okay, none of that is an answer to my question, but let's get something else out of the way first." Ray waits until Gabe meets his eyes, if only for a moment. "What the hell makes you think that you are bothering me?"

"You didn't seem particularly keen to see me." There's no reproach in Gabe's tone, just resignation, and why would he even *think* that? Ray tries to remember his last message and mostly recalls editing out any trace of eagerness. Which... Huh. Seems like he succeeded.

"I just didn't want you to feel obligated," he says after a beat, painfully aware of the vulnerable softness to Gabe's mouth, the hypnotic sweep of his dark lashes, how the woollen afternoon light saps all colour from his eyes.

"Obligated," Gabe repeats tonelessly, as though it's an alien concept.

"I may have taken it a little too far." Ray clears his throat. "Sorry about that."

Gabe is silent for a moment, shadows moving behind his eyes, "Okay," he says eventually, on a long breath. It doesn't feel okay, but moving on seems safer than insisting on how Ray really did want to see Gabe—a lot, *too much*.

"Okay," he echoes. "Now that we've established you're very welcome here: what's going on?"

Gabe's chest rises on a deep intake of air, and he ducks his head back over his tea, eyes hidden. "Apparently, *The Daily Mail* has been courting my parents for a while now." He sounds like he's reciting someone else's information. "Yesterday, they finally gave them the exclusive interview the paper's been angling for."

"That's your deeply religious parents, right?" It's a silly question. They're Gabe's only parents, obviously, but it gives Ray a moment to digest it.

"When I described them as deeply religious" —one corner of Gabe's mouth curls up, but it's devoid of humour— "it might have been an understatement. They're true believers. As in, they reject social media and fashion, divorce, same-sex relations, you name it."

"That's..." Honestly, Ray doesn't know what that is.

"Yeah." Gabe sips at his tea, gaze on his hands. "They weren't always this bad, just ... religious, yeah, but around the time I turned ten or so, my dad lost his job, and they fell in with this group of people that kept muttering about how the church in our village was too wishy-washy."

The red-rimmed eyes, the slight tremor in Gabe's voice... Ray has a bad, bad feeling about this. "Okay, so they're religious nutjobs. And they reject social media as the work of the devil or whatever, but they talked to *The Daily Mail*, of all things?"

"Funny, isn't it?" Gabe doesn't sound amused. "Looks like the article will break tomorrow, but I bet you the rumours are already out there. Hotel's probably surrounded by now."

Fucking hell.

So Gabe's parents went to the press with breaking news about their son. It's unlikely that Gabe erring off his destined path to priesthood would be particularly newsworthy, but Ray doesn't want to jump to conclusions.

"Do you know what exactly they said?" he asks, carefully watching Gabe's face over the rim of his cup.

"Not word for word. But *The Daily Mail* called my agent for a comment, so yeah, I know the gist. *'Scoop shock breaking news: Gabe Duke's dad says: My son is gay!'*" Gabe snorts, but it catches in his throat, and the line of his mouth remains grim. "Not that my dad would call it that. More like, 'chooses a lifestyle of sin' or something like that."

"And you, um." Ray puts his cup down. Fuck, he shouldn't even ask this right now, but there's a part of him that needs to know. "You are gay?"

"Yeah." Briefly, their eyes meet, before Gabe's gaze skitters away again. He's got one hand wrapped around his cup, the other absently bunching up Ray's duvet before smoothing it out again. "Sorry, probably should have led with that. I'm just not used to … putting it out there. Like, there are maybe five people who know—like my sister and Charlie, and my therapist, and now you." His mouth twists. "And my agent as of when he got the call, of course. And my parents, obviously, and the entire staff at *The Daily Mail*, and then tomorrow it'll be the whole fucking world."

Ray can tell the exact moment it hits Gabe: his attempt at a sarcastic smile dies, suddenly wiped out, just before his face crumbles.

"*Fuck*," he whispers, chin dropping to his chest, and then Ray is out of the desk chair and crawling across the mattress to pull Gabe in for a hug.

"I'm sorry." Ray repeats it, "I'm sorry," while he can feel Gabe shaking against him—not crying, Ray doesn't think so, just shivering as though he spent the past ten minutes in below-freezing surroundings, turning into Ray with his whole body, holding on, one hand still wrapped around the cup that's digging into Ray's hip.

Don't worry, boy, tomorrow is a new day.

It's his dad's voice Ray hears, the words laced with a smile, but

Ray can't promise even that. Tomorrow is a new day, yeah, but it's also when the world will start screaming in technicolour about Gabe's personal life.

"I'm so, so sorry," Ray tells the soft skin at the side of Gabe's neck.

"You know what's ironic?" Gabe's voice is slow, dream-like, as he burrows deeper into Ray's embrace. "Like, cosmic irony, I guess. Or maybe just coincidental." A huff. "I was always so careful. Always worried that someone outside the industry could sell me out. Turns out it's the devil you know."

This moment isn't about Ray. It's not about them, about their impossible friendship, about how Gabe is gay—maybe that changes something or maybe it doesn't. Right now, it doesn't matter because this moment belongs to Gabe, and that's why Ray will hold on for as long as Gabe lets him and half a second beyond that.

Just to make a point.

～

THE SOUND of a key in the door, then a crash. "Ray! Some help, please?"

"Andrew," Ray supplies when Gabe visibly startles. "My other flatmate. Unlike Patrick, he truly is mostly harmless."

Understandably, Gabe doesn't look much reassured, but he nods with the expression of a man who has no choice but to accept the course fate has chosen for him. Ray wishes there was anything he could say in reassurance, but Gabe already met Patrick, so Ray figures that at least it's all uphill from here.

"I'll be right back," Ray tells him, scrambling off the bed they'd been sharing for the past half hour, cross-legged and facing each other as Gabe talked about his hometown, about his parents and his sister, in a halting voice.

On the threshold, Ray pauses just long enough for a backwards glance.

Gabe, on Ray's bed. Real and alive and three-dimensional, after weeks of text messages. It's surreal and wonderful and sad all at once because even though Ray is glad to see him, he's also devastated that anyone, much less Gabe's own parents, would betray him like this—would serve him up like a sacrificial lamb, ready to be devoured by the wolves howling just outside the door.

"Ray!" Andrew shouts again.

"Coming!"

Ray makes it to the door right as a can of beans is about to slip from Andrew's grasp. The paper bag of groceries must have broken. Honestly, serves Andrew right for refusing to use the blue Ikea carrier bag that Ray and Patrick gravitate towards, while Andrew deems it a symbol of capitalism. Is it fashionable? No. Is it light-weight, sturdy, and small enough to fit into Ray's backpack so he can simply unfold it when he drops by the supermarket on his way home from work? A hundred times yes.

"Defying capitalism, one paper bag at a time?" Ray asks dryly as he retrieves the can of beans, along with a bag of flour and a packet of sugar. Looks like Andrew intends to bake something, which is really the main reason they keep him around. That, and the fact that he balances them out and gives occasional nuggets of good advice.

"Revolutions have to start somewhere." Andrew waggles his eyebrows because fortunately, he's not in the habit of taking himself too seriously. "Who were you talking to? Hope I wasn't interrupting—although you still look like a bum, so I guess you're not having a hot date."

The words are at odds with the kindness in Andrew's eyes; he sat with Ray through both of Gabe's movies even though he'd already seen them, and while Patrick's reaction to the continued silence on Gabe's end was offers of alcohol and supportive ranting, Andrew simply shared his best tea and maintained that there might be more than one way to read things.

Turns out he was right.

"Not a date, no." Ray leads the way into the kitchen and deposits his haul on the counter before turning to face Andrew. "It's actually… Uh. When you said that maybe Gabe wasn't just ignoring me because a better offer had come along? You were right."

Andrew's forehead creases as he sets the torn bag down on the table. "Wait. Are you saying that the person you were talking to just now..."

"Gabe's here, yeah."

If Ray were less worried about Gabe, he'd be delighted at seeing Andrew positively freeze, looking like the proverbial deer caught in the headlights, only less deer and more giraffe, and less headlights and more struck by lightning.

"Gabe Duke?" Andrew sounds miles from his usual calm and collected self.

"Hi," Gabe says quietly from the doorway to the living room. Ray didn't hear him coming. "That'd be me, yeah. And you must be Andrew?"

Andrew swallows and adjusts his glasses before he turns wide eyes on Gabe. "Yeah. Andrew Jones, *Evening Standard*."

Fucking hell.

It must have been pure pattern recognition, Andrew's brain switching to autopilot and adding the bit that usually follows after he states his full name. Gabe, though, sucks in a sharp breath and looks like he's been punched.

"Andrew is one of the good guys!" Ray takes a step towards Gabe, both palms up. "I swear. You have nothing to fear from him." *Or me.* "He knows we've met, and that we've been texting, and he hasn't breathed a word so far, and he never would."

"Fear? From *me*?" Andrew sounds like he's just waking up to the fact that something is very, very wrong. "What is that supposed to mean?"

"Gabe's parents" —even though Ray is speaking to Andrew, he keeps his gaze on Gabe— "sold him out to *The Daily Mail*."

"His parents?" Andrew's confused gaze flicks from Gabe to Ray, and back. "What kind of parents would sell out their son?"

Gabe's mouth pulls tight. "Mine, apparently."

"That's fucked up, mate. Really sorry to hear that." Finally, Andrew seems to regain his proper footing. He leans back against the kitchen table, everything about him projecting a non-threatening air. "But Ray's right: you've got nothing to fear from me."

"Yeah?" With Gabe's tone as cautious as his expression, Andrew continues.

"Seriously. First off, Ray is one of my best friends, which makes you my second-degree good friend, and that matters more than the frankly shitty paper I work for." He purses his mouth. "Secondly, I write a commuter column, meaning I interview random people on the train about pet peeves like suitcases with squeaky wheels and idiots who watch videos on public transport with the sound on."

Briefly, Ray forgets the point Andrew's trying to make because, "That *is* fucking annoying. There's this one guy who always does that in the break room at work, and I swear he's both blind and deaf because it's bloody loud, and it's like he doesn't even see how people are glaring at him to turn it down. What is up with that?"

"Schoolyard bullies who grew up into public annoyances?" Gabe looks slightly more at ease than he did a minute ago.

"Common rudeness." Andrew shrugs. "Failure of their parents to teach basic empathy because good ol' manners don't matter when a guy with a bucket on his head would make for a better Prime Minister than any of our recent disappointments."

Ray has learned to recognise the early warning signs of Andrew getting into a full-blown political ramble, so he shoots Gabe a pointed look. "If you want to escape without an ear bleed, don't encourage Andrew. He can talk politics for five hours without a toilet break, and your active participation is not required for the conversation to go on."

"Piss off," Andrew says comfortably, and somehow, that appears to be the moment Gabe decides that Andrew can be trusted because his smile is small but real.

"Some other day, maybe? I'd actually be interested. Just, you know, not when there are paps stalking my hotel and my agent wants to know whether I'm planning to address the public or not."

Andrew's eyes narrow like he's about to ask for details, then he nods. "Fair enough. But do let me know if you're ever up for an interview about all the pesky downsides to travelling First Class, will you?"

Too far?

It could go either way. Ray holds his breath, keeping Gabe on the edge of his vision as he starts unpacking the groceries. Gabe's chuckle loosens something in Ray's chest, and maybe this is exactly what Gabe needs: some gentle teasing, being treated like he isn't made of twigs and porcelain.

"Well." Gabe hooks both thumbs into the waistband of his tailored jeans, pushing out his flat stomach to give himself the appearance of a belly. "Just between us, the champagne really isn't what it used to be." Spoken in the brisk, clipped tones of a middle-aged, upper-class prick. "And would you believe that last time, I had to carry my own suitcase? Britain's going down the drain, is what I keep saying."

Ray mimes a slow clap. "Well played, Sir! It's almost like you're an actor or something."

"Or something, yeah." Gabe's face darkens as he seems to contemplate the future of his career. He snaps out of it almost immediately, gaze falling to the groceries lined up on the table. "Is that for Christmas baking?"

Andrew glances over from where he's started putting things into the fridge. "Yeah, I was going to make a batch of stollen Christmas biscuits, and maybe some ginger ones too. Feel free to help."

It's said in jest, but Gabe's eyes light up. "Yeah?"

"Um." Andrew seems to rearrange some preconceived notions in his head before he grins—one of those goofy ones that make him look like a five-year-old boy in a thirty-five-year-old body. "Sure. Have you done this before?"

"Baking?" Gabe continues without waiting for a response. "Yeah. Been a few years, but I love it. My sister and I used to do a cake most Sundays." He throws Ray a glance that's meant to be shrewd, offset by the momentary twist to his mouth. "Guess that should have been a clue for my parents, huh?"

"Your parents are idiots," Ray tells him softly.

"They're the only ones I have, though."

And if that isn't like a punch to the gut. Ray, at least, still has his mum.

"I'm so sorry." He holds Gabe's gaze to show he means it and considers pulling him in for another hug. But before he can make up his mind, Gabe inhales deeply, pastes a smile on his face, and turns to Andrew.

"So. Stollen biscuits, you said?"

∼

THERE'S something soothing about Andrew's presence, Gabe finds. While Patrick brings the energy of a live wire and Ray makes Gabe feel too many things at once, Andrew doesn't say much as they divide up the two recipes, Gabe on double ginger biscuit duty while Andrew takes the stollen upon himself.

It's just them, for now, with Patrick still at work and Ray having kindly offered to pick up the suitcase that Gabe left at the Savoy. Accompanied by pleasant, chill pop music that Andrew put on the kitchen speaker, they mostly talk to ask for ingredients or, in Gabe's case, where he can find things like spoons and measuring cups.

For the first time since Walter called, it gives Gabe a chance to breathe and assess the situation.

He needs to call his sister. He needs to set up a call with his therapist, too, and make sure he talks to Charlie before the article hits the newspaper stands first thing tomorrow morning.

Charlie will drop everything to be with Gabe.

While there's a selfish part of Gabe that wants that, a selfish part that needs his best friend right there by his side, he's been leaning on Charlie too much in recent weeks and months and *years*, really. He can't always expect Charlie to be his crutches because, at some point, Charlie will grow tired of it, and then what's left?

"All right?" Andrew asks, and Gabe realises he's been staring at the dough instead of kneading it.

"Yeah, sorry. Just blanked out for a second there."

"No worries." Andrew doesn't push, and maybe that's why Gabe feels comfortable with offering more.

"In that interview that'll be in *The Daily Mail* tomorrow, my parents will out me."

Andrew doesn't look surprised, just keeps on dividing the marzipan into even pieces. "I figured as much. How will you respond?"

Gabe notices that Andrew doesn't ask if it's true—maybe because he's drawn his own conclusions from the fact that Gabe is here, of all places, or from the way Gabe can't help but gravitate towards Ray.

"I don't know yet," he admits, keeping his attention on the dough and the way it feels in his hands, a tad sticky but not too much so. "Part of me just wants to stuff my fingers in my ears and hope it all goes away."

"A tried and true technique that usually fails." Andrew's tone is wry, at odds with the kindness in his eyes when he turns to look at Gabe. He reminds Gabe of Gordon, in more than just the age. "Although with Christmas coming up, you might have a chance to get away with it in this particular case."

Gabe snorts. "Mate, I appreciate the lie, but this isn't my first time at this rodeo."

"Well, I tried." Andrew's smile is lopsided. "It'll buy you some time, though. Just tell your agent to be unavailable for comments, and things should be mostly on hold until after the holidays."

"The internet never sleeps."

"Nah, but the internet might also cast you as the secret love child of George Clooney and Prince Joshua, and peddle proof that you're half reptile."

Gabe gives it some serious consideration. "You raise a good point."

"It's my true calling in life."

They're quiet while Gabe starts sectioning off pieces of dough that he rolls into sausages the width of a finger. He's first to break the pleasant silence. "Can I ask you something? About Ray."

Andrew's eyes narrow. "You can ask, yeah. I don't commit to answering."

Gabe possibly likes him even better for that. "Ray seems to be in the habit of dating dickheads."

"That's your question?"

"No. Just ... *why*?" Gabe pauses to reach for a knife. "Is it because of that twat he dated when he was, like, seventeen?"

"He told you about that?" Andrew sounds impressed. "And yeah, that's part of it. Add guilt about his dad and his embarrassment about losing that scholarship, and you end up with someone who feels they don't deserve good things."

Ray feels guilt about his dad? It's a conversation for another time, and with Ray.

Gabe rolls dough for another quiet minute. This time, it's Andrew who speaks first.

"What are your plans for the next few days? I'm gonna go out on a limb here and assume you won't exchange presents under the tree with your dear mum and dad while Silent Night is softly playing in the background."

Gabe laughs at the absurdity of the image, the sound scraping along the back of his throat. "Who knows, maybe that was their devious plan all along: out me just before Christmas so that the public outcry will have me crawling back to them like a good little repentant sinner."

"Hard to predict the twisted workings of a crazy person's mind," Andrew agrees.

"I honestly can't be bothered to even try." Gabe transfers the first batch of medallion-shaped dough onto a baking tray. "And to answer your question: I don't know yet. Ray's leaving tomorrow, right, so my time here is limited—and thanks, by the way, for being cool with me staying even just for tonight—"

Andrew waves him off. "Don't mention it. Kind of nice to have a baking mate for once, what with how Ray and Patrick have the miraculous skill to ruin even the simplest recipe."

"Still, thank you." Gabe starts on another dough sausage, keeping his gaze on his hands. "But yeah, anyway, I haven't really planned past tomorrow. Fly to the Caribbean, maybe? I know I'd be welcome at my best friend's place but he's from my hometown, so..."

"Yeah, I see how that would come with some mixed emotions." Andrew's tone is dry. "Anyway, two things: one, I'll be here until the 25th since my parents are still on a trip, and you're welcome to stay until then, or even after. Two, you could always go with Ray. I went with him once, so I can tell you first-hand that it'll be madness with all his sisters there and one of them's got two kids now, too, but maybe that's exactly what you need right now."

It sounds nice. God, it does—out of all the church activities Gabe experienced growing up, his favourite part was how excited the children in the community got around Christmas. The nativity plays, the pretty fake presents, the tree bowing under the weight of red and gold baubles...

Ray's family might celebrate differently, of course, or not at all. And anyway, Ray hasn't said a word about inviting Gabe along.

Gabe pulls his bottom lip into his mouth and glances over at Andrew. "I don't want to be a bother."

"Jesus fucking Christ, it's like two peas in a pod." Andrew heaves a dramatic sigh. "If Ray hasn't asked you yet, it's because he assumes you've got better plans."

"You don't know that." Gabe isn't sure what, exactly, he's defending Ray from, but he feels like he should.

"Oh, trust me, I do know that. I've been living with that guy for long enough to know the twisted workings of his brain."

"It's his time with his family." Still defending Ray against what might be windmills. "Maybe he doesn't want a stranger hanging around."

"Lord help me." Andrew turns his eyes heavenward. "You're hardly a stranger, Gabe. He'd want you there, trust me."

"Well, I'm not just going to *ask*."

"And why not?"

"Because then he might feel pressured to invite me."

"Funny." Andrew's tone implies the opposite. "This feels *just* like that conversation Patrick and I had with Ray some days ago."

"It's good to be considerate," Gabe protests.

"And did you feel terribly inconvenienced by Ray's invitation?"

Invitation? Oh—the message that read like a brush-off.

"Well, no." Gabe dusts his hands with more flour to keep the dough from sticking to his fingers. "He didn't sound keen to see me, so I didn't know there was an invitation to be inconvenienced by. If I had known, I wouldn't have been."

"Thank you for proving my point." Andrew flattens a piece of dough in his palm before he places marzipan at the centre and rolls the whole thing into a ball.

"Your point?"

"There's considerate, and then there's going overboard some fifty miles from port. Ray is a pro at the latter, and I'm starting to suspect you're not far behind."

If Charlie were here, he would offer Andrew a high-five.

"Please don't take this the wrong way," Gabe begins, and Andrew interrupts with a chuckle.

"Nothing good ever came after a line like that."

"No, I swear I don't mean it in a bad way. Not, like, contrarian or anything. Just..." Gabe meets Andrew's eyes as he raises his flour-dusted hands with a small shrug. "But what I mean is, why do you care how I spend my Christmas? You barely know me."

"Ha. You'd be surprised at how much I've heard about you in the last couple of months." Andrew moves on smoothly, before Gabe has a chance to ask just what, exactly, Ray said about him. "Also, you seem like a good lad, and on top of all that, it's almost Christmas. What better time to nudge a couple of blind men onto the path to enlightenment?"

Gabe picks up the knife again to produce more medallion-shaped slices of dough. "I honestly can't tell if you're serious right now."

"That's for me to know and for you to puzzle over for the rest of the evening." Andrew's grin rivals the Cheshire Cat's. For some reason, it makes Gabe grin right back, maybe because it's been a bit of a day, and it somehow led him to a point where he's baking

Christmas biscuits with a man he just met, who insists on giving him life advice.

"You're a bit mean aren't you?"

"Only on Sundays." Andrew says it as though it's cause for pride.

"It's Thursday."

"Oh. Must have woken up on the wrong side of the bed, in that case."

Gabe puffs out a laugh before he sobers. "Hey, Andrew? Thank you. For letting me hang around, for sharing your baking tools, for ... caring to talk to me like I'm a real person, I guess."

"You're welcome." Andrew's voice is gruff in that way people use when they're trying to avoid a show of emotions. "Also, if you get a chance? Please tell your parents to fuck off from me."

Gabe has no plans to see his parents in the foreseeable future—or speak to them, for that matter. He appreciates the sentiment, though, so he sends Andrew a smile that feels only the slightest bit off. "It will be my pleasure."

Andrew bumps their shoulders together in silent acknowledgement, and when they both turn back to work on their respective doughs, Gabe's heart feels marginally lighter than it did before.

He's still not going to ask Ray for a Christmas invitation, though.

9

"Those *fuckers*." Deborah sounds livid. The laptop screen shows her leaning into the camera, her hands balled into fists, eyes reduced to angry slits.

Gabe exhales. It's not like he expected her to announce that she had her own interview lined up, but something in him still loosens. "I don't want you to take sides."

"Oh, I'm taking sides. I'm taking sides, all right." She utters a string of what Gabe suspects are French curses before switching back to English. "And I'm done making excuses for them. *Done!*"

This is Deborah at both her best and most volatile. Ninety-five per cent of the time, she carries herself with the kind of calm, rational composure Gabe can only hope to achieve one day—it's those remaining five per cent when she explodes into action and, say, moves to France on a whim, or dyes her hair purple only to dye it back to black for the next family occasion, or loses her virginity in the backseat of a car because their parents forbade her to attend a friend's birthday party.

"Don't do anything rash, please?" Gabe sits up straight on Ray's desk chair and hopes his voice conveys how serious he is. "I don't want you to, like, walk out on them after telling them to burn in hell, and then you regret it a month from now, and it's all kind of my fault."

"I won't regret it, and it's not your fault either way. This has been a long time coming."

"Deborah..."

"Gabe." Deborah's tone effectively stops whatever he meant to say. "If I want to tell them to go to hell, that's my prerogative. Now, once I'm through with them: where do I find you?"

"What about the money?" Gabe asks in a last-ditch effort to make her pause, *think*. "They still pay for your studies, don't they? So unless you change your tune and start accepting money from me..."

"I will not live off my little brother's riches," she shoots back, just like Gabe expected. "And I'll figure it out. Don't worry your pretty little head."

"But if you don't?"

"I will." She sounds confident enough for the two of them, and Gabe knows that for now this is the best he'll get.

"Okay. *Fine*." He leans back in Ray's chair, crossing his arms and jutting out his bottom lip. "Have it your way. As per usual."

"Thanks, I think I will. Now, Christmas?"

Good question. It's not like Gabe attaches heightened emotional importance to Christmas; a couple of years ago, he spent it at an exclusive yoga retreat, and last year, he did charity events—which won't be an option this year, not unless he wants the paps to shove their way into a children's hospital and shout intrusive questions while he's handing out board games and stuffed animals that his assistant helped him wrap.

"Can I let you know tomorrow?" he asks.

Sadness briefly touches her eyes before she smiles. "Sure. If it's Hawaii, you may have to cover my flight after all."

He smiles back. "Don't tempt me."

They say their goodbyes, then Gabe shuts down the laptop. Once the screen turns black, he buries his head in his hands and just *breathes*—in, and out, and in.

A gentle knock on the door makes him open his eyes and sit up. "Yeah?"

Ray peers into the room before he opens the door fully and comes in, bringing with him the lingering scent of freshly baked biscuits. He looks soft and comfortable in his pj's, the small stud in his ear missing. "I didn't hear voices anymore, so I thought you might be done. How did it go?"

Gabe is hit by a rush of gratitude that leaves him faintly lightheaded. Here's this man who took him in without question, who's been nothing but kind and generous all day, who picked up his suitcase and offers hugs when Gabe needs them, who asks about his sister. How can Gabe ever repay him?

He blinks through the fog. "Good? I think. Although she's dead-set now on telling our parents where to stick it, and it'll be my fault if they're no longer talking."

"Maybe she should have done that a long time ago." Ray's voice is quiet, the lamplight painting him in golden hues. "Like when they kicked you out, for example."

"She thinks it was my decision to leave. I made her swear not to bring it up with our parents because I knew they wouldn't." What's intended to be a snort gets stuck in Gabe's throat. "I mean, I'm practically dead to them. Unless they're discussing me with *The Daily Mail*, I suppose."

Ray raises his brows. "So you lied to your sister?"

"I didn't want to drag her into it!" Gabe flicks his hand at nothing. "She hadn't done anything wrong."

"Neither had you."

"I know that!"

It's silent for a beat.

"Rationally, I know that." Gabe deflates. "I don't feel guilty about being gay, but they're my *parents*. No child wants to be a disappointment."

Ray perches on the edge of the bed, facing Gabe. "Yeah, I get that. Honestly, it's a miracle you're as well-adjusted as you are."

"Probably got Charlie to thank for that. He never made me feel like there was anything odd about me." Just the memory makes Gabe smile. "One day, he just goes, 'So, you've got a crush on the preacher's son, eh?' And that was that. No drama. He just accepted it and moved on."

"The preacher's son?" Ray tucks a smirk into the corners of his mouth. "Was he called Billy Ray?"

"He was not." Gabe grins back, a distant, warm glow burning in his chest. "Incidentally, he was also not the only boy who could ever teach me."

Too late, he realises how flirty that sounds. Ray must notice too because his gaze drops to Gabe's mouth, tension stretching thick between them.

Not the time.

Gabe's got too much on his plate right now, and if he starts something with Ray, he wants to do it *right*. He doesn't want a fleeting thing, waking up in the morning to remember that his life is a mess and he has no right to drag anyone else into it. What he wants is football arguments and text messages and conversations about books they love or disagree on, about classic films and the reproduction rate of cells and their crazy friends. He wants kisses as well, wants to drop to his knees for Ray, wants naked skin and slow hands and muffled groans—but not just for a night.

He reaches for a teasing smile and finds it in a drawer of his mind, pulls it out. "Not that this particular son of a preacher man was ever interested in teaching me anything but the intricacies of the Bible. Dusty Springfield would be so disappointed."

Ray breathes out a laugh, gaze sliding away. "Can't win them all."

"No, you really can't." Gabe gives a shrug, suddenly aware of how tired he is. "Anyway, think I'm too knackered to call Charlie now. I'll just send him a text. He'll probably want my hide for not calling once he sees what's going on, but that's a problem for tomorrow."

"Sounds like a healthy approach to life."

"Exactly. Why do today what you can delay until tomorrow?"

With a chuckle, Ray gets up from the bed and busies himself with slotting a few scattered books into what seem to be their rightful places on the shelf. For a second only, Gabe lets his eyes linger on the curve of Ray's bum, nicely outlined by the thin pyjama bottoms. Then he turns to his phone and starts a new message to Charlie.

'Oops, my parents did it again... I'm okay, though. Honest! Pretty tired, but I'll call you first thing tomorrow, okay? Love you, man.'

Once it's sent, he puts the phone face down on Ray's desk and gets up, abruptly uncertain. They haven't discussed sleeping arrangements, and Gabe isn't quite sure how to bring it up. Is he expected to sleep on the sofa? It's too short and would probably screw up his back for the next few weeks, so he might be better off on the carpet—it'll be like the good old times on the floor of Charlie's student room. He'll still need some kind of blanket, though, and a pillow maybe.

"So, um." He stops, unsure how to continue.

Ray turns and, for a beat, simply looks at Gabe as he appears to ponder something. Then he straightens, rolling his shoulders back as he firms his jaw. "Okay, so this is probably silly, right?" A crooked grin quirks his mouth, the words rushed. "But Andrew dared me, *so*. I'm sure you have better things to do, right, but just in case you don't—you would be welcome at mine. For Christmas."

Wow. Andrew was right?

Gabe lets the corners of his mouth tug up. "Well, my current plan is to get some fucking sleep. Beyond that? I've got nothing." He brushes a hand down the side of his jeans and glances away, then back at Ray. "So no, I've got nothing better to do. And actually, I'd love to come. If you're sure it's not an imposition?"

"You ... want to?" Ray looks as though Gabe just told him that Santa Claus is real, surprise plain in his features. Then he gathers himself. "Not an imposition, no, not at all. You'd be very welcome. Just be prepared for, like, my sisters being utter terrors—they wouldn't rat you out, not that, but they cheat at Monopoly, and they're *loud*. And there's a Christmas tree and the kids get presents, but mostly it's just everyone getting drunk and eating too much, so if you're expecting a real Christmas-y Christmas..."

Amusement pools in Gabe's stomach. "Are you trying to put me off?"

"No! Just giving you a fair warning, is all."

"It all sounds great."

A slow grin spreads over Ray's face and brightens his eyes to a rich whiskey colour. "Yeah?"

Warmth settling deep in his bones, Gabe grins back. "Yeah."

∼

RAY ISN'T PREPARED for the sight of Gabe in boxers and an oversized T-shirt. There's no reason why it would hit him quite like this, breath catching in his throat, heat rising to his cheeks. Maybe it's the visual reminder that Gabe will spend the night in Ray's bed—alone, of course—or maybe it's because right here, right now, Gabe looks like he could be Ray's.

"Found everything all right?" Ray asks to gloss over his reaction, closing the book he'd been pretending to read at the desk.

"Yeah, thanks." Gabe lingers on the threshold, and for the first time since they met, he seems small. "Any chance you could find me a blanket and a pillow?"

Ray nods towards the bed. "Already put fresh sheets on for you. I'll kip with Patrick."

Gabe's eyes widen. "I'm not kicking you out of bed! I thought I could just, like, sleep in the living room or something."

Is he for real? Ray snickers. "You've sat on that sofa, right? Because friendly reminder, it's lumpy and definitely too small for you."

"Yeah, no." Gabe ducks his head, smiling a little. "Thought I might sleep on the carpet."

"I wouldn't recommend it, given I don't remember the last time we had it cleaned." Ray shakes his head and gets up from the chair. "Seriously, Gabe. Friends don't let their friends sleep on the carpet."

"Well, friends don't kick their friends out of bed."

"It's really not a problem—I've known Patrick since we were both in diapers, so it's hardly the first time." Temporary insanity, pure and simple, has Ray add the next bit. "Either that, or you and I can share. Not like my bed isn't big enough for two."

Holy shit, what was he *thinking*? Gabe needs a place to hide, not Ray overstepping the boundaries of their friendship.

Briefly, Gabe's gaze flickers to the bed, then back to Ray. "I don't mind sharing."

He ... doesn't mind sharing.

"Okay." Ray narrowly avoids clearing his throat. "Um. Right, yeah. If you're quite sure it's fine?"

Gabe presses his lips together, lashes dark smudges against his cheek. "I'm sure, yeah." His voice dips low. "To be honest, maybe I'd be kind of grateful not to be alone tonight."

Friends.

"So that's settled." Ray aims for casual and thinks he mostly succeeds. "Do you want to turn in now? I know you're not much of a night owl, plus it's been a hell of a day."

"If you don't mind?" Gabe sits down on the edge of the bed, and bloody hell, it's neither the time nor place, but there's no way Ray won't mentally revisit this particular image—except he'll have a hand down his pants and the Gabe in his mind will invite him closer with a hot look.

Ugh, *stop* it. Gabe has enough people perving over him.

"Nah, it's fine." Ray is failing as a friend, but other than that, it's all just peachy. "Let me just grab my stuff from Patrick's room and tell him he's on his own tonight after all."

"Don't forget to check for monsters under his bed, in that case."

"Gabe, listen." Ray moulds his tone to convey regret. "I know this will come as a shock, but there are no monsters living under beds. Also, Santa isn't real."

In a move he blatantly copied off the Green Hunter, Gabe falls back onto the bed as though he's been shot, clutching his chest. "My worldview! Shattered to pieces!"

Ray doesn't notice Gabe's splayed thighs and the bare, creamy skin there. He does not. "Are you sure you did movies?" he asks. "Because that looked more like slapstick theatre to me."

Gabe's grin is at odds with the shadows still lurking around his eyes. "You honour me."

It takes Ray conscious effort to keep his attention on Gabe's face. Accordingly, he can't quite think of a good response, so he retreats with a wiggle of his fingers and ducks into Patrick's room.

"I am *doomed*," he hisses.

Patrick glances up from his laptop but doesn't bother hitting pause on the movie he's watching. "What else is new?"

"No, I mean it." Ray rakes a hand through his hair. "I suggested we share a bed as a *joke*, except he said yes? I can't share a bed with him. But I also can't admit that I can't do it."

"The struggle is real," Patrick drawls.

"I intuit a certain lack of moral support here."

"That's correct." Patrick's smirk shows off his sharp incisors. "I figure that since you invited him to spend Christmas with you, we've passed the point of no return. You've made your bed, pun intended, now go and lie in it. I'll be right here with the popcorn."

"Bitch," Ray mutters.

"Prick." Patrick hesitates. "Hey. You know what you're doing, right?"

"Nope." Ray throws him a bitter smile. "No clue whatsoever."

"That's kind of what happens when you catch feelings," Patrick tells him, his answering smile uncommonly kind. "Now, off with you. Be with your boy and leave me to enjoy my movie, will you?"

"Not my boy." The protest is weak, and Patrick doesn't bother with a response as Ray gathers his bedding in his arms and mumbles a good night.

"Sleep well," Patrick says, sugary sweet.

Because that's likely.

When Ray returns to his own room, Gabe is already nestled under the covers, taking up the bed half that's further from the door. At the dip of the mattress under Ray's weight, Gabe's eyes blink open, half-lidded. "Hey," he rasps out. "This okay? Didn't know which side you'd prefer."

"No preference." Ray busies himself with setting out his own twin duvet and fluffing up the pillow. "I usually just sleep in the middle. Been about a year since I last shared a bed with anyone, so…"

"You haven't—" Gabe flashes Ray a tired look. "In a *year*?"

On the list of topics Ray wants to discuss while Gabe is in his bed, this ranks roughly on the same level as 'child slaves used in cocoa production' and 'the varied and awful methods employed by industrial fishing.'

"Not for sleeping," he says curtly, and Gabe gazes at him for a moment too long before he nods, his curls whispering against the pillow.

"Fair enough."

They're both quiet after that, Ray opting to slide under the covers in his pj's even though he's used to sleeping naked. "Ready for me to turn off the light?" he asks once he's settled comfortably, a safe arm's width of space between them.

"Please." It's barely more than a gust of breath.

Once Ray flicks the switch, darkness wraps around them. It heightens his other senses, makes him intimately aware of every single breath that Gabe takes, of the warmth he imagines emanating from the other side of the bed, maybe even the faintest hint of Ray's shower gel that Gabe must have used earlier.

It's going to be a long and restless night.

When Ray turns his head, he can make out the faintest outline of Gabe's profile. "Good night," he tells the shadows between them.

Gabe draws an audible breath. "Thank you, Ray. For everything you did today. I have very few people in my life that I trust completely, and you're one of them."

"Anytime, Gabe." The thing is, Ray means it. *Need a friend in your corner? Need a hug, a fuck, or a kidney? You've got my number.* He swallows around the mild taste of panic.

"Thank you," Gabe repeats, his voice melting into the darkness like honey that dissolves in a glass of whiskey.

"You're welcome."

"Good night, Ray." No more than a whisper.

Silence settles after that, and Ray wills himself to slow down the swirl of his thoughts, just like when he meditated for ten minutes every morning before school, years ago. He finds a comfortable position, arms by his side, and lets his eyes drift shut, mentally scans his body from head to toe, then focuses on inhaling and exhaling, regular like waves washing up on the shore, while his thoughts float like clouds across the sky.

A hitched breath to his right.

Ray's eyes fly open. He lies motionless, listening to make sure he didn't imagine it—and there it is again: the tiny hitch of Gabe's breath, as though he's trying his hardest to suppress the sound.

Ray could leave him be.

"Gabe?" he murmurs instead, shifting to face him.

For a few, dragging seconds, there is silence. Then Gabe rasps out a "Sorry."

Ray matches Gabe's low tone of voice. "What for?"

"Just..." Gabe turns his face away and curls in on himself. "It's stupid." Another hitched breath. "I just... *Fuck*. I promised myself I'm done crying."

Ray's entire body is aching with the need to reach for Gabe, so he does—a tentative hand on Gabe's back to feel Gabe's muscles coiled tight like springs. "Not stupid," Ray says softly. "They're your parents, Gabe. How could you not care?"

Gabe inhales as if to reply, but in the end, all he does is sniffle quietly. Ray's heart maybe breaks a little for him.

When Gabe moves incrementally closer, his back still to Ray, the shift is so small Ray needs a moment to decide whether he imagined it. No. No, he didn't. Slowly, carefully, he smooths his hand along Gabe's back, down to Gabe's waist and around to the centre of his chest.

This time, Gabe doesn't try to hide how he burrows closer. It's... They're spooning. Ray is basically *spooning* Gabe, palm flat on Gabe's chest, only their duvets maintaining an illusion of platonic distance between them.

Ray's earlier meditative calm has been shattered into a million pieces. He strives to rebuild it, consciously sitting with the thought of what he wants Gabe to be to him for a couple of deep breaths. Then he lets it go because Gabe *trusts* him, and Ray would rather cut off his own foot than betray that.

"Okay?" he whispers.

"Yeah. It's... It's nice." Gabe exhales on a quiet sigh. "Never been held in bed before."

"Never?" Ray didn't mean to sound so incredulous, but ... *never*? If Gabe wanted to, he could have a different person in his bed all night, every night, and twice on Sundays. Ray ignores the unwarranted jealousy that flickers in his stomach like a case of mercury poisoning.

Gabe's chuckle turns out watery. "I'm not a blushing virgin. Just ... not much experience in the romance department, I guess."

Because he's in the closet. At least until his parents drag him out and into the plain light of day first thing tomorrow morning.

Fuck them.

"Sorry for your loss." Ray aims for a droll tone and hopes he lands in the general vicinity. "If there's one thing I miss about dating, it's the romance. Sex is easy to come by, but holding hands, kissing, lying in bed just like this? Not the kind of thing you get just from walking into a bar."

Of course, romance is also what fades first. The sex, it seems, is the one thing about Ray that doesn't get boring after a month, at least based on the relative interest shown by his previous boyfriends.

"I can see why," Gabe says quietly, almost like an admission. "This is nice."

God. It is, yes—the touch of Gabe's body against his, Ray's nose tucked into Gabe's neck, curls lightly tickling Ray's forehead. Under his palm, through the thin fabric of Gabe's T-shirt, Ray imagines he can feel the rhythm of Gabe's heart, slower now, his breathing easier.

"It is nice, yeah." Ray swallows around the gentle burn in his throat, something that feels a little like tears. "You should try to get some sleep, all right? Big day tomorrow." Shit, that's the last thing Gabe needs to be reminded of. Ray casts around for a quick, harmless reason and lands on, "Because you don't want to meet my sisters running on an empty tank, trust me."

"I do," Gabe says simply. "Trust you, I mean."

This isn't real, Ray reminds himself. This is just for tonight, or for a few days. Just until Gabe gets back on his feet and remembers there's a world out there—a world that will be waiting for him to make his next move. Ray, for one, has no doubt that he'll hit the ground running.

"Good." Ray closes his eyes and tightens his hold by just a tiny bit. "Then sleep."

A whispered "Okay" as Gabe's chest rises on a long, deep intake of air. A moment later, he exhales, most of the tension in his muscles draining away.

It isn't long until Gabe drifts off, relaxing further into Ray's hold. Ray, on the other hand, is awake for a long while after, too aware of every precious second that ticks by, of every tiny change in Gabe's breathing and the warmth of his body—too aware of Gabe, Gabe, Gabe.

When Ray finally sinks into sleep, he dreams of green eyes and empty corridors.

10

Gabe's first thought is *No.*

Please, not his alarm. Not another flight, another interview. Not when he's comfortable for once, and warm.

"You gonna get that?" Ray rumbles from behind him, and, oh. *Ray.*

Also—not Gabe's alarm, but his phone.

It's tempting, so very tempting to just ignore it and keep lying right there, in Ray's arms. Can't the rest of the world just wait for a while?

Blessedly, the phone stops ringing before Gabe is forced to make a grab for where he left it, somewhere on the floor. He closes his eyes.

Only for his phone to start ringing again.

Charlie, then. Bloody hell.

With a groan, Gabe twists his upper body so he can reach the floor, trying not to dislodge Ray's arm as he blindly feels around for the phone. *There.* He confirms it's Charlie and accepts the call with a "What do you want?"

"What do I want?" Charlie sounds outraged. "What do *I* want?! How about a best mate who tells me things!"

Things...

Ah, shit.

"I did! I sent you a text."

"A text. He sent me a *text*." Concern grapples with irritation in Charlie's voice. "Here's a hint, Gabe—next time your parents fucking out you in *The Daily Mail*, you give me a call immediately so I know you're okay."

"Technically, they can only out me once." It probably wasn't the smartest response Gabe could have picked, but his brain is still operating at reduced speed, half of his focus on the solid warmth of Ray's body against him—except Ray makes as if to pull away, mumbling something about giving Gabe privacy to talk. Gabe doesn't want privacy.

"Oh, you're fucking hilarious," Charlie gripes.

Gabe hums an acknowledgment even as he holds on to Ray's hand, turning his head just enough to meet Ray's eyes. 'Stay,' he mouths, and after a moment, Ray settles back against him, flat palm coming to rest against Gabe's ribs.

"Gabriel Jacob." Charlie's tone suggests it might be his second or third attempt to get a response.

"Sorry, yeah. I'm here." Gabe switches the phone to his other ear so he can rest his head on the pillow. "And I'm sorry I didn't call you last night. I was just ... fucking exhausted, really. It's been a brutal promo window, and after Walter called me about my parents, I just wanted to crawl into bed and sleep for about a century."

"Fuck, mate. I'm sorry." Charlie's voice has lost its sharp edge. "Anything I can do? Does Deb know?"

"Yeah." Gabe sighs. "She knows, and she's planning to tell our parents where they can shove it."

"Honestly, she should've done it a long time ago. Would've too, if you'd told her the truth."

It's not a new discussion—Charlie has always maintained that it isn't Gabe's job to protect Deborah, but Charlie doesn't have siblings, so he can't possibly understand. Since Gabe doesn't want to get into it right now, he chooses not to acknowledge Charlie's point.

After a second, Charlie moves on. "Anyway, Gee, where are you? Still in London? Tell me you made it out before the paps got to you."

"No paps. I left the hotel in time." It's the truth, if not all of it—Gabe has no interest in explaining where, exactly, he's hiding out while Ray is right there, listening in. Even if all Ray gets is Gabe's side of the conversation, it would be too revealing.

"Okay, good. *Great*." Relief brightens Charlie's voice. "Now, where do I meet you? Unless—I assume you wouldn't want to spend Christmas with us, right? Too close?"

Easy questions, difficult answers. Gabe blinks at the green curtains that allow a trickle of morning light into the room. When did he last sleep past dawn? It feels like a decade ago.

He decides to answer the second question first. "Too close, yeah. Plus it's not a secret you're my best mate, and I don't want to encourage a stakeout in front of your house. "

"Too late. I spotted the first pap when I opened the blinds." Charlie doesn't sound particularly bothered. "It's how I knew something was seriously up."

"Shit." Gabe groans. "Your mum will have my hide."

"Mate, my mum loves you more than I do most days, so you'll be forgiven. But, yeah. Not much of a secret safe house, this." The tapping of keys on Charlie's end, then, "All right, I'm ready to book my trip. Plane or train?"

Christ, it would be good to see Charlie. Gabe swallows around the lump in his throat. "I can't always expect you to drop everything the minute I've got it tough."

"Oh my God, shut *up*." Charlie puffs out an annoyed breath. "You'd do the same for me. You *have*. Remember Nora?"

Of course Gabe does. She was whiplash smart and funny, and when she moved back to the US, she snapped Charlie's heart in two. Gabe rescheduled a watch ad campaign he'd been meant to shoot and instead camped out in Charlie's tiny studio flat for a week, making sure that Charlie ate some food that didn't come out of a microwave and drank some liquid that didn't come out of a bottle with a per mille sign.

"I remember Nora, yeah."

"Good. So I repeat: plane or train?"

Gabe isn't getting out of this. He doesn't want to, even—but it means telling Charlie where he'll be while Ray is right there. The only way to handle it is like ripping off a band-aid: quickly and decisively.

"Train. I'm still in London, but we're planning to leave here around ten, and then it should be a four-hour drive or so."

"*We.*" Charlie manages to pour a world of meaning into the word.

"Ray's family lives east of Leeds—"

"Colforth," Ray supplies.

"Colforth," Gabe echoes dutifully, silently begging Charlie to accept the information and move on. No such luck, of course.

"Ray's family. Right." Years of familiarity make it easy to picture Charlie's face as he says it. "Okay, I've got just two questions for you. Yes and no answers will suffice."

Gabe presses the phone more tightly to his ear. "Shoot."

"One: Ray invited you to spend Christmas with his family?"

Well, that's an easy one. "Yes."

"Good, thank you for playing." Charlie pauses ominously. "Two: I woke you up, and yet he's right next to you."

"That's a statement," Gabe tells Charlie because no would be a lie, but yes feels like admitting to more than this is, and with Ray right there, Gabe can't elaborate.

Charlie snorts. "I'll take that as a yes."

"It's your prerogative to do so."

"Look who's unpacking the big words." The clacking of a keyboard underlines Charlie's words. "All right. I'll need about three hours to get there, plus some extra time to make sure I don't bring the lone pap here right to your door. How about I arrive at five?"

"That sounds—" Gabe cuts himself off because he can't just invite people to Ray's family home, now can he? "Give me a sec."

He moves the phone away from his ear and twists around to face Ray. For a beat, he's caught by how *close* Ray is, then he shakes himself out of it and focuses on the matter at hand. "Is there a hotel in Colforth?"

The corners of Ray's eyes crinkle with a warm smile. "I take it Charlie's coming?"

"Yeah." When Gabe smiles back, it's effortless—maybe it's because right here, with the curtains mostly closed, reality seems very far away. "Like he'd miss the drama."

"He's a good friend." Ray doesn't phrase it as a question, and there's nothing in his tone to suggest he's fishing, but Gabe still feels a need to clarify. Just in case.

"He's the brother I never had. Like you and Patrick."

"I had a crush on Patrick in Sixth Form," Ray offers blithely. "It lasted about three seconds. Don't tell him, or he'll be insufferable."

Huh, the more you know. Gabe snorts. "Random, but thanks for the information, I guess? Anyway, um. About that hotel?"

"There's a tiny B&B, yeah, but unless he's allergic to cats, he might as well stay with us, too. Farah won't get in until tomorrow, so her old room will be empty tonight, and the bed's big enough for both of you to share."

So Gabe won't be sharing with Ray. That's okay. He didn't assume he would be, what with Ray's mum right there and all, hardly the moment to crawl into her son's bed—not that anything even *happened*, other than Ray holding Gabe all through the night.

It felt big.

At least it did to Gabe. For Ray, it was probably nothing all that special even though he said he missed that aspect of dating. It definitely wasn't *new* for him.

Get back to the point.

"You sure your family won't mind? You told your mum about me, right?"

"I said I'm bringing a friend, yeah—not who you are, though. We'll cross that bridge when Allie sees you."

Since Gabe insisted on learning at least the basics about Ray's family, his mind fills in the details. Allie, also known as Alisha: Ray's youngest sister and the one he deemed most likely to freak out, although he sounded confident that she could keep a secret.

"But anyway," Ray continues. "You're very welcome, I promise. And Charlie would be welcome, too, as long as he isn't a picky eater."

"Ha. More the kind of person who'll eat you out of house and home." It's true, too—if there's one thing Gabe envies Charlie for, it's that Charlie has the metabolism of a hummingbird. He can eat anything he wants without gaining so much as a pound, while Gabe is stuck in a tug of war with his muscle-to-fat ratio.

Granted, Gabe's therapist suggested that it's primarily a way for him to feel in control. Maybe she's right, but he'll still feel better if he finds some way to stay active over the coming days. Colforth is small; there must be some nature running options around.

One problem at a time, though, and Charlie's waiting for an answer.

"You sure it won't be an imposition?" Gabe asks, watching Ray's face closely for any sign of doubt. There is none.

"Seriously, it'll be absolutely fine. My mum loves a full house." Ray grimaces. "Or, in her words, 'I know how to use protection, so four kids were a choice, not an accident. I'd have eight running around if it were up to me.'" Even though Ray's imitation of his mum is mocking, it's coated in a layer of deep, genuine affection.

"I'm looking forward to meeting her," Gabe says, quite honestly. "And you're sure that—"

He doesn't get to finish because Ray reaches past him to swipe the phone. With a shrewd look, Ray brings it to his ear. "Hi, mate. Charlie, right? This is Ray. You fine with a homemade dinner tonight, and staying at my family's place rather than some hotel?"

"Ray!" Gabe hisses.

Ray easily evades Gabe's attempt to reclaim the phone, rolling away from Gabe as he listens to whatever Charlie is saying. *Don't let it be anything embarrassing, please.* Gabe considers draping himself over Ray to make another grab for the phone, but he's only in his boxers and a T-shirt, and it seems like a risky idea to start wrestling with Ray in bed.

In the end, he acknowledges that there isn't much of a point in trying to stop this. If things go according to plan, Ray and Charlie will meet tonight—two important parts of Gabe's world colliding. God, he wants them to get along.

He falls onto his back and idly listens to what sounds like a focused discussion of logistics. It's only a couple of minutes before Ray passes the phone back, leaving Gabe to say goodbye to Charlie while Ray shuffles out of bed to brush his teeth and get packed up.

Gabe tries not to notice how Ray's pyjama bottoms cling to his arse. He fails.

∽

SINCE GABE LEARNED how to drive in the US where the cars are big but the roads are bigger, London city traffic requires his full attention. If anyone asks, he can blame it on the British oddity of driving on the left.

Fortunately, Ray and Patrick seem to sense that he needs to concentrate. It's only once traffic starts to thin considerably that Ray starts fiddling with the audio system of the rental car that Gabe's assistant organised, cursing when the bluetooth and his phone refuse to cooperate.

"Try mine," Gabe suggests with a jerk of his chin at where he placed his phone in the tray between his seat and Ray's. Last he checked, it was overflowing with messages that he didn't feel mentally equipped to open—one day, he'll take a class in Adulting 101, but today is not that day.

"Yours?" Ray asks, as though it's a foreign concept. "Like, your phone? I don't want—I could accidentally see something."

"Unlikely. All my naked selfies are protected by an extra password, and if you're looking for George Clooney's number, I'm afraid I don't have it."

Ray huffs out a low laugh. "Not looking for a sugar daddy, as a matter of fact."

What are you looking for, then?

Gabe doesn't ask. Partly because he can't afford to care about the answer, not right now, and partly because Patrick is in the backseat and Gabe isn't quite sure what to make of him. While Patrick has been friendly enough and appeared genuinely sorry for Gabe's bad luck in the parent department, he's also been watchful—a quick, sharp glance when Ray helped Gabe hide his recognisable curls under a baseball cap, a curious tilt of the head at how Gabe had Ray's coffee waiting when Ray returned from his morning shower.

Post-Nora, Gabe would act the same around any potential new girlfriend of Charlie's. So if that's what Patrick is doing, Gabe can respect it.

"Adam Driver?" he offers with a brief look at the cut of Ray's profile. "Pretty sure I do have his number."

"Getting warmer," Ray says with another laugh. "But I'm good. One movie star is all the excitement I can handle."

There's a flirty comeback about to trip off Gabe's tongue. He swallows it back down and tells Ray his code instead. For a minute, it's quiet in the car as Ray successfully connects Gabe's phone, then scrolls through his music.

"Why are all your playlists either heavy beats or chill piano classical?"

"And podcasts." Gabe checks the mirrors before overtaking a truck that's crawling along. "The beats are for working out, the piano is for trying to sleep on a flight."

Ray shakes his head. "Your carbon footprint must be gigantic."

"Yeah, 'fraid it is." Back into the left lane just as the GPS chirps about an upcoming exit. "My assistant makes sure to offset each flight, but it's probably just a modern version of selling indulgences. Guess my parents will be gratified to see me rotting in hell after all—if there is one."

He means to make a joke of it, but can't quite help the bitterness creeping into his tone. While Ray doesn't respond, he reaches over to briefly touch Gabe's hand on the wheel, fingertips light against Gabe's skin. After a deep breath, Gabe sends him a grateful smile that Ray returns.

"Are we there yet?" Patrick pipes up from the backseat. It might be an indirect slight against Gabe given he's the reason they're driving when the train would have been faster, but the rearview mirror shows an impish gleam in Patrick's eyes.

Ray appears to draw a similar conclusion because he twists around, voice careful. "You know it'll be another three hours, so what's your play here?"

"Can I have some ice cream?" Patrick volleys back. "I want ice cream! *And* I need to pee!"

Gabe bites the inside of his cheek to stop himself from grinning. "How long," he asks, directed at Ray, "do you think he can keep this up?"

"It's Patrick," Ray says. "Indefinitely would be a safe guess."

"Hey!" Patrick leans into the gap between the two front seats. "I resent the implication. Just trying to hold up my part of the deal. If mummy and daddy are sitting upfront, the rowdy kid in the back needs to keep up a steady string of complaints."

"Please don't." Ray's tone holds little hope.

"I'm *bored*." Patrick bounces in place, grinning. "Entertain me."

"How about some jazzy Christmas tunes?" Ray asks the car at large. "If we turn it up real loud, it may drown Patrick out."

"I want the Three Investigators."

"I want a new best mate."

"Harsh!" Patrick clasps a hand to his chest. "It's like you don't love me anymore. Have I been replaced? I know I don't have luscious curls and soulful green eyes—"

"Soulful?" Gabe interrupts, amusement tickling the back of his throat. "Have you been hanging around the comment sections of my social media profiles?"

Patrick gives a grave nod. "The internet is a dark and scary place, mate."

"Don't I know it." Unbidden, Gabe's mind flashes to imagining his fans' reactions to the news. Will they feel betrayed? His sexuality may not be as big a deal as it would have been ten or twenty years ago, but it also won't be met with shoulder shrugs and smalltalk about the weather.

Some of his thoughts must show on his face because Ray taps his hand again. "Hey, I'm sure it won't be that bad."

"I hope so." Gabe keeps his gaze fixed on the road. "Like, my career is kind of built on me being cute and theoretically available. I can handle a paycheck cut—might need to sell the Porsche—but what if I suddenly don't get movie roles anymore?" Sparks of light flit through his vision, and he blinks to clear them away. "I don't have a theatre voice."

"*Breathe*," Ray orders, quiet but firm. His fingers dig into Gabe's elbow, the contact oddly grounding.

Gabe sucks in a harsh breath. "Sorry." Another breath. He realises he's gripping the wheel too tightly and forces himself to loosen his hold.

"Better?" Ray's tone is devoid of judgment.

"Yeah. Sorry, I didn't mean to... I've got strategies for this, I swear." Again, Gabe inhales and holds the air for a moment before letting it go on a controlled exhalation. He glances away from the road just long enough to find Ray watching him with calm eyes. "How did you notice before I did?"

"I used to get panic attacks sometimes—in the mornings, when I had to go to school." Ray sighs. "Physical contact helped. And someone talking me through it, especially when it was right at the start."

"You never told me that." It's Patrick, voice a near-whisper.

On the periphery of his vision, Gabe catches Ray turning his upper body to face Patrick in the backseat. "I figured you were worried enough about me."

For a beat, Patrick is silent. When he speaks again, it's with an iron edge. "Okay, here's the deal: if I see Xander, I'm going to kill him. You two can be my alibi."

"That's the arsehole you dated in school, right?" Gabe shoots another glance at Ray, then at Patrick via the rearview mirror. "Because if yes? Deal."

"Good. I like you." Patrick nods, as if to himself.

"All right, stop." Ray raises both hands, along with his voice. "Can we all just settle down, please, and lower the testosterone level in this car? And can we maybe also acknowledge that I'm a proper adult and don't need you two wannabe warriors defending my honour and good name?"

"I know how to hit a moving target with an arrow," Gabe informs Patrick, as though Ray hadn't said a word.

"Excellent." Patrick rubs his hands. "And I know the most vulnerable places in a person's body. I think we're set."

Gabe throws a quick grin over his shoulder. "You know, if the acting thing doesn't work out for me, maybe you and I could start a murder-for-hire business? We'll only accept targets that deserve to be eliminated."

"Sounds good. I'm getting kind of bored with physical therapy anyway."

"Why me?" Ray asks no one in particular, but there's a tinge of amusement to his tone. It fades when he continues, though. "And Gabe, I'm sure there'll be plenty of roles waiting for you after this. Maybe not the lead in a hetero rom-com, but—"

"That's a load of rubbish," Patrick interjects. "Did anyone ask Heath Ledger and whatshisname—Jake something?—for their gay cred before casting them in *Brokeback Mountain*? Nope. So there."

"I wish it was that simple," Gabe tells him.

"Well, it should be. It's called acting for a reason, isn't it?" Patrick's tone is matter-of-fact. "And at the risk of sounding like a fawning fan boy: you, my friend, actually have a talent for acting."

The compliment is unexpected, especially from Patrick. Maybe all it took was a murder scheme for his caution to evaporate.

"Thank you." Gabe lets the words sit for a moment before he sighs. "And I really do wish it was that simple, but see, the key difference is the target audience. Rightfully or not, the assumption is that any movie with a mainly romantic narrative will appeal to a female audience. And that female audience will want an attractive male lead they can pin their hopes and dreams to—which is a harder sell if he's gay."

"Sounds like you thought about this a bit." Ray's frown colours his tone. "But you're not even in predominantly romantic roles, so why does it matter?"

"Because the assumption—again, rightfully or not—is that for action movies, it's guys who want to watch them. Add some male eye candy, and they'll have an easier time getting their girlfriends to come along."

"Jesus fucking Christ." Patrick's chuckle carries a heavy note of sarcasm. "This sounds like a theory from the sixties, when the recommended treatment for female depression was a haircut and a make-up tutorial."

Gabe shrugs. "Yeah, well. Welcome to traditional Hollywood, where clocks run a little more slowly. To be fair, things are changing. Just ... not particularly quickly."

"What about all the streaming services that are out there now? Like Netflix and Amazon and so on. They're less traditional, right?" Ray sounds hopeful. "Because, you know, Patrick is right: you're not just a pretty face. You're talented, and surely that has to count for something."

Coming from Patrick, it was a nice surprise; coming from Ray, it lights a warm glow in Gabe's chest. "I thought you hadn't seen the movies?"

"I watched them a few days ago." Ray sounds distinctly vague.

In the backseat, Patrick chortles. "True, that. Andrew and I sacrificed a precious half-day to rewatch them with you, all just so you'd be prepared for the premiere if Gabe doubled down on his invitation. Which" —directed at Gabe— "you did not."

"Because Ray's message made it pretty clear he didn't want to be there," Gabe points out. "And I assumed from his tone that he wasn't particularly keen to see me. I can take a hint."

"Well, you know what they say about assuming," Ray mutters, frowning.

"Assuming makes an ass out of you and Ming?" Gabe asks.

"Well played," Patrick comments from the backseat. For some reason, he sounds delighted by this entire exchange.

"Look, Gabe—" Ray's tone makes Gabe glance over long enough for their eyes to meet before Gabe has to return his attention to the road. "I didn't want you to invite me just because you promised we'd meet again and you wanted to keep your word."

This feels like a conversation they've had before.

"I didn't feel obligated." Orange lights flashing up ahead make Gabe slow down the car: two lanes merging into one. He indicates right and waits for someone to let him in before he shoots Ray another look. "Why do you find it so hard to believe that I" —*like you* — "enjoy spending time with you?"

"Because you're you!" Ray makes it sound like the obvious answer to an obvious question, and two can play this game.

Gabe snaps his fingers. "Oh, I know this one! What is: a potentially out-of-work actor who, at twenty-one, may have already seen his best days?"

It earns him a glare, which is kind of fun. "Stop it."

"Stop what?"

"Putting yourself down."

Gabe smirks. "You first."

"I want ice cream," Patrick says from the backseat, sounding utterly pitiful.

They're all silent for a couple of seconds.

Gabe is first to burst out laughing, and Ray and Patrick aren't far behind. Maybe it's a simple reaction to the tension that's been heavy in Gabe's bones since Walter's call yesterday, like a pendulum swinging the other way, but whatever it is—in this very moment, Gabe feels ready to face the world head-on.

His confidence fades almost immediately, but he holds on to the memory as Ray finally finds a playlist he approves of. While Patrick belts out lyrics he seems to be making up on the fly, Ray chiming in occasionally, Gabe keeps his hands on the wheel and refuses to plan any further than the drive.

Mostly, it works.

11

They drop Patrick off at his parents' house, just a block from where Ray grew up until the age of eleven. After that, it's just Ray and Gabe in the car, and Ray is aware of that in ways he isn't sure he wants to be.

Fortunately, jazzy Christmas tunes bridge the momentary silence that descends in the wake of Patrick's departure, and it's only a minute before Gabe clears his throat. "So, any words of advice?"

Well, that's delightfully generic.

"If you put a tea bag in your whiskey, no one will judge you for daytime drinking."

"You got that from Patrick," Gabe guesses, quite accurately. "And I meant advice about meeting your family. Any dos and don'ts?"

Gabe sounds nervous. Which, well... Which would be perfectly natural given he's about to enter a house full of strangers after his waste-of-space parents sold him out to *The Daily Mail*, of all things. Surely they could have picked some ultra-Christian church bulletin if it was all about getting the truth out there—except that would have meant leaving a nice paycheck on the table. Seems like moral righteousness only gets you so far when it's time to pay the bills.

Anyway, advice. Ray tries to take a mental step back and assess his family objectively. There's too much love woven into his perception, though.

"Ignore anything that comes out of Allie's and Jazmin's mouths, as much as you possibly can. Fay—Farah—is the oldest, so she's less likely to embarrass me, herself, or you. Also, she's a mum, so she probably has to be a bit more mature."

"Two kids, you said?"

"Jasper and Jess, yeah. Their father decided he's not a family man after all, so he's not in the picture."

A frown wrinkles Gabe's forehead. "Isn't that the kind of thing one should decide before having kids?"

"Amen, brother. Take a right here." Familiar rows of semi-detached red brick houses glide by outside the window. *Home*. "As for my mum, don't insult the royal family where she can hear you. I honestly think she believes in the Queen Louise more than she believes in Jesus, at this point."

Gabe chuckles. "Not a problem. I actually like the royal family."

"You've met them?" Ray doesn't know why he's surprised. Maybe because, for minutes at a time, he keeps forgetting that Gabe isn't just Gabe; that he's Gabe Duke, the kind of guy to make headlines.

"Only in passing. The prince's husband is funny."

"Of course he is." Ray shakes his head, more amused than annoyed by how nonchalantly Gabe talks about people that most Brits will only ever see on TV. "So, anyway, I think that just about covers the dos and don'ts."

"I didn't bring any presents." Gabe sounds as though he only just realised a gross oversight on his part.

"No one expects you to. Stop worrying, please." Ray flicks his hand at the last house along the road, a two-story detached home with patchwork renovations done to it over the years. It sits right next to the train line, open fields beyond. "Number two, over there. You can park on the road."

Gabe obediently pulls over and turns off the engine before he looks up at the house. Briefly, Ray wonders what Gabe sees. The wooden window frames that haven't seen a fresh coat of paint since

Ray's grandparents lived here? The patchy lawn or the mossy roof? It must be a far cry from the house Gabe owns in L.A.

"I love how close to the fields it is," Gabe says, smiling. "We should go for a run later."

"By 'we,' I assume you mean the royal we, correct?"

"'We' as in 'you and I.' Andrew told me you used to be a runner—no time like the present to start again." Gabe's grin shows off white, even teeth, and Ray shields his eyes with a hand.

"Stop that. I need another coffee before I can handle your movie star smile."

Gabe leans closer, still grinning. "Is that a yes?"

"It's a 'wait in the car while I prepare my mum and sister for who you are.'"

"That sounds suspiciously like a yes to me."

"It's a maybe." Ray ignores Gabe's triumphant cheer as he opens the passenger door and gets out of the car. "Be right back. Don't talk to any strangers while I'm gone."

"Yes, sir." For good measure, Gabe adds a military salute before he unbuckles himself and relaxes into the driver's seat. Ray takes one second to rake his gaze over him, then he turns to face the house and the music.

The door opens before Ray can ring the bell, and then his mum's right there, pulling him into a tight hug that smells like vanilla and home, calling for Allie to get downstairs and say hello to her brother. Allie's there a moment later, sticking out her tongue at him before she jumps into his arms and holds on for longer than she'd ever admit to.

"Why did your friend stay in the car?" Ray's mum asks when they finally separate.

"Right, about that." Best to get it over and done with—just like jumping into an ice-cold lake. Ray tilts his head at Allie. "Remember how I said I probably wouldn't see Gabe Duke again?"

She narrows her eyes. "Yeah...?"

"Turns out I was wrong."

"What..." Understanding flashes over her face. "That's not funny."

"It isn't meant to be." Well, maybe it's a tiny bit funny—Allie likes to pretend she's cool, so seeing her rattled like this is a rare treat. "You probably saw what broke this morning, right? He's got nowhere else to go, so I invited him to spend Christmas with us."

"You invited him..." Allie's clever brain works through the implications even as she's staring fixedly at him. "Wait, so you're—"

"We're *not*," Ray interrupts. "Just friends. His hotel was surrounded, and he doesn't really know people in London other than me."

"Can someone fill me in, please?" Ray's mum affects her patient nurse's voice.

"Gabe Duke," Allie says, like that explains it all.

"Is he that actor you had up on your wall?" Mum asks Allie, and oh, this is good. This is *excellent*. "The one who went with Ray to that football match?"

"You had his poster on the wall?" If Ray is smirking like a shark smelling blood, well, so what of it?

"I was *sixteen*," Allie states, with all the dignity of her recently-turned-eighteen years. Ray bites down on the temptation to mock her —he needs her on her best behaviour, and tickling her combative reflexes won't do him any good.

"Okay," Ray says pleasantly. "So you're well and truly over it, meaning you won't mind if he spends Christmas with us. And you won't breathe a word of it to anyone. Because that's just how much of a grownup you are."

"I can tell when you're manipulating me, you know." Yet she looks vaguely proud, so he's pretty sure he hauled her in hook, line, and sinker. Next up: his mum.

Ray gives her his best sheepish smile. "Gabe is a bit famous, yeah, but mostly, he's a nice guy with awful parents. They outed him in *The Daily Mail* this morning, and I just figured that in the spirit of Christmas, the least we can do is give him a place to hide for a few days."

Also Charlie and possibly Gabe's sister Deborah. But Ray will introduce those additional pieces of information when the time is right.

"Christ, that poor boy." Mum glances past Ray towards the car. "Isn't he nineteen or so? Far too young to be in the spotlight like that."

Ray wonders if his mum just experienced a flashback to how much Ray struggled—and for him, it was only a few classmates harassing him, not professionals with cameras and microphones.

"He's twenty-one," Ray corrects. "But yeah."

A huff suggests that Ray's mum considers those two years to be perfectly irrelevant. "Well, of course he's welcome. Don't make him wait out there, will you? Does he have any dietary requirements I should be aware of?"

Typical—as far as Ray's mum is concerned, few things can't be fixed with good food and a cuppa.

"None that I'm aware of." He hesitates. "Although he does kind of watch what he eats, I think. What with the whole ... being-featured-shirtless-in-movies thing."

Allie giggles, but blessedly, Ray's mum limits her commentary to a raised eyebrow. "What are you waiting for? Get him inside, and I'll make you both a cup of hot chocolate. He's had a rough day, by all accounts."

"Several rough days, more like." Ray takes a step back, then jerks his chin at his sister. "You'll be cool? No telling anyone about this until after?"

"Cross my heart," she says in a throwback to when Ray was a teenager and made his younger sister promise to cover for his late-night movie escapades into the city, in return for a bag of sweets. The only time she broke her word was when he got on her bad side the day after by finishing her favourite cereal.

It's as good an insurance as he's going to get.

"Thank you." He puts meaning behind it. "Don't tell Fay and Jaz, but you're totally my favourite."

"Ray!" Mum sounds scandalised.

"I'm kidding, Mum! Come on, we're siblings—we're meant to joke and tease each other."

"It's part of the job description," Allie jumps in.

"Definitely my favourite," he stage whispers to her, and she dimples prettily while clasping a hand to her heart.

When Mum shakes her head, it's with a smile. "Oh, fine. Now go get your boy so he doesn't think he's been forgotten out there."

Not my boy, Ray wants to say, but the knowing look in his mum's eyes stops him. He should be ready for a conversation that will happen sooner rather than later, and since it's his mum, it will be bluntly to the point where his dad would have let Ray approach the topic at his own pace.

Fuck, Ray misses him. Still. Always.

"Yeah, okay." He exhales around the gaping hole in his chest that just won't close. "I'll go get him."

When Andrew stayed for Christmas, it wasn't a big deal. Ray decides it doesn't have to be a big deal with Gabe either, but he's lying to himself, and he knows it.

∼

IT FEELS LIKE AN AUDITION. Not like the one for the Green Hunter when Gabe was too despondent to have any expectations, but like the one for the farmer's son in a small-town drama, which he didn't get because they wanted a rougher look. He did get James Watson, though.

The woman at the door has Ray's smile. Somehow, it's enough to make Gabe relax a fraction.

He sets his suitcase down and checks his posture before he offers his hand with an answering smile. "Thank you so much for allowing me to spend Christmas with your family, Mrs Fadil." Shit—he should have checked with Ray whether his mum really did accept her husband's name.

"Margaret," she corrects, enveloping his hand in both of hers for a warm, supportive moment. "No need for formalities, Gabe. I'm very sorry to hear about your parents—you're welcome to stay with us for as long as you like."

He blinks and swallows. "Thank you. Really."

"You're most welcome. Now, stop tripping over your gratitude and come on in." Margaret picks up his suitcase and leaves the door open so he can follow. While Gabe considers protesting that he should be the one dealing with his own luggage, something about her resolute air tells him it'd be a futile effort. With Ray right on his heels, Gabe enters the house.

"And that," Ray says just as Gabe notices the young woman in the hallway, lingering on the threshold to what might be the living room, "would be my baby sister Allie."

The way Allie scrunches up her nose clearly conveys she objects to being called the baby sister. Gabe grins at her before he shoots Ray a look. "I'm pretty sure that when you called her Baby just now, it occurred to her to mind."

"Holy shit, did you just quote *Dirty Dancing*?" Ray dramatically widens his eyes. "I've brought you into the light and expect nothing less than a prominent mention in your Oscar acceptance speech."

Allie groans. "Oh my *God*, Ray. Could you be any more gay?"

Ray arches an eloquent eyebrow in response, while Margaret stops on her way to the stairs. "Young lady! I thought I'd raised you to think before you speak."

It's a second before Allie seems to realise the bigger context and flushes, obvious even against her darker skin tone. "I am so sorry," she tells Gabe, sounding genuinely contrite. "I didn't mean—I'm just teasing. It's what Ray and I do."

Gabe sends her a genuine smile. "Don't worry. I actually said something very similar to Ray not that long ago, plus I know what it's like—I've got a sister of my own."

"I know," Allie says, then flushes even harder while Ray coughs to disguise a laugh.

"Allie is a fan," he informs Gabe.

"Used to be!" she protests.

Ha. Gabe manages to conceal his amusement under a layer of sorrow and a soft, doleful, "Oh."

"You're still cool," Allie rushes to assure him. "It's just, I'm older now, and I kind of prefer to have crushes on real guys—you are real, of course, but, like..." She trails off, looking utterly mortified, and Gabe takes pity on her because he doesn't think Ray or Margaret will.

"Hey, I'm just teasing." He gives her elbow a friendly squeeze. "Sorry about that—blame your brother's bad influence. It's really nice to meet you, and thank you, too, for putting up with me for the holidays."

"It's nice to meet you, too." Her smile is beautiful, eyes the same colour as Ray's. "And I swear that I'm not usually this much of a mess. Someone" —a pointed glare at Ray— "failed to give us a fair warning that we'd be hosting a rather prominent guest for Christmas."

"Where'd be the fun in that?" Ray asks.

"For starters, it might have saved you from waking up to something slimy on your pillow."

Halfway up the stairs, Margaret heaves a long-suffering sigh. "Kids, *please*. I know we said no gifts, but if there's one thing I want for Christmas, it's the illusion of having raised a bunch of well-behaved, polite children who can be unleashed on the world without a second thought."

"You want us to *lie*?" Allie sounds scandalised.

"Way to teach us the importance of honesty and authenticity," Ray chimes in.

Another sigh before Margaret pointedly ignores her children by addressing Gabe. "I'll get you set up in Farah's room for the night. Please make yourself comfortable—there's a late lunch in the kitchen for you and my demon spawn, and I'll be down in a minute to make you both some hot chocolate."

It's a good thing Gabe's planning a run later, hopefully before the light fades fully. "Thank you so much," he tells her. "For everything."

"You're most welcome, sweetheart." Her tone is so kind that it just about makes him want to cry. "It's through no fault of your own that you're having a rough time, and if there's anything we can do to help, just ask."

"This *is* helping," he tells her, and it is—the sense of normalcy,

Ray bickering with his sister, the entrance area that's cluttered with shoes, rain jackets, and scarves... There's something deeply comforting about the untarnished reality of it all.

"Well, good." She nods, smiling. "Welcome to our home, Gabe. Treat it like it's yours, please."

Since there is no immediately available response bar another thank you, he smiles back, abruptly reminded of when he was twelve years old and his mum praised him for reciting Luke's Christmas story by heart. It's one of the few memories he has of measuring up.

Ray's light touch to his shoulder nudges Gabe out of it. "Come on," Ray says. "I'll show you around. Not that there's much to see, but just in case you're the first one up tomorrow and are looking for coffee or some such."

"It's great," Gabe tells him.

Ray scoffs. "You haven't seen anything other than the hallway."

"It's great," Gabe repeats, with emphasis. He means it, and it's obvious that Ray gets the message when the corners of his mouth tilt up into a pleased curve.

"I'm glad," is all he says, though, and there's this moment when they're quietly looking at each other, Ray's eyes a honey-rich almond colour, his face just as beautiful as when they first met, yet familiar, too.

Ray glances away first, and it's only then that Gabe remembers they're not alone.

Golden warmth settles in his bones. It feels tentative and precious, too fragile to examine closely just yet—so he lets it fade to a background hum and follows Ray further into the house.

∼

HALFWAY THROUGH LUNCH, Ray's twenty-year-old sister Jazmin breezes in: pink hair, a nose stud, and an admirably zen attitude about the train delays and missed connections that extended her journey home by two hours. According to Ray, she's part of some artist community in Edinburgh and doesn't even recognise Gabe until Ray explains the situation to her.

"Gabe Duke? Right. Think I might have seen you on a poster in Allie's room," Jazmin tells Gabe with a shrug, to which Allie reacts by burying her head in her hands and lamenting the curse that is being born into this family.

"So I've heard." Gabe gives Allie's shoulder a supportive squeeze. "But raise your hand if you managed to live through your teenage years without any missteps in taste."

"Anyone actually tempted to raise their hand," Margaret puts in, "please keep in mind that I have a wide and varied collection of photos of all of you, ages zero to now."

Ray pulls a face. "Parents don't usually phrase that as a threat, Mum."

"Just defending my youngest."

"Fair." Jazmin generously salts her roasted potatoes. She's got a tiny sun tattoo on her wrist that briefly holds Gabe's attention. When he looks up, he finds her fixing him with a stare. "Okay, question for you. That outfit you wore in Allie's poster—pretty tight in certain places. Is it as uncomfortable as it looks?"

Gabe releases an undignified snort of laughter. "Well, they did tailor it to my exact measurements. Let's just say I can't afford to gain weight if I still want it to fit. And on that note..." He nudges Ray with his toes. "You're still up for a run, right?"

"*You?*" Allie turns to Ray with an exaggeratedly shocked expression. "You haven't gone for a run in, like, decades."

"A couple of years," Ray grumbles. "And I said maybe."

This is where Gabe needs to tread carefully. If he pushes too hard, Ray is the type to dig in his heels out of principle, so gentle insistence is a more likely route to success. It's not like Gabe couldn't go by himself, of course—usually, at this point, he'd value the chance to spend some time alone and in his own head, but Ray's company doesn't feel like an imposition, doesn't drain him of energy the way most people do. It's similar to Charlie, yet wholly different, too.

In between Patrick earlier, Ray's family now, and Charlie arriving later today, it would be nice to have a bit of time with just Ray.

"I don't really know the area." Gabe aims for a deliberately plaintive tone. "My sense of orientation is rubbish, so I could very well manage to get lost in the fields around here. So, you know. It'd be great if you could come along, show me around a bit? At least this one time."

Ray squints at Gabe, a suspicious tilt to his mouth. "Are you just saying that so I'll come?"

Ignoring the curious, but mostly amused glances he catches from Ray's mum and sisters, Gabe does his best to look guileless. "Why would I do that?"

"I'm not sure. Because you like to mock my pain?"

Gabe widens his eyes. "Would I do such a thing?"

Ray's tongue presses against the back of his teeth, his gaze moving from Gabe's face to his own empty plate. "I didn't bring any running shoes." He sounds uncertain, a sure sign that victory is within reach.

"You've got an old pair here," Margaret says. Bless her.

"Not sure it's a good idea to run in old shoes," Ray tries.

"We're not gonna go for very long." Gabe unpacks his most brilliant smile. "Please?"

Ray's shoulders rise with a deep, resigned intake of air. "Fine. But if I'm sore tomorrow, expect non-stop complaining."

There's a dirty joke somewhere in there, but one, this is not the time for flirting given Gabe needs to sort out his own shit first, and two, Ray's mum is right there. So Gabe leaves it at, "Duly noted."

Half an hour later, they're heading out into the fields. It's a fairly mild winter day, no wind and mostly cloudy, so Gabe is in running tights and a tight, functional long-sleeve shirt, while Ray is in old jogging bottoms and a hoodie he dug out of his wardrobe. At an easy trot, they cross the railway tracks. Once they trade the cluster of houses for open sky, Gabe draws what feels like his first real breath in days, *weeks*.

"I missed this," he tells Ray.

Ray throws him a sceptical look. He's slightly out of breath, but seems to be keeping up well otherwise. "You missed Colforth?"

"Nature running." Gabe gestures at their surroundings. "In L.A., it's mostly the treadmill for me, and scenic videos only get you so far. Last time I got to do a proper run outside was when I was filming in the Flow Country, back in November."

For a few steps, Ray is quiet. When he speaks again, his gaze is on the ground, voice low. "We used to live just around the corner from Patrick, bit further from the fields. The house here belonged to my grandparents, and when they died, my dad paid out his brother and we moved here."

It seems like a rare occasion for Ray to bring up his father unprompted, so Gabe is careful to keep his tone light and gentle. "Did he grow up in that house?"

"Yeah. Mixed memories, I think—like I said, his parents were very religious, very strict, and they weren't a fan of him getting with my mum." Ray points them towards a tiny agricultural road, hedges on one side and utility poles and a muddy field on the other.

"They came around?" Gabe guesses.

"Not until Fay was born." Ray's gaze flicks to Gabe. "My uncle—my dad's brother—had already moved to Germany by that point. So, with Fay being the first grandchild, I suppose it made them realise they needed to get out of their own way, or they might be left with no kids, and no grandkids either."

Gabe isn't sure if it's meant to give him hope for his own parents. Even if they did a U-turn tomorrow and welcomed him back with open arms, would he find it possible to forgive them? Not trust them, no—that ship has sailed. But could he find a way to allow them back into his life without constantly looking over his shoulder?

For Ray's sake, he smiles. "I'm glad they came around."

"Yeah." Ray is silent for another few steps. "After we moved here, I started running 'cause I thought it'd help me be better at football. Went with my dad sometimes. There's a community golf club further ahead where we stopped in summer—they've got a fountain with drinking water. Occasionally got some ice cream at the clubhouse and walked some of the way back."

"He was really loved, wasn't he?" Gabe sneaks a glance at Ray's profile—the serious line of his mouth, his prominent cheekbones, the warmth to his complexion even on an overcast day. "There seem to be all these traces of him in the house, like tons of pictures and books, and Jazmin said he took the photo in the living room. The one with the foggy railway tracks?"

"Yeah." A smile plays around Ray's lips. "He took it less than a kilometre from home. An early autumn morning, before he went to work."

"What did he do?"

"Construction. My mum's a nurse, my dad was a gaffer—you can probably imagine how proud they were when I got that scholarship." The smile flickers and dies. "At least he didn't have to watch me squander it away. Small blessings, I guess."

The strong current of pain in Ray's voice makes it harder for Gabe to breathe. He slows down slightly and grapples for how to respond. By all accounts, Ray did just fine in university until his dad's death threw him for a loop, but that hardly counts as comfort. Also, didn't Andrew mention that Ray felt guilty about his dad?

"We actually held the funeral reception at the golf club." Ray sounds far away. "Mum wasn't in any shape to host people at our house, so it was just easier. Don't think I'll ever smell devilled eggs again without wanting to puke."

"How did he die?" Gabe asks softly.

"Cardiac arrest." Ray gives a harsh, humourless chuckle. "He was always first to carry the heavy stuff, help out, give someone a hand. Super hot summer day, probably overexerted himself on the construction site. By the time the ambulance arrived, it was already too late."

"I'm so, so sorry, Ray." It's perfectly inadequate, yet it's the best Gabe has. "If you want us to turn around...?"

For several steps, Ray doesn't respond. "I should have seen it coming!" he bursts out all of a sudden. "I was studying medicine, and I couldn't even save my own dad."

Oh, Jesus. Is this what Ray's been carrying around with him for the past three years? Gabe pulls Ray to a halt, doesn't really *think* before he draws him into a hug and holds on until Ray melts into him, arms coming up around Gabe, breath hiccuping once before it steadies. They're both a little sweaty, and Gabe closes his eyes, lets the distant rush of traffic fade to the back of his mind. His heart feels heavy and light at the same time.

"What are the symptoms?" he murmurs, nose tucked against Ray's cheek.

"It depends." Ray inhales deeply and makes no move to let go. "Sometimes none. Sometimes there can be chest pain, shortness of breath, dizziness,..."

"Would he have told you? Or—" Wow, Ray's mum is a nurse. Does she carry the same burden as her son? "Would he have told your mum?"

"Probably not, but I should have known." Ray draws back enough to look at Gabe, eyes wide and sad. "I should have *known*."

"How?"

"He was my dad." Ray's voice is filled with a quiet sense of dejection that makes Gabe's heart break just a little for him. In his large hoodie, the sleeves reaching past his wrists, Ray looks younger than his twenty-five years.

"It sounds like he was a fantastic guy." Gabe slides his hands down to Ray's elbows and squeezes. "I doubt he'd want you blaming yourself for something that isn't your fault."

Their eyes hold for a moment, then Ray drops his gaze, dark lashes shielding his eyes. "I don't know how to stop."

Talk to someone.

It's not Gabe's place to forward advice that he himself received not too long ago. "Maybe," he suggests after a pause, "you could start by acknowledging that your dad would want the very best in life for you?"

The grey afternoon light softens Ray's features, his mouth a sensitive curve. When he frees his left arm, Gabe worries that he held on too long—but Ray doesn't move back, just holds out his hand for Gabe to inspect the crescent tattoo by the side of Ray's thumb.

Gabe skims a fingertip over the lines of ink, then glances up to find Ray watching him, something unreadable in his eyes. Gabe's breath stutters at how close they are, but God, *not* the time.

"Jazmin has a sun tattoo," he observes quietly, afraid to break this tentative spell between them. "On her wrist."

"They all do—Allie's is on her ankle, Fay has hers on her thumb, like me."

"In memory of your dad?"

"Yeah." Ray exhales heavily, his gaze far away, the tiniest curve of a smile to his lips. "In Arabic, the sun is female and the moon male. He used to call us his moon and suns."

"That's beautiful," Gabe says, so low it's almost a whisper.

"I just..." Ray swallows visibly. "I just miss him so fucking *much*. But at least I had him in my life for twenty-two years, right? I got to grow up with a fantastic dad who loved me just the way I am, and that's a lot, isn't it?"

"It really is," Gabe tells him, careful to avoid any thoughts of his own parents. Something must show on his face, though, because Ray shakes his head and pulls back.

"Fuck, look at me whining about how tough I've got it. Meanwhile, your dad is a piece of shit who doesn't deserve to have a son in the first place."

"It's not a competition." Gabe tries for a laugh that turns out a little watery. He looks away, at the cluster of trees on a nearby hill, the grass below a muted, wintery green. "You lost something really wonderful. Me, I didn't have much to lose in the first place. It's just varying shades of sad, isn't it?"

"I guess so," Ray says slowly, and this time, he's the one who pulls Gabe into a hug that lasts for several warm seconds. When they separate, Gabe resists the impulse to wipe at his eyes. He's *fine*.

"So." He huffs out a breath, rolls his shoulders back, and straightens his spine. "Break is over. Ready to continue?"

"Not at all," Ray says, but he follows it up with a wink and the tiniest of grins that, while not entirely convincing, doesn't look fake either. It's a start.

"Race you to the end of the fence?" Gabe suggests.

Ray scoffs. "Absolutely not."

"I dare you."

"Oh, fuck *off*," Ray says. And starts running.

With a small whoop, Gabe follows.

12

In between ducking his sisters' questions and setting Gabe up with everything he needs for a shower, Ray's been too preoccupied to worry about meeting Gabe's best friend. The way Gabe tells it, Charlie is a legend. They've known each other forever, so there's a very real chance that as soon as Charlie arrives, Ray will be relegated to the sidelines.

He feels selfish even thinking it.

It's not that Ray intends to keep Gabe all to himself—he wants him to be happy and supported and loved, he *does*. But he also wants to be part of that, however small, and if Charlie is even just a bit like Patrick in that he's a magnet for attention and people like Ray fade to grey in comparison... *Selfish.*

When Ray comes downstairs after his own shower, legs comfortably tired in a way he's almost forgotten, he can already hear excited voices in the kitchen—Gabe and Ray's mum, Allie, and someone distantly familiar from that one brief exchange on the phone.

Ray stops to listen for a second. Charlie sounds bright and friendly even as he's griping about all the ways pre-Christmas train travel sucks, keeping up a steady stream of conversation that Ray suspects is designed to envelop Gabe in a comforting blanket of normalcy. It's the kind of thing Patrick would do, and somehow, Ray finds the thought reassuring.

He enters the kitchen with a ready smile and lingers on the threshold.

"Ray!" It's Gabe who first catches sight of him, lighting up even as he remains tucked up against a lithe guy who's a tad shorter than Gabe, with blond hair and blue eyes, a face that seems designed to smile easily, and often. "Come meet my friend Charlie. Charlie, this is Ray."

The guy—Charlie—assesses Ray with a quick, cheerful expression before he removes himself from Gabe's side, walks right over, and pulls Ray into a hug. "Thank you," he whispers, low enough for only Ray to hear.

Surprised, Ray pats him on the back. "What for?" he asks, equally low.

"Being good for him." Charlie draws back and beams at Ray like nothing at all passed between them. "Real pleasure to meet you, mate. Not sure I approve of your taste in football clubs, but I'm sure it's something we can work on."

"What if I'm happy with my choices?" Ray returns.

"Stockholm syndrome," Charlie says with an enviable measure of confidence. "I study psychology, so you can trust me."

"Don't," Gabe advises from behind Charlie. "Until he finally gets his act together and starts actively working on his bachelor's thesis, he can't be trusted."

"No one asked you," Charlie tells Gabe.

"As someone who's known you since day one of primary school, it is my duty to warn the general public."

Charlie strikes a pose as though he's in some old western. "As someone who's known you just as long, it is my duty to make fun of you as often and as much as I can. Do you" —directed at Ray now— "care to hear about that time Gabe tried to skip school, but felt so guilty about it he turned himself in halfway through the second period?"

Gabe rucks up the back of his hair. "I was a good kid! Nothing wrong with that."

"Ray always—" Allie begins, and Ray crosses over to her in two big steps, clapping a hand over her mouth.

"Not a *word*."

She licks his hand. As it's exactly what he expected, he limits his reaction to a superior smirk.

"That all you've got, midget?"

"You know you can't silence her forever, right?" Gabe asks. "Because I, for one, am actually curious about the things you always did."

Ray adjusts his hold so he's half-hugging Allie from behind, grinning at Gabe over her shoulder. "What do you mean, I can't silence her forever?"

"*Rafayet.*" Both the name and the tone imply that Ray's mum means serious business. "Stop bullying your sister."

With a flinch, Ray lets Allie go. She dusts herself off with a dignified expression, belied by the mischievous glint in her smile as she echoes Mum with a plaintive air. "Exactly, Rafayet. Stop bullying me."

"Rafayet?" Gabe mouths.

Fortunately, that's the precise moment the family cat stages her first appearance: Pinky strolls into the kitchen with her tail held high, the tip curled into a reverse question mark, and brushes up against Gabe's leg on her way to Ray. He drops down to the floor to give her a chin rub that she leans into with her entire body, purring like there's no tomorrow.

"*That's* Pinky?" Gabe kneels down beside Ray, offering Pinky his hand for a sniff. She accepts it with a delicate twitch of her whiskers.

"Choose your next words carefully," Ray warns him. "Other than Patrick, Pinky was my closest ally when things at school sucked."

"I'll pretend I didn't hear that," Mum says.

Ray sends her a smile. "You're my mum, so it's totally different."

She smiles back. "Fine, I'll let it slide."

"I just meant..." Gabe's fingers brush against Ray's. "It's just that when you told me there's a cat named Pinky, I expected something a little more colourful than black."

"Her original name was Blacky." The memory makes Ray grin. "But she was young and silly and had a knack for getting herself into trouble. So when Dad and I were painting Allie's room…" He tosses her a wink before he focuses back on Gabe. "You see, Allie was eight and going through a full-blown princess phase."

"I'm still a princess," Allie says. "The rest of you losers just don't understand."

In the interest of getting on with the story, Ray ignores her. "Which is why her room needed to be pink. It was her birthday present, and Dad and I got to do the honours. Except Pinky—Blacky, back then—managed to sneak in when we weren't paying attention, and all of a sudden there's this shocked mewl, and our formerly black kitten is partially pink when she dashes out of the room, leaving equally pink paw prints on the carpet."

When Gabe laughs, head thrown back, all heaviness falls off him. He's so beautiful it *hurts*, and surely everyone must see it, surely Ray isn't the only one who can't bear to look away. But when he manages to finally avert his eyes, Charlie is watching him, not Gabe. There's a faint smile on Charlie's face as he nods at Ray, and since Ray doesn't know what else to do, he nods back.

He's quiet while Allie tells more stories of Pinky's adventures and recent squabbles with a neighbourhood cat, Allie's initial nervousness around Gabe seemingly forgotten. Charlie contributes his own stories of the cat he had when growing up, Gabe chiming in with details that make it clear they spent years living in each other's pockets.

Ray is okay with that. Before meeting Charlie, he would have felt nervous about the depth of their bond—his own friendship with Gabe is still new, still fragile. How could he possibly compete with what connects Gabe to Charlie?

Now that he sees them together, he realises he doesn't want to. They tease each other like brothers, comfortable and affectionate, no concept of personal space. It reminds Ray of Allie and Jazmin and Farah, of Patrick.

Somehow, Gabe is in a separate category.

And while Ray isn't ready to examine that too closely, it makes it easier to believe that there might be space for him in Gabe's life, too. So when his mum asks him to prepare dinner so she can lie down for a nap ahead of her night shift at the hospital, Ray waves away Gabe's offer of help and tells him to go spend some time with Charlie instead, a chance for the two of them to catch up.

With darkness having fallen an hour ago, the temperature has dropped close to freezing, so Gabe and Charlie bundle up in jackets, scarves, and hats to brave the cold outside for a walk. Just before they leave, Gabe ducks into the kitchen. In the mismatched, bulky winter clothes he borrowed off Ray, he's far from the stylish movie star who took Ray to the Arsenal game; rather he looks like someone who could have grown up here, just another boy from a small town where the supermarket cashier knows your name and neighbours have an opinion on who you should marry when you're older.

If possible, Ray likes him even more for it.

For a moment, Gabe simply stands on the threshold, watching as Ray cuts up spring onions for a salad. Without even trying, Ray feels his lips tug into a smile. "You look like the puffy Marshmallow Man from the *Ghostbusters* movie."

Gabe's chuckle is quiet, almost intimate. "Guess there's an alternate career path in there for me."

"You won't need one," Ray tells him, "because you'll be just fine."

While a brief smile flits over Gabe's face, he doesn't respond as he draws closer on socked feet. Ray has learned that Gabe is someone who enjoys silences, who doesn't need to fill every gap with words and more words—but somehow, this feels different, expectant.

"Need anything else?" Ray asks, turning to face Gabe fully.

"No, all good." Gabe leans his hip against the dark oak wood counter, something heavy in the way he studies Ray's face. He's close enough that Ray could easily touch him, just reach out and cup Gabe's cheek, feel the warmth of his smoothly-shaven skin.

"Good," Ray says, breathless for no reason.

"Yeah." Gabe tilts his head, green eyes brightened by the stark overhead light of the kitchen, a faint flush to his cheeks that might be down to how, bundled up like that, he must be on the brink of overheating. "You said you miss the small things about dating, right? Like holding hands, cuddling, kisses."

In all honesty, it's not like Ray's limited number of relationships provided him with an abundance of those things—it was typically on him to initiate it, and he didn't want to come across as overly needy.

"Well, yeah." Ray lifts a shoulder. "It's no big deal, though. Why do you ask?"

"Oh, just... See, I was thinking. And, like." Gabe's teeth pull on his bottom lip, gaze bouncing from Ray's eyes to his mouth, and back up.

"Like...?" Ray prompts.

Gabe seems to make some kind of decision because he smiles quite suddenly, swaying closer. "Thank you," he says simply.

And kisses the corner of Ray's mouth.

It's the shortest touch of Gabe's lips against Ray's skin, so brief that Ray might have imagined it but for the more pronounced blush on Gabe's cheeks when he steps back, the same smile still in place. Ray is staring, knows he should say something and doesn't know what because ... Gabe just kissed him.

Gabe just kissed *him*.

"You don't, um." Ray clears his throat, licks his dry lips. "You don't have to do that. Certainly not out of gratitude. It's not—I told you it's not a big deal. It wasn't meant to be, like ... a thing you feel you have to do."

"I know." Whatever Gabe sees in Ray's face makes his smile widen. "I wanted to, though. See you in half an hour or so, yeah?"

"Sure," Ray manages, and then Gabe's left the kitchen. A brief exchange with Charlie in the entrance area before the front door opens and closes. Silence settles in the house's old frame.

I wanted to.

Ray draws a deep, confused breath. Exhales, just as confused. In the bright glare of the kitchen lights, the memory of Gabe's lips on his skin seems surreal.

He didn't imagine it, though. It definitely happened, and while he has no idea what it means—whether it means anything at all—he won't solve this riddle by staring at the spot where he last saw Gabe. So, since there's nothing else he can do, Ray returns his attention to the cutting board and slowly, methodically continues slicing spring onions into even rings.

It takes a minute or so for his hands to steady.

~

DINNER IS, unsurprisingly, a rowdy affair.

Ray is happy to lean back and listen while Allie, Jazmin, and Charlie debate some internet meme that Ray hasn't kept up with, his mum and Gabe contributing the occasional comment. Something about blue-painted people doing handstands in public places? Afterwards, they migrate to the living room to watch one of the Harry Potter movies that's featured as part of a Christmas marathon, while Gabe is upstairs to deal with urgent phone calls he's apparently delayed for as long as he possibly can.

When Gabe joins them, some forty minutes into the movie, he looks pensive, quietly folding himself into the space Charlie and Ray clear for him. "All right?" Ray asks him in an undertone.

Gabe is slow to react, his thoughts seeming miles away. His lashes sweep down in a hypnotic blink before his eyes find Ray's. "Yeah. Just…" He appears to forget what he was going to say, trailing off, gaze sliding away.

Ray brushes their hands together. "Gabe?"

Gabe refocuses. "My agent says they're just about knocking down his door. I'll have to make a statement eventually."

The news broke only this morning. It seems unfair that Gabe isn't given the time he deserves—is given no time at all because that's the logic of news on fibreglass speed, twenty-four hours a day, no holidays or weekends, keep 'em coming, keep it fresh, hustle for that bustle, rake in those clicks.

"Fuck them." This time, Ray keeps his hand right there, knuckles resting against the backs of Gabe's fingers. "If you need a week, take a week. If you need a month, take a month. The world won't end just because you don't make yourself available for the first microphone they shove under your nose."

"Preach it, brother," Charlie agrees in a murmur from Gabe's other side. "The only timeline that matters is the one you choose."

Gabe's hair tickles Ray's neck when he shakes his head. "It's not that easy."

"Why the hell not?" Charlie asks, while on screen, poor Harry Potter is getting increasingly desperate in his search for a way to breathe underwater. Pinky, in her usual spot under the sofa table, stretches, yawns, and curls up again in a different sleep position.

"Because..." Gabe flutters a helpless hand. "I want to work again eventually. And I've got people who depend on me, like my assistant and my social media person. Like, my agent's got other clients, but my assistant has two kids, and there's no dad in the picture. So if I can't pay her anymore—"

"Gabe. *Gee.*" Charlie leans right into Gabe's space, one of his hands landing on Gabe's knee. "First off, your money won't run out anytime soon. Secondly, you'll be fine. Yeah, it's your parents who planned this party, but you can decide whether you want to show up, and if yes, whether you want to change the music and serve champagne, or bring something nasty to spike the punch."

"I don't even know what that means," Gabe mumbles, but he already seems calmer. Ray uses his index finger to draw circles into the back of Gabe's hand.

"It means," Ray says, "that you have some power here. You're not just a pinball to your parents' whims."

Charlie nods. "What he said."

There are a few seconds of silence as they watch Neville hand Harry the solution to his no-gills problem. Over Gabe's bent head, Ray catches Charlie's eye, a moment of understanding passing between them.

"Maybe," Gabe says eventually, and since Ray knows it's the best they can expect for now, he starts paying proper attention to the movie even as he keeps drawing circles into Gabe's skin.

TEETH BRUSHED, Ray lingers on the threshold of Farah's room. "You're all set?"

"All good, man." Charlie gives a thumbs-up from where he's digging through his overnight backpack for a sleep T-shirt—he's bare-chested, and in a different context, Ray might think him a rather attractive if slightly scrawny guy.

Gabe, already under his own duvet, blinks sleepy eyes up at Ray. "Thank you."

For the briefest of instants, Ray's mind flashes back to that moment in the kitchen: the same words and then Gabe's lips on the corner of Ray's mouth. "You're welcome," Ray tells him with just enough of a delay that he wonders if Gabe notices.

After bidding them goodnight, he steps out into the hallway and closes the door.

Last night, Gabe slept in Ray's bed; now that Charlie is here, it wasn't even a discussion. And that's okay, really—Gabe and Charlie have been friends for half an eternity, and Ray never expected Gabe to pick him anyway. It's not like it's a competition because if it was, Charlie would win, hands down.

Which, fuck. That makes it sound like Ray doesn't like Charlie when he *does*. Charlie is one of those people who seem to lift everyone's mood just by being around, and he's been nothing but gracious towards Ray. It's just...

God. It was kind of nice to be needed, and now that Charlie is here, Ray is happy that Gabe has the support of his best friend, he really is—but he feels maybe just a tad useless.

Ray is fucking selfish, is what he is.

Hating himself just a little, he settles in for bed. The first night in his teenage bedroom is always weird, like traveling back in time because nothing much has changed since he completed his A-levels, not even when he moved back here for a short while after his dad's death. Half of the walls are still red, the other half plastered with maps of cities and countries he wants to see one day. In one corner, a black bean bag is shoved up against a shelf filled with books he picked up in all sorts of places, from yard sales to book swap boxes to birthday gifts, interspersed with knickknacks like a globe, and a defunct record player, and the sole Spider-Man figure he kept when he sold the rest of his collection.

It's home, more so than his room in the flat he shares with Patrick and Andrew. Yet sometimes, he can't help but feel like it's not just this room that's stuck in the past.

With his brain still churning, he grabs a book at random—Harari's *Sapiens* doesn't lend itself to bedtime reading, so he reaches for the book next to it, which turns out to be the memoir of a London couple after moving to Southern France. He sinks into the familiar pages that describe sun-soaked January lunches and the mission impossible that is French paperwork, inconsiderate visitors from back home and intricate greeting rituals between men and women in the closest Luberon village.

Back in school, books like this made Ray dream about escape, about living somewhere else one day. The scholarship had been his entry ticket to that—a fresh start in a new place.

He might have lost the scholarship, but unlike some of his classmates, he at least made it out of town. Last he heard, Xander was still helping out in his dad's catering business when he'd always talked about moving to the big city.

But then, things change.

It's nearing midnight by the time Ray turns off the light. The freshly washed sheets smell of a different laundry detergent than what he uses in London, and he closes his eyes and lets his mind drift back to the night before—Gabe's warm weight against him, Ray tucking his nose into Gabe's hair, the faint scent of aftershave mixed with something more inherently *Gabe*, sweet and a tad musky.

Gabe came to him for help. That makes it wrong, *so* wrong for Ray to submit to the slow heat pooling in his belly. Yet he slides a hand down his stomach, bare skin that feels warm to the touch, already spreading his thighs in anticipation of the first brush of his fingers against his dick.

A quiet knock on the door stops him cold.

He jerks his hand back and lies motionless, listening. There: another knock, then the door creeps open by a fraction.

"Ray?" Gabe whispers.

"Gabe?" Ray sits up, the duvet falling down to his hips before he remembers that he's naked. In the faint light of a street lamp that squeezes through a gap between the curtains, he doubts Gabe can see much, but ... still. "Something wrong?"

"Charlie snores." Gabe takes a shuffling step into the room, voice the colour of shadows. "And he's got cold feet."

Ray is pretty sure he can follow those words to their logical conclusion, but he doesn't want to say it first. "Okay...?"

"Can I..." Another shuffling step. "Would it be okay if I shared with you?"

Once he strains to make out more than Gabe's silhouette, Ray can tell that Gabe brought his duvet and a pillow. And fuck, Ray's still a bit hard, and he's not prepared for this, but there's no part of him that wants to turn Gabe away.

Gabe, who kissed the corner of his mouth earlier.

Ray shoves the thought away. "Yeah, 'course. Just let me put some clothes on. I sleep naked, usually."

"Oh." It's said on a quick breath, then Gabe turns away to close the door. "Sure. I can just..."

He doesn't finish, but Ray assumes he's offering to stay like that, face averted, to give Ray some privacy. A dangerous thrill runs through Ray at the idea of Gabe watching him, trying to guess at details in the dark.

Stop it.

Ray slides out of bed and crosses over to his wardrobe, digs out a fresh pair of boxers and a T-shirt, and slides into both. "All safe," he tells Gabe.

"Okay, great." Gabe's voice is barely above a murmur, but he sounds just a hint affected—not uncomfortable, Ray doesn't think so, and it's nice to feel like he isn't the only one who's aware of the pull between them. It's the wrong time for them, of course. The wrong time, the wrong place and constellation. Maybe if they'd met ten years from now, with Gabe just a little less famous and Ray just a little less of a failure...

Maybe then.

The thought squeezes down on his chest. He needs a second to regain his composure, glad that the darkness hides his features, before he can hope to sound anywhere near calm. "All right. Come on, then. You still prefer the right side?"

"I kind of ... um." Gabe pauses halfway to the bed, the night reducing him to a cutout. "I prefer the side that's further from the door, if you don't mind? I know it's silly."

Ray is wholly unprepared for the wave of affection that rolls over him. "Not silly, no. I slept with a nightlight until I was twelve."

"Well, I'm twenty-one, and I still feel reassured if I'm not right next to the door. Even when I'm in a hotel, I always sleep on the far side." Gabe's tone is self-deprecating, and since Ray is no stranger to negative self-talk, he reaches for Gabe's shoulder.

"Stop that. Everyone's got their thing, don't they? Yours happens to be sleeping positions in relation to doors, mine's about big groups. Patrick can't swim out into the middle of a lake ever since he saw *Jaws*, and Andrew hates it when people peel eggs with their fingernails."

"Charlie gets creeped out by the idea of running his fingers over rough wood. Something about the sound it makes." The embarrassed note to Gabe's voice has melted away, just like Ray intended.

"See? Everyone's got their thing." After a squeeze to Gabe's shoulder, Ray lets go. "So, left side for you?"

"Yes, please." A smile filters through the words. "And thank you."

"No need. Like I said, I kind of enjoy the whole cuddling thing." It veers close to the exchange that led up to Gabe almost-kissing him, so Ray is quick to add, "And Patrick makes for a terrible cuddle partner. Always wants to be the big spoon even though he's, like, a head shorter than me. Which—not to assume that we'll be cuddling! Just in general."

"I don't mind being the little spoon." The smile in Gabe's voice is more pronounced now.

"Well, good. So that's settled. Great." Ray needs to stop talking before he digs himself into a hole. With that thought in mind, he turns away and tugs his pillow and duvet from the middle of the bed over to the right side, making room for Gabe on the left.

Gabe carries his bundle over to the far side, the mattress dipping when he slides under the covers. For an awkward moment, they're both just lying there, breathing, waiting for some kind of cue.

It's Gabe who shifts towards the middle of the bed, rolling onto his side so Ray can easily fit himself into the space behind him. Ray knows an invitation when he sees one, so he shuffles closer and slips an arm around Gabe's chest. "This okay?"

Gabe tucks himself closer, covering Ray's hand with his own. "Yeah."

Ray should let him sleep. Gabe must be exhausted, and Ray's questions aren't in need of urgent answers. But... "Earlier, in the kitchen." It's not a complete sentence, of course, except Ray doesn't know how to finish it.

Thankfully, Gabe doesn't fake ignorance. "It just felt like something I wanted to do? I know you like that sort of thing, and I've never really ... you know. Had a chance."

"Oh." Ray isn't sure if he's disappointed—isn't sure whether he expected any particular answer at all.

"It doesn't have to be a big deal, right?" Gabe twists his head around so they can kind of look at each other in the dark. "Just, like ... a friends thing?"

Ray frowns. "As in friends with benefits?"

"Not, like ... sex." The night turns Gabe into a relief of grey and black, his voice low to match the atmosphere. "I mean, you're *very* attractive, that's not—it's just that it could get confusing. If we had sex."

Ray isn't sure he quite follows Gabe's logic given that, sex or not, he's plenty confused. For Gabe's sake, though, he can pretend. "So you mean, like ... cuddle buddies?"

"Exactly." The faint gleam of teeth when Gabe grins. "You get to fill the void caused by your no-dating policy, and I get to try out some new stuff with someone I trust, see what I've been missing out on, or not. Win-win."

It sounds so simple, put like that—yet Ray can feel the accelerated pace of Gabe's heartbeat, at odds with his calm tone. Does Gabe want this more than he lets on?

If Ray had any sense of self-preservation, he'd say no.

Except that might mean he won't get another chance at holding Gabe like this. He won't get to be the first man Gabe kisses just because, not because it's meant to lead somewhere. It's hard to think clearly with Gabe right up against him, warm and solid, Gabe's hand covering Ray's, the night wrapping them up like a protective blanket.

For a moment, Ray is gripped by a sense of vertigo, like standing at the top of a precipice. He blinks, and the room shifts back into focus, the beating of Gabe's heart the realest thing around.

"Ray?" A thread of insecurity is woven through Gabe's voice, and Ray can't remember what he's scared of.

"That sounds like fun," he says, and it's not a lie, but it isn't quite the truth either.

"Yeah?" Even in the darkness, Ray catches the glint of Gabe's smile, close enough to kiss it right off Gabe's lips. He could, now.

"Yeah." Ray swallows and finds that his answering smile is just a breath away. "But first: sleep."

"Sleep," Gabe repeats, like a prayer.

Ray tightens his arm around Gabe's chest by a tiny increment, enough to make a point. "Good night, Gabe."

Gabe inhales, then lifts their joined hands so he can drop a kiss to Ray's thumb. "Night," he whispers, guiding their hands back to their original position, his heartbeat slower now, calm.

Ray closes his eyes. This time, sleep claims him within minutes—like falling backwards into warm water, floating, *safe*.

13

For the second time in as many days, Gabe wakes up in Ray's bed. It's a different bed, granted, but the boy lying next to him is the same. For a few precious moments, Gabe lets himself pretend that it's real. That he's ready for the big jump, that Ray is fine with dating as long as it's Gabe, that the arm wrapped around Gabe means more than friendship and comfort.

This is not that movie, though.

Voices filtering through the door intrude upon the peaceful bubble—Ray's mum, back from her night shift, and Allie, who Gabe wouldn't have pegged for an early riser. Which … huh. A glance at the retro alarm clock on the bedside table reveals that it's a quarter to ten, meaning that Gabe slept for more than nine hours. He can't remember the last time he did that. Possibly kindergarten. Possibly the *womb*.

He luxuriates in Ray's embrace for another minute before carefully extracting himself to look at him. A combination of sleep and curtain-filtered light softens Ray's features, smoothing away any trace of worry, no lines marring his forehead. Dark lashes fan out against his cheeks, eyebrows a proud arch. Fuck, but he's beautiful.

Without thinking, Gabe leans in to kiss Ray's cheek. He jolts back when Ray stirs at the touch, then remembers that he's allowed.

Another kiss, light as a feather, and Ray's lids flutter open. He looks disoriented for a moment, staring at Gabe as though he's trying to draw a line between dream and reality. It makes Gabe smile.

"G'morning."

Ray's eyes narrow a fraction, sifting through some kind of reflections. Then he yawns and smiles back. "Morning, Gabe." His voice is sleep-rough, and somehow, Gabe isn't prepared for that.

He hides his reaction by starting to gather his things. "I've got to go. Charlie's probably still asleep, but your mum is back, and Allie is up, too. Unless" —he shoots Ray a sly glance— "you want to explain this to them?"

"Let me think." Ray sits up and shoves a hand through his hair before he sends Gabe a quick, bright grin. "Since it's you who crawled into my bed, I don't feel like it's my story to tell."

Gabe fakes an air of affront. "Why, sir, if that isn't the response of an utter poltroon, I don't know what is."

"A what?"

Gabe lets his own grin shine through. "A coward in the world of Shakespeare. Charlie and I have this thing where we end most of our phone calls with a battle of outlandish insults. This won me the last round."

"I'm not sure whether congratulations are in order," Ray says dryly.

"Well, Charlie won the previous round by calling me a gentleman of four outs."

"Meaning?"

"A gentleman of four withouts—wit, manners, good looks, and ... money, I think?"

Ray huffs in amusement. "Hardly accurate."

"Accuracy is not the point."

"I see." The corners of Ray's eyes crinkle as he seems to take Gabe in for a beat. "Okay, so. I'm afraid to ask, but: did you just kiss me awake? Because, mate, I know it's an easy mistake to make, but I'm not some hundred-year-old princess sleeping her life away in a castle that's overgrown with roses."

All right, okay. So they're doing this, but it comes with a side of joking. That's good, that's brilliant. Gabe can roll with that.

"I'd prefer a prince, personally, so I thought I might try my hand at turning this particular frog," he shoots back, adding a wink to show he's kidding, and also because he knows it'll make Ray wince theatrically.

"First off, it takes a princess to do that. Secondly, your winks are an abomination."

"First off," Gabe counters, "'princess' is a state of mind, and no one can take that away from me. Secondly, feel free to critique Deb's teaching prowess when she arrives later. Just let me get the popcorn first, please."

Deborah. Gabe will see Deborah today. Christ, it's been *months*. She came to visit him in the summer, but he didn't manage to fulfil his promise of a return visit in the autumn because he had to reshoot one Green Hunter scene in a different location, and several others due to a change in love interest.

Whatever shows on Gabe's face makes Ray reach out, then freeze for a moment with his hand hovering in the air, an uncertain tilt to his mouth. Gabe could make the decision for both of them, simply by turning into the touch. But it feels like this is Ray's bridge to cross—so Gabe waits, hardly daring to breathe.

Ray's hand is gentle when he cups Gabe's cheek, careful, like Gabe is something fragile and precious. "You really miss her, don't you?" Ray asks in an undertone.

"Yeah." Gabe exhales and leans into the touch, letting his eyes close for a moment. "I thought... I thought I might lose her, too."

"Sounds like she found it a rather easy choice between you and your parents."

"Yeah. Guess I was worried about nothing."

"Guess you were." A pause before Ray adds, low like a promise, "You'll be fine, Gabe. You'll be *fine*." As if to underline the statement, his thumb drifts to the corner of Gabe's mouth, moving in small, feathery-light circles.

If circumstances were different, Gabe could snake out his tongue, wrap his lips around Ray's thumb in blatant invitation. Even as it sends an excited shiver through him, the idea is daunting. It's not like it'd be a first—Gabe has both given and received blowjobs. He's had casual sex, no matter what Charlie thinks. He's just ... never had it mean something. And while he's always cared about making it good for the other person—he's not a selfish prick, thank you very much—it would be different with Ray, *more*. Gabe would want to make it so, *so* good, erase all memories of those bastards who came before him and made Ray feel inadequate.

If they ever crossed that line, Gabe doesn't think he could find his way back.

With a smile, he turns his head and kisses the pad of Ray's thumb, then moves off the bed to gather his twin duvet and pillow. "I should get going. Maybe you can poke your head into the hallway, see if the coast is clear?"

"I can do that." Yet it's another moment before Ray crawls out of bed and crosses over to the door. His boxers cling to his small, tight arse, leaving very little to the imagination when he ducks halfway out the door, and Jesus, that bundle of Gabe's bedding sure is coming in handy right now.

"Clear?" he asks, proud of how even his voice sounds.

"Clear." Ray steps aside to let Gabe pass, his fingers briefly skirting down Gabe's arm. "See you at breakfast."

Since Gabe doesn't trust himself to reply, he nods, smiles again, and escapes into the hallway. He tries to be quiet when he sneaks into the room he's supposed to share with Charlie, but he needn't have bothered: the room is bathed in daylight, Charlie sitting cross-legged on the bed with his phone in hand. Wordlessly, he watches Gabe enter the room, close the door, and place the bundle in his arms back on the bed.

Silence.

"You snore," Gabe tries.

Charlie tilts his head with a haughty look in his eyes.

"Also, your feet are freezing. *And* you steal my duvet even though you have your own."

Still Charlie doesn't respond.

"Fine!" Gabe raises his hands, palms up, and sends Charlie a pleading look. "It's just ... Fuck, it's just *nice*, okay? Nothing happened. We just slept, I swear, but he said he misses aspects of dating like holding hands, kissing, sleeping in the same bed, and I... I've never experienced that in the first place, so..."

"Oh, *Gabe*." Charlie is off the bed in a heartbeat, pulling Gabe into a full-body embrace. Gabe clings to him, thinks *Don't leave* and isn't self-centred enough to ask because Charlie would stay even though he's got parents who love him, parents who aren't getting any younger and want to see their only child for Christmas.

"I'm fine," Gabe tells Charlie's shoulder. "Honest."

"'Course you are." Charlie sounds like he actually believes it. "I'm just worried, yeah? It's my job. And I like Ray, I really do—great lad, seems to genuinely care about you, and if I were gay, I'd hit that."

"Jesus, Charlie—*images!*"

"Don't think Jesus's got anything to do with it." Charlie's smirk colours his voice before he pulls back a little to look at Gabe, hands steady on Gabe's elbows as all mirth fades from his expression. "So, like I said: I like him. You went to him for a reason, and I don't think it's just that he's the one person you know in London. Far as I can see, he's earned that trust. I expected to come here and find you a wreck—"

"Hey!" Gabe protests.

"Your fucking parents outed you to the entire world, mate. No shame in having a good, old-fashioned breakdown over it."

Gabe bites down on the inside of his cheek, using the pain to focus his emotions. "Like I'd give them the satisfaction."

"That's the spirit." Charlie squeezes Gabe's elbows, eyes kind. "Thing is, I can see how great Ray's been for you. As your best mate, I'm just about ready to buy him a pony to say thanks. But I can also see the way he looks at you."

This is treacherous territory. Gabe shouldn't care, not until he's ready to deal with the utter clusterfuck that's become his life, but... God, he still wants to know. "How does he look at me?"

"Like you're the Elizabeth Bennet to his Mr Darcy." Charlie chuckles softly before he shakes his head, sadness flitting over his features. "I want that for you, Gee. I want someone who looks at you like that for the rest of your fucking *life*, and maybe Ray could be that person. But, just. Holy shit, between your parents and the paps and the question of what you want to do with it all, you've got your plate not just full, but fucking overflowing, right? It's a hell of a lot to deal with. So maybe this is not the time to rush headfirst into something that, if it goes wrong..." A pause, then Charlie finishes in a whisper. "Fuck, Gabe. I don't want to see you break."

Gabe thinks of Nora. Thinks of Charlie crying on the sofa the first night Gabe got there, of Charlie refusing to shave for days and drinking too much. Thinks of himself after his parents kicked him out, sleeping on Charlie's floor with no plan, no hope, no future.

Ray could do that to him.

Not yet, not quite—but if Gabe let himself fall, just jumped right in without a safety net, it would be easy to lose himself in Ray.

It's Gabe who reaches for Charlie this time, pulling him back into a hug that's just as tight, just as close. "I'll be careful," he promises, and he's not sure if it's for Charlie's sake or his own.

If, maybe, it's already too late.

~

WATCHING Charlie leave will never be easy.

Video calls help, yeah, but an hour of scheduled time won't ever measure up to simply existing in the same space, talking or not, to spontaneous spoon battles over cereal and lounging around in front of the telly, exchanging comments about nothing of importance.

It's going on noon, a pale sun gracing the cloudless December sky, so it's a calculated risk for Gabe to walk Charlie to the train station.

But if he can't take a risk for his best friend in the whole wide world, what even is the point?

Decked out in a fluffy jacket, a beanie, and sunglasses, Gabe figures he looks sufficiently different from his polished image to get away with this daytime outing. It's a twenty-minute walk through quiet neighbourhoods of mostly single-storey homes and one small, old church made of beige brick stones, then along the town's main road that takes them past a single, closed pub and what must be Ray's old primary school. It's a sleeper community without a town centre to speak of, its main selling point being the direct train line to Leeds.

There's not much foot traffic. The only people they encounter seem to be in a hurry and don't spare them more than a glance and a nod. On the platform, it's just them and an elderly woman who's well past the age of Gabe's target audience, so he relaxes and lets himself enjoy his final minutes with Charlie.

The train arrives far too soon.

He walks home by himself, the first time in two days that he's truly alone. A stiff breeze makes his eyes water so he has to blink repeatedly to clear his vision, refusing to use his hands because that would make it feel too much like crying. He's not. It's just the wind, the cold air in his face.

The house is quiet when he lets himself in with his borrowed key, Ray off to get groceries at the bigger supermarket one town over, Allie and Jazmin out with friends after swearing up and down they won't breathe a word about Gabe, and Ray's mum catching up on lost sleep after her night shift.

Gabe uses the time for a bodyweight workout in the living room, which is better than nothing. He's just finishing up with some stretches when Ray's mum enters with a steaming cup of tea, turning on the tree lights before she sits down on the sofa. Her smile erases his sudden concern that she might object to seeing her living room treated like a makeshift gym.

"Sorry for working out in here," he says anyway. "I should have asked."

She blows on her tea. "Don't worry about it. I can only imagine how much pressure you're under to stay in shape."

"Well, yeah." He lies back on the towel he's been using as a replacement mat and pulls one knee up to his chest. "But it's much worse for female actors."

Margaret watches him over the rim of her cup, the smile lingering mostly around her eyes now. "You're not in the habit of complaining, are you?"

"I was raised to believe that whatever happens, God has a plan, and it isn't my job to question it." Gabe aims for joking and instead lands on the bitter taste of ashes.

"Funny." Margaret's tone is dry. "I was raised to believe that faith holds us accountable to certain values, and among those would be that we strive to lift our children up rather than hold them down. Not that my parents *quite* succeeded when I fell in love with someone who didn't fit with their expectations, but at least they didn't actively try to tear me apart."

Gabe sits up and hugs both knees to his chest, sudden tiredness clawing at the edge of his vision. "How did you come to terms with it? Being a disappointment, I mean."

"Oh, honey." Margaret shakes her head. "I wish I could give you an easy solution, but I think you're still a bit young for kids. Because, see, it's when you have children that you understand they're *meant* to disappoint you—and it's a blessing that they do."

"You're ... disappointed in your children?" That's not the impression Gabe got from seeing the Fadil family together. They bicker more than Gabe's parents would have tolerated, but there's an undercurrent of affection running through their interactions that takes the sting out of every insult.

"Yes." Margaret leans forward, fixing Gabe with clear, blue eyes. "And no. Not at all, not even a little."

"I don't understand."

The corners of her mouth tug upwards. "I didn't expect you to. Let me try to explain, all right? See, let's take Ray. We were so *proud* when he started med school—me, a nurse, would have a doctor for a son. I was thrilled, and so was my husband." Shadows flicker in her eyes as she pauses for a breath. "It wasn't until much later that I realised Ray wasn't suited to being a doctor. He would have hated the weight of responsibility, of telling patients what was wrong with them, having to make fateful decisions, often on insufficient evidence and educated guesswork."

"So…" Gabe frowns. "He didn't live up to your expectations, but it's good that he didn't?"

"Because our expectations were wrong for him. For a while, he was happy because we were happy, but even before my husband died" —another flicker of grief— "he'd lost his enthusiasm. He went through the motions, yes, and he kept his grades up, but it just wasn't right."

"What happened with the scholarship?"

"Once Al died, Ray simply stopped caring." Margaret's voice is like stained glass. "I wasn't in a good place at the time, and Fay is my oldest, but she was pregnant, and then her husband left. So Ray, being the second oldest… I suppose he felt it was his responsibility to carry us."

Ray would have been around Gabe's age at the time, maybe a year or two older. Gabe can't imagine being strong enough to carry a family when he can barely carry himself, some days.

"My point is…" She sighs, swirling her tea. "As a mother, I have to accept that my children need to do things their way, at their pace. And I'll be proud of them no matter what."

Embarrassingly, Gabe finds himself blinking back tears. It's not common for him to set up camp this close to the water, but it's just been one of those days. Several, really. "You should tell Ray that."

She nods. "I suspect I should."

They're both quiet while Margaret takes a sip of tea and Gabe goes back to stretching, the Christmas tree twinkling in the corner.

"Thank you," Gabe says eventually. "I know I've said it before, but I really appreciate you letting me stay here, and being okay with Charlie and my sister dropping by. I… That's no small thing."

"Don't worry about it, sweetheart. We won't be serving lobster and caviar, but we've certainly got more space than I know what to do with most days." It's lighthearted, not meant as a slight, so Gabe doesn't take offense. He also refrains from offering to pay her—when he tested the idea with Ray, it landed like a bag of stones.

"Sounds like you don't love this house," Gabe says instead.

Margaret sways her head. "It's always felt like the house of my husband's parents, even after they passed away."

Gabe moves out of his final stretch, lying on his back for a moment as he takes in the off-white ceiling and the wood-panelled walls. His own house is much more modern, with floor-to-ceiling windows taking up two sides of the living room and an adjacent open kitchen filled with state-of-the-art appliances that he never uses, yet he knows the feeling of being a guest in your own home all too well.

There are a lot of things he could say, but in the end, he settles on, "I'm very sorry about your husband."

"Thank you, Gabe." Margaret's voice matches the grey curtains, dropping to a near-whisper, before she visibly pulls herself together and sends him a faint smile. "And just so we're clear, it's a pleasure to have you with us. You're a lovely boy, and I'm glad Ray met someone like you."

It seems to imply things that aren't true—and yet Gabe doesn't want to correct her. "You've created a wonderful family," he says instead. "I'm just grateful that I can be a part of it for a little while."

"I've done all right, huh?" Her entire face brightens with the words, and Gabe feels lighter just looking at her.

"You certainly have." He rises to his feet, momentarily off-balance before he finds his centre and excuses himself to take a shower. When he glances back, on his way out of the room, Margaret has picked up a book, her tea sitting on the sofa table as she searches for the right page, the Christmas tree lit in yellow and gold.

Charlie's house is the closest thing to a home Gabe has ever known. This, here, doesn't feel all that far off, and maybe, *probably*, that means something. Gabe made a promise to Charlie, though, and for a good reason—it truly is the wrong time.

But what if it's the right person?

14

Ray's oldest sister Farah arrives in the afternoon, kids and a suitcase filled with presents in tow. She's clearly been warned about Gabe's presence because the flicker of recognition on her face comes without an element of surprise. Out of all of Ray's sisters, she looks the most like him: the same prominent cheekbones and almond eyes, the same shock of black hair. She looks tired, though, older than her thirty years, a seriousness to her that makes Gabe think she hasn't had the easiest year, or several of them.

Gabe introduces himself after hugs have been passed around like candy, then focuses on the kids because kids are *easy*—at least at ages three and five, they are. All they really want is for someone to run around with them, engage with their stories and activities, someone who isn't afraid to act silly. Gabe's just the man for the job.

All the while, he keeps an ear out for the doorbell.

Deborah has been oddly mysterious about when, exactly, she'd be arriving. Her earlier text message had been short and to the point: *'Dealt with parents, on my way. Expect me late afternoon.'*

His offer to pick her up at the train station was marked as read and met with silence. Which can really only mean one thing:

Deborah knows. She knows Gabe wasn't honest about how he left home, and chances are she's pissed.

The Fadil clan plus Gabe just sat down for a late tea—with a splash of rum for the adults—when a car stops on the road, right in front of the house. From the kitchen, they have an excellent view of it, so Gabe gets to watch his sister emerge on the passenger side and lean down to say something to the driver, who starts the car up again a moment later. She remains on the pavement, and Gabe's brain trips over the fact that she didn't bring a suitcase.

She isn't planning to stay.

"Gabe?" Ray murmurs, leaning close enough that his lips brush the shell of Gabe's ear. It jolts Gabe out of his stupor. "All right, there?"

"Yeah." Gabe releases the word in a rush of air and meets Ray's eyes. "Just ... no suitcase."

Ray gets it immediately. Under the table, his hand finds Gabe's knee for a tight squeeze that provides Gabe with a much-needed point of focus. "I'll come open the door with you," Ray says, right as the bell rings.

"Thank you." It nowhere near covers all the things Gabe wants to tell Ray, but for now, it will have to do.

"Gabe and I will be the welcome committee," Ray announces to the table at large in a rare show of him taking charge. "You lot stay here, no need for everyone to scramble for the door."

Gabe gets up when Ray nudges him, and if anyone is giving them odd looks, Gabe is too focused on Ray to notice. They exit into the dimly lit hallway, and fuck, it's been *months* since Gabe saw Deborah, but she isn't here to stay. Heaviness pools in his belly, slows down his steps.

"Hey. *Gee.*"

The unaccustomed nickname makes Gabe glance up. A moment later, Ray is right there in Gabe's space. His eyes are warm, just like his fingertips when he tilts Gabe's chin up and brushes their mouths together. The contact is brief, barely there at all, and Gabe finds himself chasing more when Ray pulls back.

"It'll be fine," Ray promises in an undertone.

You don't know that.

Gabe nods and manages a wobbly smile. When Ray steps away, Gabe rolls back his shoulders and raises his head, breathing deeply before he opens the door just as Deborah is about to ring the bell once more.

She got her ears pierced.

That's the one thing Gabe notices before she pulls him in for a hug that's just like he remembers—an invitation to believe that no matter the problem, his big sister is there to fix it. She holds onto him long enough for his heartbeat to settle into a different, calmer pattern.

When she pushes him back, it's gentle, but there's an edge to it. As he doesn't expect it, he stumbles a little, and it's Ray who steadies him.

Deborah's gaze flits to Ray before she focuses back on Gabe. "*You!*" She jabs a finger towards his stomach. "You *lied* to me!"

"Deb..." That's it. That's the extent of what Gabe has to say for himself because yes, he did. For good reasons, but he did.

"Don't you dare *Deb* me, Gabe—"

"Inside," Ray orders, slicing right through whatever Deborah was about to say. "Gabe doesn't need our neighbours taking an interest."

Deborah squints at Ray for a beat longer this time, taking him in properly. "And you are?"

"Someone I trust," Gabe cuts in.

Apparently, that's enough for now because Deborah gives a sharp nod and follows them into the house. As soon as she's inside, she sheds her jacket where she stands and rounds on Gabe again. "You fucking *lied* to me, Gabe! What the hell?"

There's no way Ray's family in the adjacent room didn't hear her.

"Deborah, *please.*" Gabe drops his arms by his sides and sends her a pleading look. Ray's presence is a warm anchor of comfort next to him. "I'm a guest here, and there are kids in the next room."

Deborah inhales deeply, shoulders rising with it. When she speaks again, the words are much quieter. "Fine, I'll play nice. But first, I deserve an explanation. Like, why the *fuck* did my own little brother claim it was a mutual decision for him to leave home when, in fact, our bloody parents kicked him out *years* ago? Don't you think that's information I deserved?" Her steady gaze is belied by the tremble in her voice. "Or was it handled on a need-to-know basis?"

"Whatever you're thinking? Please stop." Gabe reaches for her wrist, relieved when she lets him. "I just... *God.*" Words. He needs to find them and set this right. "I lied, yeah, but not because I didn't trust you or some rubbish like that—I'd trust you with my *life*, Deb."

"Oh, really?" She snorts. "Then why, pray tell, didn't you just tell me the fucking *truth*?"

"I didn't want you to feel like you had to choose."

"You didn't want me to choose?" Deborah's laugh is like nails on a board, her eyes filling with tears. "Jesus, Gabe. I didn't realise you're that much of a bloody idiot. It's been *years* since our parents knew anything real about my life. There's no fucking choice here—you're the only family I have. And I get to see you, like, once in a blue moon."

It's as though his ribs are clamping down on his heart. "Then why aren't you staying?"

Her forehead crinkles as she sends him a watery, confused look. "What?"

"You didn't bring a suitcase."

Eyes clearing, she turns her hand around and tangles their fingers. "I didn't want to impose on your friend's" —she glances at Ray, a quiet presence by Gabe's side— "family. There's a B&B just a five-minute drive from here; I got a room there."

Gabe recognises fishy when he smells it. "And by 'I' you mean 'we'?"

A tentative smile curls her lips. "I might have met someone."

"*When?*" Gabe tamps down on the betrayed note to the question —he misled Deborah for years about his falling out with their parents, so he's got no right to be upset that she isn't sharing every minute aspect of her life with him. "Last we talked, you were ranting about how that German engineer guy courted you for weeks, and the moment you sleep with him, he's gone like Casper the ghost."

"He's a biologist, and turns out it was a miscommunication." Her smile is fully pronounced now. "He was supposed to go back to Hamburg for the spring semester. After we... He had to scramble to get things reorganised before all the admin people were off for the Christmas break."

"Wow. So he's staying in Paris for you, and now he's spending Christmas with you as well?"

It will never be anything less than hilarious to see his big sister blush like a teenager. "Don't think it's much of a sacrifice—ours aren't the only parents who suck, you know. His seem to believe that throwing money at their son is the extent of their responsibilities. "

Ray's chuckle is edged with wistfulness. "Well, don't they say that every unhappy family is unhappy in their own way?"

"Did you just" —Deborah narrows eyes as green as Gabe's— "casually quote Tolstoy at me?"

"Yeah. Sorry." Ray ducks his head, peering up at Deborah through his lashes. "Was trying to lighten the mood and landed straight on pretentious. Especially since I never actually finished Anna Karenina."

Jesus fucking Christ, he's *wonderful*. Gabe wants him so much it hurts.

He drags his gaze away just in time to find Deborah scrutinising him. The lines of her face soften as her attention returns to Ray. "I like you. You can stay."

"Thanks, I think?" Something loosens around Ray's eyes, almost as though he really was worried about whether or not Deborah would like him. "I'm Ray."

"Deborah." She shoots him a smirk. "Don't say it's nice to meet me because it'd be a lie. I'm good now, though—take me to meet the in-laws."

"*Deb*." Gabe groans to hide the stupid quiver in his stomach.

"Oh, relax." Her smirk eases into a smile. "I'm kidding, boys. I promise I'll behave."

"That would be a first," Gabe grumbles, but when she keeps smiling at him, he finds it's impossible to hold on to his sour expression. Deborah is here, and she knows, and she's with him, she's *staying*.

As far as Christmas presents go, this one's pretty damn fantastic.

~

It's like a switch flicked somewhere between the hallway and Deborah entering the living room. Ray watches her greet his family with polite grace, miles removed from the forceful, fast-talking woman who first exploded into the house. And yet it doesn't feel fake, more like equally valid nuances of her personality, pressure that needed to be released.

Afternoon tea is followed by a walk to expel some energy. As per usual with a diverse group like that, it turns into a pearl string of people walking in twos or threes, the stragglers catching up whenever the fastest group stops and waits, only to fall behind again.

Ray sticks with Gabe and Deborah to hear her recount the confrontation with their parents. The way she tells it, she didn't even make it into the house. "Not much of a surprise, given my opening statement was 'Hello, darling parents—you think my *brother* is a sinner?'" Her smile reveals dimples just like Gabe's. "'Then how's this? I lost my virginity at sixteen, and the only time I go to church is when you can see me.'"

"Easing into it isn't your style, is it?" Ray asks, partly to give Gabe a moment to move past his obvious discomfort at inspiring the final rift between his sister and his parents.

Deborah snorts rather inelegantly. "I swear that I'm a calm, rational person ninety per cent of the time. You just happened to meet me in a highly emotional situation that brings out the other ten per cent."

"So what happened after?" Gabe asks. His frown lingers, but at least he doesn't look nauseous anymore.

"They yelled a bit, I yelled a bit, neighbours came out to stare, and eventually, Dad told me they should have kicked me out years ago just like they did with you." Deborah introduces a meaningful pause. "Which, as you know, was news to me."

Gabe ducks his head. "Sorry."

"You better be." The initial raw edge of hurt is gone from Deborah's tone, and Gabe tosses her the tiniest of smiles in response. It feels fragile, though, so Ray decides to give them a moment.

He drops back to walk with his mum and Jazmin instead, abruptly, *fiercely* grateful to have them in his life. Jazmin entertains them with tales of her artist friends, her words painting a life that is wildly different from Ray's routine of taking the same train to work most mornings, sitting down for his prepared lunch between twelve and one, and leaving between five and six, broken only by the occasional Saturday or Sunday stint. He doesn't want to trade places, but something about the passion in her voice prods at the pockets of doubt in his mind that he's become so adept at ignoring.

When Jazmin runs off to chase a laughing Jasper, Ray shoves his hands into his pockets and keeps his gaze on the ground.

"What's the matter, love?" his mum asks after a few steps, and it occurs to him that she's been doing that more—encouraging emotional conversations in an attempt to fill one of the gaps left by his dad's death.

"Oh, nothing." He huffs. "Just wondering if I'm wasting my life, is all."

"Because you dropped out of med school?" There's no judgment in her tone, and when he glances at her profile, she has her face tilted into the low-standing sun.

He swallows. They've never really talked about it, at least not this bluntly. "I guess, yeah."

"Hmm."

"I mean, I don't know if I'd have made a good doctor. Probably not —I don't have that natural authority. And, like." He swallows again and stares at the orange glow of the beginning sunset. "I mean, I couldn't even see what was wrong with my own dad, right?"

"Oh, *honey*." His mum stops walking. "Admittedly, this took me a while to see, but it isn't anyone's fault. Not mine, certainly not yours."

"You…" Embarrassingly, his voice cracks. "So you wondered, too? If there's something we could have done differently?"

"Of course." Her tone is matter-of-fact, but her expression is not. "I'm a nurse. It is my *job* to spot health complications before they arise, and yet I missed what was wrong with my own husband."

Somehow, it never occurred to Ray that his mum might have experienced a carbon copy of his own guilt. "Mum, you know he wouldn't have told you. Even if he'd had any symptoms like … you know, chest tightness or shortness of breath, something like that—you know what he was like. He wouldn't have said a word. How could you have known?"

"How could *you* have known?" she returns.

He opens his mouth to reply—and draws a blank. Anything he could say she could easily throw back to him.

I should have known because he was my dad.

So should I have known because he was my husband?

Of course not.

That's what he would tell her because no, he doesn't blame her. He never did—not for a minute, not for a second. 'Then why do you blame yourself?' she'd ask, and he wouldn't know how to answer.

"I don't know," he says quietly, to both her question in his mind and the one she actually asked.

"Me neither," is her equally quiet response. "So maybe there simply isn't anyone to blame."

Since his throat is too tight for words, he nods and looks away. After a moment, his mum nudges his hand and starts walking again. He falls into step with just a second's delay, and they're quiet for a minute, only the sound of the others' voices drifting to them.

"What you said earlier, love," his mum says then, voice still low as she glances at him. "About wasting your life. I do hope you know that I don't need you to become a doctor. All I ever wanted was for you to find something you're passionate about."

Passionate.

Ray thinks of Gabe and the way he talks about stepping into a character, that spark he describes when it all connects. There are moments like that at the lab, when things don't work and then they *do* —cells that grow far better in treated water, increasing room humidity to improve cell attachment after thawing. Those are the moments Ray relishes. And yet...

He feels around for the right way to describe it. "I do enjoy some of the lab work—mostly the occasional challenges, I guess. But I also get kind of bored sometimes, you know? Like, all I do is carry out other people's ideas."

"Listen, sweetheart." She turns her head to study him with a warm, serious expression. "I have no doubt that you will find your path. It may take a little while, but you will."

The certainty in her voice makes him feel heavy with something he can't quite name. He lets his gaze drift over the fields and the cluster of trees, the orange-flooded western edge of the sky. "Thank you, Mum."

"Thank Gabe." Humour brightens the words. "He's the one who suggested I should tell you how proud I am of the man you're becoming, rather than just assume you'll know."

"You're proud of me?" Ray wishes it didn't come out quite like that, small and young, needy.

His mum stops to take him by the shoulders and turns him so they're facing each other, her gaze steady. "Always, Ray. *Always*."

He's too fucking old to cry over his mum's praise, so he settles on a wobbly smile instead. "Thank you."

With a small squeeze, she lets him go, and they resume walking. Behind them, Ray hears Jess's high-pitched giggles, Jasper shouting about duckies, and Farah, Allie, and Jazmin all laughing about something. Further up ahead, Gabe and Deborah look like they're in a serious discussion, heads bent close together, her hands sketching patterns in the air while Gabe nods and interjects occasionally.

Gabe.

Ray clears his throat. "Speaking of Gabe..."

She quirks a brow at him. "Yes?"

"I thought I'd set him up in my room for tonight. No need to put anyone out, right?" He should leave it at that. Except his mum is watching him, an expectant air about her, and he stumbles over his resolve to forgo any explanation or justification that will only arouse suspicion. "I mean, Andrew stayed with me too when he was here, and Patrick slept over plenty of times."

"Love." She shakes her head, eyes kind and knowing. "Gabe isn't Andrew or Patrick."

Any denial he might have offered dries right up. He ducks his head, unable to hold her gaze for more than a second. "Yeah. I know."

She's silent for a step or two, then breathes out a small laugh. "Sometimes, I forget you're not my baby anymore. Yes, of course you can set Gabe up in your room." A pause. "He's a very nice boy."

But he won't be mine.

Ray catches the words before they trip off his tongue. It's true, and yet, for just a moment, he wants to pretend that Gabe might stay, that the world out there won't claim him back—that Gabe could belong with Ray instead of those rich, beautiful people who usually surround him.

Just like Ray taught himself in school, he sits with the thought for a few conscious seconds before he releases it. Watches it drift away into the approaching evening, like a soap bubble that will burst upon contact.

∼

DEBORAH LEAVES JUST before dinner to spend the evening with her new beau, but promises to be back tomorrow after breakfast. Since Gabe doesn't know where he'll be a week from now, he feels like a fairytale dragon, greedily hoarding this treasure of precious minutes and hours spent together, piling them up for a rainy day.

He feels the same way about Ray—each covert brush of their hands a new trinket for his collection, each conversation a bauble, each bump of their elbows as they brush their teeth a plastic bead that he lines up on his mental string.

After a quick pee, he follows Ray to the room they'll be officially sharing tonight. When Ray's mum mentioned it in the course of discussing sleeping arrangements over dinner, Allie's eyebrows rose so high they just about touched her hairline, Jazmin smirked at her brother as though she was privy to a secret, and Farah was too busy cleaning up Jasper's spilt apple juice to take much notice. Fortunately, Deborah was already gone by that time, or Gabe would have faced another round of questions about Ray that he isn't quite sure how to answer.

"You'll get there," Deborah had told him during the family walk. "That's always been your thing, right? You're like an egg that needs to hatch, but once it does, what comes out is chirping and ready to go."

He'd nudged her side. "Wow, thanks. Being compared to a baby chick makes me feel particularly manly on this fine afternoon."

"Get over it," had been her unsympathetic response.

He thinks back to it now, entering Ray's bedroom to find Ray already under the covers. It's their third night of sharing a bed, and while the quiet little thrill is still there, it's now complemented by an early sense of familiarity.

"All right?" Ray asks once Gabe is settled comfortably.

Gabe shuffles towards the middle of the mattress, rolling onto his side so Ray can fit himself right up against his back. "Yeah."

Ray flicks off the light, plunging the room into a darkness that will lift slightly once their eyes accommodate. Right now, though, Gabe has to rely on his hearing to pinpoint Ray shifting closer, then a warm brush of lips against the back of Gabe's neck. With a sigh, Gabe tilts his head for better access, but Ray moves away almost immediately.

Gabe doesn't know how to ask for more without crossing a line.

"How're you holding up?" Ray's voice is a murmur that seeps into Gabe's skin and fills him up with brightness.

"Okay, I think. Still processing." Gabe considers it for a second. "According to my sister, I'm in the habit of brooding over stuff until I'm suddenly ready to spread my wings and fly. Or run around like a freshly hatched baby chick, as she would put it."

"Sounds about right." With a low chuckle, Ray trails his hand around to the centre of Gabe's chest. Gabe covers it with his own, sliding his fingers into the gaps between Ray's.

"Walter—my agent—says reactions mostly range from neutral to supportive. A few bigots, of course, but most criticism actually seems to target my parents. *The New York Times* apparently wrote a piece on the ethics of forced celebrity outings."

"Good." The steel in Ray's voice is at odds with the way his arm tightens around Gabe.

Now that Gabe's eyes have adjusted, he can make out vague shapes, the vertical line that marks the gap between the curtains. He hesitates for a moment. "Your mum's pretty great."

"Yeah." Ray tucks his nose into Gabe's hair. "I'm lucky."

"She seems to think you won't go back to med school."

Ray is still for several beats, simply breathing. "Even if I wanted to, I threw away my scholarship. I work full-time right now at the lab, and I'm fairly frugal, yeah, but I couldn't easily put aside enough to even cover the tuition for part-time students." Another pause, shorter this time. "And you've seen this house—my mum barely has the money for necessary renovations. There's no way I could ask her for anything."

Gabe knows it's a mistake even before he says it. "I have money. I mean, assuming I still have a career, which seems at least likely. And it wouldn't have to be medicine either—you could do something more research-oriented, like ... biology, I guess?"

"Gabe..." The 'no' is plain in Ray's voice, and Gabe should give it a rest, he really should, but *damn* it.

"What good is my money if I can't use it to help a friend?"

"I get that." Ray squeezes Gabe's fingers. "But what good is this friendship if you can't be sure I'm in it for the right reasons?"

"I know you're not like that."

"No, Gabe." Ray's voice is gentle, the words accompanied by another squeeze. "I need us to be equals. If I take your money, I'll become your charity case."

"It could be a loan. No interest, and you could pay me back in flexible instalments, whenever it suits you." But Gabe knows he's lost this fight—can read it in how Ray doesn't relax his hold, no indication that he's even considering Gabe's offer. Gabe puffs out a sigh. "Seriously, what good *is* my money? I don't need another car, I've got more clothes than I can wear in a year, Charlie's got enough money of his own because his parents are loaded, and you and Deborah won't take it."

"It's because we love you." Ray continues quickly, words a little rushed. "You could buy a yacht?"

It's because we love you.

Ray didn't mean it like that—of course he didn't. It was said in conjunction to Gabe's sister, so clearly it's no different from Charlie's occasional 'Love ya, man' that never made Gabe trip over his own heart, breath catching in his throat.

Right, okay. *Focus.* Buying a yacht.

"One," Gabe says, "I'm not that rich. Two, my dick is an okay size, so I don't feel a need to compensate."

Jesus fucking *Christ.* Ray says something about love, and Gabe's brain filter switches right off and doesn't stop his flying leap into a sea of too much information. On the other hand, it's the kind of joke Gabe would one-hundred per cent make around Charlie, so maybe it's fine.

"Um." Ray sounds a little choked, and that's a bad thing, probably. "Good to know?"

Gabe aims for a quiet, breathy laugh. "Yep. Just so you know what to say in case *The Daily Mail* or *The Sun* ask."

While Gabe was joking, Ray sounds horrified. "I wouldn't."

Gabe twists in Ray's hold, turning enough for their eyes to meet. In the darkness, Ray's irises seem black, the pupils huge. "I was kidding," Gabe tells him. "I know you wouldn't, Ray. I *know*."

Since Ray looks unconvinced, Gabe kisses him. It's all closed mouths and light, gentle contact, yet it's enough to get Gabe's heart racing in a way that Ray must notice, *surely* he must, and he'll pull back and ask Gabe how something so simple can set Gabe on fire, and Gabe won't have an answer.

Or maybe he does.

When he pulls back, it's in increments—retreat and come back for another brush of their lips, again, lengthening the pauses between kisses like ebbing waves of water. Eventually, Gabe settles back against Ray, warm and safe and *home* in a way he hasn't felt since he was a kid.

Love you, too.

He thinks the words but doesn't speak them, too aware that his meaning might differ from Ray's. "Good night," he says instead.

"Sleep well, Gabe," Ray returns.

Gabe bites his lip against any words that might strive to escape. He falls asleep with Ray's hand flat against his chest, a little off from where his heart is.

INTERMISSION

BUZZ IS UZZ
Posted December 25, 11:23 a.m.

BUT REALLY, where is Gabe Duke?

Last seen exiting his swanky London hotel just hours before daddy dearest outed him to anyone not buried under a pile of Christmas to-dos, Gabe Duke can be forgiven for needing a moment. Or two. Maybe the Green Hunter could ask to borrow Harry Potter's invisibility cloak, from one hero to another? Better skip the sugar, though, what with how Potter is married with kids these days!

But really, where is Duke? With nothing better to do other than putting our least favourite gifts up for sale (another vase, anyone?), here are our theories:

1. Hugging it out with the parents

Ha. Ha. Ha.

2. Gone fishing

Did Duke get a secret getaway tip from Monica Lewinsky, the world's most famous intern? Rumour has it she once hid in a secluded luxury resort located directly on the Great Barrier Reef. If there are rules about fishing by arrow, we haven't found them, so those mackerel, queenfish, and trevally better watch out!

3. Friends forever

There's no shortage of Duke proudly showing off his bestie Charlie Doyle. We fancy the Manchester-based psychology student for his boy-next-door good looks and the big smile he always seems to wear around Duke. More than friends? Who knows! All we know is that Doyle left his parents' home on the 23rd and didn't make it back until the evening of the 24th. Make of that what you will...

15

Christmas Day rushes by in a blur of activity.

As soon as Ray's mum gets home from her night shift, the kids attack the presents that Santa left in exchange for a glass of wine and one of the ginger biscuits Gabe baked with Andrew. Ray isn't usually one for ginger, but he has to agree with Santa Farah: the biscuits are excellent, and Gabe might have missed his true calling.

"I'll keep it in mind in case the acting thing goes sideways," Gabe says when both Ray and Farah praise his baking over breakfast. While Ray is pretty sure that at this point, Gabe is mostly joking, he still bumps their knees together under the table and, when Gabe doesn't move away, just ends up keeping his leg there.

Deborah and her boyfriend Lars spend most of the day with them. While the guy seems understandably daunted by the noise level that comes with Ray's family, Ray also pegs him as a kindred spirit who is genuinely fine with sidestepping the spotlight and seems passionate about his molecular biology studies in a way Ray envies.

When Gabe mentions his original misrepresentation of Lars's

study subject, Lars cracks a shy grin. "Not every German is an engineer, you know."

"Shame." Gabe's sigh is dramatic. "Life is made so much easier by stereotyping."

From there, the conversation moves on to Jasper's new dog puzzle, Allie's plans for a second tattoo, Farah's classroom stories, and quality of life in Paris versus Edinburgh versus London versus L.A. It's people talking over and around each other, the conversation dominated by Ray's family and Deborah, while Ray, Gabe, and Lars are mostly listening.

"My English isn't that good," Lars admits at some point, when specifically asked why he isn't defending his hometown Hamburg in their battle of cities.

"Your English is great," Gabe tells him. "Certainly better than my French or German, which are mediocre and nonexistent, respectively."

Right, thanks. Because the idea of Gabe murmuring quiet words in French is beneficial to Ray's piece of mind.

In the afternoon, Ray meets up with Patrick to go see a movie in Leeds. They share a nostalgic portion of nachos between them, and Ray doesn't mention holding hands and nighttime kisses, mostly because he wouldn't know how to explain it. Patrick must notice on some level, though, because when they hug goodbye, he holds on for a second longer than usual before he asks if Ray is all right.

"I am, yeah." Ray means it—he really is fine. Just a little confused, and walking around with skin that's a size too small even as he feels bright and weightless and more like himself than he's felt in a long time, calm yet ready to burst into a rainbow of colours all at once.

With another hug, Patrick rushes off to help his parents set up dinner. Ray walks home alone, taking his time, drinking in the lit houses and Christmas trees that show through windows, ignoring the insistent breeze that snakes cool tendrils under his clothes.

When he arrives at the house, it's to raucous laughter drifting over from the kitchen—Gabe and Allie duking it out with a zucchini and a salami that they're meant to slice up for the pizzas Ray's mum is preparing, Jasper and Jess cheering them on while Farah pretends to be much more annoyed by the play-with-your-food display than she truly is.

Dinner is even rowdier than breakfast, mostly because alcohol is added to the mix, and extends late into the evening as Ray's mum managed to trade tonight's shift in for working New Year's Eve. With ruddy cheeks and quick hands that dance with tales of movie sets and media circuits, Gabe looks like he fits right in—like he belongs with Ray's family, with *Ray*. Just a normal boy with a brilliant smile and a beautiful mind.

They tumble into bed well past midnight, tired and drunk and overfed. Ray falls asleep to the rhythm of Gabe's breathing and imagines he can feel Gabe's heartbeat, calm and steady under his palm.

Maybe this is happiness.

~

RAY IS NOT ENTIRELY clear on how Gabe convinced him of another run when his legs are still a tad tired from their first one. But then, it's a chance to get away for an hour or so, just the two of them, which might be reason enough. Perhaps Ray also enjoyed the exercise more than he is ready to admit—the sense of freedom, the slight soreness afterwards to remind him that he didn't just sit around all day, eating biscuits and drinking wine.

They leave a couple of hours after breakfast, Ray dressed in whatever he found at the bottom of his wardrobe, Gabe decked out in stylish workout clothes that look like they were tailored to him, probably because they were. His hair is hidden under a baseball cap, but since it's an overcast, windy day, he forwent the sunglasses, his eyes bright and cheerful as they set off.

Their conversation meanders just like the dirt paths they take through the fields, interspersed with occasional clusters of trees. Few people are out—a handful of agricultural vehicles, the occasional dog walker or family, Ray stopping a couple of times to greet a familiar face while Gabe hangs back and tries to look unobtrusive.

"It's like a reverse version of the Arsenal game," Ray tells Gabe with a laugh after he bid goodbye to a neighbour's daughter who's home for the holidays. Three years older than Ray, she hung out with Farah sometimes, but left town before things went sour for him. It's easier with people like that, people who don't look at him with either pity or mild suspicion.

"A reverse?" Gabe moves in a sure, light-footed trot next to Ray, his breathing barely even accelerated.

"The way I remember it, the Arsenal game included me trying to blend into the tapestry while you were humouring people who wanted selfies." Ray offers a grin. "Not that I'm a star around here—infamous to some, at best."

Gabe purses his mouth. "Not your fault that some of your classmates were dickheads."

"Nah. But I'm glad that at least my secondary school wasn't in town, so it didn't make the rounds here quite as much. Even gladder to have gotten out entirely."

"You really do love London, huh?"

"I love the anonymity, I guess. The side streets, the history of it, the old squares and Victorian buildings, all that. I could do without bumping elbows in the Tube every morning, though." Ray glances at the lines of Gabe's profile—the generous bow of his mouth and his dark lashes, the slightly stubborn tilt of his nose. "Why? You getting tired of L.A.?"

"Maybe." Gabe's smile comes with a quick flash of white, even teeth. "I like London. Been thinking about getting a flat there. Although when I'm out like this... I do love being in the countryside, you know? There's more space here."

"All hail Captain Obvious." Ray gives the words a teasing twist, steering carefully clear of Gabe's throwaway comment about a flat in London. Even if Gabe did get a pied-à-terre—well, it might not mean very much because he's *busy*. It's obvious how much he loves his sister, yet he rarely sees her. How could Ray expect any different?

"*Hey*." Gabe laughs again, and it's the most lively Ray has seen him since he washed up on Ray's doorstep, four days and a lifetime ago. "Stop making fun of me. I'm kind of a big deal, you know."

"Sorry, excuse me!" Ray gestures grandly at people who don't exist. "Can you please make some way for this guy's ego? Thank you!"

They're both grinning now, Ray's breath coming in sharp little bursts, but he doesn't want to slow down, wants to stay in this moment until the lights go down and the band begins to play.

"Left or right?" Gabe asks, and Ray didn't even realise they've come up to a familiar fork in the road—left is an agricultural path that would take them back in a fairly direct route, right means a detour past the golf course. Ray hasn't been there since the funeral reception, but he can't spend the rest of his life trying to outrun his triggers.

"Right," he tells Gabe. "We can have some water at the golf course before we turn around. Shouldn't be too busy today, so I don't think it'll be a problem with the whole…" He gestures at Gabe's face. "You being you thing. Most of the people there are older anyway."

"Well, I'll have to reenter society at some point." A fraction of Gabe's mirth fades, but it doesn't disappear entirely. "Lead the way."

A winding road takes them through patches of bare trees and overgrown bushes, held back by a wooden fence on one side and a low brick wall on the other. They're just a minute away from the clubhouse, perhaps two, when Ray notices snatches of music drifting towards them—the familiar strains of a Beatles song that blends into *Singin' In the Rain*. He stops, and Gabe draws to a halt a couple of steps ahead.

"What's wrong?"

"They don't usually play music."

Gabe's forehead wrinkles. "Some kind of party?"

"Maybe." A car approaches from behind them, and Ray takes a step to the side to make room on the narrow road. "What do you want to do?"

Gabe inhales and holds the air for a moment before he exhales in a rush. "I can't hide forever," he says, even as he tugs the baseball cap down and angles away as the car passes them.

"We can turn around," Ray offers.

"Let's not." Gabe's smile is delayed by half a beat, tentative. "You said there's a drinking fountain, right?"

"Yeah." Ray watches Gabe for another moment, just in case he changes his mind, but Gabe's face is determined, a stubborn set to his mouth.

All right, then. If anyone recognises Gabe... It seems unlikely that reporters would come running based on some random claim about a Gabe Duke sighting. As long as there are no pictures, the risk should be limited.

"Hey, it'll be fine." Gabe sounds more certain now, his smile growing, brightening. "I walked Charlie to the train station, and no one even gave me a second glance. People are much more likely to recognise me in places where I'm expected to be, and this isn't one."

It really isn't, and in his workout clothes, with the baseball cap hiding his trademark curls, Gabe looks a far cry from his polished Hollywood image. Of course a real fan would recognise him, but if they stick to the edges of the parking lot, stop quickly at the water fountain, and then continue along the footpath that winds through the golf court, the chances of running into someone with a Green Hunter poster on the wall are rather slim.

"Should have dyed your hair blue," he tells Gabe. "That would throw them off."

"Would make me blend right in at an Avatar convention, too," Gabe agrees.

"There are Avatar conventions?"

"Probably part of Comic Con." When Gabe sets back into motion at an easy pace, Ray falls into step with him. "Can't say I ever paid much attention—I usually just sign some stuff and hang around for whatever panel I'm on. Could be fun to get dressed up and just drift with the crowd."

"Think they'd let you borrow your Green Hunter costume for that? You could enter a Gabe Duke look-alike contest. Might even win."

"Ha." Gabe releases an undignified snort, eyes dancing. "Tempting, but if anything happened to the costume, the studio would have my hide."

"I keep forgetting that you never got around to collecting your sense of adventure from the dry cleaners."

It's a throwback to when they were just getting to know each other. Gabe's mind might be travelling along a similar path because his lips tug up. "Hey, whatever happened to the pictures of that skeleton picnic?"

"Patrick added them to our online photo album of dares."

"There's an album and no one told me? I thought we were friends!"

"I'll show you when we get back."

The clubhouse appears around the corner—it's nothing special, just a painfully average, orange-painted stone building with a sprawling parking lot out front, but when the town council reclaimed ownership of it some years ago, they planted native trees, added wildflower areas to attract pollinators, and made memberships affordable to normal people like Patrick's parents.

A sign outside the house announces a private function, faint voices now mingling with the music, but to Ray's relief, the wind seems to keep people inside. Other than a couple of smokers near the entrance, he doesn't spot any movement around the parking lot. The car that just arrived seems to have emptied out already.

Funny—Ray remembers a time when he didn't scan his surroundings for potentially hostile life forms.

They arrive at the water fountain without any incident, both of them quiet, Ray's thoughts zipping back to the funeral reception. It's been only three years, but Allie had looked so much younger then. Jazmin's hair was still black rather than pink, Farah pregnant and leaning on her husband who walked out on her some three months later, and Ray's mum so very pale, narrowly keeping it together. His own grief had taken a backseat to organising the buffet, narrowing down the choice of urns, thanking people for showing up, for flowers and cards.

Absently, Ray waves for Gabe to have some water first, the music swelling behind him for a moment before Ben E. King resumes asking his darling to stand by him at a reduced volume.

"I haven't been here since my dad's funeral." Ray isn't sure why he feels a need for Gabe to know. "Things were so fucked up back then —Jaz drifted for a bit, probably did some drugs as well, and Fay's idiot husband left her and the kids not long after, and Allie had to grow up so quickly, you know?"

Gabe steps back from the fountain, his eyes huge and of an almost translucent green. "I'm so sorry, Ray. Your dad sounds like such a great person. I would have loved to meet him."

"He would have liked you." The words get stuck in Ray's throat, and he has to look away from Gabe so he doesn't cry. "I still miss him, even now."

"Of course you do." Gabe reaches for Ray's wrist, his fingers wet from the fountain, yet the touch is still comforting. He's about to add something when his gaze flicks to the side, eyes narrowing at something.

"Ray?" someone asks.

The voice is familiar. Ray whips his head around, instantly on high alert, adrenaline flooding his system before he recognises the face.

Xander.

Fucking *Xander*, carrying a box with used plates, clearly on his way to the van parked just steps away. *Lee & Son Catering* is scrawled across its side in big, blue letters, and if Ray hadn't been so distracted by memories and watching out for Gabe, he would have noticed.

"Xander. Hi."

It's rusty nails on wallpaper, Ray's tongue slow like a drunkard's, and hi? *Hi*?! 'Screw you' is what he should have said. Except his body is stuck between fight and flight, ice flowing through his veins, hot shivers zapping along his skin. *Fuck*.

Xander sets the plates down and draws a couple of steps closer, gaze raking Ray. "How've you been?" he asks—as though they're friends, as though he wasn't a big part of why Ray suffered from panic attacks some mornings before school. It wasn't like they beat him up, nothing that overt, but any corner he turned, a derisive comment could be waiting, whispers and stares following him, half-muffled laughter that only stopped when Patrick was around because Patrick fought dirty and never lost a war of words.

"I'm..."

Mostly all right most of my days. Glad to have gotten the hell out of this town. Still fucked up by what you put me through.

"Hey!" It's Gabe, his tone bright and bubbly in a way that feels immediately off, and oh no, oh *fuck*. Gabe shouldn't be talking to anyone, shouldn't be talking to Xander, of all people. The bright burst of concern shakes Ray out of his daze.

He tries to manoeuvre himself between them, but it's too late: Xander's gaze snags to Gabe's face. Gabe has taken off his baseball cap, and Christ, why would he do that, can't he see that Xander is foe not friend, is not someone to *trust*? Yet Gabe seems utterly at ease, his arm winding around Ray's waist and drawing them close together.

"Hi," Xander mumbles, even that one word conveying effort. His attention drops to where Gabe's fingers are curled into Ray's hoodie.

"Hi, how's it going?" A multimillion dollar smile and a tiny pause before Gabe adds, "I'm Gabe—Gabe Duke."

What is he *doing*? It's an unnecessary clarification, too, given Xander's dad has been an avid subscriber to *The Daily Mail* for years —back when they pretended to be just friends, Ray was no stranger to the Lee household.

"I'm..." Xander appears to need a moment to locate his own name, and Ray idly wonders if Xander is actually a fan, whether he jerked off to shirtless pictures of Gabe before he went back to faking an interest in whatever girl would please his parents. "Xander. Uh, Lee. A friend of Ray's from school."

Ray can't help the tiny snort that escapes him.

"A friend?" Gabe repeats it slowly, as though he's doing a mental review of everything Ray would have told him about his miserable A-Levels experience. "Xander, huh... Unusual name."

Gabe's thumb is rubbing circles into Ray's waist, and suddenly,

Ray gets it. Gabe *knows*, and he's chosen to prop Ray up rather than protect himself by fading into the background. Fuck, Ray loves him.

Ray loves him.

The rush of blood to his head almost makes him miss out on Gabe's next words.

"Wait, you're that guy Ray dated briefly, right?" Gabe leans forward, smile sharpening, and 'briefly' meant half a year, but who's counting? "Your loss is my gain, mate. Hope you got over your internalised heterosexism, though."

"Everyone's an idiot at seventeen," Xander states weakly, and fuck him. Ray's still dizzy with the enormity of his realisation, a hollow ache in his bones, but *fuck* Xander. He has no right to casually imply that what he did was no worse than staying out late or failing to hand in a piece of homework.

"Everyone's an idiot?" Ray surprises himself with how steady he sounds. "Is that all you have to say for yourself, really? *Everyone's an idiot?*"

Xander's nostrils flare. "You know what my dad's like!"

"I didn't expect you to hold my hand while waving a fucking rainbow flag!" Ray gives a harsh laugh, and fuck, it feels good to say this. "It was my decision to come out, and I knew you didn't have it in you. That was fine. What's not fine, though, is how you turned around and appointed yourself the bloody leader of the homophobia united brigade."

"They never laid a hand on you!" The words sound squeezed and Xander follows them up with a hectic glance around because it seems that some things just don't change. Ray leans into Gabe's warmth and reaches for a sarcastic smile.

"Oh, so you're going to take credit for that?"

"They might have, if I hadn't steered things."

The protest is weak, and Ray shakes his head. "Yeah, sure. Or they might have lost interest in me after five minutes and moved on to the next thing."

Xander looks ill, and Ray expected to draw satisfaction from that, but somehow, it just makes him realise how much he doesn't care. If

Xander wants to spend the rest of his life stuck in this town pretending to be straight, that's his choice. It's got nothing to do with Ray.

"Anyway." Quite deliberately, Ray turns to look at Gabe and feels an effortless smile slide onto his face, something that sits warm and golden in his chest. "I think we're done here. Let's go?"

"Let's," Gabe agrees—and instead draws Ray into a kiss that starts out no different than the ones they've shared before, a gentle brush of lips, Ray curving further into it with his fingertips coming to rest against the side of Gabe's neck. It's pure inspiration or momentary insanity that prompts him to nudge at the seam of Gabe's mouth with his tongue. Gabe opens easily, beautifully, like a flower angling towards the sun.

When Ray draws back, his entire world is reduced to the flutter of Gabe's lashes, irises a slim ring of green around his blown-out pupils. Ray's heart slides up into his throat.

"Let's go?" he repeats, a whisper, distantly aware that Xander is moving away, that there's still a world beyond Gabe, but none of it truly matters.

Gabe breathes, smiles. "Yeah. Let's go."

16

It's sweet torture.

When they return, lunch is ready, and then Deborah wants to go for a walk. Gabe loves his sister, he does, but with electricity still humming in his bones, he's not as focused on their conversation as he should be.

"What's with you today?" she asks eventually, when he barely reacts to her teasing about how he should reach out to his celebrity crush Ben Jimmer, see if the guy's marriage could use a bit of spice.

"I think..." Gabe stops walking, and it's only once he says it that he realises it's true. "I think I'm ready now. To, like ... face the world again. Talk to the press, tell my side of the story. Come out properly, you know?"

She purses her mouth, considering him. "You know you don't owe it to anyone, right?"

"I know." He does, mostly. But the reality is that his job comes with a price tag, and media attention and regular invasions of privacy are part of that calculation—if he can't stand the heat, he can always get out of the kitchen. Staying is a choice, and it's the one he's making. "I want to, though. Our parents forced my hand, yeah, but I get to decide where I go from here. Feels like I've been hiding long enough."

Hiding out with Ray and, for years now, hiding in the closet. Not everyone will love Gabe for showing just a little more of who he truly is, but that's okay; you can't win them all.

"Really?" Deborah grips his shoulder, beaming. "*Good* for you."

"Thank you." He covers his hand with her own and holds on for a second, inhaling until no more air will fit into his lungs. There are arrangements he needs to make, arrangements such as informing his agent, for a start, and none of that will yet solve the question of how Ray is going to fit into Gabe's future although Gabe knows for sure that he wants Ray in it.

Maybe Gabe doesn't need to have all the answers just yet.

Deborah gives his hand a squeeze, her entire face softening. "Proud of you, little bro."

"Thank you," he repeats, and because he's tired of feeling like he's just about to cry, he changes the topic to a potential spring trip to Paris.

When they get back, it's to a full house, and Gabe plays with Jess for a bit, helping her assemble a magic Lego castle that's meant for kids a little older than her. All the while, Gabe is aware of Ray's presence in the room, of the heaviness in Ray's eyes every time their gazes meet.

They should pause, *think*.

Gabe doesn't want to think. When Ray gets up, muttering something about fetching a book from his room, it feels like an invitation. So Gabe waits for a couple of minutes before he extracts himself and makes as if to head for the bathroom on the ground floor, then turns to sneak up the stairs instead, his socked feet soundless on the steps.

The moment Gabe creaks open the door, Ray fists a hand in the front of Gabe's jumper and drags him fully into the room. Gabe has never been kissed like this before—pushed up against the wall, bracketed in by Ray's body, noses bumping before they find the right angle. Then it's open mouths and soft, desperate noises, the quiet smack of their lips when they separate and come back together, daylight painting the back of Gabe's lids in silvered shadows. He's aware of every single point of contact—Ray's thigh a solid weight against Gabe's groin, Ray's fingers digging into the dent by Gabe's hipbone, the warm gust of breath each time Ray exhales.

A thump just outside the door makes them jolt apart. Jasper starts wailing a second after, clearly awoken from his afternoon nap in a bit of a strut.

"Later." Ray makes it sound like a promise, the slight rasp to his voice more pronounced than usual.

Gabe thinks of a line they'd drawn just days ago, washed away by the incoming tide.

He ducks back in for one more kiss and lets his hands skate down Ray's sides, imagines dropping to his knees right here, in broad daylight, the curtains open to a grey sky. Pictures Ray watching him, fingers in Gabe's hair, biting his lip to stay quiet.

Pulling away is not the hardest thing Gabe has ever done, but it isn't terribly far off either.

"Later," he agrees. One last look at Ray's parted lips, then he forces himself to slip out of Ray's room before his resolve caves in.

※

THERE'S something excruciatingly delicious about having to wait.

Gabe's previous encounters tended to be quite to the point—a distinct vibe he caught from someone, some banter to test the water, and an unambiguous plan to meet away from prying eyes. This is different. It's stolen glances and the secret brush of Ray's knuckles against Gabe's arse as they pass each other in the kitchen, it's their feet bumping under the table, it's Ray watching Gabe's mouth close around a spoonful of ice cream.

By the time Ray's mum is gone and it's socially acceptable to get ready for bed, Gabe feels flushed, his heart glowing and his skin on fire.

Ray is sitting on the edge of the bed when Gabe walks in, a book open in his lap, still in jeans but with his shirt off. The curtains are drawn, only the gentle gleam of the lamp on the bedside table illuminating the scene.

Gabe closes the door with a soft snap. "Fuck. *Look* at you."

"That's my line." Ray sets the book aside and rises to his feet. He's leaner than Gabe, subtly muscled, and Gabe drinks him in, thinks about taking his own T-shirt off but wants Ray to do it for him. With a smile, he leans back against the wall, tipping his hips forward as he holds Ray's gaze.

"Bloody hell," Ray mutters. Then he's in Gabe's space, right up against him, crushed together from head to toe. *Kiss me*, Gabe thinks —says, maybe, because Ray does, his thumb against the dip between Gabe's collarbones, and Gabe tilts his head back just a tiny bit and lets himself fall.

Then there's nothing, Gabe's hands grasping at air.

He slits his eyes open and finds Ray an arm's length away, watching Gabe with a heavy, glittering gaze. "Let me see you," he whispers, and for a moment, Gabe is confused because Ray already *is* —this is Gabe, all of him, everything he has.

Then his brain stutters back into gear. Clothes, right.

Something about the way Ray looks at him invites Gabe to take his time, so he does—lets his fingers linger on the button of his jeans before he moves to grasp the hem of his T-shirt, tugging it up with a slow smile. He's never been self-conscious about his body, but the way Ray focuses on him as though Gabe is all he sees... Jesus, it's addictive.

When Gabe's naked, there's a pause, as though the world is holding its breath while Ray looks his fill. Gabe deliberately widens his smile, unashamed to use the dimples God gave him. "Kiss me, please?"

"In a minute. Let me just..." With a grin, Ray uses his hands to frame Gabe for an imaginary shot with an invisible camera. "There."

It's silly and perfect, reminding Gabe that they're still *them*. He flexes his biceps for another pretend shot, laughing when Ray takes it, and then they're kissing again, Gabe gripping Ray's shoulders, Ray dragging his knuckles over Gabe's abs and down to the base of Gabe's erection.

"Think I want your mouth on my dick," Ray says into the space between two kisses, and God, yes, Gabe is so very down with that. He pulls them over to the bed and sits down on the edge of the mattress, bringing Ray in with both hands on the curve of his bum.

It feels like burning up, running a fever Gabe doesn't want to sweat out, and that's a song title, isn't it? His mind trips over details like Ray's stifled groan when Gabe unzips his jeans and takes Ray in for the first time, the heady scent of arousal, the intense focus on Ray's face as though he's afraid to look away. When Ray nudges Gabe back with gentle hands cupping his face, Gabe resists for a second before he glances up through his lashes.

Ray's Adam's apple bobs when he swallows. "What do you want?"

Gabe rests his cheek against Ray's stomach as he considers his answer. If he has his way, this will be the first time of many, many more, so there's no rush. And yet...

"Anything. *Everything.*" He turns his head to kiss Ray's stomach. "I want you to take me. If that's, you know. Something you'd enjoy."

"Something I'd enjoy?" Ray repeats incredulously. Since Gabe catches the twitch of Ray's dick, he's pretty sure of Ray's answer even before Ray abruptly curses and pushes Gabe over onto his back, following him down. Then they're back to kissing, Ray twisting fully out of his jeans before he slithers down Gabe's body to settle between his legs, mouthing at Gabe's dick while he works him open with lube from the bedside drawer, Gabe biting his own hand to stifle any sounds that could otherwise escape.

He must lose track of time because it might be minutes or hours later when Ray makes his way back up Gabe's body, mapping the path with small, feather-light kisses. His eyes are dark and half-lidded when they meet Gabe's. "I don't have condoms."

We don't need them.

God, Gabe wants that. It'd be a first, but no matter how much he trusts Ray, no matter how convinced he is that he himself is clean— they should get tested first, just in case.

"My suitcase," he says. "The lid. Small inside pocket."

"Okay." Ray nods, a faint downward twist to his mouth as he slides off the bed. It might be nothing, or he might be wondering how often Gabe gets laid, whether this is business as usual for him. It couldn't be farther from that.

Gabe props himself up on his elbows, both because it shows off his chest and also allows him to watch as Ray crosses the room and bends down by Gabe's suitcase. "Check the expiry date," he tells Ray, even though he knows it's fine. "Been quite a while since … you know. I think they're still good, though."

Ray turns the box over as he returns to the bed. "They're fine," he says, the odd twist to his mouth replaced by a smile.

"Awesome." Gabe lets his thighs fall open and smiles back. "How do you want me, then?"

"Any way I can have you." Ray glances away immediately after, ducking his head, and it's only after Gabe kisses him long and hard that Ray meets his eyes again. He shines bright like a beacon, and fuck, Gabe would pick him out of any crowd, any day.

"Ray," he whispers, not even sure whether it's a request or a confession.

"Yeah." It feels like an answer and blends right into another deep kiss, so many of them added up by now that any hint of the minty toothpaste is gone. They didn't turn off the bedside lamp, and Gabe is glad for it—he nearly loses his breath watching Ray roll on the condom with a concentrated frown, biting his lip, dark eyebrows pulled together.

Everything flows.

Ray moving into and over Gabe. Gabe's arms around Ray, his legs on Ray's shoulders. Hot air caught between them, and no one has ever meant this much, pulled Gabe under and lifted him up, loved him like this, been loved by him like this.

No one.

Just Ray.

Ray.

17

Gabe wakes up in increments, like a hypnotically slow fade-in.

Sunlight, turning the dark brown curtains a warm shade of amber. The weight of Ray's arm around him. Naked skin, legs tangled, their bodies pressed together under a duvet that's meant for one.

Ray's mum—her laughter drifting through the closed door along with Jasper's morning giggles. She must have woken him up after returning from her night shift.

Shit, they need to get up. Jasper has taken a real shine to Gabe, and at three years, he is able to open a door but not respect the reasons for why it might be closed. Gabe doesn't want to keep this a secret, but he'd prefer for Ray's family to learn about them in a way that doesn't include finding them naked and wrapped around each other in a room that might still smell like sex.

"Ray."

No reaction.

Gabe turns in Ray's embrace and runs a finger from Ray's forehead down the bridge of his nose, lets it rest against his bottom lip. "Hey. *Ray.*"

Ray drags in a slow breath before his eyes open, taking a second to focus. Once they do, he stares at Gabe for a long moment as though his brain is lagging several beats behind reality.

"Good morning," Gabe says, grinning a little as he taps Ray on the nose.

God, he's in love with him. He is, and maybe Ray isn't quite there yet, but if last night is any indication, he can't be far behind. They can make this *work*.

"Gabe?" Ray's voice sounds as though he's still waking up, and it makes Gabe's grin widen.

"Who else?" He doesn't wait for an answer. "Now, much as I'd love to spend the day in bed…" Silly as it is, he taps Ray's nose again before he leans in for a close-mouthed kiss, only pulling back once Ray starts responding. "Much as I'd love to spend the day in bed, we should put in an appearance before your family decides to wake us up."

"Right." Ray still sounds half asleep, and when Gabe smiles, it's a beat before Ray smiles back, gaze sliding away. Something ugly quivers in Gabe's stomach, but he ignores it.

Ray isn't much of a morning person. Surely that's all there is to it.

Gabe rolls out of bed and stretches leisurely, reassured when Ray's gaze snags to him like it's instinct, like he couldn't look away even if he wanted to. It's heady, and Gabe exaggerates the sway of his hips just the tiniest bit when he walks over to his suitcase and crouches down to dig for some fresh clothes.

When he glances over his shoulder, Ray is sitting up in bed, staring at his hands with an almost pained expression. *Not a morning person.*

Gabe bundles his clothes in his arms and stops by the side of the mattress, ducks down for another kiss. To his relief, Ray responds immediately this time, almost desperately—he raises a hand that he tangles in Gabe's curls to hold him in place, nudges Gabe's mouth open with his own.

Well, Gabe can worry about morning breath, or he can kiss Ray. It's not a difficult choice.

After they separate, they stare at each other for a moment, breathing, Gabe's heart throwing itself against the cage of his ribs in an attempt to escape. *I love you*, he thinks, very nearly says it, but this isn't the right time.

Soon, though. Soon.

He makes it to the bathroom without running into anyone, gets cleaned up and tames his hair, turning himself into a presentable young man who doesn't look like he stayed up late having sex with the family's only son—something he would very much like to repeat, for the record.

By the time he joins Margaret, Allie, Farah, and both her kids in the kitchen, Ray already beat him there. He must have used the bathroom on the ground floor and moved more quickly than Gabe, wasted a little less time grinning at himself in the mirror. When Gabe enters, Ray glances up, smiles, and returns his full focus to his eggs.

"Your phone's on the kitchen counter, love," Margaret informs Gabe with an absent flick of her hand before she turns a page of the morning paper. "You must have forgotten it last night. It's been buzzing a few times since I sat down, so you may want to check that."

"It's been buzzing basically non-stop for years," Gabe says, "and worse in the last few days. Whatever it is can wait."

"That's the spirit," Farah says. "Show your phone who's boss."

"That'd be me." Gabe sits down, but doesn't help himself to some food right away. While he'd prefer to do this with Jazmin present, he doesn't want to wait until lunch to say what's been itching under his skin since his walk with Deborah yesterday. This morning, he feels more certain than ever.

"D'you want some orange juice?" Allie, seated next to Gabe, holds up the bottle after serving herself.

"Thanks, yes." He draws a deep breath and tries to catch Ray's eyes, but doesn't succeed. All right, here goes nothing. Addressing the table at large, Gabe announces, "So, I've been thinking."

"Dangerous habit," Allie says.

Ray looks up with a smirk that doesn't quite reach his eyes. "For you, maybe."

Jess giggles while Margaret sighs, shaking her head.

Sudden hesitation grips Gabe. Should he have this discussion with Ray first? After all, if Gabe has anything to say about it, Ray will be directly affected. Gabe could still swerve to another topic, but Ray's family has been nothing but amazing, taking him in as a guest over the holidays, making him feel more welcome, more at home, than his own parents did even before they kicked him out.

"Gabe?" It's Margaret, her voice gentle. "Something you wanted to say?"

"Yeah." This time, Gabe manages to hold Ray's eyes, if only for a moment, before he expands his attention to the entire table. "I think I'm ready to face things. You've all been *so* fantastic, and I honestly don't know how I can possibly thank you—"

"Chris Hemsworth's number would be a start." Allie again, and Gabe grins at her, his big announcement feeling a lot lighter already, like yes, he can face the media and his fans, and the world will keep on turning, no big deal.

"I'll see what I can do."

"You said you're ready to face things?" Margaret reaches across the table to give Gabe's hand a squeeze. "Are you sure? There's no shame in taking a few more days—whatever time you need."

"*Mum*," Jasper demands, and Farah shushes him, gesturing for Gabe to continue.

"I'm sure, yeah." Gabe lets his smile show and hopes it conveys the certainty he feels. Enough hiding—to use Charlie's analogy, it's about time for Gabe to swagger into his parents' party, change the music, and ask the bouncer to throw the previous hosts out on their arses. "I'll ask my agent to set up an interview with someone like Oprah or Jimmy Kimmel or Monica Muswell, assuming they're interested. Not sure how soon it'd be, but ... yeah. Next few days, I hope."

"Excuse me," Ray mumbles. His fork clutters to the table, and then he's out of his seat and out of the kitchen. A moment later, there's some commotion in the entrance area, followed by the slam of the front door. Gabe remains in his chair, staring at the empty space where Ray was only moments ago.

What just happened?

Brief silence settles in the kitchen, even Jasper seeming to sense the shift in atmosphere, pausing in his attempts to wheedle another Christmas biscuit out of his mum.

"Oh dear." Margaret is first to speak again, her eyes sharp and knowing when she finds Gabe's. "I take it you didn't think to inform my son that you're leaving?"

"I'm not leaving!" Gabe protests. "I mean, yeah, the interview will be in L.A., probably, so I'll be gone for a bit, but I'm not *leaving*. I'm..." *I'm in love with him.* He can't tell Ray's family before he tells Ray himself, so he finishes on another, "I'm *not* leaving."

"And does Ray know that?" Margaret asks, gentler now.

"He... I mean, he should." Gabe glances around the kitchen—at Allie's quirked eyebrow and Farah's patient smile, Jess's confused expression, Jasper drinking from a glass of water that he holds with both hands—before he looks back at Ray's mum, feeling all the air escape from his lungs. "I thought it was obvious."

The hint of a grin deepens the faint lines around Margaret's eyes. "Well, you may want to go after him, then. Just to make sure he understands how obvious it is."

"Right, yeah. Good idea." Gabe jumps to his feet, then stops halfway to the door. "Any idea where he would go?"

Allie waves a hand. "If you don't catch him heading towards the fields, try Patrick."

Patrick. Of course—just like Gabe would run to Charlie, Ray will turn to Patrick. The address should still be saved in the GPS from when Gabe dropped Patrick off a few days ago.

"Thank you," Gabe tells Allie before he dashes out of the kitchen.

"Run, Forrest, run!" Allie calls after him, and even though Gabe's stomach is twisted up in sick little knots, he huffs out a small laugh as he shoves his feet into his shoes and grabs the jacket Ray has been letting him wear off its hook.

It's just a misunderstanding. That's all it is. He'll catch up to Ray, and he'll explain, and he'll *fix* this.

He will.

~

Icy morning air hits Gabe like a slap in the face, chasing away the last dregs of confusion. The temperature must have dropped by several degrees overnight, the sun still pale and weak at this hour.

Where did Ray go?

He's got maybe three minutes on Gabe—not a big head start, not as such, but enough for Ray to disappear if Gabe turns the wrong way. Except…

Gabe squints at the lone figure on the other side of the train tracks, skirting along the edges of a field. With the sun in his eyes, Gabe struggles to make out details, but something in him knows it's Ray—instinctive pattern recognition, fast thinking, whatever Charlie likes rambling about whenever they get drunk and Gabe is only half-listening. It's Ray, closer than Gabe expected, and Gabe's gut clenches at the possibility of Ray pausing outside the house, waiting for Gabe to jump up and follow him right away, counting to ten, to thirty, to sixty, before giving up.

Giving up on *Gabe*.

Well, that's not going to fly. Gabe heads left at a fast trot, towards the crossing, and then turns right as soon as he's over the tracks, choosing a dirt path that Ray must have taken, too. It doesn't look as though Gabe has been noticed just yet; now that he's closer, he can tell that Ray is walking with his head down, shoulders up against the cold, hands shoved into the pockets of his winter jacket.

Maybe Gabe can get him to wear the Burberry coat. Since it's tailored to Gabe's body, it would be a bit big around Ray's shoulders, but he's got the height and face to cut a dramatic figure in it. Does it count as Gabe fulfilling his endorsement obligations if it's his boyfriend wearing the clothes?

Getting ahead of himself here.

Or maybe not, because Ray *cares*. He wouldn't have left like that if he didn't.

Gabe's close enough now that all it would take is for Ray to lift his head and glance back, but he doesn't. The dry ground is clumpy with tractor tracks, so Gabe has to watch his step even as he picks up the pace.

"Ray!"

Ray jerks around as though he's been hit by a rubber bullet. The sun is behind him, flowing around his silhouette and washing out the details of his face. "Gabe."

He sounds ... resigned, Gabe decides. After crossing the final few metres between them in a jog, Gabe draws to a halt in front of Ray and takes a moment to drink in his face, both of their breaths coming out in little clouds.

Gabe tilts his head and widens his eyes. "I'm sorry about earlier. I should have spoken to you first—didn't realise how it was going to sound."

Ray blinks, shadows dancing around his expression. "It's fine. I'm sorry, too—I didn't mean to make a scene."

It's not quite what Gabe was expecting. "You didn't mean to make a scene?"

"Yeah. I mean, it's on me, right?" Ray exhales in a small burst of fog. "Not like you promised me anything, so it's really not your fault."

"My fault?"

"It's not," Ray clarifies, except it doesn't clarify a thing for Gabe.

"What, exactly, is it that's not my fault?"

Ray raises his gaze, eyebrows drawn together, something deliberately brave about the way he holds Gabe's eyes. "That I was stupid enough to fall in love with you."

He says it like it's news of a diagnosis—*terribly sorry to inform you that little Johnny here is suffering from asthma*. Gabe starts forward, smiling, a weightless feeling in his chest as though he's been released from gravity.

"Me too. *Me too*, Ray."

Ray shies away, and it stops Gabe cold. For a few moments, they're simply breathing, a gap between them that could be easily bridged in two steps, but Gabe doesn't dare move.

"What's wrong?" he asks, gravity wrapping its tendrils around him once more.

"This won't work." Ray sounds no less resigned than he did when Gabe caught up with him, and that doesn't make *sense*.

"What do you mean?" Gabe shakes his head. "I'm in love with you, Ray. I'm in love with you, and you just told me you're in love with me. It's simple, isn't it?"

"It's really not." And now Ray's voice rises, his arms crossed against the cold, his gaze fixed on a point just above Gabe's shoulder. "Your world is crazy, Gabe. There's no space in it for someone like me."

"I'd like to think it's *my* decision who I make space for in my life."

"But it's not!" Briefly, their gazes tangle and hold, then Ray's flits away again, skittish like a nocturnal animal fleeing the light. "You've got fans, and an image, and the media is all over you. I don't belong there. I'd be laughed out of the room."

"Is this about the attention?" Gabe's attempt at a scoff scrapes painfully along the back of his throat. "I mean, *really*? You're rejecting me because strangers might be mean on the internet?"

Ray tips his chin up. "I don't want to be the guy Gabe Duke dated for five seconds before he got bored."

Any irritation Gabe might have felt drains away, leaving him light-headed. "You think I'll ditch you, just like those dickheads you dated. *Ray*." He tries for a smile, tries to catch Ray's eyes as he takes a tiny, tiny step forward. "I'm in *love* with you."

Ray ducks his head and looks away.

"You don't believe me."

Silence, again.

"I'm not—with the interview, yeah, I'd probably do that in L.A. because the biggest shows are there. I do travel for work, but that doesn't mean that I'm *leaving*. Like, my homebase doesn't have to be in the US" The more Gabe talks, the faster the words come. "I was going to look for a flat in London. You think I'd do that if I wasn't planning long-term?"

Ray is beautiful, so very beautiful, but his derisive chuckle is ugly. "People like you don't stay, Gabe."

It feels like someone emptied a bucket of ice water over Gabe's head. He sucks in a breath, winter in his lungs. "People like me?"

A flicker of regret, then Ray clenches his jaw and meets Gabe's gaze. "You've left before. You'll do it again."

"I fucking *love* you, Ray!" Again, like a broken record, but it's all Gabe has. He can't fall to his knees and beg, he can't whip out a ring or recite some heartfelt poem—if Ray doesn't believe that Gabe is worth the risk, there's just ... nothing.

Absolutely nothing.

"It doesn't matter, does it?" Gabe's entire body feels like one big bruise, with his chest having borne the worst of the impact. "You don't believe me, so whatever I say, it all means nothing."

Ray's silence is answer enough.

"Okay." Gabe bites his lip, the sharp sting of pain providing him with a focus point. He squints against the biting cold and allows himself one last look at Ray—the curve of his mouth, the regal arch of his eyebrows—before he turns away and starts walking.

The dirt path requires all his attention, and Gabe keeps his gaze on the ground, vision swimming until he blinks to clear it. He tells himself that he isn't hoping for Ray to call him back.

It's good that he isn't, because Ray never does.

～

BY THE TIME Gabe throws his suitcase into the car, there's still no sign of Ray. It's just as well—Gabe doesn't feel like getting his heart run over some more.

He doesn't tell Ray's family much, just that they should ask Ray about what happened because Gabe doesn't really understand it either. Before he leaves, he hugs Ray's sisters one by one, picks Jasper up for a cuddle, and kisses the back of Jess's hand as though she's a princess.

"You'll always be welcome here, Gabe," Margaret says before she draws him in for a hug. When they separate, Gabe has to wipe away a small, useless tear because the reality is that he'll never see these people again.

"Thank you." It comes out choked, and Gabe presses his tongue against the roof of his mouth until grey dots stop dancing in front of his eyes and he feels like he can breathe again.

Ray's family is still gathered on the front lawn when Gabe drives off, waving at him until he turns a corner.

It isn't until he stops for petrol, about an hour later, that he sees Walter's message about the emergence of new pictures that show Gabe and Ray, supplied by an anonymous source. They're in their running gear, about to leave the parking lot of the golf club, and fortunately there's nothing compromising—just two guys out for a run, with one of them happening to be famous. Maybe Xander took them, or maybe it was someone in one of the parked cars.

In the end, it doesn't really matter. Gabe will make sure to be spotted at an airport to draw all attention to himself, and if he's ever asked about Ray, he can truthfully say that there's nothing between them.

Nothing at all.

18

Take a healthy amount of Hollywood fame and stir in some gay scandal, serve hot with a side of family drama.

It must make for an irresistible combination because there's no shortage of willing interviewers. Gabe ends up following Walter's advice by going with Monica Muswell, who started out as a stand-up comedian and sports reporter before she moved to the US for her own talk show. As a fellow Brit, she tends to bring out Gabe's accent, which Walter considers beneficial to the revised image they're trying to build.

Once this is over, Walter deserves an amazing bonus for going above and beyond the call of duty.

When Gabe told him as much, though, Walter dismissed it. "This ain't nothing, kid. I've been in this business for thirty years, and it's a damn luxury that by now, I can afford to take on only clients that I actually like. Until you break five laws in one night, urinate in public, or punch a reporter in front of running cameras, you're one of them."

He's waiting off to the side now along with Gabe's assistant Jade, both of them doing their very best to stay out of the way while showing support. It probably says something about Gabe that his agent and his PA are the closest he got to making real friends in L.A.

—or maybe it just says that he's got the golden touch when it comes to hiring the right people.

Charlie is there as well, bless him. He flew in yesterday and will stay until early January because, in his words, "where there's drama, there is Charlie." They're both pretending it's got nothing to do with keeping Gabe from drifting around his empty house by himself, clutching a bottle of quality vodka.

"Gabe, my dear!" Monica waved at him earlier from across the room, stuck in a makeup chair. Now, she smells of face powder and hairspray, but her smile is real. "How's my favourite superhero?"

"A little less super these days." He gets up to kiss her cheek, then sits back down in his assigned spot on the dark blue sofa. The set was originally built for some online course on interior design, and the eclectic mix of colours and patterns is strangely comforting, like he won't be the only oddity in the room.

"Every hero feels like a zero once in a while. It's good for character development, you see?" She settles in her own assigned spot, the distance between them calculated to convey a friendly atmosphere without dipping into chummy.

"That's fair. But I wouldn't mind skipping to the part where the bad guys are in chains, and it's sunny skies and ice cream for everyone."

"I'm sorry, honey. The despairing-hero-gazing-at-the-burning-world scene is a tried and true classic, and you look so very pretty when you cry." Quite deliberately, she adds a smarmy twist to the compliment that makes him crack a genuine smile. It reminds him that they didn't pick her for the British accent only, but also because his two prior appearances on her show were some of the most relaxed he's ever felt with a talk show host—they fell into an easy rhythm that danced between friendly banter and comical flirting. Gabe's fans had eaten it up.

He hopes that this one, while very different in format from a live audience, will be equally well received.

"It's the magic power of a tragic, lone tear falling from my eye," he confides. "Two wouldn't be manly, but one is *just* right."

Monica is suitably up-to-date on internet trends—part of the job, really—and clearly catches the reference to a Green Hunter meme that made the rounds a year ago, of Gabe's character arriving too late to stop his childhood village from burning to the ground. They'd shot variations of his reaction, but the single slow-motion tear had won, and subsequent captions of the screenshot ranged from *'Me having to wake up before 10 a.m.'* to *'When you're getting roasted in the group chat but text back LOL'*.

"Speaking of rehydrating to combat the loss of blood, sweat, and tears..." Monica nods at someone behind Gabe. "We're about to roll, so just checking if someone already offered you some water, coffee, tea? Whiskey?"

"Flat, no ice."

"The water or the whiskey?"

"As someone recently told me, you can disguise your daytime drinking by hanging a tea bag in your whiskey." He smiles through a flutter of grief. "But water, for now. Thank you."

A glass is put in front of him moments later, and he thanks the young man who brought it. Immediately after, he wonders if he needs to be careful with that kind of thing now, if his every interaction with a guy, any guy, will be scrutinised much more closely from now on.

"Ready?" Monica asks right into that thought.

Gabe turns to face her and breathes in deeply. They told her to ask whatever she wanted because blacklisting topics would only delay the inevitable. Since Gabe spent the past two days pulling eight-hour shifts with his media coach, he's as ready as he'll ever be.

"Hit me," he says with a deliberate, calm authority that settles his own heartbeat.

Monica leans forward to give his knee a gentle pat. "All right, here's what it will look like: we'll start with an intro about who you are—some Green Hunter shots, one as James Watson, a few pictures from events, stuff like that. Cut to *The Daily Mail* headline, add reactions from a couple of your coworkers."

Gordon will be one of them; he checked whether Gabe was fine with him providing a flattering soundbite. Gabe isn't sure who else they asked, but since he's not in the habit of screaming at people or voicing outrageous demands, he hopes it will be another positive comment.

"Clear," he tells Monica.

"Good." She sends him a sweet, soothing smile. "You've got this, Gabe."

Another deep breath. "Thank you."

She nods at someone, and then they're both quiet as they're counted in. *Three*, and Gabe blocks out the rush of blood in his ears; *two*, and he refuses to wonder whether Ray will be watching this at any point; *one*, and he sinks into himself as though it's a role he's playing.

Gabe Duke, Hollywood actor. Boyish charm, killer abs, gay.

Go.

"Some kids," Monica addresses a camera, right on cue, "get Xboxes for Christmas, or maybe a puppy. My guest today, though? His parents decided to surprise him with an exclusive interview for *The Daily Mail*, one in which they just so happened to out him as gay. Tell me, Gabe..." She turns to face him, voice and eyes sympathetic. "Was that an item off your wish list?"

"Not exactly." He flashes his dimples. "Personally, I'd have been happier with a kitschy card and an Amazon voucher."

"Other brands are available," Monica supplies, grinning back. "Now, publicly, you haven't really shared much about your childhood. I know you're from a small village in central England, but that's just about it."

"Yeah, well. I had my reasons." Gabe lets his gaze drift past Monica as well as the camera positioned just over her shoulder that's focused on his face—*one Mississippi, two Mississippi*—then snaps his attention back to her. "The truth is, my parents kicked me out when I was eighteen."

Out of the corner of his eye, he catches a ripple of reactions at his announcement—an assistant clapping a hand to her mouth, the young man who brought Gabe's water straightening abruptly. The production team is too professional to destroy the illusion of it being just Gabe and Monica, though, and so is Gabe: he keeps his gaze on her and waits for the question that will inevitably follow the look of surprised concern on her face.

"Because you were gay?"

And there it is.

Gabe lifts his head and aims for a mix of proud and vulnerable. "Yeah. Because I'm gay."

It's the money shot. He knows it, and Monica does, too. For a moment, neither of them speaks, granting the words the space they deserve.

Monica's eyebrows draw together. "That must have been tough," she says, quiet yet clearly enunciated. "Being kicked out at eighteen."

"Yeah, it wasn't a laugh." Gabe lets one corner of his mouth tug up. "I ended up sleeping on the floor of my friend Charlie's uni room—he's the one who dared me to audition for the Green Hunter. He's here, incidentally." It's a definitive breach of the fourth wall when Gabe nods at a spot off-camera.

"Charlie Doyle, is it?" To her credit, Monica rolls with it. "Lots of rumours flying around about the two of you. You want to comment?"

A real laugh tickles Gabe's throat. "Right. Funny enough, it's actually Charlie who showed me some of that. People ... shipping us? Because they think we're in a relationship, so that makes them shippers?"

"I believe that's the correct term." Grinning, Monica raises a brow. "So?"

"No. I'm sorry—I love the guy to bits, but—"

"Love you too, mate," Charlie calls from off to the side, and one of the cameras swivels around to capture him even if the exchange might end up on the cutting room floor.

"But," Gabe continues, "we've been friends for, like, fifteen years. *Just* friends. He's straight, I'm not, and guess what? It's entirely possible for a gay man to have platonic male friends without falling in love or lust."

"Shocker," Monica says with a sardonic smile.

"I *know*."

A brief pause while the cameras record their faces from various angles.

"Well, if we're talking rumours..." Monica crosses her right leg over the left, her smile softening. "There's another handsome young man we've seen you with a couple of times now—a football match, I believe, and recently, just after Christmas, out for a run?"

It's the one question Gabe didn't train for—not because he didn't see it coming, but because he couldn't stomach the idea of sitting through hours of his media coach grilling him about Ray, about how they'd met, how Gabe felt about him.

Gabe blinks, his composure splintering for just an instant before he claws back control. "He's a friend."

"A friend," Monica repeats, as though it's a concept that needs clarification. Gabe knows the trick and falls for it anyway.

"Yeah. I'm not saying I didn't wish for more than that, but anyone dating me will have to deal with a hefty amount of public attention. It's ... a lot to ask for."

This is where some interviewers might smell blood and go in for the kill—not that Monica didn't already get enough quotes to make it worth her while, but an investigative journalist wouldn't leave it at that. It would change the tone of the interview, though.

"I sense a story there," she says, "but maybe not one you wish to share today." A barely noticeable pause in case he wants to prove her wrong, then she moves on. "Now, some might actually welcome that attention. I remember a few rather public dates—I guess we can still call them that—that you had with singer Cora Wells?"

This one he did prepare. Walter got in touch with Cora's team yesterday to get the stories straight, and she called him a few hours later to wish him luck.

Gabe relaxes slightly and smiles, tilting his head in a way that implies a hint of bashfulness. "She's a friend. I wasn't ready to come out yet, so she did me a favour. Just for the record, though, and since the new year is almost upon us..." He lifts the corners of his mouth. "I wouldn't recommend the Champs Elysees on New Year's Eve as a romantic outing. Gets pretty crowded."

"You don't say." Monica winks, and it reminds Gabe of how Ray used to tease him about that—Gabe's supposed incompetence at winking. He pulls his mind back on track for the next question. "You just said that a year ago, when you were publicly dating Cora Wells, you weren't ready to come out. You're ready now?"

Gabe could turn the other cheek.

He discussed it with his team, whether he should play it safe and stick to his nice, sweet, charming persona, or whether there is room for more complexity. It's the one area where he decided to veer off Walter's preferred path—he has no plans to see his parents anytime soon, so this is the closest he'll get to saying his piece.

"Ready or not—I don't have much of a choice, do I?" There's just a tinge of steel to his tone, and he sits forward, narrowing his eyes and inviting Monica to probe further.

"No, I guess you don't," Monica murmurs, sympathy colouring her words and expression.

"I'm only twenty-one," Gabe says. "It's daunting, putting myself out there like this. If it had been up to me, I'd have waited another year or so, explored a range of other roles, hopefully made more of a name for myself as a character actor." He shakes his head and glances away. "Honestly, I'm still working on my belief that I can bring more to the table than a pretty face."

That was more candid than he'd intended. Monica has the good sense to let the statement sit, her entire body language projecting that she's listening.

"So." Gabe inhales and throws the camera a hard look. "It sucks a bit, having what should have been *my* story, *my* choice, taken away from me by people who were meant to protect me."

Could he have turned the other cheek? Yes. But it feels *good* to have his say. Even if his parents may never watch this, some people in the village will, and it might make them think. In fact, Charlie mentioned that the preacher's son had stopped him on the road for a quick chat about how Gabe was doing, and to make it clear that interviews with *The Daily Mail* weren't the kind of behaviour endorsed by the local church. It's nice to think that in terms of personality, Gabe's first crush wasn't entirely misplaced.

"'A bit' seems like an understatement," Monica says.

The conversation moves on from there—LGBT+ representation in Hollywood, conservative attitudes, and roles Gabe would love to play next. "A good, old-school villain," he says, "or the romantic male lead in a straight rom-com, just to prove that it can be done." Monica picks up on that with no small amount of glee, and together, they riff on the storyline of that rom-com: a meet-cute prompted by Gabe starring in a shampoo commercial, followed by miscommunication and the inevitable big gesture at the end.

By the time they finish the interview, Gabe feels better than he has in days. There's still that fissure in his chest where the wind whistles through, but he suspects it will take a lot more than just a few days for that to close.

It will, though. Given time, it will.

~

"Where is he?"

Ray sits up with a start, his book snapping shut. *Patrick*. Downstairs, voice carrying through the entire house.

"Where *is* that bloody idiot?" Patrick sounds as though he's out for blood, and Ray knows it will be a matter of seconds until the door to his bedroom bangs open.

So. Patrick watched the interview, then.

Ray's family did too, gathered around the telly like it was the mandatory evening news in the sixties. Ray himself left halfway through the opening sequence, just as an attractive BAFTA Award winner called Gabe a class act and actor. He just couldn't make himself sit through watching Gabe smile and be fine without Ray, not when the past two days already tortured him with constant reminders, sideways glances in the supermarket, neighbours asking whether it was really Ray running with that young, gay actor.

Since the interview aired, he's successfully ignored any and all knocks by his family, feigning sleep that he isn't getting at night. There's no chance Patrick will be similarly deterred, though, so Ray shoves a hand through his hair and readies himself for the inevitable.

Patrick doesn't even bother knocking. He just breezes right in, kicks the door shut, and throws himself onto Ray's bed, a tablet bouncing down next to him.

"Come on in, please," Ray says dryly. "Make yourself right at home."

"Shut up, arsehole." Patrick's index finger finds Ray's stomach and gives it a hard jab. "You fucking *lied* to me. You said Gabe left because he wanted to."

"I didn't say that."

Implied it, maybe—after Gabe left, four days ago, Ray walked until his fingers felt as numb as the rest of him, then wound up at Patrick's, who took one look at him and asked, "He left?" When Ray nodded, Patrick pulled him into a hug and started ranting, but quickly stopped when Ray refused to engage.

"You bloody well knew what it looked like when you showed up looking like death warmed over." Another hard prod. "You didn't correct me. Potato, potahto."

"Well, he *left*." Ray can't hold Patrick's gaze so he drops his own, stares down at the bedspread until the pattern starts to blur. "Does it matter why?"

For a beat, Patrick is silent. "Did you watch it?"

"Did I watch what?" Ray asks, deliberately obtuse.

"Don't play dumb. Did you *watch* it?" Each word deserves its own full stop, based on Patrick's pointed emphasis.

Ray swallows. "No. Couldn't handle it."

"See if I care." Patrick huffs. "You, my friend, are on thin ice. So you will shut up, and you will watch what I'm about to show you, and then you and I will have a fucking *talk*."

There's no way out of this—one benefit of having known Patrick since they were both in diapers is that Ray knows a lost battle when he sees it. This is one of them, and even though he feels sick just thinking about Gabe's face and smile, his elegant hands and the rumble of his voice ... *fuck*. The only way Patrick might let this go is if Ray throws up, and he isn't prepared to go quite that far.

His chest is far too small for the mess that fills it. "Okay."

Patrick looks as though he wants to say something in response, then contends himself with a hard stare as he reaches for the tablet. It wakes up to Gabe's smiling face, and maybe Ray will throw up after all.

Fuck, he misses Gabe. Not all the time, just ... most of the minutes of most of his days.

He made the right choice, though. Gabe might have wanted Ray here, tucked away between open fields and a train line that connects to the fourth-largest city in the UK that wouldn't even make it into the US top ten—maybe he did, yeah. But send Gabe back to the real world, to glitzy Los Angeles and people shouting his name, and Ray will seem like a flash of temporary insanity, a *burden*.

He refuses to be anyone's burden, ever again.

"Well," the female interviewer says the moment Patrick presses play. The warm timbre of her voice cuts through Ray's thoughts. "If we're talking rumours... There's another handsome young man we've seen you with a couple of times now—a football match, I believe, and recently, just after Christmas, out for a run?"

And Gabe...

Gabe's entire face falls.

It's a quick thing, maybe a second: Gabe's eyes fill with shadows and loss. Then his lashes quiver, and it's like a screen comes up, a veil pulled over an emotional abyss.

"He's a friend," Gabe says, and Ray wants to scream because he's not; that's not what they are.

"A friend," the host repeats, head tilted and tone curious.

"Yeah." Gabe's voice is low and serious, but the veil stays in place. "I'm not saying I didn't wish for more than that, but anyone dating me will have to deal with a hefty amount of public attention. It's ... a lot to ask for."

The host's focus doesn't waver. "I sense a story there," she says, "but maybe not one you wish to share today."

The tiniest pause, and then the conversation moves on to other things—women Gabe used to date, and how he wasn't ready to come out, not really. Even as Ray aches for him, there's a new, jagged wound that's opened up in his own heart because he didn't *mean* to do this.

He didn't mean to hurt Gabe. All he meant was to protect himself from the inevitable fallout.

Patrick hits pause. "That," he says, quiet now, "was not the face of someone who left because he wanted to."

Ray's breath rattles around the broken glass in his chest. He's still staring at the screen, Gabe's eyes a vibrant green against his winter-pale skin, and Ray loves him so much it feels like a physical weight that's about to crush him.

"I think..." He draws another breath, can't get enough air into his lungs, and turns to meet Patrick's eyes. "I think I messed up."

"I think you did," Patrick agrees, not unkindly.

"He told me he loves me."

No surprise shows on Patrick's face. "And—let me guess—you didn't believe him."

Ray hesitates, thinking back to that stark, icy morning, to Gabe's voice and the look in his eyes. "I believed that he thought he did."

"You just didn't trust him to know himself."

That sounds perhaps even worse, so Ray stays silent.

"Is this about the likes of Xander?" Patrick asks. "Because if it is, I swear to fucking *God*—"

"It's not," Ray interrupts. "I mean, maybe a little. But mostly, it's about Gabe, about... He's *famous*, Pat."

"Oh, is he?" Patrick's tone is sardonic. "I hadn't realised."

"I don't fit into that."

"Because the public scrutiny creeps you out, or because you're not good enough?"

Ray presses his lips together, tugging on the bedspread. "Little bit of A, little bit of B?"

"Prince Joshua," Patrick says. "Jon Bon Jovi, Meryl Streep, Gal Gadot, George Clooney."

"Excuse me?"

"Famous people who married their normal partners."

"I hardly think one of the top human rights lawyers in the world counts as a normal person."

Patrick narrows his eyes. "Ben fucking Jimmer and Henry Brown."

"Jimmer is nowhere near as famous as Gabe, especially nowadays."

"Oh, for fuck's *sake*, Ray! Could you get out of your own fucking way for maybe half a second and entertain the possibility that things with Gabe weren't doomed from the start?"

Ray is about to protest when he remembers Gabe's face—how lost he'd looked, if only for a moment. How small and sad.

Patrick must read something in Ray's silence because his tone softens. "Here's what I think: you'd be okay with the attention if you felt better about yourself. Maybe you wouldn't love it, sure. But you'd handle it."

Fuck. Each time Ray blinks, he sees the shadow of grief in Gabe's eyes.

"Ray?"

"I thought, um." It feels like admitting to a substantial flaw. But this is *Patrick*—the guy who stood by Ray when no one else would, who's been his rock for years and years. "It's the 31st, so I thought I could write down a list of everything that's wrong with my life, decide what changes I want to make. It's just ... New Year's resolutions are kind of silly, right? Not like that ever works."

"I think it's brilliant." Patrick reaches out as if to poke Ray again, but instead, he grips Ray's arm. "And maybe it doesn't work most of the time, but that's because I'm not around to kick some *arse*."

Ray was fully prepared to drop it. He frowns, sitting up a little straighter. "You think it's a good idea?"

"*Yes.*" Patrick's tone brooks no room for doubt.

"Oh." Ray exhales, then covers Patrick's hand with his own, letting the contact ground him. "Okay. I guess I've got some work to do before we go watch the fireworks, then."

"That you do, my friend." With a smile, Patrick clambers off the bed and stands looking at Ray for a moment. Slowly, his face grows sombre. "Do you love him?"

"Yeah." It shouldn't hurt to admit it. "But right now, with the way things are, I don't fit into his life."

Patrick nods, and for once, he seems to be all out of words.

He leaves soon after, and instead of returning to his book, Ray picks up his phone and pulls up Gabe's name, their thread of messages. None since Gabe showed up at Ray's flat in London, ten days ago.

'I'm sorry,' Ray writes.

He stares at it for a long minute. If he sent it, it would be for his own sake much more than for Gabe's—as long as Ray isn't ready for the public side of Gabe's life, he deserves no part in it.

Letter by careful letter, he deletes the message. Sets his phone aside, picks up a pen and a piece of paper, and starts writing.

19

Days slide by like weeks, and weeks like months.

At some point, Gabe stops sleeping on his side, with his back to the door. He still wakes up to the ghost of an arm around his chest, though.

It doesn't mean anything.

20

March brings spring flowers along with Gabe smouldering at Ray most mornings—from a poster advertising Gabe's latest film, cruelly displayed at the entrance of the nearest Tube station so Ray walks by it every day that he doesn't run to work or the university. In the picture, familiar rows of wet specimens are lined up in jars on a shelf behind Gabe, and next to him is the BAFTA Award winner who'd called Gabe a class act.

Ray doesn't Google whether they're a thing.

He also doesn't check whether Gabe will be in London for the movie premiere. It's been three months, and Ray is not Alanis Morissette, showing up to wish Gabe the best and ask whether he thinks of Ray when he fucks whoever keeps his bed warm now. No matter how Ray feels at the idea of Gabe with someone else, it's none of his business. He himself made sure of that.

He still loves Gabe, yeah—but surely his quota of life-altering second chances was exhausted when his lab supervisor agreed to cover his part-time bachelor's in cellular and molecular biology. It's contingent on him working at the lab for another five years and throughout a mutually agreed master's research project, but it's the kind of deal he never even hoped for when he asked about reducing his hours after researching student loans. He didn't expect to be valued.

So, yeah. It's fine. Ray is *fine*.

In fact, by most accounts, he's better than he's been in years. He might have been happy, even—at least if it weren't for the Gabe-shaped hole in his heart.

So...

He's fine. He is.

~

DRAMATIC ENTRANCES and declarations are mostly Patrick's thing. So when the front door bangs open while Patrick is right beside Ray on the sofa, they both startle.

A second later, Andrew appears in the doorframe. "I," he announces grandly, "am Spartacus!"

Patrick subjects him to a critical once-over. "That's rather a lot of clothes for a gladiator."

Ray nods. "Should be loincloth only. Maybe a metal one, though—got to protect the goods."

"We're talking figurative here, lads." Andrew strolls into the room as though he's walking into a party. He strikes a pose in front of the sofa, clad in dark skinny jeans, a knit sweater, and thin, wire-rimmed glasses.

"You ... offered to die for us?" Patrick guesses.

"Solid proof of an education in classic movies." Andrew nods his approval before he brandishes what looks like some kind of ticket. "You wouldn't *believe* how many people I had to sleep with to get this."

"A free ride on the London Eye?" Ray suggests.

Patrick snaps his fingers. "A ten-penny discount on a Big Mac with a side of fries!"

Andrew's expression is nothing short of smug. "A red-carpet ticket to the premiere of *The Code of Life*. Featuring—just in case you weren't aware—one Gabe Duke."

Ray's heart stumbles, twists, and resumes beating at twice its normal rate, accelerated like that of a small animal. Hummingbird hearts beat more than a thousand times a minute, more than ten times the human rate, and he doesn't know why his brain latches onto that bit of trivia. Maybe because it's *safe*—just like Patrick was safe when Ray fancied himself in love with him, the very opposite of everything Gabe stands for.

"Holy shit." Patrick whistles. "Way to go, man. That is worth selling your body for."

Andrew gives a humble nod. "Anything for a friend."

For a friend. For *Ray*.

"I..." Ray exhales to clear the fog from his brain. "Is that... But I *can't*."

"Why not?" Patrick frowns, his voice rising. "Mate, you've come so far. You go to a grief support group, you hit the gym, you're going back to uni... I'm fucking *proud* of you, and if you aren't proud of yourself, there's something wrong here."

There might be something wrong with Ray, yeah, but not that—he is proud, a little, of the changes he's made. But he can't waltz right back into Gabe's life and expect to be welcome.

"No, I *know*. I swear this isn't about me, like, not deserving love or something like that." Ray rises from the sofa, can't sit still when his heart is still hammering away in his chest. "But, it's just ... *three months*, all right? More than three months, even. It's been more than three months since I had any contact with him, and I can't just show up at his premiere and be like, 'Hi, remember me? Because I'd *love* to pick up where we left off.'"

"Why not?" Andrew this time, his tone reasonable even though the question is not.

"Because!" Ray throws up his hands. "What if he doesn't want to see me?"

The moment it's out, all the fight drains from him. It's been three months, God. Ray hasn't moved on, but what if Gabe did? He'd have people throwing themselves at him every single day—*beautiful* people, beautiful *men*.

"Then at least you know." Andrew shakes his head, his eyes clear when they meet Ray's. "What's the worst that could happen?"

Worst-case scenarios are Ray's forte. He's been better lately, consciously tries to catch himself before his thoughts derail, but years of practice make this an easy one. "It's been months. He could show up with someone on his arm—maybe the guy who's with him in the movie, Gordon ... something?" Like a puppet with its strings cut, he drops back onto the sofa. "And then I'll be the desperate stalker from his past who really should have sent him a text before showing up uninvited to a public event. That's if Gabe hasn't blocked my number."

It's quiet for a few seconds, then Patrick slides into the space next to Ray, bumping him gently with an elbow. Andrew sits down on Ray's other side even though the sofa isn't meant for three. "Just so you know, Gordon Robinson just had a baby with his wife. He seems rather into it."

Ray makes a noise to convey that he heard what Andrew said, but it doesn't really change the bigger picture.

"You know what?" Patrick tucks one foot under his body, hugs the other knee to his chest, and sets his chin on it, studying Ray with a heavy air of consideration. "I think there's more to it."

"More to it?" Ray doesn't manage to hold Patrick's gaze for more than a beat.

"Yeah." Patrick sounds more certain of himself by the second. "I know the way your brain works, remember? You've been in a better place not just since yesterday—you could have reached out to Gabe at any point in the last month, told him you're ready now if he'll still have you. But you didn't."

Since Gabe left, Ray can't even count the number of times he picked up his phone and stared at the very last message he sent to Gabe, the one Gabe misread as a brush-off and never answered before he showed up on Ray's doorstep. In his mind, Ray wrote Gabe a hundred messages since—*'I'm sorry'* and *'I miss you'* and *'I'm better now but I still love you.'*

He didn't send even one.

"I didn't know what to say," he tells Patrick.

"That's a load of rubbish." Patrick's forehead creases as he shakes his head. "No, I think you feel like you deserve to lose him."

"That's not—I'm better now," Ray protests. "You said it yourself."

"Not like that." Patrick's eyes narrow as though he's trying to see right through Ray. It's a weighted moment before he speaks again. "You messed up. You *did*. But it doesn't mean you don't deserve a second chance."

Fuck.

"I should have been there." The words scrape along Ray's throat like a shovel on concrete. "His bloody parents forced him to come out, and it must have been so fucking *hard*, and I wasn't there. I should have held his fucking hand and—"

"You're not Xander," Patrick cuts in sharply. "You could have spoken to any single one of those reporters who showed up at your mum's, and you didn't. Hell, you could have given your own exclusive to the fucking *Sun* or *Daily Mail*."

He doesn't get it.

Patrick just doesn't *get* it, and Ray slides down on the sofa until his bum is on the edge and he's nearly horizontal, chin pressed awkwardly against his chest. "I wasn't there for him," he says, low and quiet now. Fuck, he's tired. "I say I love him—I do, I fucking *still* do—and then how do I prove it? By fucking right off when he needs me because I can't get out of my own fucking way."

"That's fair," Andrew says. It's so rare for him to jump into the middle of an exchange like this that Ray twists his head to look at him.

"I *know* it's fair."

"Right. Then want to know how to fix it?" Andrew pauses to make his point. "Apologise. And be there next time."

Everything in Ray stills.

He opens his mouth and closes it again, before he finally manages, "But what if he doesn't want to hear it?"

"Then at least you tried." Patrick this time, a tiny smile tugging at the edges of his mouth. He leans down until his nose is almost touching Ray's, filling Ray's entire vision with blue eyes framed by lashes that are bleached at the tips.

"What?" Ray asks when it's clear Patrick won't speak until prompted.

Laugh lines bloom around the corners of Patrick's eyes, his voice warm and soft. "I dare you."

Oh, screw him.

"Screw you," Ray whispers, stomach dropping to somewhere around his feet, ribs squeezing down on his lungs as he stares at Patrick, and fuck, maybe he wants to go. Wants to see for himself what it's like for Gabe, walking down a red carpet with people screaming his name, wants to see what Gabe's world looks like—expensive suits and dresses, white smiles, lobster canapés, and champagne.

It's not Ray's world. But if Gabe wants him—still wants him—maybe Ray could handle being a visitor, at least once in a while.

"I'll go," he says and pretends he doesn't tear up just a little when Patrick and Andrew cheer for him.

~

Leicester Square is lit up like a Christmas tree—not a typical British one in restrained red and gold, but an American one, a myriad of colours and blinking lights, just like in the movies.

Ray has never been to the US, barely even made it to continental Europe. How can he possibly hope to fit into Gabe's life?

But he's here now. And he hasn't had a panic attack in years, but it's a little like that when he shows his ticket, the suit he borrowed from Andrew slightly too tight in the shoulders—breath falling short of truly filling his lungs, a hint of dizziness, things shifting and dancing at the edge of his vision.

The ticket checker sends him a practised smile, no doubt one of many she will have to spare this evening. Her dress fits like a glove and must have cost far more than Ray's suit. "Enjoy the evening!"

With a deep breath that strains the buttons of his jacket, he moves forward.

When he sets foot onto the red carpet, noise presses in on him from both sides, fans crowding against the barriers, the black granite facade of the cinema looming up ahead. *The Code of Life* glows in neon letters, enormous versions of Gabe and Gordon Robinson judging the world from a lit display far above.

Left foot. Right foot. People are staring at Ray, assessing, as he moves towards the entrance. He shoots glances at the crowd and catches sight of a few signs clearly meant for Gabe—*'Still my hero!'* and *'I want to be your surrogate!'* printed onto a big, winking emoji. It makes Ray chuckle under his breath even as he focuses on getting past the crowds and inside without tripping or otherwise drawing attention, loosely aware of photographers gathered near the entrance, cameras and flashbulbs poised to capture any person of interest. Ray is pretty sure that after three months, he doesn't qualify.

No one takes note when he passes.

Most of the noise dies when he enters the building. He expected a reception before the film, a chance to somehow catch Gabe's eye. Instead, he is encouraged to move right to his seat, smiling hosts and hostesses keeping things moving in preparation for the arrival of the actual stars of the night. People like Ray aren't meant to linger.

He doesn't dare ask how he can catch Gabe alone; he doesn't want to get arrested for stalking. So he moves to his assigned seat in the bottom quarter of the huge room, rows upon rows of artificial leather chairs that fit several hundred people, more than half already taken. The screen shows scenes from the red carpet, the first familiar faces starting to arrive—minor and medium celebrities that stop for the occasional autograph, but are quickly shuffled forward as soon as someone more important arrives. It's like watching an animal documentary on pecking orders, with clearly defined roles and hierarchies; *out of the way, beta, here come the alphas!*

When they do come, it's like someone turned up the volume. The smaller names arrive first, people Ray doesn't recognise because he couldn't bring himself to watch the trailer, but they sign memorabilia, pose for photos, and stop for brief interviews while more seats fill up. Then it's the female actor playing Rosalind Franklin, arriving in a car with the guy cast as Maurice Wilkins. They take longer to make their way to the entrance, and Ray realises he's gripping the armrest of his seat and forces himself to let go, lacing his hands in his lap instead.

Another car.

Gordon Robinson. He gets out to a wall of screaming from the crowd, waves once, and holds the door for the director, a woman by the name of Karine Gladwell. The crowd gets louder.

And then there's Gabe.

A deafening roar fills the room as the crowd surges towards the barriers. Ray's heart stops. Stutters back to life once he understands that it's not a bad thing—Gabe is *safe*, all they want is to get closer, scream their support and love at him. "There he is," someone says in the row behind Ray, just as the screen cuts to Gabe's brilliant smile. He looks like he was born for this: radiant and beautiful, comfortable with all eyes on him, a true star.

Ray knew that Gabe was famous. But *seeing* it—fuck, it's different. What can Ray even hope to offer him?

He slides lower in his seat while Gabe and the two others make their way along the red carpet, stopping for autographs and selfies, then professional photos and interviews that are broadcast onto the big screen. Gabe's suit is cut to accentuate his body in all the right ways, his voice filling the very last corners of Ray's mind. A hundred metres—it can't be much more that separates them, yet Gabe is untouchable, moving in a bubble that puts him beyond Ray's reach.

Ray shouldn't have come here. It's too late to leave now, though, it'd only draw attention. So he'll sit through the screening and the torturous knowledge that Gabe is in the same room and on a different planet, and then, quietly, he'll fade away. Numbly, he watches as things wrap up on the red carpet, Gabe ushered inside along with Gordon Robinson and the director. The screen goes black.

Minutes pass.

A murmur rises along the rows of seats. It starts in the front and spreads quickly, like water ripples that travel outwards after a stone was cast. Applause as the lights turn up and the movie cast walks out in front of the screen to form a smiling, black-clad line with Gabe at the centre, the only one Ray sees.

There must be seven hundred people in here. Eight hundred. If Ray got up right now—maybe then Gabe would spot him, but what's the *point*? So, while everyone else leans forward to cheer for the stars of the night, Ray sinks further into his seat and tries to turn himself invisible.

Maybe that's what does it: an oddity, an unexpected break in the uniform line of happy faces. Gabe's bright gaze glides over Ray's row, moves past him—and snaps back like it's a rubber band, the smile falling off Gabe's face.

It's a second, maybe less. They stare at each other, twenty metres and a universe between them.

Then Gabe tears his eyes away, a smile slipping right back onto his face as though it never left. Together with the rest of the cast, he takes a bow and then his seat in the front row, never even sparing Ray a second glance.

So ... that's it. That's it, then.

Ray thought he was ready for Gabe's indifference, but that's been the thing with Gabe from the start, hasn't it? That Ray was never ready for him. As the lights go down, he tries to breathe around the wound that's reopened in his chest, to keep the jagged edges from gaping apart, shivering even though most people around him have donned their jackets and jumpers.

He'll be okay. All he has to do is get through the next two hours, wait until the crowd thins, and slip out unnoticed.

Falling apart wasn't on his New Year's list, and so he won't.

∼

IT'S A MOVIE. It's a *good* movie—maybe, probably. Ray doesn't actually know because only fragments filter through, most of his focus on blending in with his surroundings as larger-than-life images of Gabe show him variations of everything he cannot have.

When his phone buzzes with a message, he welcomes the distraction. He has just enough self-awareness to pick a moment when the big screen lights up with calculations written on a white sheet of paper, making the glare of his phone less obvious as he pulls it out of his pocket.

It's Gabe.

'What are you doing here?'

Ray stares at the letters until they start to blur. He can't tell whether Gabe is upset, curious, angry—but if Gabe bothered to send this in the middle of his own premiere, he's not indifferent.

'I wanted to see you,' Ray replies because there's no point in lying, is there?

He locks his phone so the screen will go dark, but keeps it in his hand. It's only a minute before he feels another telltale buzz against his palm.

'You hate crowds.'

Still impossible to glean any emotion from it. Ray hesitates for a long minute, finger poised over the keyboard. And really, he's got nothing to lose, does he?

'I wanted to see you more than I hate crowds.'

Nothing.

Three minutes, four. Ray keeps checking the screen just to make sure he didn't miss it, ignoring his seat neighbour's irritated sideways glances. When the reply finally arrives, Ray nearly drops his phone.

'The after-party is in the bar upstairs. You're on the guest list.'

After-party. There's an after-party? It will mean more people, groups of strangers having a good time while Ray watches from afar, everyone flocking to Gabe. But if that's the one chance Ray gets to talk to him? He'll take it.

'I'll be there,' he answers.

There's no reply, but then, he didn't really expect one.

MORE APPLAUSE, more bowing. In Ray's inexperienced view, it seems like a great audience response—a standing ovation that seems to go on forever, and when he leaves the auditorium, just one body floating in a sea of hundreds, the snippets of reactions that he catches are mostly positive.

"—what it tells us about our modern-day geniuses like, say, Elon Musk."

"—not sure why it was set in a bog, but can't say I really—"

"Great chemistry between Robinson and Duke—"

"—so the basic message is that genius and obsessive pursuit of a goal come at a price."

Since Ray doesn't want to be the first one at the after-party, then wait around clutching a glass of wine until Gabe makes it there, he hides out in the toilets for a bit, updating Patrick and Andrew on what's going on. They're varying shades of encouraging, with Patrick changing the name of their group chat to 'Every Duke Needs a Ray of Light', which is so cheesy it makes Ray laugh in spite of the twisting weight in his belly.

Once he locates the party, he has to wait while the hostess looks for his name on the guest list. For a sickening instant, Ray wonders if this is Gabe's revenge—embarrass Ray by leaving him stranded at the entrance. But that's not who Gabe is.

"I was added just, like, a couple of hours ago or so," he tries, and her face clears.

"Oh, you should have led with that." She flicks to a separate page that's been tacked onto the main list, a manicured fingernail sliding down the printed names. "*There.* Personal guest of Gabe Duke, is it?"

"I ... yeah. Thank you."

"Enjoy the party!" she chirps and turns to the couple waiting behind him.

It's a nice setting: high ceilings and herringbone parquet, modern chandeliers suspended above turquoise chairs and marble tables, plenty of floor space to mingle, and an entire wall of glass overlooking Leicester Square. Dozens and dozens of people. Ray grabs a glass of prosecco off a tray and tries to get his bearings.

Gabe is easy to find—people are flocking to him, and he's smiling, gesticulating, dimples pressing twin shadows into his cheeks. Watching from afar, Ray wouldn't know how much the promo season exhausts him. 'It's like method acting,' Gabe had explained in one of their texts. *'Like I'm stepping into the skin of someone who's outgoing and exuberant, happy to mingle and talk about himself, life of the party, and I have to hold the pose for a couple of weeks at a time.'*

He's holding it now.

Ray drifts closer, trying to look casual as he leans against a nearby wall and takes tiny, tiny sips of prosecco. It's a little too sweet for his taste, especially since he's been making an effort to reduce his sugar consumption, but the glass is something to cling to, so he does.

Laughter as Gabe and Gordon Robinson recount an evening in a village pub while filming up in Scotland. As it peters out, Gabe's gaze flickers over to Ray for a moment so brief Ray might have imagined it. He thinks about pulling out his phone, just for something to do, but he doesn't want to look antisocial or discourage Gabe from coming over.

Gabe won't come over, though. Will he? It's on Ray to make a move.

In the end, Ray takes his glass of prosecco and himself to the very edge of the group clustered around Gabe and Robinson, and attempts to look like he belongs. Another glance at Ray, then Gabe ducks in to tell Robinson something meant for just the two of them. Ray looks away.

They seem comfortable together—no surprise, maybe, given that they must have spent a lot of time together during filming, and more now, during this promo tour. Ray has never been the jealous type, but no matter what Andrew said about Robinson just having had a baby, well, who really knows, right? And if Gabe's choice is between Ray and someone who was nominated for an Oscar a few years ago...

No. That's the kind of thinking that made Ray walk away from the best thing he never had. He is *worthy*.

Ray glances back up just in time to watch Robinson move away to welcome a group of newcomers—friends, it seems. It makes Ray wonder why Charlie isn't here. Busy with uni perhaps, or couldn't be bothered when he's almost certainly attended other premieres and might have been forced to wait around, bored, while Gabe did his job. Because that's what this is: part of Gabe's job rather than a fun occasion to booze it up with friends.

Maybe Ray shouldn't have come. But he's here now, and Gabe cared enough to put him on the guest list, so Ray isn't wasting this glimpse at a second chance he was given.

By now, the director has joined Gabe's group, which seems to have expanded even further, people laughing, congratulating Gabe and Karine Gladwell, both of them shaking hands, answering questions, and posing for photos. Ray counts at least two guys who are hoping for more than just a picture with Gabe. He lets himself be pushed to the fringes, sets his glass down on a bar table, and waits for a break in the tide.

There is none.

When someone sets a full glass down next to his, Ray deliberately doesn't glance over. Usually, he'd be glad for a few minutes of conversation to help him belong, but what if Gabe slips away while he isn't looking?

"Ray, right?" a familiar voice says next to him—familiar because Ray spent some of the last three hours listening to it.

When Ray turns his head, he finds himself subjected to Gordon Robinson's frank regard. He clears his throat and does his best to look friendly rather than wary. "Uh, yeah. Congrats on the movie. And, um. My friend says you had a baby?"

Way to awkwardly fish for information.

"Yeah. Bane of my existence and love of my life—other than my wife, of course." Robinson's expressive face flashes to open delight.

"Congratulations," Ray says. This time, he means it.

"Thanks." Robinson picks up the glass he set down, but merely to study Ray over the rim. With Gabe still holding court nearby, Ray isn't going anywhere, so he meets Robinson's gaze, but can't quite help himself from glancing over at Gabe again two seconds later. He's just ... magnetic, *Christ*.

When Ray returns his focus to Robinson, the man's lips twitch.

"What?" Ray asks.

"You're not subtle," Robinson says.

It doesn't feel like an attack, so Ray keeps his tone even. "I'm not trying to be."

"Good." Robinson nods once, as if to himself, and takes a quick sip from his glass. "Then I'm going to let you in on a secret, Ray. You won't catch him alone. You want to talk to him, you'll have to muscle your way in."

Ray honestly could have done without this inconvenient confirmation of what he was beginning to suspect. "I can't just, like ... elbow people out of the way. That'd be sure to get me thrown out on my arse."

"So you're just going to stare from afar and eventually go back home, having accomplished nothing?" Robinson raises an eyebrow that is not quite mocking, not quite dismissive. Challenging, maybe?

"I..." Ray inhales before he shakes his head. "No."

"Glad to hear it." Robinson takes another sip from his glass, his tone crisp. "Because you're the one who walked away. He won't come to you, so unless you make a move, and soon..."

Message received.

After another glance at Gabe, Ray empties the rest of his prosecco. His blood isn't exactly bubbling with liquid cottage, but something about the action felt good, decisive. "Why bother telling me anything?" he asks Robinson.

"Based on what I heard from Gabe, you seem like a good guy who got scared." Robinson's smile eases the stark expressiveness of his features. "We've all been scared before, haven't we? But I find it's the chances we didn't take that haunt us."

"Thank you," Ray says around the sudden lump in his throat.

With another smile but no further words of advice, Robinson slips away. Ray returns his focus to Gabe's throng of admirers—and isn't Ray just another one of them?

But he's not.

He knows Gabe. Knows how it feels to hold him through the night, knows the slow blink of his eyes in the morning, his boyish glee at animal-related humour, the scent of his aftershave, and the way his voice gets deeper when he's turned on.

He *knows* Gabe, in a way none of the people surrounding him could ever even hope to. So why should he politely wait his turn?

Ray raises his head, straightens his spine, and rolls back his shoulders. Takes one step towards the group. *Treat it like a dare.* Is this what Gabe feels like when he steps into a role?

"Excuse me," Ray says.

No reaction by the people that separate him from Gabe. Still too quiet, too unused to commanding attention—yet it was enough to draw Gabe's gaze. Their eyes meet, hold for a beat longer this time, and when Gabe glances away, it feels as though Ray's been doused in ice water. *Look at me, dammit!*

"Excuse me!" Much louder this time, trying to pour authority into his voice that he doesn't feel. Heads turn to assess him. "Sorry to interrupt." He isn't. "Gabe, when you're done with this round of pictures, may I borrow you for a minute?"

Ray is pretty sure that he just placed himself on the receiving end of myriad glares, but Gabe's is the only face he sees. It's hard to read Gabe's expression—pale even under a subtle layer of makeup that can't quite mask the circles under his eyes, tired, and so very beautiful that Ray aches with it.

He breathes. Waits.

"Yeah." Gabe's smile stutters as though his facial muscles temporarily forgot how to perform their functions. "Just a moment."

Ray keeps his eyes on Gabe. "Sure."

It's hard to say how long he waits—could be a minute, could be ten. His pulse slows to a meditative rate, his entire focus on Gabe. So what if people are watching him, wondering who he is? Some might even recognise him, and if so, the story is bound to get out. Ray couldn't care less.

Eventually, the crowd parts to let Gabe through. With a smile, Ray nods towards the glass section that overlooks the square. There's no answering smile, but Gabe falls into step as Ray starts moving.

He finds a dimly lit corner that gives them a measure of privacy and turns to face Gabe. Outside, the bright facades of historical buildings and restaurants glow like ships in the night, fans still crowded around the barriers in front of the cinema. Briefly, Ray wonders if he and Gabe are visible or if it's just their silhouettes that will show behind the glass, and then decides that he only minds if Gabe does.

"This okay?"

Gabe spares a glance at the bustling square. "It's fine."

"Good." Words. There are so many in Ray's head, clamouring for attention, that he struggles to choose. "You look tired."

"Promo season." Gabe draws a sudden, harsh breath. "You just forced your way into an entire group of people."

The raw edge to Gabe's voice pulls Ray up short. "I wanted to talk to you," is what he settles on eventually, quiet and more desperate than he intended.

Gabe gazes at him for a beat, then lifts his chin. "So talk."

Too many words, yet again, so Ray stays silent as he sifts through them, trying to find the perfect ones to make Gabe understand. He's staring at Gabe, couldn't look away if he tried, so he catches the moment Gabe's face shutters.

"I should have been there," Ray blurts out. It's far from perfect but it's a start, and once the first words are out there, the next are much easier. "I *wanted* to be there. For you. I really did, but I got stuck in my own head because it's a little hard to believe I've got anything to offer you. I got scared and I wasn't ready, but now I am. If…" He stops to clear his throat. "If you'll have me again."

Nothing. Just the background murmur of other people that don't matter because only Gabe does. In the dim light, the green of his eyes is muted to grey, his pupils huge.

"Please say something," Ray whispers.

"I…" Gabe shakes his head, gently, as if to clear it. "I went through all the fucking stages of grief, you know? Like denial, anger, all of it.

And I finally landed on something like acceptance, and *now* you want me back?"

It's... It's not a no, is it? It's not Gabe saying he's completely over Ray, that he's moved on, thanks but no thanks.

"I'm in love with you—still in love with you." Ray holds Gabe's eyes as he says it, doesn't care if Gabe sees too much. "And I'm not scared anymore."

"I've got a flight to catch." Gabe sounds as though the words have been dragged up from somewhere deep within him. He doesn't move, though. He doesn't *move*, and it's what gives Ray the courage to reach out and touch, just a light brush of his knuckles down Gabe's arm.

"Please stay."

Gabe's lashes flutter. "Give me a reason."

Ray is ready to give him a million reasons, if that's what it takes. "I still sleep on the side of the bed that's closer to the door."

Gabe swallows and drops his gaze.

"I love you." Ray leans in and waits for Gabe to look at him again, Gabe's eyes wide and wet. Ray wants to wrap him up in his arms and never let go, but he's not allowed. Not just yet. "Please give me a chance to prove that next time, I will be there."

A second passes, two. Then something changes around Gabe's mouth—a slight firming of his lips, his gaze direct when he meets Ray's eyes. "You know how when we met, it was kind of fun that you didn't know who I was? But truth is, I come with baggage."

"I know." Ray doesn't hesitate, doesn't even blink. "I'll never love the attention. But if it means I get to be with you?" He pauses. "I'll take it. I'll take it a hundred times over."

It's like balancing on a razor-sharp wire, rocks on one side and crashing waves on the other. Ray keeps his gaze on Gabe and refuses to look down.

It's a minute shift—the faintest hint of a smile settling in the corners of Gabe's eyes. When he straightens and holds out a hand for Ray to shake, the smile grows into something real and tangible. "Hi," he says. "Gabe Duke, Hollywood actor."

Ray takes Gabe's hand. Of course he does—wraps his fingers

around Gabe's and holds on. "Ray Fadil. Lab technician and biology student."

Gabe's eyebrows raise in a silent question.

"I'll tell you later." Grinning, Ray keeps his hold on Gabe's hand.

"Later," Gabe agrees. Briefly, his gaze sweeps around the room before it returns to Ray, lips curving up into what might be a challenge or an invitation. "People are staring."

"Let them," Ray says.

And kisses Gabe, right there for the world to see.

EPILOGUE

When the bell rings, Ray isn't ready.

That doesn't matter, though. It's been six weeks, six bloody *weeks* since they last saw each other, so he drops the hoover where he stands and lets Gabe in, waiting by the door like a seafarer's wife expecting her sailor's return. He hears hurried steps before Gabe rounds the corner and takes the last flight of stairs, two steps at a time.

White T-shirt and black jeans, as beautiful as ever. That's just about all Ray sees before they collide.

They stumble over the hoover on their way to Ray's room, and Gabe tears his mouth away long enough to ask, "Cleaning up for me? I feel so special."

"Fresh sheets on the bed, too," Ray tells him, and then they have better things to do than talk.

Afterwards, they lie with the window open, slowing breaths and bare skin, the sounds of a city evening floating in on a summer breeze. "Missed you," Ray admits in a whisper, and Gabe rolls them over so he can stretch out on top of Ray, getting lost in easy kisses, all earlier urgency dissipated.

"Missed you, too," Gabe says eventually.

Ray tangles a hand in Gabe's hair and just *exists* for a minute, his chest light, his body heavy and content. That's until he realises—"Shit, did we leave your suitcase in the stairway?"

Gabe raises his head for a dimpled smile. "Don't worry about it."

"Don't worry about it," Ray echoes. "Don't *worry* about you showing up without a suitcase? You're not breaking up with me, are you?"

He's joking. Well, mostly joking. He's never felt this happy in a relationship, but it hasn't been without its challenges—with Gabe based in L.A. and travelling a lot, they haven't seen each other nearly as often as Ray would like, and even though he is working on it, he still gets jealous. Gabe isn't good with time zones, and he's thrown himself into his current project with the verve of a man possessed, convinced that if the hetero rom-com he's filming fails at the box office, it will set other gay actors back by a decade. Some days, he was too exhausted to do more than fall asleep with Ray still on the phone, listening to each other's breathing.

What if Gabe *is* breaking up with him?

Gabe scoffs. "Don't be ridiculous."

Ray allows himself to relax by only a fraction. "That's not a no."

"It's a *fuck* no. You're an idiot, and I love you."

"Oh." Ray smiles, wide and stupid and irrationally relieved. "Okay. Good."

"'Good'?" Gabe repeats, gently mocking. "It's been six weeks, and all you have to say to me is 'good'?"

"Good, yeah." Ray inserts a pointed pause, then grins. "And I love you, too."

"Better." With a little sigh, Gabe sits up and rakes a hand through his curls. Even in the fading light, they're hopelessly messy, and Ray's never been the possessive type, but he draws no small measure of delight from seeing such blatant evidence of his own good work.

He doesn't look away when Gabe catches him staring. Why would he?

Gabe's lips curl into a slow, private smile. All he says, though, is, "Hey, let's take a walk."

"A walk?" Granted, it may not be entirely surprising that Gabe isn't sleepy yet given his body is stuck in a different time zone, but, "You just got here."

"I've been cooped up on a flight for ten hours—"

"With extra leg room," Ray interrupts. "Also, free champagne and an hourly foot massage, most likely."

"—and I feel like a nighttime London walk," Gabe finishes, ignoring Ray's input. Which, fair. It's what Ray does when Gabe teases him about the supposed abundance of holidays granted to university students.

While it doesn't escape Ray's notice that Gabe has yet to reveal the whereabouts of his suitcase, he assumes it might be a repeat of Gabe getting them a surprise hotel suite so they can enjoy some privacy. Ray called it splashy and unnecessary—at least until he realised it meant they could lounge around in bed most of the day without anyone knocking on the door just to be a dick, and also because it meant another chance for him to cajole Gabe into demolishing Ray's Black Forest dessert together.

"Should I bring my toothbrush?" Ray asks, just to prove that he isn't fooled.

Gabe shoots him a bright sideways glance. "No need."

Uh-huh. Well, if it makes Gabe happy, Ray will humour him.

They get dressed and exit the flat before either Patrick or Andrew return. Theirs is not a particularly nice neighbourhood, so Ray and Gabe direct their steps towards one that is, just like the other times they've done these nighttime outings, talking and exploring historical side streets and quiet Victorian squares under the cover of darkness.

Ray updates Gabe on his latest essay on science communication, life at the lab, and Allie's plan to work and travel for a year in Australia—things that hardly ever make it into a message or a rushed phone call. Gabe talks about how the rom-com was intense, but the vibe on set was some of the most convivial he's experienced, far better than the multi-character universe the Green Hunter inhabits, which can lead to constantly changing acting constellations. Apparently, there are also rumours that Gabe's performance in *The Code of Life* might earn him an Oscar or BAFTA nomination, which he laughs off as, one, unlikely; two, if it happens, it would be at least partially motivated by the respective committees trying to boost their 'woke' credentials; and three, Ray would deserve some of the credit for helping Gabe feel more at ease with the role.

"Or maybe it would be simply because you deserve it," Ray says.

Gabe bumps their elbows together. "You hardly even remembered the movie."

"I remember it just fine!"

"After watching it a second time."

"First time I saw it, I was a bit busy freaking out about whether I'd blown any chance with you, babe."

"Babe?" Gabe repeats, as if testing the word.

"Too much?" Ray asks.

"Just new." Gabe turns into a short side street that connects to a garden square, his voice blending in with the quiet night as he smiles over at Ray. "I think I like it."

"Good." Ray smiles back. "So, for the sake of curiosity, are we heading somewhere particular?"

"Yep," Gabe says brightly. He's got one hand in his pocket, the other reaching for Ray's as he pulls them towards one of several narrow red-brick buildings that surround the square. "In fact, we're here."

"Here as in…?"

By way of an answer, Gabe tugs Ray into an enclosed awning and pulls out a key to unlock the front door, then holds it open for Ray. "After you. Third floor."

Ray stops on the threshold of the nineteenth century building to look at Gabe, illuminated from above by an ancient metal cage lamp. This is… It *must* be. Like, this is Gabe with the key to a London house, so surely it isn't just wishful thinking. Right? Except Gabe just redecorated his L.A. house to make it feel more like home—sending Ray pictures of sofas and lamps, requesting input that Ray was reluctant to provide because … well. He's selfish, and so he struggles with the idea of Gabe investing heavily in a place that's so far away from Ray.

"You just redecorated your place," Ray says slowly, frowning.

"I did." Gabe sounds pretty damn happy with himself.

Ray squints at him. "Your place in L.A."

Gabe's grin turns downright smug. "I never said that. No point if it goes up for sale tomorrow, is there?"

"You..." Ray draws a sharp breath, knocked off-kilter, heat rising to his cheeks. It won't mean that Gabe will be around constantly; that's not how his job works. But if his home is in London, a twenty-minute walk from Ray, instead of a half-day flight... *Oh.* Ray doesn't dare smile, not yet. "You're not just having me on, right?"

"*Ray.*" Gabe shakes his head, eyes soft. "Let's have a look at my new flat, shall we?"

And there's no way Ray can't kiss him after that, so he does. It feels private, just the two of them tucked into the roofed entrance area, warm summer air and Gabe real and alive and *there*.

When they finally make their way up the polished wood stairs, Ray feels like he's glowing. It's not like Gabe did this just for Ray—Gabe has never felt truly at home in L.A., and Charlie mentioned the possibility of moving to London for his master's. But ... it's not like Gabe didn't do it at least a little bit for Ray, too.

The flat is beautiful. While fairly narrow like the building itself, its high ceilings make it seem airy and welcoming even at night, restored oak boards lining a floor that feels smooth and warm under the soles of Ray's bare feet, his shoes left by the entrance, next to Gabe's suitcase.

"There's an office and a guest room through there." Gabe points to the right, then to modern glass stairs that lead up to a second level. "Master bedroom—smaller, but overlooks the garden square outside, so I think you'll like it."

Does he sound ... nervous?

"Kitchen and living room are up ahead, also overlooking the square." Gabe heads in that direction and Ray trails him but stops in front of a map that's been put up on the wall beside the kitchen. It reminds Ray a little of the maps he still has up in the bedroom at his mum's, except this one's magnetic and littered with dots in three different colours.

"Places you've been?" Ray asks.

Gabe joins him, close enough for their arms to bump. "The blue dots, yeah. Green is where you've been—the UK, obviously, plus France and Belgium, right? And the US when you visited me in May."

"And Italy once, when I was a kid." Ray looks from the map to Gabe's profile, and Christ, it's probably not healthy, the way his heart is trying to hammer a path out of his chest. "What's yellow?"

"That's the places I really want to take you." Gabe's smile is the most beautiful thing Ray has seen all day. *God.* They'll need to talk about it because Ray's standard for holidays is a tent in Scotland while Gabe's is a private resort in the Seychelles, but maybe it's a conversation that can wait a little longer. Say, when Ray is a little less blinded by this wave of sheer, beaming affection that would make him agree to anything as long as it keeps the smile on Gabe's face.

He wraps an arm around Gabe's shoulders to tug him close for a quick kiss to the temple before letting him go. "All right. Show me the rest, babe."

The rest, as it turns out, means a fairly simple kitchen and a bathroom with tiles from the seventies, a gorgeous living room with built-in book niches that are only partially filled, and a modular sofa that Ray recognises from pictures Gabe sent, its fabric showing the colourful pattern they chose together. The principal bedroom on the second level comes with an expensive box spring bed Ray had only joked about getting, and a reading nook fitted into a corner with floor-to-ceiling bay windows.

"Do you like it?" Gabe asks when Ray sits down on the floor cushions, the lights dimmed to almost nothing to better show the square outside. "I know it's a bit further for you to the lab and to uni, too. But it's just two more stops on the Tube, and if you run, it's mostly along the Thames."

Fuck, he's *amazing*. Ray isn't sure how he got this lucky, but somehow, he did, and he plans to hold onto it with both hands.

Smiling, he pats the space next to him. "Come here."

Gabe hesitates before he complies, folding himself into the nook next to Ray, barely touching, the cautious tilt to his mouth obvious even in the shadowed room. Well, that just won't do. Ray shifts, caging Gabe in between his thighs, and lets his smile widen.

"Ask me."

Gabe wraps both hands around Ray's knees and tilts his head. "Ask you what?"

It's crazy and wild and reckless. But Gabe bought a London flat he decorated with Ray in mind, and Patrick has been making noises about moving in with Lauren, and Andrew's been mumbling about how, at some point, a self-respecting thirty-something-year old needs to live on his own rather than with flatmates who never put the orange juice back in the fridge.

Ray leans forward until his nose is nearly touching Gabe's, close enough for Gabe's features to blur. "Ask me to move in."

Gabe swallows audibly, his voice a whisper. "Are you sure?"

A thread of insecurity tries to wind itself around Ray. He shakes it off like a spiderweb. "Yeah. I mean, if you want me to."

"Well, let me think…" Gabe's hands run up and down Ray's calves. "A third of the wardrobe is empty. Pretty sure I left enough space for your books, too, and I guess someone has to use the key that's got your name engraved on it."

"You engraved a key with my name?" Ray knows he's grinning like an idiot, his entire body light like a hot air balloon.

"It's supposed to be, like, a romantic gesture." Gabe grins back, teeth gleaming white in the shadows that surround them. "But hey, if you don't want it, I guess I could hand it to my other boyfriend named Ray?"

"Oh, *shut* up," Ray says, "and kiss me."

Blessedly, Gabe does.

AUTHOR'S NOTE

Hiiii! You made it! And I hope there's a smile on your face right now.

Now, writing is not my day job. It has to fit into the nooks and crannies of my life—a passion that is often relegated to the sideline, taking a backseat to work that pays the bills, to sports and friends and family, to our two adorable cats demanding attention, to unwanted adult responsibilities like doing the laundry and figuring out what's for dinner.

This is why I am so grateful for every reader who takes the time to write a review or drop me a note. If I can leave even just two or three people with smiles on their faces, in a slightly better place than where I found them? That's what makes it worth it. In addition, reviews nudge a book higher up in search results because the sad truth is that if it isn't on the first page? It might as well be invisible... So if you enjoyed this book, **I'd be enormously grateful if you took the time to write a review.** *Thank* you.

Let's stay in touch!

- Check my website for bonus content, or join my newsletter

for updates and even more extra stuff: **www.zarahdetand.com,**
- My **Facebook readers group Zarah's Zarlings** features book chatter, things that make me laugh, sneak peeks, and bonus content, or
- Find me on Instagram **@zarahdetand**.

Writing a book is always a journey, and at times, it can be a lonely one—spending weeks and months with characters that only I know. Not this time, though! I was fortunate to find three amazing and inspiring travel companions: the socktastic Barb, the medically capable Lisa, and my resident film industry expert Jana. Your suggestions, thoughts, humour, and enthusiasm kept me company on this long and winding road, and I couldn't be more grateful. Thank you all.

—*Zarah*

P.S. I should mention that this is a self-published work of writing without any financial resources behind it. While a lot of care went into catching mistakes, some may have slipped through the cracks. If you spot any, I'd love it if you let me know via my website.

MORE BOOKS BY ZARAH DETAND

This Shifting Ground: A law student and part-time waiter befriends a new-to-town customer seeking casual connections. This slow-burn MM romance novella combines fast-paced dialogue with a simmering attraction that blurs the lines of friendship until they cease to exist. **Free on my website!**

Amid Our Lines: In this small-town romance set in the Swiss Alps, London songwriter Eric recognises his new boss Adrian as the adult film star he fancied as a teenager. Their awkward encounter sparks a comedic, slow-burning friends-with-benefits arrangement, amidst a backdrop of snowy charm and heartwarming romance.

Be My Endgame: Liverpool midfielder Alex Beaufort and Manchester United striker Lee Taylor go from rivals to roommates during England's World Cup campaign in Spain. This MM sports romance tackles family legacies and personal struggles as unexpected feelings kick in. A love story as thrilling as a last-minute goal. (Prince Joshua and Leo appear for a couple of scenes!)

Wear It Like a Crown: In this MM royalty romance, an ex-noble is hired to handle a blackmailer threatening to expose the sexuality of Prince Joshua, second-in-line to the throne. This is my most popular book and perfect if you want to lose yourself in a long read.

You're My Beat: In this slow-burn friends-to-lovers tale, a dancer and a rockstar rekindle an old connection during a world tour. Realistically messy feelings meet lighthearted banter for a hard-won happily ever after.

Pull Me Under: After accidentally outing himself, a soccer player enters a fake relationship with an openly gay music student. As they navigate public appearances and the media spotlight, their friendship deepens and romantic feelings emerge, leading to a heartwarming and cheerful tale of love in the limelight.

...and several more!

Printed in Great Britain
by Amazon